In the Best Interests

Tim Hind

Copyright © Tim Hind, 2019
Published: June 2019 by
The Book Reality Experience
Western Australia

ISBN: 978-0-6485198-5-0
Paperback Edition

Typeset in 11pt Garamond

Cover Design by Luke Buxton | www.lukebuxton.com

Dedication

For

Mum, Dad
&
Jamie

This book is based on actual events.
Names, locations, times and details
have been changed to protect the innocent...
and the guilty.

Coming Soon

The Luke Frankland Novels

Pick a Packet or Two

1

Hong Kong, Sunday, 22 August 1999

'Lily, finish up and come help me.'

The girl looked up from the computer screen and frowned, but she knew better than to argue.

'Okay. Give me one minute.' Her fingers danced across the keyboard, typing in a rapid sequence of characters and causing multiple command line boxes to close down. The programs they were running saved their progress and terminated themselves. Lily only paused when a fresh gust of wind and rain hit the living room window.

Tropical storms were common in Hong Kong, but this one was stronger than many and most definitely wetter. The rain was heavier than anything Lily could remember and her mother had said the same. Not that flooding would be a problem, nineteen floors up in a high-rise. Even this cheap and nasty tower block, which Lily regarded as a vertical slum, was built to withstand most of what Mother Nature could throw at it.

She wondered how their old house would be fairing down in Mong Tseng Tsuen. It had been a beautiful colonial-style two storey with separate bedrooms for her and her twin brother, Paul. There was even a nursery for baby Ethan right next to her parent's room. But the road used to flood in heavy rain and there had been landslides in the mountains above. This downpour would definitely cause problems. She thought of her old friends and neighbours still living down there and gave a silent prayer that they and her former home would be safe.

'Come on Lily, I need help,' her mother said behind a cloud of steam coming from a cast-iron wok.

'Leave the computer on Lil, I want to play on it,' Paul called as he got up from the floor, leaving Ethan to chew on a ragged teddy bear.

'You still killing dragons, Sir Never Best?'

'Shut up. And it's Ever Quest.'

'Yeah, like I said. Never Best.'

Lily ignored the middle finger gestured towards her as it was accompanied by Paul's usual wide grin. Despite being infuriating at times, he was still her best friend. She couldn't understand her classmates who seemed to hate their siblings. Paul and she had always been close, but they'd become closer still since their father had been taken. Especially when Paul had insisted on quitting school and getting a job, even though Lily pleaded with him that he was the brightest.

'That's not true and we both know it. Anyway, I can get a higher paid job labouring than you could. I'll work full-time, Mum will work part-time and you'll go to school. Get educated, become rich. Buy back our house.'

She intended to do exactly that. One day.

Leaving the PC running, it took her two strides to cross the living area to the tiny kitchen. She began to serve the rice as her mother turned the electric stove off and gave the vegetables and meat in the wok one last stir.

A stronger gust of wind, laden with rain, crashed itself against the building and even Ethan looked up at the noise. The rain drenched windows mottled the lights of the neighbouring apartment blocks and the little bit of Downtown that they could glimpse. Lily thought it was like looking through wavy glass, or perhaps the kaleidoscope that her father had brought her home from one of his trips. She caught her breath and steadied her hand.

Two years on and still she was surprised by the depth of her grief. Not when she rationally thought about it, but on moments like this where a sight or sound made her think of something in particular. Like a silly toy. Just one more thing that had been lost to her.

Her mother prompted her to serve the rest of the rice before spooning the contents of the wok onto each plate.

'Paul, turn that computer off or pause it or whatever you do with it and move the screen off the table. Come on, we have to ea—'

The wooden door of the apartment splintered from the frame and sagged on its top hinge. Lily jumped and knocked one of the plates off the small bench, adding to the wave of sound in the living room. She heard her mother and baby Ethan scream at the same time and watched Paul begin to rise from his seat at the table.

Two men wearing balaclavas and dressed in olive green moved swiftly into the room. They called out no warning, they didn't identify themselves like she'd seen in the movies, but they wore the sword insignia of the Chinese Special Police Group. Before Paul had managed to fully stand they grabbed him and thrust him against the wall. Lily froze, but her mother reacted with a speed that Lily never thought possible. Her diminutive form leapt across the space towards the two men. A raised hand, still holding a metal serving spoon about to be used as a weapon.

She never got the chance. A third man, almost too large to fit through the ruptured door frame, slapped her across the face so forcefully that Lily saw the shower of blood from her mother's nose fly across the tiny room. It coated Lily's face and she tasted the coppery metallic tang on her lips. Her mother crumpled to the floor. Ethan screamed and cried. Paul was held firm against the wall and his struggles were as ineffective as Ethan's would have been. Lily stood rooted to the spot, unable to breathe.

The third man wore no balaclava. He had sharp features, intense eyes and a half-smile playing across his lips. He looked down at Lily's mother, who was trying unsuccessfully to regain her feet, like she was an amusing distraction. He called in a fourth officer.

'Lift her up and put her with the sister.'

'Yes, Captain.'

He waited until Lily and her mother stood side by side. Then he turned to Paul.

'Taking time for some amusement?' he said, glancing back to the PC screen. Lily followed his gaze. An immense dragon hovered, facing off against a diminutive knight in armour.

Paul stammered to reply but failed.

'What's your name, boy?'

'P…p, Paul Wai.'

A flick of the head by the Captain and one of the two officers punched Paul in the stomach. He retched and coughed, doubling over before being hauled upright again.

'We are not in British Hong Kong anymore, boy. What is your proper name? Your Chinese name?'

Paul coughed again before managing to say, 'Zhang Yong, Zhang Yong Wai.'

'Good. We have the right person. Well, Zhang Yong Wai, you are under arrest for the deliberate and malicious misuse of computer equipment. I would have happily given you a couple of good beatings and left you here, but it seems whatever you did you've annoyed and embarrassed some very senior Party members. Look on the bright side, not many criminals are arrested by the Special Police Unit of the Chinese People's Armed Police Force. You should be honoured.'

Lily's mother tried to move towards Paul again. The fourth officer held her fast but could do little to stop a mother's cries. Two more men, these dressed in People's Liberation Army uniforms, entered the apartment. The Captain waved them towards the PC and signalled for Paul to be taken away. As he was being manhandled through the shattered door, his eyes met Lily's and she was at last released from her paralysis.

'Stop! Stop. It wasn't him. It was me.'

Her outburst had the effect of stopping all movement in the tiny space.

The Captain tilted his head and looked at her before letting out a long and deep sigh that drowned out the incessant noise of the wind and rain. 'Of course it was. How noble. I should have expected a twin sister to sacrifice herself for her brother.'

Lily's mind registered that this Captain of Special Police knew a lot about her family. It was no surprise.

'Take him away and let's get out of here.'

'It's true. I'm the one that hacked it. Let him go.'

The Captain took a single stride and towered over Lily.

'It's Min Hui, isn't it?' He asked, calling her by her Chinese name.

She glared up at him, trembling inside but determined not to show her fear.

'Well? Is it?'

The aggression in his voice forced a nod from her.

'Good. Then I suggest you shut your mouth or I'll drag you in for obstruction. And maybe your mother and that runt of a baby too. Do you want th—'

'The hack was done to the Legislative Council's main server. The communique that was due to be sent by the Council to the central Politburo's standing committee was replaced with the text of Thomas Paine's Rights of Man, but only when the email was opened at the receiving end. The names of the Hong Kong Legislative Council within every Government server were changed to be the signatories of the American Declaration of Independence.'

The Captain turned to the two soldiers who were about to shut down and seize the PC sitting on the table.

'Well, is she right?'

The soldiers swapped surprised looks.

'Come on. Is she?'

'Eh yes, Sir. Yes, she's correct.'

Lily felt her mother's hand grasping for hers, but she pressed on. 'No one else would know that. Certainly not my brother. He only plays games about dragons on the computer. I'm who they want and you should probably make sure you take the right person into custody. Like you said, there were some very senior people who were embarrassed by this. They probably don't want to be embarrassed again.'

When she remembered it later, Ethan had stopped crying and there was a lull in the storm. The whole apartment fell quiet while the Captain contemplated her words. It had felt like hours but had been mere seconds.

A flick of the Captain's head and Paul was thrown back into the living room, landing heavily on the floor. The Captain grabbed Lily by the arm and dragged her out through the door. Lily's mother struggled against the officer still holding her and Paul sprang to his feet. His face distorted in rage he charged at the retreating police officers. Lily shouted at him to stop, that it would be alright, that everything would be alright but still he fought for her freedom. He lashed out and one of the police officers responded by striking the onrushing boy with a baton. Lily, twisting in the Captain's grip saw her beloved brother fall backwards. His head crashed against the table so hard that the PC screen was knocked flying. Her last sight of her family was her mother sobbing and crying, Ethan sitting wide-legged on the floor bawling, his face infused red with the confusion of an innocent and her twin, lying on his side, staring at her with unseeing eyes.

2

Baghdad Airport, 26 April 2004

The ramp of the C-130J Super Hercules transport aircraft came to rest gently on the tarmac of the world's most dangerous airport. A warm breeze, like some giant's hairdryer, flooded the expansive cabin and enveloped me. I stood up, already sweating and followed the other two passengers towards the opening. The sweet, and I always thought intoxicating, smell of aviation fuel filled my lungs. I rated it somewhere between the scent of a really good cigar and the base notes of vanilla. Just a shame you couldn't get a diffuser fragrance called "Essence of Aviator".

'Excuse me, Sir. Flight Lieutenant Frankland?'

I turned back to see the aircraft's Loadmaster looking up at me from a crouched position next to the weapon storage pallets arrayed up the middle of the cargo bay.

'Yes, Sergeant?'

He unshackled a retaining hook and stood up.

'I'm afraid you can't get off Sir.'

'Umm, why not?'

'Because your body armour doesn't have any Kevlar plates in it. No one's allowed to get off in Baghdad unless they have full body armour.'

'But I have to get to the terminal building. I've got to take a really vital phone call in there. It's been set up for ages.'

The Sergeant stayed quite impassive. I hadn't realised he was as tall as he was. He had a good few inches on my six foot two, but he was far from being tall and skinny. His desert combats were surprisingly well fitted, outlining muscular upper arms, legs and a torso that was obviously athletically toned. The whole effect reminded me of a carefully sculpted statue, although the headset atop the Sergeant's head rather detracted from the look. With one ear covered and one exposed, and a long-lead trailing to the side of the airframe, I revised my thoughts on statues and decided he looked like an extra from *Top Gun*. I imagined he would have been right at home in the beach-volleyball scene. He might even have upstaged the rest of the actors. Regardless of how he looked, I had a problem and I hoped to convince him to see things my way.

'You know what the comms back to the UK have been like. I've had this call booked for over a week. I need to take it, Sergeant.' I punctuated my sentence by turning neatly on the balls of my feet and wondered if it had perhaps looked a bit too much like a pirouette rather than the definitive exclamation mark I had hoped for. It didn't matter.

'Sir. I won't say with all due respect as I think it is patronising in the extreme, but I will say that you are mistaken if you think your rank outweighs my authority in this particular matter. I wasn't asking you not to get off. I am telling you that under UK Military regulations and in particular the Royal Air Force's standing orders for Baghdad Airfield, no one without full body armour is allowed to walk across the tarmac.'

He ended his speech with a casual smile that worked to dissipate whatever tension might have been building up.

'You've used that before, haven't you, Sergeant?'

'Oh yes.'

'To people way more senior to me?'

'Oh, most definitely, Sir, yes.'

'Any of them ever decide to ignore you?'

'Not so far.' Another broader grin.

I bowed my head in submission and retook my seat on the canvas webbing strung low along the sides of the aircraft. 'Fair enough, Sergeant…?'

'O'Malley, Sir.'

'Let me guess, they call you Thomas?'

He waved for the ground crew and cargo handlers to come on board. 'Yeah. That's exactly what they call me. It's even what I have on—' He pointed to his left breast where in peacetime his aircrew name badge would have been. Not so in a warzone. 'Ah well, you know.'

I did. I watched him manoeuvre his way around the various cargo pallets with ease. He moved with an assuredness that made me wonder how long he had been in the Service, as he looked even younger than I thought I did.

'So what is the phone call, Sir?' he called over from the other side of a pallet of air-to-ground missiles.

'It's my desk officer,' I said and knew that Thomas would automatically understand the urgency. Desk officers within the Air Force meant the men and women who arranged postings. They were supposed to put round pegs into round holes. Most times they settled for sort of round pegs in sort of round holes. Sometimes they wedged decidedly square pegs into triangular holes. I'd been waiting for weeks to hear from mine. I was homeward bound after six months in Qatar and had no clue where my next tour of duty was going to be. If I didn't speak to him it was likely that I'd go on a month's post-deployment leave and then get told with one day's notice where I was expected to pitch up to. It was hardly ideal.

'Is it at a set time?' Thomas asked.

I glanced down at my watch. 'In half an hour.'

'Why don't I have a word up front and get it patched through to the cockpit? You can take it on that headset next to you if you want.'

'Really?'

'Yeah. That's easy and I'm sorry you can't get off and stretch your legs, but seriously, we're a kilometre away from the terminal and there's always some small arms fire coming in. I mean they never hit nowt, but the powers that be want to be careful.'

'The powers that be want to pull their fingers out and equip us with flaming body armour. Or sort out some more flights.' I pointed down to the limp vest jacket that was meant to be my protection. 'I got thrown this in Qatar and when I asked where the Kevlar inserts were, was told they hadn't arrived. Then they told me it'd be best to sit on my helmet as the aircraft taking me home would be going via Basra and Baghdad. It's a shambles.'

'Sit on your helmet? Ha, that's great. Mind you, I'm sure you heard what happened to that soldier a while ago?'

I shook my head.

'Small arms on approach into here, a one-in-a-million chance. It came through the fuselage and hit him in the backside.'

'You're kidding, right?'

'Not at all. Seriously, they reckon it came up through the gap when the main undercarriage was lowered. Poor bug—'

The call of the ground crew chief interrupted him. Thomas raised the cargo ramp until it was level and the ground crew positioned a stand underneath it. The first pallet of cargo was pushed to the edge and the tines of the waiting forklift engaged. As the driver began to back away and I could hear the rubber tyres squelching on the hot tarmac, I heard another noise. A low thud and dull explosion from somewhere in front of the aircraft. I knew what it was. The forklift driver stopped, dismounted, climbed up the stand, rolled onto the ramp and took a seat opposite.

Thomas walked past me towards the cockpit. 'Mortars, Sir.'

I nodded.

The next couple of minutes were filled with thud, dull crack, pause, thud, dull crack, pause. Thomas came back into the cargo bay and plonked himself down beside me.

'Your call is booked to be patched through.'

'Thanks.'

'For a man with no body armour and who's spent his war in Qatar, you're very calm for being under mortar fire, Sir. I'm impressed.'

'Don't be too impressed. I have insider information.'

He raised one eyebrow. 'Really?'

'I may have spent my 6-month war in Qatar but I'm Air Intelligence. My boss and I spent a large chunk of our time analysing the mortar strikes on Baghdad Airfield. We figured out where the likely launch points for mortars were around the perimeter and even what the insurgents were using to cue their attacks.' I hadn't said it for effect, it was true, but Thomas sat back a little and appraised me.

'Are you responsible for the reports that moved us into different parking spots around the airfield?'

'Afraid so. Well, not only me, my boss led the effort. But yes, we're the reason you're parked up in this very spot. We know where they can launch from and we know what they can and can't hit. We even got to the point of being able to predict where the insurgents would be on some occasions and started taking out more and more of their mortar crews before they got a chance to fire.'

'I'm even more impressed. Me and the rest of the crew probably owe you a drink. We used to get really nervous about coming in and out of here. It's been a lot better recently.'

I decided against saying that it had been me who saw the pattern initially. It seemed immodest and I was never comfortable with blowing my own trumpet, even if it was true. I'd only been out of military intelligence school for three years, so in terms of experience I was a novice, but it turned out I had a knack for recognising things that proved to be significant. I'd never expected to have a talent for it and it was as much a surprise to me as to my bosses, but there it was. I put it down to learning music at a young age and being slightly dyslexic. To see notes or to read words my mind conjured the separate parts, almost spinning them in 3D to be able to see them properly. It made me hold patterns in my mind's eye. I couldn't explain how I did it, it simply came naturally and it allowed me to see when patterns were wrong and when they were right. There was a strange emotional state that accompanied it. A feeling that had taken me by complete surprise when I first encountered it during my initial tour of duty, but one that became stronger and more recognisable whilst in Qatar. It had allowed me to recognise how the insurgents had been targeting our aircraft.

My boss had taken my misgivings and using his experience turned them into a real and worthwhile intelligence product. A method to not only protect our troops, but to go after the enemy. I had felt a tremendous sense of self-worth and an ongoing surprise that I was good at something I had never suspected. But I wouldn't bore Thomas with the details. Instead, in response to his thanks, I mimed doffing a cap.

'You're welcome. That said, we don't know if and when they'll get their hands on new mortars with longer ranges, so I'd still be a bit nervous about that…and the RPGs. I can't say I'm entirely thrilled about that prospect.'

'Ah, it's okay Sir. They can't hit a barn door with an RPG and look on the bright side, if they do get a new longer range mortar, or they get lucky with an RPG you won't have to worry.'

'How come?'

Thomas pushed himself back up and the forklift driver went back to his vehicle.

'Because if they do hit us the flash to bang will be so quick and the explosion of the aviation fuel so large that you quite literally won't have a clue what happened.'

'Well that's reassuring. Thanks, Thomas.'

He guided the next pallet to the edge of the ramp and supervised the lifting of ammunition boxes with unhurried yet precise movements. I was captivated by someone doing what I considered a complex job with consummate ease.

As the forklift trundled away, Thomas checked his watch. 'Right then. Not much more to go and then we'll get loaded up. I'm afraid we have a whole contingent of Royal Scots due to come home with us, so you'll have to bunch up a bit.'

'But I'll have time for my call?'

'Yeah, definitely. It won't be that quick. But once we get the Jocks in we'll be on our way.' He checked his watch. 'Stores off-loaded, passengers on-boarded, incoming mortar attack survived and home in time for tea and medals.'

'Ah, good old *Blackadder*. Where would we be without him? I've never known a briefing that couldn't be improved without quoting from that show. But as for medals, I'll admit I'm not a fan.'

'Why's that?' Thomas asked, waving more ground crew in.

'Ah, I'm not that comfortable about the way we do it. We give the same medal to soldiers, like the Royal Scots, who've been on the ground patrolling and getting shot at, probably on a daily basis. Or it goes to you and the rest of the aircrew who have to fly in and out of some really dodgy places with the risk of being shot down. I'm okay with that, but then they go and give exactly the same medal to someone like me who sits inside a massive great airbase with kilometres of protection between him and the enemy. It doesn't seem right. I think there should be one for those in real danger and a different one for those supporting from positions of relative safety.'

'Mmm, guess so. I never really thought about it.'

'To be honest I'd rather the politicians saved the money on medals and spent it on,' I pointed down to the weightless desert camouflaged vest, 'Kevlar. Complete spineless morons.'

'Not a fan?'

'Definitely not. Untrustworthy, worthless, dishonourable liars the majority of them. Especially this New Labour lot. Can't make their minds up about who they are or what they believe in.' Thomas's surprised look made me realise how much resentment I had put into my last sentence. 'I didn't say that out loud, did I Sergeant?'

'No, Sir. Not at all.' He flashed another grin and added, 'I never thought about the medal thing before. Personally, I'd swap some of mine for some home time.'

'Some of yours? How many have you got?'

He guided the last forklift into place and the final pallet of ammunition started to lift.

'Umm, seven,' he said.

'Now I'm impressed. How did you manage that? I mean, you look even younger than me.'

'I'm twenty-seven. How old are you Sir?'

'Seriously?'

He grinned again and I couldn't help but reciprocate.

'You're twenty-seven?' I asked, surprised he hadn't said nineteen.

'Yeah, I know, good genes, what can I say. And you?'

'Twenty-four. Well, twenty-five next month, so I guess you're not actually that much older. How do you get seven medals?'

'Joined up when I was eighteen. Finished training by the time I was twenty and been on the Herc fleet out of Lyneham ever since. We're like the old-fashioned Transport Command I guess. Anywhere there's hassle, we're usually the first ones in and last ones out. So we get to see the world's shit holes and in return we get medals thrown at us. You know how it goes though, don't you?'

He watched the forklift back away, threw the driver a mock salute and came to sit next to me again whilst the ground crew removed the stand and lowered the ramp onto the tarmac. As I made to speak Thomas held a finger up, clicked the button on the long-lead and spoke into his headset's mic. 'Roger that.' He lowered the mic stalk away from his mouth.

'Sorry, you were saying...about how it goes?' I asked.

'Oh, yeah, medals. You get medals for being brave, being there and being around at the right time.'

I frowned. 'Do you?'

'Yeah. I haven't been brave. I've been there and been in for a while. Every medal I measure in days and weeks and months of being away from home. It adds up to years.'

'Do you have a family?'

'Yeah. Despite all of that I did manage to get married and have kids, but sometimes I feel like I'm missing out on an awful lot of stuff.'

I felt a twinge of regret and he looked profoundly sad. I had to stop myself from reaching out and patting the back of his hand. Definitely not the done thing. In the time I wondered how to respond, he perked back up again.

'Ahh listen to me complaining. Could be worse. I could be Army. Ha!'

'Exactly! What is it? We check in and they dig in?'

He laughed. 'Yep. Probably don't mention that to the lads coming on.' He raised a hand to adjust his headset. 'Roger.' He clicked off the mic and standing, said, 'Your call is on the way through Sir, I'll leave you to it. Don't forget it'll be a radio patch so you'll have to press the mic button to speak and use radio protocols.' He handed me the spare headset and I put it on. Thomas gave me a thumbs up and walked away. I didn't think I looked in any way as rugged or credible wearing the headphones and boom mic as he had, but as long as it functioned it was fine.

'Flight Lieutenant Frankland?' A thin and tinny, but surprisingly clear voice sounded in my ears.

'Yes.'

'Go ahead Sir, you're connected.' A click and a patch of static and then the voice of the man who was responsible for putting me somewhere for the next two to three years of my life. Squadron Leader Tony Dennis. Everyone called him Les. But not to his face. He was a native of nowhere in particular that I could figure, but his voice always sounded to me like he was trying to affect something close to a Knightsbridge 'Sloan-Ranger' accent.

'Luke? Can you hear me okay? Over.'

'Yes, Sir. Crystal. Over.'

'I'm told you're in the back of a Herc sitting on the pan at Baghdad. That's quite ironic really. Given what I have for you. What do you know about the Lyneham Fleet? Over.'

I gazed at Thomas across the empty cargo bay as he checked the web-strapping seats along the length of the aircraft. 'More than I did, Sir. Why's that? Over'

'Well, I'm thrilled to tell you we have a terrifically exciting and dynamic job up for grabs now. Just as well really, as the only other thing I have at present is some nondescript, boring as bat-poo job in MoD. Something to do with computers or some such nonsense, but they have expressly mentioned that the incumbent does not have to be technical. Must be capable of briefing senior types and networking. They actually asked for you by name, but it's hardly the sort of job you want, I'm sure. It's working in London, wearing suits and sounds seriously tedious, not exactly enthralling. Over.'

I laughed and Thomas turned sideways to look across at me. The sidearm strapped to his leg holster caught the glint of light from the rear door as a distant low thud and dull explosion echoed across the open tarmac and into the belly of the Hercules.

'Oh, I don't know Sir, I wouldn't necessarily say that. If it's a posting to MoD, where would I live? Over'

'Umm, hang on.'

I could hear the disappointment in Les's tone across the miles. He obviously thought junior Intelligence Officers should be gung-ho and looking for thrills. Hardly commuting through London to some boring job with computers. Even I had to baulk at that last bit. I was terrible with technology. I barely knew how to look after my emails, but he'd expressly said not technical. I wondered what it could be. I was also enamoured at the prospect of wearing a suit each day, choosing my own colour of tie to wear, reclaiming my identity from the banality of uniformity.

'Hello? Apparently there is a London SSSA flat in-cluded…near Vauxhall. In a place called St George's Wharf…I don't know where that is. Over'

'Me neither, Sir. But I guess it must be on the river somewhere. Over'

'Really? Why's that? Over'

'Umm, the wharf bit? Over'

'Oh! Yes, quite. Actually, wait, there is a note that says it's near to Vauxhall Cross. That's the MI6 building. Over.'

I restrained myself from telling him they weren't called MI6 officially anymore, but what was the point. He was an Operations Officer who was filling the role of posting Intelligence Officers to jobs he understood little about and could be told less. I was lucky he knew my name.

'What's an SSA? Over.'

'SSSA. It's Substitute Single Service Accommodation. Your own digs but paid for by the MoD. I'm sorry Luke, but are you saying you like the sound of this. Are you sure you don't fancy—'

I missed his next word or two as they were masked by yet an-other dull crump of a mortar. It dawned on me there was no whis-tle accompanying the incoming round like you hear in the old films. Maybe I was too distant from the launch point. Probably not a bad thing. I watched Thomas stretch the canvas seats taught. The first of the Royal Scots came up the ramp. That canvas web-seating would be theirs and my only comfort for the next twelve hours. I returned my attention to Les.

'-opportunities to get out and about and brief aircrew and get down range with them. Lyneham Intelligence is a terrific prospect. Others would be snapping my hand off, but I said to myself that I'd offer it to young Luke first. So what do you say? Over.'

'Can you give me a second, Sir? Just a moment. Over.'

'Yes, but I need a decision toot suite. Over.'

The Royal Scots were streaming in now.

'Sergeant O'Malley.' I called and beckoned him over. 'When you're down range on Ops, where do you and the crew stay?'

'Hotels usually, if they have them. Like you said, we're Air Force, not animals,' he added quietly, looking around at the young infantrymen filing into the space, but giving me his trademark grin again.

'And when there aren't hotels?'

'Tents, hangars, the back of the aircraft. We can sling hammocks across the middle here,' he added, pointing up to hooks set into the airframe. 'Anywhere we can whilst taking it in turns to stay up and guard the airframe. That depends on the risk level where we are. Why's that?'

'No reason especially. Just wondering. Thanks.' I pointed to my headset and he sauntered off to settle the troops.

I clicked the mic button. 'Sir, I really appreciate it, I do. But if it's all the same, I think I might give London a go. If that's alright? Over'

'Well, yes, of course. I wanted you to have a choice but if you're sure. Can't say I'm not a little surprised and even a little disappointed in you Frankland, but if you want Whitehall and the politics of the MoD, then I shall make the arrangements. If you are absolutely sure? Over.'

'I'm sure, Sir. Thank you. Over.'

'Right. Well, safe trip home and I'll send through the paperwork to your leave address in a few days. Out.'

The line went dead, the squaddies squeezed in, the ramp went up and in the headset I heard the cockpit crew and Thomas running through their final checks. As we began to taxi, Thomas caught my eye and gave me a waggle of his thumb. I knew what he meant. Good call, bad call, good posting option, lousy? Are you happy?

I raised my right hand like a Roman Emperor, holding it mid-chest, drawing out the moment. Then I gave him a wink and the thumbs up.

3

London, May 2004

Centrepoint Needle Exchange. The sign hung precariously above a door that looked like it was reinforced with a main battle tank's armour. I pulled a piece of paper from my inside suit pocket and checked the address again. Apparently I was in the right place. I couldn't be in the right place. This was meant to be a Ministry of Defence office, not a needle exchange for drug addicts. I turned a full circle, taking in the Dominion Theatre across the street, the busy junction of Tottenham Court Road and came back to face the building that had been one of London's first skyscrapers. I saw a concierge at the reception desk in the tower's foyer and figured he'd be my best option. He pointed me back into the street and told me to go past the door of the needle exchange and around the corner.

A narrow wooden door this time, secured with a Simplex lock. I double checked my piece of paper again and entered the code I'd been given. Sure enough the door opened and I stepped into a bleak corridor with a double width elevator. My instructions said to take the lift to the first floor. I couldn't decide if the instructions were leading me to a great clandestine adventure, or if it was because my new department couldn't be bothered to come down and meet me.

The elevator made a groaning, shaky ascent and when the doors opened I was greeted by an open plan office sporting faded portraits of Her Majesty The Queen and Prince Phillip, albeit hanging a little crookedly between yellowed net curtain covered windows on the far wall. Slightly more suitable than a needle exchange.

Three of the half a dozen metal-framed, wooden-topped desks in the expansive space were occupied, but none of the men looked up. Set into the corner furthest from the elevator was a glass partitioned office. It was home to an imposing dark-wood desk and an executive leather chair in which sat a man, who although also looking down, bore a remarkable similarity to Mr Burns from *The Simpsons*.

I stepped out of the lift before the doors began to close and waited patiently. I wondered if I should cough discreetly or perhaps shout a cheery, 'Hello', but given that every one of the four men I could see, including Mr Burns, was at the very least twice my age and in some cases looked nearer to three times it, I decided it probably wouldn't be the ideal way to announce my arrival. One of the old codgers in particular looked like he could peg out if I startled him with a loud noise.

I took a breath. And another one. This was ridiculous. I settled on approaching the nearest man and stepped forward only to be almost steamrollered by a rotund woman who bustled out of a door set into the same wall as the elevator. The stack of MoD file covers, A4 lawyers pad, stapler, pencils and sundry other stationery items she had in her arms spilled onto the floor as she, or rather I, bounced back before we mutually reached out to steady one another.

'Oh! I am so sorry. I didn't see you there. I've always said that store room door is far too close to the lift. Oh my,' she paused and looked up at me and I felt her hands tighten a little on my upper arms. 'Oh! Hello. Can I?'

I looked down at her round face, round eyes and a mouth that was shaping a very round "O". She couldn't have been more than five feet tall, seemed to be in a similar age range to the rest of the office, wore an appropriate amount of make-up but an indecent amount of a perfume which now filled my nostrils. It was robust, heavy, very sweet and I figured, on first impressions, remarkably suitable. I knew it would forever make me think of this moment were I to smell it in the future. I waited for her to finish her sentence but she didn't.

'Can you…?' I asked, letting go of her arms.

'Sorry?' She said, not letting go of mine.

'You said, can you. Can you what?'

'Oh! Yes, Sorry. Can I help you?' She released me and stood back.

'I'm Flight Lieutenant Frankland. I've been posted here?'

'Ah, yes! Of course you are. I was expecting you. In fact that's all yours,' she said, pointing to the stationery cascaded across the pale green, and much the worse for wear, carpet.

She knelt down to start picking the items off the floor and gave an involuntary, "Oooffh" as she settled on one knee. Her black skirt and white blouse seemed equally stressed about being forced into the position.

'Allow me,' I said, helping her to her feet before I stooped to pick the items up. I judiciously ignored the popped button on her blouse that now gaped and afforded a view of a bra that looked industrial strength.

'Thank you. I'm Steph. Officially the administration manager,' she inclined her head towards the rest of the office and whispered, 'but to this lot, I'm office Mum.'

'I'm Luke. Nice to bump into you,' I said, straightening up with my stationery supplies secured.

Steph snorted deeply and laughed with a pitch that was at the upper reaches of soprano and could well have been sending the canine inmates at the Battersea Dogs and Cats Home wild with distraction. The men in the office still didn't look up from their desks. What were they concentrating on?

'Oh that is funny. You and I will get on famously,' she said, beckoning me to follow and guiding me to one of the empty desks. It sat as far away from the rest of the office occupants as could be managed.

I set my cargo down on top of a desk that appeared to have been scratched, scored, gouged and graffitied for decades before my birth.

'Here you are, home sweet home. Humble, I know but we're very proud of it,' Steph said gesturing with an outflung arm to both my desk and the whole of the office. I masked my thoughts about the desk and managed to "genuinely" fake a beaming smile of gratitude.

'Now. I'll show you the facilities, make you a cuppa, you can tell me all about yourself and then,' she checked her watch, 'when the boys are finished, I'll make the introductions. I know the boss is very, very keen to meet you. Oh you'll have a great time here.'

'Umm, Steph, what are they working on? Is it a priority tasking?'

She bustled off again, waving me to follow and heading to an open door in the same wall as the store from which she'd emerged earlier. I could see it was equipped as a small kitchen.

'I wouldn't really call it that, but it is an important part of our routine. Tea?'

'Please.' I waited as she filled the kettle and then when she wasn't more forthcoming prompted her to continue.

'Oh! Yes. Well we get four copies of each paper. That reminds me, I shall have to up that to five now that you're here. Shan't I? Sugar? Milk?'

'Julie Andrews,' I said, and then immediately wondered if this civilian lady would either know what that was or be offended by the Service slang. 'Sorry, white none I mean.'

'Oh! No. Don't you worry. I know what a Julie Andrews is, Luke. I was Royal Navy Reserve for twenty-five years. We might look old and civvy, but we were once in the Services. Well, apart from Jim. He's Malaysian.'

I felt that given half a chance Steph would launch into the explanations behind each and every one of the office, but I was keener to find out what the routine was that could hold the four men so enthralled. 'So, the thing with the papers?'

'Oh! Yes. At eight each morning I put a copy of *The Times* on their desks and the first one to finish the cryptic crossword,' she frowned and looked exceeding serious, 'and have the rest verify the result,' she relaxed her features and took a breath. 'Doesn't have to buy their round of drinks after work.'

I looked back through the kitchen door and wondered if sharing a canvas bunk in the back of a Herc with Sergeant O'Malley hadn't been the better option after all.

4

London, May 2004

Colonel Charles Henry Cowling won the crossword competition that morning. The men assembled in Mr Burns's
glass office. They pored over Colonel Cowling's finished
puzzle, then each in turn nodded, shook hands and the Colonel,
Jim the Malaysian and Dave, the one in particular I thought would
croak if I shouted hello, came back into the main space. Steph
made the introductions and Colonel Charles asked me to pull a
seat up next to his desk.

'Other side if you would Luke. Afraid I'm the stereotypical
former artillery officer. Deaf as a post in my left ear. Not that great
in my right if I'm honest. Any-hooo, welcome to the Joint Operations Centre for Coordinated Security or as we are known, the
JOCCSy, but we pronounce it Joxy. Damned happy to have you on
board. I assume Steph has shown you around and sorted you out?'

'Yes, Sir. She's been great.'

'Course she has. She's wonderful. Not sure anything would get
done here if not for her. Now, to you. The old man,' Colonel
Charles gestured over his shoulder to the glass office, 'will want to
meet you after morning tea, but for now, I'll run you through what
you'll be up to and what we expect.'

'Excellent. I must admit I have no clue what I'm here to do. My desk officer told me it was something with computers, but that's about all I know. I did tell him I wasn't technical, but he said that wa—'

'Bah. Computers. Lot of nonsense. Typical that the likes of a desk-bound type wouldn't understand. Don't you worry. Yes, we deal with the impact of computers, but let me just say that you can understand the implications and impact of a Pack How coming in on the top of your position, without having to fire the gun yourself.'

I considered blagging my way through the conversation, but decided it was probably easier in the long run to admit my ignorance. 'I'm sorry, Sir, but a Pack what?'

'Ah, right. You're Air Force. Sorry about that. A one hundred and five millimetre field artillery gun. You don't have to know how to fire one to understand what happens when it lands. We're the same here. You don't have to understand how computers work to understand the implications when bad things happen with them.'

'And do bad things happen with them? I mean other than them crashing. Every computer I've ever used ends up with the blue screen of death at least once a month. But it doesn't really cause me that much angst.'

The Colonel laughed with a bass effect. I wondered if he and Steph ever contemplated a duet.

'How right you are. How right you are. That's precisely what most people think, but nowadays, what with the expansion of computer networks, and I don't mean dialling up your modem to the Internet, I mean big Government networks, one man's blue screen of death could quickly become a lot of people's problems. Now, tell me this…'

He paused and leaned forward on his desk, his face close enough to see the intricate network of tiny red veins that were bumping their way across his nose. I felt I should reciprocate his movement and leaned in close. He tried to whisper conspiratorially, but his deafness meant his words were still delivered at a resounding volume.

'What do you think would happen if all the computers in the Army, Navy and Air Force crashed at the same time? Eh? Tell me that? What do you think?'

We'd have a lot more time to do crosswords was my initial thought, but I reflected that it might not be the best answer on my opening morning. I sat back and as genuine as my earlier fake smile to Steph, frowned in my pondering. Bizarrely, as I pretended to contemplate a matter I had never once thought of before, I realised that in fact, I had. Of a sort. I sat upright and the fake frown left me. This was exactly the same sort of problem I'd considered before, both during my training as an Intelligence Officer and subsequently in supporting operations in the Middle East. This was an example of a low probability, high impact event. An unlikely, almost impossible scenario that would have massive consequences. This was aliens landing. Low probability, massive repercussions. This was life expectancy increasing to two hundred, with the resultant impact on society. This was, in its worst ever realisation, almost unimaginable yet with horrendous consequences, 9/11.

I realised I was clenching my jaw and my fists. My mind whirled through the knock-on effects of every computer system I had ever used in the military being denied to me. What about the flight control systems, or shipborne navigation, or aiming control mechanisms for weapons? What about the background systems? The ones used to process pay and allowances. How quickly would family morale and cohesion break down if no one was getting money? How quickly would every unit of every Service run out of parts and supplies if the computers that tracked and ordered the items simply stopped? I had a mate who was a supply officer and I was pretty sure she didn't keep the physical records on cards or paper anymore. The Colonel boomed across my thoughts.

'Are you okay, Luke?'

'Uh, yes. Yes I'm fine. Why?'

'You've gone quite clammy. I didn't want you to give me an answer straight away you know. It was only rhetorical.'

'No, Sir. I'm fine. I was just considering something I hadn't thought of before. If we lost our computers, we'd be pretty much defenceless as a Nation State.'

'Quite! Exactly. That's exactly right and that is exactly why we are here.'

I glanced around at the threadbare office. The battleship grey paint on the walls was faded to an unattractive off-white. The carpet, which had looked bad near the elevator looked even worse next to the Colonel's chair. The empty desks which outnumbered the occupied.

'When you say, we, Sir. Are there more of us?'

'Not at present. There are quite a few slots that aren't filled. Probably won't be what with budget cuts, but don't be too worried. I mean I asked you to think about it, but let's be serious. Computers don't really go wrong like that.'

'Don't they?'

'No. So don't be worrying. It's like that programme on the television. You know, where they show the re-enactments of crimes and then tell you not to worry and to sleep well. That's the same as my little question. We need to be on guard, but within reason. We have enough here to do our job.'

'And what exactly is our job?'

'We scan the papers and magazines and anything we can find on the Internet for shady goings-on with computers and then we collate it into an intelligence summary, write it up on a daily basis and send it through to the higher-ups and *the Minister.*' He ended by placing a lot of emphasis on the Minister. I felt he wanted me to be impressed.

'The Minister?' I repeated the phrase, trying to get incredulity into my voice. I wasn't sure I succeeded but the Colonel looked happy.

'Yes. Straight to the Minster. The Secretary of State for Defence himself. That's quite the responsibility for a junior officer like you, so this is an exceptional opportunity for your career progression.'

'My reports will go straight to his desk?' I was a little shocked by the thought. That certainly wasn't how the military worked. I needn't have worried. It obviously wasn't how the MoD worked either as the Colonel gave another deep rumbling chuckle.

'Not quite on your own Luke, no. You'll write them up and then Jim will check any technical details. He's our self-confessed technology wiz. Then Dave will edit and shape it into our preferred style of writing. I check and edit Dave's words to make sure they meet what I know are our boss's expectations and then he signs it off for release.'

'And we do that every day?'

'Every day. Monday to Friday.'

'And what else?' I asked it innocently enough as in every previous job, my colleagues and I would turn out an intelligence summary as a single task in a day made up of ten or twenty more tasks. It was the Colonel's turn to straighten in his seat. I wasn't sure how to read his expression but it was somewhere between surprise, shock and disappointment. Like finding you had stepped on chewing gum and trudged it through your house.

'Else? That's more than enough to keep us busy.'

'Yes. Of course. Sorry.'

'No need to apologise. I like enthusiasm as much as the next chap and you will be an extra set of hands, so we shall maybe get things done a little faster. I must admit your predecessor wasn't up to much.'

'There was an Air Force officer here before me?'

'Yes. A chap called Marrtins. Dutch descent. Pretty damned useless.'

'I didn't know we had someone here. My desk officer didn't mention it. Was he intelligence?'

'God no. And that was the problem. He was some former Jaguar pilot. Almost as old as me and I'm as old as the hills. Didn't like using the computers to write the summaries. Used to handwrite his bit and then Dave had to type it in. Took a devil of a long time. We've actually been much quicker since he left back in October. Been hanging out to get a replacement though and now you're here things will be improved immeasurably, of that I have no doubt.'

'I hope I'll be of use, Sir.'

'I don't doubt it at all, Luke but don't run before you can walk. Anyway, we'll be moving soon.'

'We will?'

'Yes. This old place was home to an older organisation. Back when the Soviets were a problem and it is rather showing its age. Don't you think?'

'I hadn't noticed, Sir.'

'We'll be off to bigger and brighter soon. I'm sure you know the MoD Main Building is being given a complete refurbishment?'

He looked at me like this was common knowledge and that I should obviously have been completely au fait with it. I thought a nod wouldn't go amiss and the Colonel seemed happy to press on.

'As part of the revamp, we've been given a new home. Top floor with windows looking out to the river. Marvellous aspect. Can't wait to get in and then we'll give this whole thought about doing something else a look over. New start and all that. Yes?'

I wasn't convinced, but the Colonel was getting to his feet. I guessed my welcome interview was over.

'Go and meet the other chaps properly, get Steph to make you another cuppa and then the old man will want a word at about eleven.'

I checked the wall clock. It wasn't nine yet. A quick glance into the glass office revealed the old man, sadly not called Mr Burns, but Mr John Leofric, a Civil Servant equivalent to a one-star General, having a read of the latest *Computer Weekly* magazine.

I met Jim the computer expert. Malaysian, came to England in the sixties. Worked at a variety of jobs which he listed in his sing-along accent. When he ended by telling me he'd been a bus conductor and then joined the Civil Service in the eighties, I was fascinated to know how he ended up as a computer engineer. Jim didn't answer but took a cigarette packet from his pocket and abruptly wandered off to the elevator. I was bemused.

'Come along young man.'

I looked up to see Steph. She hastened me to the kitchen and insisted on making me yet another cup of tea.

'Don't worry about Jim. He's a little sensitive. The Air Force pilot who was here before you used to tease him about having no formal qualifications.'

'So how did he get the job?'

'He answered an internal Civil Service advert. They were looking for someone with an interest in the technical side of computers.'

'And what's his?'

'Now I don't really know about these things, so I might not even be saying it right, but apparently he had an At-a-hari and used to program the BBC's computers. Although I'm not sure about that either as he's been a Civil Servant for twenty years. It all must be quite good though as he got the job. All gobbeldy-gook to me. I don't really like them.'

I almost choked on my tea. 'Steph, you surprise me. You don't like Malaysians?'

'No! I don't like computers.'

'Oh right. Sorry. I did wonder.'

'I like all of the boys. We all get on. Though Jim doesn't like Dave that much. He sa—'

She stopped abruptly, but I knew she was desperate to tell me.

'Aww, we can't have secrets, Steph.'

She sidled a little closer. 'Dave was army. Conscripted into National Service in the late fifties, so you can guess how old he is. He went to Malaysia and then when his time was up he joined the regulars. Been all over the place has Dave. Aden, Germany, lots of Northern Ireland. Was in a bus going back to the camp with a bunch of his young soldiers when it was blown up over there.' She paused and looked sad. Genuinely sad. None of your fake emotions for Steph.

I waited for the moment to pass. 'Why does Jim not like him?'

'He thinks Dave's regiment was responsible for burning his village in Malaysia.'

Had I still been drinking my tea I think I may have spat it all over poor Steph. 'Oh God! You're serious? When was that?'

'Nineteen fifty-eight. Dave was eighteen. Jim was eight.'

'And he seriously thinks Dave was there?'

Steph rolled her eyes. 'I know. What's worse is Dave never gives him a straight answer on it so poor Jim fumes when it comes up.'

'But you said their crossword competition was about rounds in the pub?'

'Yes.'

'So do Jim and Dave socialise together?'

'Oh! Yes,' she chortled. 'I see what you mean, but yes, of course. In fact, the two of them are normally the last to leave the pub. Well...'

Another look of concern passed over her face. I sidled a little closer to her this time.

'Truth is Dave's always the first to get there and the last to leave. Most times though Jim stays to make sure he gets home safe.'

She finished her tea and I went back to my desk. After an hour or more I finally managed to finish getting registered on the MoD computer systems. Another half an hour and Dave and I had become acquainted, although the smell of drink coming off the man was heavier than Steph's perfume. Our conversation came to an end when he took his pipe out and went to light it. I pointed out that he couldn't smoke inside and he swore, told me it was political correctness gone crazy and stomped off to the elevator. Steph told me not to feel bad about it.

'I have to tell him the same four or five times a day. It's one of his quirks. Anyway, time for you to go and see Mr Leofric.'

I went to stand but Steph put her hand on my shoulder.

'Just a little thing, Luke. Mr Leofric used to be a defence attaché.'

She said the word with exquisite French pronunciation.

'Umm, yes?'

'In the Middle East. He collected a lot of expensive rugs and he brought them in to hang on his office walls, but he only really has one wall, the other has a window in it and the other two are glass.'

'I'm a bit confused, Steph.'

'Well, he had to put some on the floor. But you're not allowed to stand or walk on them. He gets very angry. Probably not the best way to start off. Just a tip.'

I reached up and gave her hand a gentle squeeze. Her already vibrant personality seemed to shine even brighter.

I crossed the thirty steps to Leofric's door and by the time I got there he was waiting to greet me. My initial impression had been a bit off. He didn't just bear a resemblance to Mr Burns, he could have been his double. As tall as me, slender, large nose, a marked overbite, small chin and a half halo of grey hair that had slipped off the top of his head and was clinging on to his ears in a final attempt to battle complete baldness. That said, he carried an air of authority which, up close, was almost tangible. I reached to shake his hand and introduce myself, but he spoke first.

'Welcome young man. Do come in.'

He gave me a quick look up and down, then stepped aside and I, being careful not to step on the two rugs on the floor, positioned myself in front of his desk.

'And may I say, BZ. BZ indeed. So what ship have you come off?'

For the second time that morning I thought about blagging it and for the second time decided I couldn't. 'I'm sorry, Sir, I haven't come off a ship and I'm not entirely sure what BZ means.'

He sat in his expensive looking chair, behind his expensive looking desk, the only two things I had seen even close to luxurious all morning and waved me to sit down.

'But I would have assumed a Navy chap would know what BZ was. You know. Well done?'

'Umm. Perhaps Sir. But I'm Air Force.'

He sat forward. 'Really? Are you sure?'

I nodded. 'Definitely, Sir. Flight Lieutenant Luke Frankland. Royal Air Force.'

'Well, bugger me. Charles said we were getting a new fellow in and I didn't think to ask. I didn't think we would replace like for like.'

'I'm not a pilot, Sir. I'm Intelligence, so not an actual like for like.'

'Oh I don't give a buggery about that. I meant that other chap wore slacks and polo shirts to work.'

'Oh, I see.' I said, even though I really didn't. 'And you thought I would be from the Navy?'

'Not really, but I assumed seeing you walking about the office this morning that you were, and on shaking your hand I was convinced.'

This time there was no need to fake a frown. I was thoroughly confused.

'It's Luke, Yes?'

'Yes, Sir.'

'You are wearing a double cuff shirt with proper links, a finely tailored suit that is most assuredly not from Next and an Old Sedberghian tie. Am I wrong?'

'No Sir, you are entirely correct.'

'And did you go to Sedbergh?'

'I did.'

'And you say you decided to join the Air Force?'

'I did.'

'How intriguing.'

There was a pause as he considered me and I considered if this was some form of joke. I waited for him to laugh in a contralto register that would complement Colonel Charles and Steph. He didn't. He merely looked me up and down again and continued.

'I thought Old Sedberghians joined the Guards or the Navy and I'd have known you if you were in the Guards.'

'You would have?'

'Of course. Guards myself, don't you know?'

I needed to take a semblance of control of this. It was a bit of a punt, but not much. 'Excellent. Cavalry?'

His smile spread across his overbite as if Mr Burns's animator had let the pencil slip. 'Of course. Of course. I must admit young Luke, I do like the cut of your gib. I think we'll get along very well. Now tell me about your time at Sedbergh. Did you still have to climb that dratted hill, *Winder*, on a morning as punishment?'

The rest of my welcome interview from the former Household Cavalry officer, John Leofric, was spent with me reminiscing about the exclusive northern England boarding school that the men in my family had attended for three generations. I'd narrowly missed out on the days of fagging seemingly trapped in the British public's idea of such an institution and I certainly never befell a proper bully, but that was mostly due to having an older and very athletic brother whose physical presence deterred even the bravest of them. Nonetheless, by the time Mr Leofric stood to invite me to lunch at his club, he and I seemed to have rather hit it off.

We caught a cab from outside the office door and meandered our way through the narrow streets towards Pall Mall.

On the short journey I made more small talk but pondered on the significance of having a one-star equivalent heading up this strange little, almost dysfunctional, team.

'Sir, how come your department was formed?'

'Oh the department was a long hangover from the Cold War. We were designed initially to look at threats to national infrastructure, but that dwindled away after the collapse of the USSR.'

'But now you've been reformed?'

'A year or so ago, a few chaps started taking an interest in computers. They thought the old infrastructure organisation could be the place to put us. Changed its name to the Joint Operations Centre for Coordinated Security, appointed a few staff members and then asked if I would head the whole thing up. Seemed a jolly sort of pastime for my last two years in harness.'

We completed the rest of the journey with him talking about horses and me thinking about why a quirky team had been reinstated. By the time we reached his club, I had determined a couple of things. One right and, as I would discover over the course of the next two years, one very wrong.

I was right that somebody, somewhere must have had the realisation I'd had at Colonel Charles's desk earlier. Computers crashing left, right and centre could be a game-changer; a Nation State game-changer. I was wrong in thinking the computers needed to crash.

5

She was woken from a shallow, fractious sleep by a kick to her bare feet, before being dragged up by her arms and hair from the thin mattress on the floor. The two guards towered over her, their grip harsh and much more severe than any needed to restrain her. She felt the wave of utter exhaustion break over her, accompanied by the stench of their breath.

Lily had no real idea how long it had been since she saw the life leave her brother's broken body. She guessed perhaps a couple of weeks, but she knew that in her confusion, brought on by sleep deprivation and routine beatings, it could have been a month. It felt like a year.

The hiss of white noise filled the cell and the single bare bulb, high up on the wall protected in a metal cage of its own, continued its pulsating blink. She waited for the first of the punches, slaps and kicks to punish her already traumatised body. Since the ordeal had begun, the tiny bit of functional, rational thought left to her had been impressed by how the guards, the eight that she had managed to identify separately, could hit her so hard yet leave no lasting damage. She could just about see out of her swollen eyes, just about breathe with her cracked ribs, just about eat the sloppy, cold rice through teeth that hadn't quite been knocked out. Her urine coloured red after a beating but not as much as she would have expected. They seemed to know exactly how to administer pain without breaking their subject too much and exactly how long to leave between beatings to allow her to recover.

She thought none of that now. The rational part of her brain grew smaller each and every timeless day and she knew, in the end, she would be left a raving psychotic. At least the crushing grief of her brother, a pain she felt more acutely than her physical state, would be lost in a crumbling mind. Insanity had a bright side.

Her lungs drew in as big a breath as they could and her body tensed as best it could to withstand the first blow. But it didn't come. She felt herself being half-dragged, half-carried out of the cell. Squinting through swollen lids, she saw a corridor with cell doors much like hers on either side. Dozens of them.

The guards, silent as ever they were, dragged her towards a bigger door, set into the wall at the end of the drab green corridor. She realised that this was probably how it ended. Through that door to a scaffold or a firing squad. A part of her, that last semblance of Lily, yelled inside a head empty of white noise for the first time in...it felt like a lifetime...to find her feet, push against the guards, desperately fight not to go through that door. Fight for her life and escape. What she managed to do was utter a low, pitiful groan and shed even more tears. With her bowed and buckled head resting almost on her chest, tears dripped from her chin onto her naked body. She willed her eyes to open a little wider, but the tears distorted her focus and she thought of the rain on the apartment windows. Her mother, her baby brother Ethan...her beloved Paul and then the handsome face of her father. Had he come up this very corridor? Had he gone through the same door to his death? In her mind she said his name and called on him to come to guide her to her death.

The door was swung open and the bright lighting of the room beyond made her wince. Her eyes worked hard to adjust to the intensity of the light but the swollen lids couldn't blink quickly, so all she could see were white and black spots dancing in front of her. Still, she willed herself to face her fate and made the huge physical effort of raising her head as much as she could. No battered submissive would go to a death in this room. Her mind's eye saw *"Liberty Leading The People"*, that her father had taken her to see in the Louvre when the family had visited Paris a few years before…A few years before. Her mind jarred at the difference in her family's circumstances from then to now. She concentrated on the painting. Lily's lips couldn't form a smile but it was there nonetheless. Her memory conjured other images. A book given to her as a gift. Read so many times, the spine cracked, the pages loose, but she took the pictures from the middle and placed them on her bedroom wall in their beautiful house. A black woman on a Montgomery bus, an Edwardian lady in a fine coat and hat being arrested outside Buckingham Palace, a drawi—

Her thoughts were stopped by being forced onto a cold metal chair, the slamming of a door and silence. A silence so loud in ears that hadn't had a single moment of respite from the hissing noise, it almost suffocated her. Lily raised her head cautiously. Her vision slowly returned.

She was sitting opposite a man about the same age as her father had been. There was no desk between them and had he reached out he could have touched her, but instead he looked her up and down. She didn't move her hands or shy away more so than her already huddled position. Her nakedness was of no concern to her. Not now. Each of her guards had hit her, punched her and touched her. Never raped her, but she had always thought it would only be a matter of time. She wondered when her modesty or efforts to cover her dignity had been stripped away as effectively as her clothes.

'Hello, Lily.'

The sound of another human's voice shocked her more than any other thing this man could have done. She wept harder than she thought possible. No one had spoken to her since the Captain of Police had delivered her to this place. Never once had her guards as much as uttered a syllable. Their fists and feet and fingers spoke as much as they needed. Her sobs became louder and her body wracked itself against the chair's cold metal. The man opposite didn't speak again. Didn't try to console or cajole her. Eventually, her body drew back from the shock. Her sobbing subsided. Her tears eased. She didn't try to reply. She'd learnt enough about speaking even a single word from her guards.

When the silence had been restored, she inclined her head submissively and glanced up at him. Then away again.

'I am Major Yuán of the People's Liberation Army.'

Lily remained quiet. The man wore a suit, not a uniform, but she had no reason to doubt him. She had no reason to care if he was speaking the truth or not. Through her narrow field of vision she noted that his clothes were well fitted. He sat upright and when she risked a glance at his face, he seemed to be looking at her stomach. She glanced again and realised he was looking lower.

At sixteen Lily knew about sex, but was still a virgin. She had had a few rough fumbles with a boy or two from school, but nothing serious. Nothing ever as intrusive as what her guards had done with their fingers. She glanced down at her body. Her small breasts heavily discoloured by bruising, her torso painted with black and blue, deep purple and red. Her thighs, where the guards had favoured hitting her over and over with rubber batons boasted two heavy lines of blackened purple, almost the same colour as the dark triangle of pubic hair that nestled between. How could this battered, bruised and bludgeoned body hold any sexual fascination for a man? Yet, there he was, staring at that black triangle.

'Lily, look at me.'

She glanced up at him. His eyes on her face now.

'I can get you out of here if you want.'

Lily opened her mouth to speak but shut it quickly.

'It's alright. You may talk.'

With effort she managed a single word. 'How?'

'We think a girl like you, who has done such a silly thing with computers, has been punished enough. The Politburo wanted you dead, but a number of people want to keep you alive.'

Lily was confused. Who would want to speak up for her? Before she was caught hacking the Legislative Council, she would only ever have been known as the daughter of a dissident. A Hong Kong Chinese man who didn't want the state to be returned to the

Chinese by the British. A man who had been vocal in his criticisms of the regime in Beijing and fully supportive of the British Government, British democracy, British freedoms. A man who had been abandoned by the British and not allowed to relocate before the handover went through. A man who had been given guarantees by both sides that no one would harm him or his family. No actions would be taken. A man who she had watched being beaten and dragged from their home and had never seen again. Lily's family had no friends in the Chinese Government.

She concentrated so hard on the memories that her brow creased and the pain in her face made her wince and groan.

Taking a shallow breath she managed, 'Why?'

'Because we can see you have a talent. The hack that you managed to carry out took a great deal of knowledge and skill. We would like to put that to good use.'

'I'm not…that talented.'

He shifted in his seat. 'What makes you say that?'

'I got caught,' she said through gritted teeth.

'True. But that was down to arrogance. Not your skill as a hacker.'

Lily glowered at him. Her voice grew strength. 'I'm not arrogant.'

'Ah, but you are. You didn't only break into the Legislative Council. Had that been a one-off, we would never have been able to find you. The camouflage and misdirection you used on the attack would have left us completely at a loss as to who the culprit was.'

Lily knew that was correct and waited for him to add something. He didn't. Her curiosity flared.

'So how did you find me?'

'Because you were arrogant.'

Her temper flared much brighter than her curiosity. 'I am NOT arrogant,' she tried to shout it at the top of her voice. It barely made a forced whisper.

'You have had a history of hacking. Getting the skills, low-level stuff, gradually getting bigger, more sophisticated. Your early work went unnoticed for the most part. It wasn't against Government, it wasn't against anything we cared about. No one noticed and no police or PLA assets were asked to track down the perpetrator, but the attacks and the history of the attacks were still out in the ether. They weren't as cleverly done as your later work and were much easier to trace. Like following breadcrumbs. Easy to identify the computer addresses. Easier to tie down to a physical location. Our only mistake was assuming it was your brother.'

At the mention of Paul she tried to straighten up, thought about launching herself at this man, realised she could barely sit up let alone stand and allowed herself to let out a small cry of pain.

'It was most regrettable that he died. The Captain and his men have been given a warning about their behaviour during the arrest. But I'm not here to discuss that. I'm here to offer you a way out.'

Lily knew there was something missing in his explanation of her getting caught. If her earlier stuff was not noticed when it was done and her big attack had been untraceable, how had they found her? She wasn't arrogant. She wasn't. But she ignored his offer of a way out. 'Tell me how you caught me?'

'Zìyóu Zuòjiā.'

Lily's closed her eyes and felt what little spirit she had left fall to the floor.

'You couldn't resist adding a personal tag into the deepest part of the code you used. Not content with replacing the documents as they were transmitted to the Politburo, you arrogantly left your mark. A signature on your masterpiece. Clouded and obscured but there nonetheless. Like some graffiti artist, wanting the world to know of their vandalism. It took our best people quite some time to see it for what it was, especially given the choice of material you decided to upload, but they found it in the end. Then we went to see if that signature had been used anywhere before and…' he paused. Lily opened her eyes. 'And here we are. You may not like it, but the very words that encapsulate the freedom you were seeking, were what led to your incarceration.'

He said nothing more and allowed the silence to stretch out. Lily went back through her memories and realised this man, this

Major, was right. Her arrogance had led to her capture. In the same instance she knew something much worse. That arrogance had gotten Paul killed. She thought she'd been at rock bottom. Now she knew there was a long way still to go.

'What do you want?'

'I'd like you to come and work for me. Put those skills of yours to greater use. I'll teach you to lose the arrogance and then you can help our nation protect itself against the rest of the world. You can be a force for good. You can protect individual freedoms like you say you want to.'

'Work for the PLA?'

The Major's lips formed a tight smile. 'Not work for…join. I want you to join the PLA. We can give you a career for your talent.'

Lily considered him. His suit. His confidence that she would be a great asset for him. For them. She decided to push a little. 'Are my mother and baby brother okay?'

He looked momentarily confused. 'Eh, yes. Why wouldn't they be? They did nothing wrong.'

This time she allowed the silence to stretch as she examined her feelings towards the offer. This time it was the Major who was compelled to speak. 'Well?'

'I'd rather join my father and twin brother.'

6

MoD, London, November 2004

Colonel Charles stepped over the rolled carpet and gave a disparaging look to the stepladder precariously resting against his desk.

'Oh bugger this! Come along troops. We'll call it a day and let these chaps finish up.'

I had to wonder what the painters and carpet fitters made of the old Colonel, but guessed as "these chaps" were contracted to do the final fitting out of the new MoD offices they had probably come across quite a few eccentric types.

Jim and Dave, not backward when it came to accepting an early knock-off, were already at the main door to the bright and shining space that was the new home of the JOCCSy.

Steph wasn't far behind them. 'Oh! Colonel Charles, we could make an afternoon of it. The Christmas Lights are being switched on in Oxford Street and there's a Christmas fair on the corner of Bond Street.'

'Excellent. Sounds good. Come along Luke. There's sure to be Gluhwein and I know you like a good drop of red.'

I checked my watch. Three-fifty. The lights would be switched on at about six. Two hours of drinking before the lights went bright and probably a few hours in a pub afterwards. Sounded good if I was honest. The Colonel was right…I'd always liked a good red. And a good G&T. And a smooth Bourbon. And more recently, a good Bavarian lager. Being in the company of the Fab Four, as I now called Charles, Steph, Dave and Jim, hadn't done anything to dissuade me from what I'd discovered as a teenager; alcohol was a fun diversion.

'I'm halfway through an email I want to send off, Colonel. I'll catch you up in a few minutes.'

'Righty-oh. See you in Bond Street. Call Steph on the old mobile if you can't find us. Toodle-pip.'

I saw the two carpet fitters rolling their eyes at the Colonel's farewell and felt a surge of annoyance at them. He might be eccentric, but he was harmless and he'd served the country for decades. I'd come to think that the Fab Four deserved to be taking it easy in their run, or rather slow meander, to retirement. That wasn't to say that on many occasions during the previous six months I wondered what the hell I had let myself in for. I was mostly bored senseless, although the frequent fuzzy heads following the daily after-hours drinking sessions made me grateful for having such a light workload. Mind you, my cryptic crossword solving had improved immeasurably and what with Mr Leofric taking quite a shine to me, I had met some useful London City types at his club. I figured networking like that could never be a bad thing.

The only major down side had been the dilapidated office, but that was in the past. Our new home on the top floor of the MoD Main Building was stunning. Views out over the Thames, modern infrastructure, bright, light, well equipped and only a fifteen minute walk along the river from my apartment. I had been bemused at how and why a nondescript little unit like ours was being so well looked after, considering our complete lack of contributing anything to the security of the UK, but satisfied myself that within the same building, billions of pounds were being squandered on equipment projects that would never see an actual product brought into service.

I returned to the email I'd been composing to one of my friends still working up at RAF Waddington, where I'd been stationed before Qatar. "Waddo" was the physical, if not necessarily spiritual, home to Royal Air Force Intelligence. There were so many intel related units at the base that Air Force Intelligence personnel seemed to be tethered to it by elastic bands. You were either posted there, just come from a posting there or were about to be posted back there. It did mean the social life on base was brilliant, but being five miles from Lincoln, in the heart of rural Lincolnshire, didn't make for a metropolis experience.

The MoD computer systems, three of which were accessible from my desk, were of course classified. The particular one I was typing my email on could handle UK and US sourced information up to Top Secret, but it didn't alter the fact you could also use it for niff naff and trivial matters, like catching up with friends. I signed off the email inviting any of the Waddo crew who fancied a freebie weekend in London to come right on down. My apartment in St George's Wharf was a two-bedroom grandiose affair that could accommodate about ten of us if we needed it to. I pressed send, waited for the icon to change signifying it had gone, scanned down the list of unread emails and moved the mouse to shut the program and the PC down…The white arrow hovered above the red-boxed X on screen as my brain registered the subject line of an email that had arrived in the previous few minutes.

UK/US TOP SECRET - SI -
SIGNIFICANT COMPUTER BREACH

I'd been here six months. I'd read the daily newspapers, I'd read *Computer Weekly, Computer Monthly* and a host of other tech-related magazines as and when they came out. I'd read the occasional classified signal and email from Canada and Australia, two nations who were about as advanced as me and the Fab Four when it came to computer attacks. I'd read an occasional snippet from the UK banking sector that had been passed through some clandestine back channels, but realistically the only worthwhile cyber intel reports came from the United States and even they were a bit scant on detail. This new email was the first computer-attack related one I had ever seen with a Top Secret banner. I double clicked it and expected to read the usual couple of lines that made up the standard US report. When the message expanded to fill the screen I saw paragraphs of text disappearing off the bottom of my monitor.

Checking that the painters and carpet fitters were on the far side of the office, I started to read and quite literally felt my mouth drop open.

'Colonel?' I said half out loud before looking up, only to remember that they had long gone. I returned to reading. Four paragraphs in, I felt my stomach knot. I double checked the distribution on the email. It had only been sent to us at the JOCCSy as we were know in emails, a single address in the Security Services, another in the Secret Intelligence Service and a final one in a department I hadn't been aware of within the Government Communications Headquarters. That was it. Only four people in the whole of the UK were reading this. MI5, MI6, GCHQ…and me. Depending on how diligently they checked their emails, I might be the first. I temporarily locked the screen on my PC and went over to John Leofric's new office. Not glass walled this one, but a proper enclosed space, adjacent to our main area. Moving his desk had been an enormous undertaking, probably the most complex bit of our whole move, but it had finally been accomplished by a team of removal men who had muscles reminiscent of Sergeant Thomas O'Malley. I'd been most impressed. Leofric's large office, with his Persian rugs now adorning the walls and not in any danger of being stood on by an errant visitor…was empty.

'Bollocks!'

I went back to my desk and using one of the four encrypted phone lines I had available, called Steph's mobile number. It went straight to voicemail. She had, as was usual for her, forgotten to turn her phone back on. No active mobile phones were allowed within our area of the Main Building. Everyone well understood the risk of communication security, and had done since before the Second World War, so the use of non-secure phones was prohibited. Not that the Colonel, Jim or Dave need have worried. They were not yet taken by the idea of a mobile phone and so Steph and I were the only ones on the team to have them. I would routinely switch mine on as I knocked off for the day. Steph would routinely not remember to turn hers back on for hours. It was a standing joke, especially if I was trying to find them when they were out on the town. But it wasn't a joke now. I unlocked my PC screen and kept reading. The further down the email I went, the further my stomach tied in knots and the further out of my depth I became. I had to get some top cover on this, some advice that could point me in the right direction. My stomach twisted even harder when I realised there was only one avenue open to me and one person I would probably end up having to talk to. I had no choice.

When I had read the reports about the insurgents using mortars in Baghdad, my mind had extrapolated the information and reached some quite shocking, but sensible propositions. I had a sense for it, I wasn't too sure how or why I had it, but it was there and that sense had read this email and extrapolated a set of new computer threats that we had never considered. Ever.

Colonel Charles, had he been here, might have listened and that would have been my job done, but he wasn't and wouldn't be until Monday. By that time the other recipients may well have begun to respond, especially GCHQ who officially worked for the Foreign Secretary. If the Defence Secretary was blindsided by this on Monday it would deplete his political acumen and that would make him very unhappy. It was my sure and certain knowledge that shit flowed downhill, so if he was upset, we would end up copping it. This needed to be raised now and it needed to be acted on by the MoD first. The problem was I had no way to tell anyone significant enough. As usual, the entire MoD had shut down for happy hour and wouldn't be opening up again until Monday morning.

I called the carpet fitters and painters together and told them that they had to leave the office for an hour. I didn't care if they took a break or an early knock-off. I couldn't exactly tell them why, but I knew they couldn't be in the office while I discussed this email on a telephone call. With no reluctance whatsoever, they decided to call it a day.

I picked up the handset of the most secure phone system we had and pressed the top speed dial button. The strange warbling ringtone sounded for one and a half rings.

'Air Intelligence Senior Watch Commander, Squadron Leader Tansley.'

'Sir, it's Flight Lieutenant Frankland, down at MoD.'

'Luke! Good to hear from you. How's swanky London town treating you? Birds, beer and...' he paused. 'I can't actually think of another B that would make that sound as funny as I'd hoped. Never mind. What can I do for you?'

'I need you to switch to TS secure,' I said and waited for the chirp on my end of the phone to be reciprocated at his.

'Well this sounds ominous. What's up?'

I knew Mike Tansley well. He'd arrived in to be head of the intelligence watch officers whilst I'd been there, so technically had been my boss for a year, although I'd been in Qatar for half of that. Light-hearted, easy going, clever and as physically fit a guy as I'd ever met. His idea of a good weekend was returning to his native Scotland and climbing a couple of Munroes. Now, though, in his delivery of 'What's up', Mike's banter had departed.

'Before I start, Sir. Do any of you actually know what I was posted down to MoD for?'

'Honestly? Not a clue. We were told they wanted someone who could brief well and fit in with high-level networking. We guessed a bit of the old grip and grin and defence attaché cocktail parties. You were the obvious choice.'

'I was?'

'A public school background still goes a long way, Luke. Don't knock it.'

'Yes, I suppose. Thing is the job description was wrong, or was misinterpreted. It isn't high-level networking, it's high-level networks. Computer security.'

'Oh shit. You could barely type an email.'

'I know. But it turns out you don't need to know how they work, just what might happen if they were denied.'

'Denied?'

'It's a thing called a denial of service. Where someone hacks your computer systems and then you can't use them anymore. Don't ask me how they'd do that, but apparently *they* can. Whoever they are.'

'Alright. So what's up?'

'For the last six months the MoD's response to any potential threat has been laughable. You remember *Dad's Army*?' I asked, referring to the old television comedy show from the 1970s. It was a British institution and followed the exploits of a misfit bunch of old fogies asked to serve their country in the dire straits of World War Two. The darkness of their situation, when it looked certain the Nazis would cross the English Channel, was a perfect foil to their well-meaning, but altogether hopeless, attempts to make a difference. The cast had even included one young, enthusiastic, but naïve soldier called Private Frank Pike. I wondered why I hadn't thought of the correlation before. The Fab Four plus me were much more like *Dad's Army* than the Beatles.

Mike Tansley knew exactly what I meant. 'Don't tell them your name, Pike?'

Even with my stomach still in knots, I had to laugh at that. 'Exactly.'

'Alright, so you and your Dad's Army are looking at computers. And?'

'And we haven't got much of a clue about anything. No one has. Apart from the US and GCHQ. I mean I'm only twenty-five but we didn't have computers when I went through school. The people I work with look at them with a mix of awe, frustration and annoyance. No one really believes there's a threat because all our computers live behind cordons and fences and are protected by armed guards. How could an attacker possibly get into them?'

The line stayed silent. I could hear Mike's breath and remembered when I'd worked for him. He would take a few moments to internally weigh issues. No brainstorming, no thinking out loud, just careful consideration of facts. When he finally gave an answer, it was best to pay attention.

'Are you ringing me to tell me someone has broken one of our systems?'

'No, Sir. That's just it. I've received an email from the US Joint Cyber Security Centre.'

'Cyber security?' Like in cyborg, science fiction?'

'It's a US thing. I don't think computer security sounded sexy enough to get money out of Congress, but cyber sounds futuristic, important and sophisticated. Like it's right out of *Terminator*.'

'Go on.'

I told him the contents of the email and the consequences that I presumed would flow from it. For the first time since I'd known him, I heard Mike Tansley swear.

'Sorry. But if that's right then…'

'Yes, Sir.'

'And you're ringing me to figure out what you should do about it?'

'Yes, Sir. Well, no. Not really. I'm ringing you so that you can take it to the CO,' I said, referring to the man who ran the Air Intelligence watch officer functions. The man who had the authority to notify higher up the chains of command. A man who, because of his position in the system, had direct links into senior government officials.

Mike paused. I waited.

'I totally agree with your rationale, Luke. Makes sense. Okay. You're going to hang up and I'm going to go brief the Group Captain. Then he can figure out how we handle it. I think you're right, this is way above our pay grades. I'll ring you back in ten minutes.'

I felt like a massive burden had been lifted. Had Mike been standing in front of me I'd have hugged him. Except for one small problem. Group Captain Norman Halson was one of the old guard of Cold War era photographic interpreters who had been renamed as Intelligence Officers during the preceding decade. The title on his resume may have changed but he was well and truly caught in the mind-set that this fancy multi-source intelligence was a bit of a waste of time. He seemed to think aerial photography could answer everything. When I and other junior officers had been in his company up at Waddo, he used to wax on and on about the primacy of photography. One night in the mess, when I might have had a few white wines more than were wise, I called bullshit on him.

'So in the 1940s, the code breakers at Bletchley Park, who Churchill and others said shortened the war by at least two years, they were for nothing? And the Special Operations Executive, sending those people into France to spy and report on the Nazis, they weren't up to much?'

'Now listen to me young ma—'

I'd scoffed and turned away. It was the mess bar. It wasn't work and I hadn't said anything explicitly derogatory, but he and the others had known what I thought of him. The man was an arse. Now it seemed like I was going to have to kiss and make up.

'Is there any chance the Group Captain you refer to is a different one than was there last year?'

Mike laughed. 'Sorry, no. It is your firm favourite, but don't worry, even he'll be able to see the ramifications of this. Talk in a bit.'

I hung up the phone and waited.

*

And waited.

Twenty minutes went by and still no call. In the interim I searched through our classified directories and found the details of the MI5, MI6 and GCHQ addressees on the email. On a separate phone line I called them in turn. No reply from any of them. I checked my watch again, for no reason as I had checked it every minute since I'd hung up from Tansley. It was 16:20. On a Friday afternoon. There was every chance that they hadn't even seen the email. There was every chance they, like the Colonel and the carpet fitters and the painters, had indulged in the timeless tradition of knocking off a bit early on a Friday. I returned to the email, printed out the full text that ran to four pages and reread it.

Spartan Storm.
1.   US Air Force Intelligence in coordination with other agencies has identified and verified a new attack vector used in

a significant and persistent computer breach at the Arapal-anta National Laboratories for Energy and Atomic Research.

2. US Army Intelligence concurrently identified a similar attack vector in use against the departments of State, Energy and Defense. Further investigations have revealed similar advanced persistent threats inherent in a wide array of networked systems, including other government agencies and a significant number of defense contracting companies.

3. Following analysis it is now believed that the attack was not designed to prevent use of the systems or to render them vulnerable to a denial of service attack. Instead the malware code searched for classified and non-classified information that included: research and development techniques, propriety design information and completed plans, designs, drawing, infrastructure requirements, staffing levels and details of key personnel. The attacks were elegantly conducted and on conclusion left resident code that would allow rapid re-entry into the systems by the instigators. It is initially estimated that the total data compromised is of significant proportions.

4. The US Intelligence Community is now certain that the attacks extend to Allied nation systems, including the Australian Signals Directorate and the United Kingdom's MoD IONA Network.

5. Details of the attack vector follow and include proven network defense techni-

I stopped reading as the phone finally warbled into life.

'Joint Operations Centre for Coordinated Security, Flight Lieutenant Fr—'

'Frankland, is that you boy?' The unmistakable drawl of Group Captain Halson. Despite his best efforts, the tinge of Black Country nasal intonation underlined his accent. He spoke the way I always imagined Orwell's pigs would have.

'Yes, Sir. Thank y—'

'Squadron Leader Tansley has briefed me on your issue, although I don't think it's an issue at all. What did you expect me to do?'

'The email says that MoD systems have been compromised, but if we look at the US example that could be the tip of an iceberg. Surely we should be getting a working gr—'

'Does it say who compromised them?'

'No, Sir. Although the full email does go into the techniques used an—'

'Then this could be the work of some pudgy child with round glasses sitting in a basement in Oklahoma. It is not an issue that we need to kneejerk react to for goodness sake. It is a Friday afternoon. Do you think even our American cousins would announce something as significant as this on a Friday and only send it to you. Who do you think you are?'

'They sent it to a few others, Sir. Vauxhall Cross, Thames House, Cheltenham,' I said, using the physical locations of MI6, MI5 and GCHQ, whilst trying to stifle my rising annoyance at the dinosaur on the other end of the phone.

'Yes, yes, well that's all lovely, but I hardly think it constitutes a national emergency. As I often find when I have need to converse with you, I will have to repeat myself. What did you expect me to do?'

I bit my tongue, tried to keep the annoyance out of my voice and relaxed my grip on the handset, 'Sir, I'm sitting isolated in an office in MoD. For all I know my team won't be back in until Monday morning. This email is very limited distribution, but seems to imply that MoD systems have been compromised and likely infers that significant information has been stolen. The American compromise is described as significant and persistent. They suggest that the systems remain compromised until active measures are taken to protect them. I really think we need to escalate it up the chain and get some sort of coordinated response in motion.'

'Oh for God's sake. You were always a little irrational. This is not a wave of Russian bombers heading over the North Sea on their way to nuke London. I suggest you calm down and take it with a pinch of salt. The Americans are always prone to hyperbole.

Let's be rationale, computers have never killed anyone.' He ended with a snort. Had he been in front of me, I would have quite cheerfully told him to piss off. As it was, the poor handset got the benefit of a grip that threatened to snap it in two.

'So you're saying you won't take this up the chain to higher authorities?'

'Of course that's what I'm saying. My God, how on earth did the desk officer choose to send you to London? You're an embarrassment. I suggest taking some time over the weekend to calm yourself down. Talk to your superiors about the email on Monday if you must do. Is that all?'

The amount of expletives that flowed through my mind was quite an avalanche. I managed to filter them before my tongue took delight in shaping them. 'Yes, Sir. Thank you.'

The line went dead.

'Prick.' I raised my middle finger in salute, slumped into my chair and gave a dramatic sigh that wanted for an audience but instead dissipated across the empty office.

I was staring unfocused at my PC screen. The email program listed the subject lines of every email in my account. At the top was a red line. I sat forward and refocused. The original email had been recalled. It was a thing that could be done on classified systems. It allowed the sender to reach out and effectively delete an email that had been sent. It prevented it from being opened and read by anyone who hadn't already clicked on it. In my case, it couldn't turn back time and stop me having read it, but it could stop me rereading it, forwarding it or being able to show it to anyone else. It effectively made it disappear. Almost. I looked down at the printout lying on my desk.

Intrigued, I clicked on the recall message. Usually the sender sent a recall notification with a short explanation, along the lines of, sorry wrong version sent out, or sorry overtaken by events or some other nondescript reason. This said nothing, other than a bland statement. "Recalled by US Department of Defense."

My phone warbled.

'Joint Operations Centre for Coordinated Security, Flight Lieutenant Frankland.'

'Hi there.' A Bostonian accent. Chirpy. 'This is Lieutenant Colonel Balowoski, at the Joint Cyber Security Centre in DC.'

'Hello, Sir. What can I do for you?'

'We had a notification that you had opened and read an email that was sent out in error.'

I knew my classified email system automatically sent both received and read receipts in the background, so his revelation wasn't anything that surprised me. A Lieutenant Colonel, two full ranks above me, ringing up about it surprised me.

'Eh, yes. That's right. Is there a problem?'

'No, no problem. Just wanted to reach out and say you can ignore the whole thing. It was sent in error. Part of an exercise. Should never have been generated. So I'm only calling to make sure you're not bouncing around reacting to something that's not real.'

'Ah, I see. Okay. No problem, Sir. Thanks for calling. But you'll have to check with the others on the address list. Do you want their numbers?'

'No, we're good. You were the only one that read it. Guess it's a good job it's nearly the weekend over there with you. A'right. Thanks for that, you have a good day.'

The line clicked off and I replaced the handset in its cradle. Then I lifted the email printout and went across to the document shredder. It sat next to the office photo copier. I made five copies. One went into my secure drawer. The other four into my personal folder within the office safe. Then I locked up the office and headed to the ground floor, the city and a rendezvous with some Gluhwein.

7

Shenzhen, China, June, 2000

Lily was brought back in to the familiar room. Her mind fiz-
zled with the sound of the white noise even though it
wasn't there. She half sat, half lay on the bare metal chair.
Curling up as much as she could. Waiting for the Major to speak.
She waited for her eyes to adjust to the light and then looked
across to him. She frowned. This wasn't Major Yuán. This man
was older. Heavier. Unfriendly looking. Like her idea of an angry
grandfather, sitting on a porch yelling at the children who tease
him for his long ears and hairy eyebrows. Their eyes met.

'Who are you?'

'General Chen, but I am not important, Lily. I am here to ask
you the same question we always ask you. Will you come and work
for us?'

'Ten.'

She watched the hairy eyebrows move together. Caterpillars
mating. She smirked. Any proof that she retained even a semblance of who she had been was worth recognising. Celebrating.
But not with a full laugh. That would only get her another beating.
A smirk would suffice.

'Ten? What do you mean by ten?'

'I've been asked that question ten times. My answer is always the same.' She hugged her knees and considered how thin her arms looked. It was not easy to see her own body in the dull, blinking light of her cell, but each time she was in this room she could examine how much more she had been broken, weakened. She thought they brought her in about once a month, although she had no real idea. Just another moment of existence in a living hell. One day she would die and that would stop them asking their question. She didn't think she'd survive much longer. Probably not get to fifteen questions. Maybe not even twelve.

'I have something for you to see,' he said. Reaching into his suit pocket he withdrew a few folded photographs and offered them across the gap.

Lily peered down at the black and white images. Her eyes struggled to focus but when they did, she sat forward with more speed and strength than she had thought possible. She snatched the pictures from the man's grasp and brought them closer. Her mother, looking so much older than she should have been, holding tightly to her baby brother Ethan. His face contorted in fear. Both surrounded by police. Doors of a vehicle open.

Lily moved the picture to look at the one underneath. Her mother having Ethan snatched from her arms. The next image, her mother being put into the back of the vehicle, like the one Lily had been put into all that time ago. The last image, Ethan being handed to a uniformed woman in the back of another car.

'Your brother will be adopted. Your mother will be brought here.'

Lily wondered where the third voice came from. It was a mix of a yell and an anguished cry. A distraught, soulless, bottomless well of despair that echoed off the walls and assailed her ears. She crumpled off the chair and onto the floor, the photographs falling from her feeble hands. Only then did she realise it was her voice. 'You said you wouldn't hurt them. You said they had done nothing wrong.'

'No. I didn't say that. My predecessor said that. He was mis-taken in his beliefs. She is the wife of, and mother to, dissidents.

Her husband was a traitor against the Chinese People. Her daughter the same. Her eldest son tried to attack a police officer. She may well raise this younger boy to hate the State and the People. So she will go to prison and he will be raised by a good family.'

Lily had no strength left to cry out. Instead she watched her silent tears drop, one by one, on to the last photo. Her baby brother. Being held out to a stranger.

'Or you can decide to come and work for us. Your mother and brother will be returned to each other and to your home. We will look after them. You can look after them. You will be well paid.'

Her tears were forming small rivulets that ran along the creases of the photo. Finding their own way to the edge. Lily traced a finger over her brother's face and asked if she could go home too. 'Please.'

'No Lily. You won't be allowed home. Not until we are sure that you will actually work for us. You are a clever girl. Too clever for your own good. So we will need to be sure. Then, maybe you can go home too.'

She lifted the last photo. Her tears slid down the black and white surface and bathed her brother, Ethan. His face reflected what he was, a child, crying, confused and scared. He had no understanding of the circumstances surrounding him and were he to be adopted would have no memories of their mother and no stories told to him of his dead father.

'Okay.'

'Okay? As in you will join us, Lily?'

'Yes. Just let them go.'

'I shall. Do not doubt me, Lily. I am an honourable man. A man of my word. They will be returned.'

8

The entrance hall to the MoD Main Building was exceedingly grand, but rather spoilt in its aesthetic by a set of nine metal and glass security pods that stretched across its width. The pods were thick glass tubes, like an electronic revolving door for one. As a means of allowing only pre-approved people in or out, they were most effective. Each was activated either by an individual's security clearance card, or remotely by the on-duty guards, ensconced behind their impressively grand mahogany desks. The nine were the only way in or out of the building and so, at busy times there could be a queue. Late Friday afternoons were not busy. Most of the building had emptied already. I was still pondering the US email as I passed through a pod and into the smaller ante-hall that led to the building's main entrance doors. This space was lined by more impressive looking mahogany desks, sequestered behind bulletproof glass, like bank clerk positions and each one, even on a Friday afternoon, manned by a uniformed member of the MoD Guard Service. Most of the guards were retired ex-Service, although some had come from private security firms. Whatever their background, they worked on the theory that recognition was the best form of security. If they recognised your face and knew who you were, then they didn't have to query why you were there. It also meant, when not busy, they could say hello or goodbye personally. It also meant that they could stop you in your tracks with a call.

'Ah! Flight Lieutenant Frankland!'

I looked around and saw a guard called Neil beckoning me with one hand whilst his other was replacing the handset of his desk phone.

'I was just trying to call you, Sir.'

In front of Neil's desk a tall, well-built man was turning round to look at me. He wore black shoes, a suit of charcoal grey, open-necked white shirt and no tie. His face was sharply featured and his hair, grey to the point of being almost silver in places, was neatly trimmed. I had no reason to think of him in any manner, but my instincts yelled at me that the man was not someone you ever wanted to cross. He stepped towards me with his hand outstretched and my brain registered that he moved with the confidence of a predator. An assuredness so far removed from my own capabilities that I wasn't envious, simply fascinated.

'Steve Jäeger. Pleased to meet you.'

In my mind's eye I had seen a tiger stalking through the grasses of India, but the announcement of his surname, the German for hunter, changed that image a little. He was most definitely well-named and now I pictured a lone figure crossing the open plains of the mid-western USA as his accent was unmistakably American, but without a discernible twang to place him any more specifically.

'Luke Frankland. Can I help?' I said and took his proffered hand.

He stepped further away from Neil's desk. 'I do hope so. In return I hope to help you too.'

'With what?'

'With an email you may have read. Recently.'

I hesitated, conscious of the fact I was frowning. 'And exactly who are you, Steve?'

'I work in the US Embassy.'

He reached into his pocket and handed me an identity card. It was an Embassy Staff ID in his name and with his photo on it, but other than that it was generic. I looked from the ID to him and back again. There was something slightly strange about his left eye. Not quite a squint, but something a bit weird. I ignored it and returned the nondescript ID to him. He could have been the Embassy's cleaner or the gardener. I doubted it. He could have been the local Head of Station. That was probably closer to the mark. Whatever he was, I was intrigued.

'Do you want to go back inside to my office?' I asked.

'Eh, no. I had hoped to invite you out for a coffee. Saves the hassle of getting visitor passes drawn up?'

He inclined his head a fraction. Enough for me to know that he would much prefer not registering his presence formally.

'I was on my way into town to catch up with my colleagues. I don't think a half hour diversion will impact too much. But it's a Friday afternoon. I need something stronger than a coffee.' I looked over to Neil, raised my hand and wished him a good weekend.

*

We sat opposite one another in a wall-side table halfway down the length of the Lord Moon of the Mall pub. It was a five minute walk from MoD and a stone's throw from the Old War Office Building so was the 'local' for a great swathe of military professionals working within London. The standing joke was that the former bank, now converted into a pub, should have been classified as a secure location, such were the number of indiscrete conversations held within its walls by Service personnel a little worse for wear.

Steve sipped froth off the top of a wide brimmed coffee cup. I took a long drink from my gin and tonic. Our walk to 'The Moon' had been spent swapping small talk like a couple of boxers feeling their way into a bout. Nothing of note had been exchanged. The weather was pleasant enough for November. The Christmas rush would soon be starting. Yes, the nights did indeed draw in quickly.

As we both set our drinks down in synch, it was like the bell had been properly rung for the second round.

I jabbed first. 'How do you know I got an email?'

'I was told by a friend in DC that the email had been sent. I was told who had opened it.'

'And now you're here to advise me, like the Lieutenant Colonel who rang me, that it was a mistake? A false email from an exercise and I should ignore it?'

'Tell me, Luke, what were your thoughts about being contacted by a US Army Lieutenant Colonel?' Steve's voice was quiet but his stare intense. He'd avoided my question. We held a strange sort of eye contact for a moment before he reached out to take another sip of coffee. I finally realised his left eye was glass. I tried not to stare at it, and failed. He set his cup back down and looked up at me. I quickly focused on anything but his eye.

'It's okay. Yes, it's a false eye.' He held up a hand to silence what were going to be my banal platitudes.

'It fazes people sometimes. Better to get it out in the open, then we can move past it. Don't be embarrassed. No need. It's not every day you sit opposite someone whose right eye is looking at you while the left is still many miles away.' He reached for his cup again, pausing mid-stretch. 'Do you want to know how I lost it?'

'No thanks! It's okay.' I blurted out.

'Ah, I do so love you Brits. You're horrified at the notion of sharing personal information. Easier to talk about the weather.' He flexed his shoulders and laughed. 'But you haven't answered me. What did you think of the phone call you received?' He asked, setting his cup back down and flexing his fingers against one another.

His movements were relaxed and unhurried, like he had all the time in the world, but I got a sense that deep down, he was a tightly coiled bundle of energy and nerves. I knew his question was a test. He wanted to know if I could put two and two together and draw out a conclusion that was more than the sum.

I took another long draw of my G&T. 'I was quite surprised. It's a much higher rank than I would have expected for a mistakenly sent email.'

'And that tells you what?'

'That tells me that before I answer your question, you need to tell me why you're asking.'

He lifted his coffee again and sat back in the faux-leather chair, with the cup held between his two hands at chest level, his gaze on it rather than me. I waited. He took a sip of coffee, then another. After what was probably half a minute, but to me felt like an hour, it appeared that whatever struggle or argument he'd been having with himself was finally settled.

'I will tell you, I promise. But I need to know your thoughts first. Why do you think you were contacted?'

My thoughts of this being like a boxing match had been wrong. This was a negotiation. I realised that he desperately wanted to tell me something, but he wouldn't tell me anything if he thought I wasn't the right person to tell. I had to give him something to grasp onto. In the end it wasn't a difficult decision. I knew exactly what I thought, it was why I'd kept the printout.

I lowered my voice to just above a whisper. 'I think somebody in the US cyber community made a mistake releasing that email. I think the information was close hold and I think it was factual. It was no exercise mock-up of a scenario and I definitely think it was never meant to be disseminated, especially not to foreigners. Certainly not to the Brits. The recall of the email and follow-up phone call were done to limit the damage and hopefully recover the situation. Because of the "Special Relationship", your compatriots will trust the Brits to let it slide into obscurity and take no more heed of it.' I stopped and watched the slightest of smiles tease at the sides of Steve's tight lipped expression.

'I see. That's an intriguing take on the situation, but I'm afraid you got one thing wrong.' He leant forward, placing his cup back in its saucer, the smile on his face now fully evident.

'Yes?' I asked. 'What?'

'The email wasn't sent by mistake.'

'Oh. That's interesting. And the person who sent it is now under military arrest and facing a court-martial?'

'Not quite. He's a defence contractor, but I wouldn't imagine he's going to be getting his contract renewed.'

'And why did he send it?'

'Because he discovered the biggest breach of classified computer systems ever to be discovered and everyone in my government and yours too is ignoring it.'

'Mine?' I was genuinely surprised. 'Mine already know?'

'At the highest levels, but no one's interested.'

'How much information are we talking?'

'Do you like football?' Steve's question threw me completely.

'Umm, do you mean American Football?'

'No, I mean your football, soccer as I'd call it,' he said. 'Do you like it?'

'It's okay. I prefer rugby. Why?'

'But you're familiar with Wembley Stadium?'

'Of course, Steve. Every Brit is familiar with Wembley. It's iconic.'

'Well take that icon in your mind and imagine it filled, from side to side and bottom to top with pieces of A4 sized paper. Millions and millions and millions of pieces of paper.'

'Eh, okay. And?'

'And that is the equivalent of how much information has been stolen from your networks.'

I tried to comprehend the image. I failed. 'You mean US networks?'

'Oh no, Luke. We've lost way more than that. The Wembley analogy is just for you. The US has lost so much more than that.'

'That's ridiculous. No one could process that amount of data. The information overload is so large that the theft would be meaningless.'

'Not quite.'

'It would be, Steve. I'm sorry but I know what trying to process incoming intelligence reports is like. Once you get past a saturation point it becomes useless.'

'True. I'd normally agree with you. Unless of course you imagine the pyramids.'

'You do like your analogies, Steve. But I'm not Egyptian and that one has quite lost me.'

'You can build the pyramids if you have enough personnel, Luke. You can process millions and billions of pieces of information if you know what you're looking for in the first place and have unimaginable resources.'

'There's no way the Russians have that type of capability,' I said and watched a wave of total confusion pass across Steve's face.

'Who mentioned the Russians? This isn't Moscow, Luke. This is the Chinese. The highest levels in Beijing are targeting Western computer systems and using the People's Liberation Army to do it. It's the PLA who are data mining and they have so many people they could build the damned pyramids in their spare time.'

9

General Chen scanned the latest report on his prodigy, Private Min Hui 'Lily' Wai. She was excelling as he had known she would from the first time he had been made aware of the girl. He stared at the photo attached to the top right of the page. Smart in her uniform, smart in her eyes, their brightness restored from the shell of a girl he had interviewed over a year before. It had taken six months to restore her to physical fitness. All the while, the General had personally overseen her transformation. Not that the techniques used within the military school were new or difficult to understand. They hadn't changed much since he had gone through the same training. Lily had been broken physically and mentally, but she'd had the benefit of good nutrition for the first sixteen years of her life, so restoring her to physical health had not been difficult. The General thought back through the decades to when he had started basic training. His city upbringing hadn't readied him for the shock of meeting hundreds of recruits gathered from rural China. Little more than peasants, they had been inherently weakened by borderline malnutrition from birth, yet the Army had built them into soldiers. He returned his gaze to the photo. Her body's restoration hadn't been the problem. Her mental restoration into a soldier, loyal to her comrades and her nation had been a more subtle challenge, but one that had been managed in every basic training school in every military throughout the world for thousands of years. With a Chinese twist of course, he thought. Loyalty to Party came first. That had been his fear with young Lily. That she would resist the needs of the Party, but she had complied, like the millions of others who served in uniform. She was young of course and both her body and mind were flexible. It was easy to comply once the truth was taught to you.

Her training included academic exercises in how the Party had led the people from destitution into enlightenment. How the needs of the nation had to come before the requirements of the individual and how, in a world that looked down on their kind and their country, the Chinese People had to protect themselves. Like they had done for thousands of years. Their history stretching back into the mists of time, when they had cities of culture and splendour, artisans producing exquisite paintings and metalwork, lacquer, textiles, and other luxuries at a time when in the West, they were living in nothing better than mud huts and suffering through the Dark Ages. China's light had kept the world bright. China's mathematicians, philosophers and scientists had forgotten more through the millennia than the West could ever know and now, with the Party's guidance, China, the pre-eminent race of mankind in numbers, would once again take its place as the pre-eminent race in capability. The West, weakened by moral decline, greed for personal wealth and a constant need to be superior would eventually be so beholden to the Chinese People that they would beg for their indulgence. The Party was key to this unfolding as it should. In the West, politicians were so transfixed by their own desire for power they couldn't plan anything past the next election cycle. A grand strategic plan in their eyes was one that lasted five, maybe seven years. They had no concept of time or strategy, submerged as they were in corruption and striving to cling onto their own positions of authority.

The General swivelled his chair slowly and gazed out through the window, in the direction of Hong Kong. He recalled the Chinese diplomatic paper that he had studied in his history lessons as a boy. In 1898 the British diplomats, delighted with having negotiated the lease of Hong Kong for ninety-nine years had wired a cable to London, saying that they had won a great victory, had reached a settlement that would see an end to the Opium War and had secured a huge concession from the Chinese. The land that was Hong Kong, Kowloon, the New Territories and over 200 outlying islands would be secured by the British Empire for a century. The text of the cable, reproduced in its original English had been on one side of the middle pages in his schoolbook.

"Foreign Office, Whitehall, London. To her most gracious Majesty Victoria, by the Grace of God, of the United Kingdom of Great Britain and Ireland Queen, Defender of the Faith, Empress of India. We have secured a foothold of Empire that will last a hundred years. British Hong Kong celebrates."

On the opposite side of his book had been a photograph of the luxurious black inked parchment so resplendent of the Chinese Civil Servants of the day. The most senior bureaucrat had written to their own Emperor, Guangxu.

"To his most Imperial Majesty. The British have agreed to only one hundred years. It is but the span of a mayfly in comparison to the dynasties of China. We will have our victory, although I doubt their Empire will last that long."

Now the Chinese people were on another path and a journey that would also pass in the span of a mayfly, yet would be inconceivable to the West. The General knew some of the overall plan. Not all of it by any means, but he knew his part in detail and he knew that his units were the spear point. Five battalions of specifically recruited and specially trained cyber warriors working towards a single goal.

He eased his chair back around to his desk and picked up Lily Wai's file again. She was the best they'd ever discovered and he had made her his own project. There might be cleverer hackers in China, but by definition that might mean they would never be found, but Lily with her arrogance had fallen into his hands. As sure as the rifle he had trained with when he'd been a junior soldier, she would become his weapon of choice.

10

London, November 2004

I declined his offer of a coffee as he rose to order a third for himself. 'Another G&T is fine, thanks.' As he went back to the bar, I tried to fathom what he'd told me. Whole army formations devoted to hoovering up information from the US, the UK, Canada, Australia and a plethora of other Western countries. None of it discovered until one lone analyst in America found some strange computer code in a system he had originally programmed. I felt a strange combination of guilt and excitement. For six months I had been in a unit allegedly looking for this type of activity but whiled away my days doing crosswords. Now though, it seemed that there was a real threat. Something I could study, analyse, report on. I looked out the bar window at the throngs of homeward bound commuters and felt a strange kick of adrenaline. Everyone had heard of fake emails claiming to be from a rich benefactor that tried to get you to send money to them, but probably none of the people passing by were aware of this new type of computer theft. Steve returned and took his seat. He handed me my drink and I took a long sip. Too much tonic, but it would do and anyway, I was filled with questions.

'Can I ask about the information in the email I got this afternoon? The breach at Arapalanta Labs?'

'Yes. I'll tell you what I can,' Steve said. 'Are you aware of those labs?'

'I'm sorry Steve, but like most everything else you've told me, I have to plead ignorance. I've never heard of them.'

'Have you heard of the Manhattan Project?'

'Of course. The World War Two project to develop an atomic bomb.'

'That's it. Well it was based in a laboratory in Los Alamos. Arapalanta Labs are like the grandchild of Los Alamos.'

'I see.' And I did. The buzz I could feel from my gin stopped and I felt a moment of calmness, like I'd reached a plateau after climbing up a near-vertical rock face. 'And this hacker that got into the system, they were stealing information on atomic weapons?'

'Yes…and no. They took information from there most certainly, but more importantly, once they had got inside that system they used it to branch out into other networks. Anything that was connected became a target but not everything. This was refined and specific.'

'Like a shoplifter working to a list of preferred goods?' I asked, trying not to get lost in the technical detail.

'Yeah. That's very much it. Like high-end car thieves, stealing to order.'

'And this is where the Wembley Stadium full of information comes in?'

Steve paused as a waitress came over with his coffee.

'Any'fink else, love?'

He shook his head and discreetly slipped her a fiver tip. Generous. She felt the note in her hand and without looking down at it gave him a wide smile. 'Aww, 'fanks. If you need any'fink else darling, you come to me.' She gave him a wink, gathered up the empty cups and glasses from the table and sashayed away. When she was out of earshot he continued. 'Yeah. This is where your Wembley comes in.' His voice carried a tinge of regret. He didn't look sad or upset, if anything he looked resigned to the facts he was telling me.

'The malware code infiltrated the mainframe at the lab and then the hacker systematically went through the complete network. He only copied particular bits of information, only navigated in and out of particular hierarchies.'

I held up my hands. Steve stopped talking. 'Look, I really need to point out that I have no real concept about how computers are organised. I am the furthest away you could get from being a techhead. I don't even know what this malware is that you mentioned.'

He looked at with a mix of confusion and amusement. 'You're not joking are you?'

I shook my head. I was quietly proud of the fact I could barely spell binary let alone know how it was used.

'How did you get a job in the UK cyber unit?'

I gave a dramatic cough, 'We are not a cyber unit. We are a security coordination centre and if I'm completely honest, it was a bit of a mistake. However, I'm there now and as I've had it explained to me, not knowing how the systems work doesn't stop me from analysing the impact of them.'

Steve shrugged. 'Hmmm. Well that fills in a blank.'

'Sorry?'

He ignored my query. 'Malware is short for malicious software.'

'Okay. And the hierarchy you mentioned?'

'Imagine an old-fashioned filing system. Everything organised logically, top-down. Our US systems are designed like that so it makes the job of a would-be thief a bit easier. Part of the reason your systems didn't get hit as badly was because the UK networks are less well designed.'

Technically savvy or not, I knew that this was a certainty. 'We'd probably say that they were cobbled together. A bit of a Heath Robinson approach.'

'Heath Robinson? The Australian actor?' Steve looked perplexed and I manged to stifle a laugh.

'Umm, no, I think that's Ledger. Heath Robinson was a…never mind. It's not important. Suffice to say that our approach to computers is a bit hit and miss. We probably didn't plan them out that well. Probably had people like me designing them.' This time I did laugh and Steve tried to smile along with me, but the expression died at his lips. He looked crestfallen. I thought I knew why.

'You came to me thinking I was going to be some sort of computer whizz?'

'Not that so much as…' He hesitated and gave a half-shrug. It was like his little movement finally made my thoughts fall into place.

'Ah! I think the penny has finally dropped. You came to me in the hope that I would be able to make some noise on this. Make the grown-ups in government listen and react?'

'Not government. I'm not expecting miracles, but perhaps get the Brit military to start reacting, we need to start fighting back and your government and mine are not taking the lead.'

'Why not?'

'Luke, I genuinely do not know. I have no idea why London and Washington are not shouting from the rooftops and jumping up and down about this…But they aren't, so I thought we could try to raise a flag in the UK. It almost worked.'

'But the email was spotted and recalled very quickly?'

'Yep.'

'And the only person who got it is not who or what you were expecting.'

'That's not true. We hoped to hell that you would see it. It's just…' He trailed off, his disappointment unsaid, yet still evident.

'You thought I was some tech whizz.'

'We figured you must have been into computers and coding in your spare time, as a hobby, yes.'

I considered what he'd said. 'In my spare time? As opposed to knowing what I did in my working career?'

He slowly lifted his cup and took a sip of coffee before replacing it carefully on the table. There was a lot of thinking going on behind his one good eye. It didn't take him long and I knew he'd decided to be honest with me before he opened his mouth.

'We have our sources, even on our friends. So yes, when you were posted in we took a look at your career path. We didn't do any more than look at your service record. There was no mention of computers, but we figured you must have been a tech-head in your own time.'

'You keep an eye on the Brits?' I paused and then hurriedly added, 'I'm sorry, I didn't mean an eye, I mean…Umm…'

A broad grin spread across his face. 'Relax, man. It's all good. God, I love how uptight you Brits are. I also love your approach to cyber. They post a guy in with no tech knowledge…Then again your strange little country does have some peculiar ways and, I'll admit, some fascinating and unique approaches to problems. Maybe it's no bad thing. Perhaps you're exactly who we need.'

'I seriously doubt that. I have no clue how the heck the team I'm part of can assist you. If you keep an e—I mean, if you keep a watch on the Brits then you'll know how dysfunctional my little lot are.'

'Yeah, but they're not who I'm talking about. There are a whole lot of disparate voices out there in your wider intelligence community that are subject matter experts in their field.'

'There are?' I was truly perplexed. I glanced behind him to the longcase grandfather clock, a feature of the building when it had been a bank. We'd been in the bar for almost ninety minutes. It wasn't yet three hours since I'd opened up the original email. During that brief period of time I had learnt about a massive computer - cyber I corrected myself - threat to my nation and now this curious American, at once affable yet dangerously assured, was telling me about my own country's capabilities.

He made as if to continue talking, but I held the tip of my index finger to my lips. Resting my elbows on the arms of my chair I steepled my fingers together and considered the options. I felt a familiar surge of emotions. A feeling I had first experienced only a few years ago when I had analysed a real-life, complex intelligence problem. It was like an inner calm, fringed by a surge of adrenaline. I didn't close my eyes, I wasn't going into some sort of Yogic trance, I merely let my eyes lose their focus on my fingertips and concentrated on the facts and opinions I'd been presented with. I could almost feel the parts of my brain twist and twirl, form and reform the potential options and possible conclusions before the problem, like some jigsaw in my head, formed a coherent whole.

I knew it had only been a minute or so and I was fully aware that Steve Jäeger had sat patiently and waited. That was a most unusual thing for someone who didn't know me to have done. It added a small, but vital adjunct to my finished puzzle.

I un-steepled my fingers. 'You specifically came to me. As soon as you got notice that I had opened that email, you made your way straight to me. You must have waited for notification that the Lieutenant Colonel had rung me from Washington before you entered the MoD building. Now you've sat there and waited while I thought through everything I've been told. I do this problem-solving thing which freaks most people out the first time they see me go into myself, but you just sat there, so that tells me some-body, somewhere briefed you quite thoroughly on me. Not about my lack of IT skills though, hence filling the gap you spoke about earlier. You didn't care about MI5, 6 or Cheltenham getting the email. You want me at MoD to kick things off in the hope that, if the Brits finally react, it might force the US into some form of action. You need me to do it sooner rather than later so you've already identified people who can help. Have I missed anything?'

'Not much.' He didn't quite smirk, but I got the impression I had passed an exam that I hadn't been aware of sitting.

'In all honesty, Luke, the 5, 6 and Cheltenham address were red herrings. Our defence contractor knew they were redundant. It was your inbox that we wanted the email to arrive in. We were just lucky you read it before it was recalled. Saying that, we'd have reached out to you again if this attempt had failed.'

He looked at his watch and then checked around the bar. 'It's getting on a bit and I'm afraid you've probably missed wherever you were going, but do you want to continue this over dinner?'

'Absolutely. Do you want to eat here? I'm sure we'll be guar-anteed good service.'

'Ha! Yeah I guess we would be, but no, I was thinking some-where perhaps a little more refined?'

I started to get up from my chair, but then realised a huge flaw in Steve's plan. I sat back down. 'I'm not sure how the US military works, but there are going to be some huge barriers in getting any of this up and running.'

'Go on.'

'I'm only a junior officer with about as much influence as that waitress who brought you your coffee and we Brits are strapped for cash. If you want me to pull a team together to help fight a Chinese cyber threat, I need to get my boss's buy-in and then he'll need to establish posts for people within MoD. In the current climate of cuts and more cuts, that's probably impossible and at best a few years' worth of staff work.'

'Yes, I'd normally agree with you, Luke. Except…'

'Except?'

'Your team and your one-star boss were reconstituted from an old Cold War unit, yes?'

I had gone past the point of being surprised by how much he knew. I merely nodded.

'Your boss was a previous defence attaché in the Middle East where he worked alongside some of my former colleagues. We've kept in touch over the years but that is a fact best left undisclosed to a wider audience. Rest assured, he will be more than happy that you've come up with this idea.' A single raised eyebrow told me more than Steve's explanation.

'And the posts?'

'Your funny throwback of a unit was originally established for a much bigger contingent. It was designed to react when the Russians crossed the inner-German border and it's more fun having a lot of people panic than a few. So you have spare posts available. In fact, you have more spare spaces than we actually need.'

'And how many do I, we, need?'

'Seven. Ideally.'

'A magnificent seven?'

'Possibly.'

'You better tell me who they are and then we can discuss them over dinner.'

Steve took a breath and reached into his inside pocket. He produced a thin notebook and flipped it open. I was reminded of a television police detective giving evidence in a courtroom. A well prepared detective. 'First things first. You need technical people with programming skills. Advanced programming skills, and preferably other skillsets too. You will definitely need a link into GCHQ, so you'll apply for the secondment of a codebreaker, encryption expert from Cheltenham, called Rob Curzon. Also, a Royal Air Force Police Flight Sergeant who is the UK military's acknowledged expert on counter-intelligence and computer security. Then—'

'Hold on. We have a computer security expert in the RAF?'

'You have a whole team of them working out of a place called Southwick Park. They are world leaders in counter-intelligence and if you wanted to stop some foreign spies from compromising the physical security of your computers then they're still the people to go to. Only problem is they aren't allowed oversight of any other networks and Flight Sergeant Mark Donoghue has gone almost hoarse trying to get people to sit up and take notice of emerging threats. He's gonna think Christmas has come early when you call him on Monday.'

'I'm amazed. Seriously amazed. Who else?'

'You'll need one of Donoghue's corporals, to do the physical security of your own networks. Donoghue can pick out his best and bring him with him. Then you could do with an RAF intel who has a good background in Signals Intelligence, Electronic Warfare and programming languages. Ritchie Adams is the best you have available. He's up at Chicksands at present. He and Rob Curzon can help you identify, decipher and decode the malware that you are going to be looking for.'

'Glad someone can,' I said and saw my sarcasm wasn't lost on Steve. I was impressed. My experience with the US military was that only the anglophiles amongst them truly got sarcastic wit.

'Then you need some people with other skills. You actually know Warrant Officer Rachel Kennedy.'

'From the MoD debriefing team?'

'The same.'

'Yes, I worked with her on debriefing middle-eastern refugees. Gosh, that was a few years ago. I was in between finishing officer training and being sent to do my formal intelligence training. They put me with Rachel to make coffees and teas, I'm sure of it, but in the end I worked alongside the debriefers and sat in on the interviews.'

'Your strange way of problem solving and analysing data didn't go unnoticed when you worked with Rachel. Or in Qatar.'

For a moment I wasn't sure if my face reflected the surprise I felt, but obviously it did.

Steve laughed. 'A few people thought you would have the ability to see the long-term implications of Spartan Storm. The email today was the final test.'

'And I passed?'

'So far so good.'

'Who in Qatar told you about me?'

'Ah…We've got eyes everywhere,' Steve said with his own hint of sarcasm before shrugging and continuing. 'That's why we specifically targeted you and your strange little unit. With John Leofric as your top cover there really isn't anything you guys can't achieve. With the right people.'

'And Rachel is one of those?' I asked.

'Warrant Officer Kennedy will be an asset. I've worked with her too, and I've never met a man who doesn't melt when she walks into a room. Quite a lot of women too. She could get them spilling their most intimate secrets before they've even sat down.'

'When did you work with her?' I asked it in hope of discovering a little more about Steve, but he dutifully deflected.

'A while ago. Somewhere far away.'

'Fair enough. Okay, so I agree, Rachel's great, but I didn't know she was into IT.'

'She's not into coding or programming, but she understands networks and much more importantly, she is a phenomenal source interrogator. You're gonna need some soft skills in getting information out of industry and others. You're also going to need a translator and administrator, but we can get both in one with a Royal Navy Writer called Ashley Young.'

'A writer?' I'd never heard of the title before.

'Geez-Us, Luke. You really are wet behind those ears in some things, aren't you?'

'I never pretended that I wasn't, but I do think asking questions when I don't understand something is preferable to bravado and bullshit. Don't you?' I delivered my riposte in a more forthright tone than I may have intended.

Steve sat back and considered me. 'The Royal Navy call their administrators, writers. And you may be wet behind the ears, but it seems you have balls kid. I knew I was gonna like you.'

'Sorry, but I don't like being called out on jargon. If you know my service record you probably also know I don't come from a family steeped in military tradition. I went to school, went to university, where I discovered the University Air Squadron, then I did my initial officer training and apart from a short while up in Lincolnshire and an even shorter while in Qatar, the rest of my time in the Air Force has been spent wearing suits and living off-base. Even when I was with Rachel on the Debriefing Team, I wore suits and lived in a hotel. I much prefer suits, ties, hotels and decent food to the alternatives, so I am not well versed in all this military stuff. It rankles me though when people think that makes me less capable at doing my job.'

It was Steve's turns to hold his hands up. 'Woah there, Luke. I didn't mean to offend you and believe me, I know you're good at your job. That's the only reason I'm sitting here.'

I felt my quickly risen annoyance dissipate. 'Okay. So we have a Navy Writer. And you say she's a translator?'

'Yeah, fluent in Cantonese and Mandarin. Also Ritchie Adams that I mentioned, he's a linguist too, but doesn't have any Asian languages in his locker.'

'That's six. Who's the seventh?'

'Well, that's where we might run into a problem. The special relationship our political masters spout on and on about had some worthwhile hangovers. When we expected the Russkies to come marching through Paris, we had the idea that, where we could, we'd embed a Brit in a US unit and vice versa. You have a US liaison officer post in your Joint Operations Centre for Coordinated Security.'

I sat upright. 'Oh thank goodness. So you're coming too?'

'Gawd no! You think you struggle with IT? I still use note-books,' Steve said and flicked the pages in his to underline the point. 'I was planning on sending you the best and brightest from the US cyber unit, but yes, we do suffer from the same restrictions you guys do and whilst the post is established and their wages are already being paid, we have no budget for accommodation or travel costs in London. I could get them a bunk in a USAF base a hundred miles away, but that isn't going to work logistically. Especially as they'd be reduced to commuting in on a pushbike. I'm afraid you'll have to be the slightly less magnificent six.'

'Six is better than where I am at present and you're sure John Leofric will sign this off?'

'Positive, Luke. Positive.'

'Then I guess you owe me a dinner?'

'Sure thing. There's a nice Italian on Villiers Street. About five minutes away.'

*

We were about halfway to the restaurant, walking along the Strand, when the thought occurred to me.

'Steve. Do you think your US liaison officer would be able to take the spare room in my apartment? It's already paid for by the MoD. I have to buy my own groceries, so he would too, but that's not a lot of personal expenditure for him to get a tour of duty in London?'

'I think that's a fantastic idea. If you're sure?'

'I'm sure. But do not send me a good ole' boy from Texas who's evangelical in his love of Bibles and bullets. I have standards to maintain.'

Steve affected a southern drawl. 'Aww schuks, Lukey boy, that's exactly whosa I was gonna send ya'all.'

'If he doesn't like being quiet over breakfast, reading a decent newspaper and enjoying a good quality G&T, then count me out.'

'I'll do the interviewing myself. How's that sound?'

We walked the rest of the way in amicable silence and arrived at the restaurant to be told there would be a ten-minute wait for a table. We agreed and stepped back outside to wait in the cool of a clear November night. The yellow pool of a streetlamp seemed to shine with a halo as the distant thumping bass from the bands playing at the switching on of the Christmas Lights drifted across the cityscape, mixed in with the occasional wailing of a police or ambulance siren, an infrequent horn of a river boat and the incessant background hum of life in the city that I adored. I let my thoughts roll around the prospect of a new start on the coming Monday. I also let my thoughts linger on that idiot of a Group Captain up in Waddo. I'd be rather glad to see his face when he finally heard about what we were up to. If he could be bothered to listen. It seemed that when it came to cyber, not many people wanted to listen.

'Steve, you and whoever else is in the background have obviously been preparing for this for some time. Why now? Is it simply to do with you being frustrated by your government not listening?'

'Mostly. We, my colleagues let's call them, and I have grown increasingly concerned over minor incursions, but this latest one, this Spartan Storm, is a game-changer and still no one is taking heed. Comes a point where you have to stand up and act in the best interests of your country.'

'And these six Brits you've told me about and who you and others have no doubt known of for some considerable time…Why haven't I have heard of them before?'

'Because you're like us. No one talks outside of their own little silos. Especially in classified workplaces, no one talks outside of anywhere. Isolated voices, screaming that there are serious problems and the only people up the ladder to hear them…ignore them.'

I watched a shadow pass across Steve's features.

'You're really worried about this.'

'Luke, I think we're facing the biggest threat to the freedoms we enjoy in the West. Period. The spread of computer networks and the reach of official, Chinese state-sponsored espionage into those networks makes the threat of the Soviet Bear in the Cold War look like a puppy on a chain.'

11

Shenzhen, China, December 2003

Lily stepped forward and saluted. The General returned her salute and leant down to pin on her collar insignia. A single chevron underlining crossed rifles and wheat ears.

'Congratulations, Corporal Wai.'

'Thank you, Sir.'

'A few years and I expect to see you apply for your commission as an officer. A few years after that, perhaps you will have my job.'

'Thank you, Sir, but no one could replace you.'

The General shook her hand. 'I believe your mother is in the audience?'

'Yes, Sir. Thank you for everything you have done.'

'It was nothing I did. You have brought great joy on her by your own work. Your skills are worthy of the People and now your mother can see you being recognised for your exemplary talent. It is fitting that you get this early advancement. You have done well these past few years.'

Lily stepped back, saluted once more and then, to the sound of applause, retook her place at the side of the expansive stage. Her movements were filled with grace and confidence. She knew that her mother would have tears and she risked a quick glance into the vast auditorium, trying to seek out that familiar face, but to no avail.

The rest of the newly promoted soldiers were called forward one by one and congratulated, their new rank pinned on, but not by the General. He had retaken his seat with the other dignitaries. A colonel was making the rest of the presentations. The symbolism wasn't lost on Lily. She was his protégé.

Lily felt a surge of pride rise within her. The old angry grandfather, as she always thought of General Chen, truly admired her for her capabilities. He thought of her as his own shining light. She had dedicated herself to pleasing him with her work and in turn he had been good to his word. Her mother and brother were well looked after and were no longer under such close surveillance. They were still not allowed to travel outside of China, but neither were they subject to de-facto house arrest. Lily too was allowed to move more freely when not in work. No longer did she have an escort following her. No longer was she denied the right to visit her mother in Hong Kong. All of it because the General had seen something in her and she had turned out to be better than he had even imagined.

The presentations finished, the closing speech was delivered by the General, thanking the families for coming, congratulating the recipients and acknowledging the great endeavours of the People's Liberation Army in the service of the Party, the People and the Nation. Then the Army Choir, stacked up at the back of the stage in teetering banks of benches, sang the *March of the Volunteers* while Lily stood rigidly at attention and everyone in the auditorium rose to their feet.

*

She hugged her mother tightly. 'Did you cry?'

'Of course I cried. How could I not? You have done amazingly well. I am so proud.'

Lily held her mother tightly. 'Are you?'

Veronica Wai released her grip and gently eased Lily back, so she could look at her daughter. 'Of course, Li— Min Hui,' she said softly. 'Why wouldn't I be? You are alive and healthy. You have provided for me and your brother. You have done everything a daughter could ever do and so much more.'

'But I have done it like this, Mum,' Lily said and pointed to her own uniform.

'You did it in the only way you could. You survived. We survived. That is what is important. That is the only thing that is important. We are all we have left. Do not forget that.'

Lily saw the effort it took for her mother not to cry again, but these would have been tears of grief, not pride. Images of two men swam through Lily's mind. 'I fear Dad would not be proud.'

'Hush now,' her mother said and glanced around the noise-filled hall. Little groups of family members were clustered around individual soldiers. Each cluster smiling and hugging, congratulating and enthusing at their loved one's achievements. 'Here is not the place to talk of your father, but I loved him and I knew him better than anyone and I know he would be proud of you. Proud of how you have survived. Proud of your achievements and proud of how you have protected our family. Focus on that and forget the rest.' She glanced nervously around once more, before whispering, 'Promise me, Lily. Do your work well and keep your thoughts inside your head.'

'I'll try Mum. I'll try.'

12

London, April 2005

Josh Long had been the corporal whom Mark Donoghue brought with him from the RAF Police Headquarters. In his mid-twenties, he was short, wide and angry looking, yet when you got past the veneer it turned out that he played the guitar, liked Mozart, would only drink non-alcoholic beer and was devoted to his dog, a Cocker-Spaniel called Marty. Now he stood in front of my desk with a look on his face that made me wonder if Marty had died.

'Josh? Is everything alright?'

'Yes, Sir. And no. We think we've found one.'

I looked past Josh, out of the office window and across the Thames. The light April showers gave a softness to the scene, with river boats gliding through calm, but rain-pitted waters and the London Eye, revolving slowly above the South Bank casting its monocular gaze back at me. The huge wheel moved so serenely and I tried to will its sedate calmness into my now knotted stomach.

It had been five months since Steve Jäeger and I had discussed the possibilities of establishing a real team of cyber experts. The man had been right about everything. The extra posts within the

JOCCSy had existed and John Leofric had been completely on board with the suggestions. Even the shifting around of the Brit personnel had been done much more smoothly than I would have thought possible. The first arrival, Warrant Officer Rachel Kennedy, as capable and, even I had to admit, as beguiling as she had been when I first met her on the Defence Debriefing Team, had turned up before Christmas.

The last Brit, Chief Petty Officer Ashley Young, arrived in the second week of February. Both women were in their early thirties and from what I knew of the normal progression through the non-commissioned ranks, both had been promoted in advance of the norm. Steve had told me the people he was recommending were the best. My initial impressions were that he had been correct. As for Ashley, Steph had almost adopted her on sight.

'We Navy girls need to stick together,' she had announced on Ashley's arrival and I was genuinely pleased. We still needed Steph to run the office and she did have a knack of making the banalities of MoD administration run more smoothly. Likewise, we still needed Colonel Charles, Dave and Jim to produce their intelligence summaries, but in my mind, that was more about giving them something to do to keep them out of harm's way than contributing anything much by way of significance. The Colonel was still my boss and was genuinely interested in the changing direction of the unit, but he had all but ceded command of the new arrivals to me. I had worried he would feel usurped, but if anything he had sounded grateful when he'd beckoned me over following Leofric's announcement of the way things were going to be.

'I think I'm a bit long in the tooth to be grasping state-of-the-art technologies, Luke. Why don't I provide you some mentorship when it comes to pulling a new team together, but you run with the day-to-day operations?'

He'd been true to his word. Dave and Jim hadn't minded and their only contribution to date had been an actual wolf-whistle when Rachel Kennedy first walked in. I could not believe that one of the two of them, or perhaps it was both, had done it, and was about to tear into them for their unprofessionalism, their complete lack of respect, their ungentlemanly conduct and whatever else I could manage through my rage, but Rachel, obviously seeing the flush of anger spreading across my face had waved me back into my seat.

'It's okay, Sir,' she had said quietly. Turning to face Dave and Jim, she'd casually walked across to their desks, leant down next to each in turn and said a few words. I had watched both men colour red in embarrassment before Rachel returned to me.

'What did you say?'

'No need to worry, Sir. It's sorted. Sticks and stones, but I doubt they'll do it again. To me or anyone else.'

The thirty-year veteran military cop, Mark Donoghue and his much younger associate, Josh Long had also arrived before Christmas, coming straight in from the RAF Police Headquarters. Rob Curzon, a tall, thin man with over twenty years' experience in GCHQ arrived in the first week of January, quickly followed by RAF Sergeant, Ritchie Adams who had come from the Intelligence School at Chicksands. Ritchie, fresh-faced with freckles and a shock of ginger hair, turned out to be not only an expert on electronic signals intelligence, but a multi-linguist, speaking four languages fluently and another two passably. I found it fascinating that he was able to communicate so effectively as I often had trouble deciphering his thick Scottish accent.

By February all that was missing was the American exchange officer we'd been promised. Steve had said it might take time to sort out, but in the interim he arranged for the US cyber team to send us the information they had on the Chinese malware that had been discovered during Spartan Storm. With Rob Curzon and his former team in GCHQ providing much needed technical expertise, we'd spent the last few months searching through the British computer networks that the US had known to be infected. We'd found every instance of where we'd been infiltrated and using the American provided solutions we had restored and protected our networks. More generally, we had started to work as a fairly cohesive team. The task was relatively simple as the hard work had been done by the US defence contractor, who according to Steve, was still severely annoyed that no one in the US Government was taking a blind bit of notice.

I had talked to John Leofric about the UK Government and, between his ever-increasingly long lunches at his club in Pall Mall, John told me to look to the operations we could do and worry about the Government later.

It had been reasonable advice and we'd finished off the Spartan Storm problems on British networks before Easter. Then we set about a logically devised, systematic approach to searching every other British Military computer network for instances that hadn't previously been discovered. Three weeks into the search and without discovering any breaches, I had been thinking that Steve's observations about the haphazard nature of our computer networks might just have saved us. That was before Josh had presented himself in front of my desk.

'Okay, let's hear it,' I said to Josh and rose from my seat. He led me to our small briefing room which, cut off from the main office, afforded even greater security and privacy. The rest of my team were already assembled and Mark Donoghue was standing next to the lectern. A projector showed a picture of a standard issue, military laptop.

'Carry on,' I said, taking my seat around the eight-seater oval table that almost filled the rest of the space.

'As you know, we've been using the original malware that was found on Spartan to see if code with similar profiles or signature methods turns up anywhere else. Last night, Rob and Ritchie found what they thought might be an instance of it within the source code of the military mobile communications network, Ptarmigan.'

I interrupted him and felt comfortable doing so. I was far from being shy about admitting when I didn't know something.

'It's a battlefield wide-area-network communications system. Originally designed for the British Army of the Rhine, it was voice only but adapted and expanded to carry data in the mid-eighties. It's now email and document transfer capable and as such it's used across deployed Army, Navy and Air Force units. It's the main go-to system if you are on a RAF Squadron, or a Royal Navy ship or in an Army battalion.'

I'd been on none of them, so was happy that I'd never come across it, but the fact it was deployed so widely made my already knotted stomach twist further. I nodded for Mark to continue.

'We set up an overnight software trace and as of this morning we got a positive hit for malware. It's deeply embedded and very well disguised but it is there and it has been active for some time.'

'How long?' I asked, dreading the answer as I saw Mark's sideways glance to Rob and the tightening of the veteran cop's facial muscles. When I'd first met Mark he'd reminded me a little of Christopher Lee, the former Dracula actor. Not really because of his looks, but there was something about his demeanour. Serious and severe. Now he looked serious, severe and saddened.

'At least two years. We've found evidence that exercise plans and exercise briefings had been siphoned off. I wasn't too worried about that as they reside on an unclassified level of the system. However, as we looked further we discovered that deployments of ships, aircraft and ground units in support of Middle-East operations have also been copied. Potentially most worrying, Special Forces deployment details, down to times and positions have also been copied off the system.'

'For the last two years?'

'Possibly longer, but certainly, the last two. Yes. It totals thousands of documents.'

I took a breath and looked up to the screen. 'And the picture of the laptop?'

'Rob and his mates at GCHQ couldn't fathom how the code could have spread so far within what is a modular system. It should have been stopped within a single regiment or squadron, not spread throughout the network. So, we ran another search code through and traced back the entry points. These laptops were bought on a major procurement initiative by the MoD procurement branch and that's Ashley's area of expertise, so I'll hand over to her,' Mark said.

'You know the MoD, Sir,' she said with a roll of her eyes. 'They couldn't just go to the nearest high street computer shop and have the whole thing done in a week. Oh no. They had to put out a call for tenders which they sent to companies back in May 1998. The original contract was for seven thousand hardened, as in military ruggedised, laptops which could withstand temperatures up to forty-three degrees and down to minus twelve. The original contract was to be met within one year and had a value of one hundred and five million pounds.'

'And by the time they actually got them into service?' I asked, fearing the usual track record of MoD procurement debacles.

'It was September 2002 and the total cost was three hundred and seventy-five million.'

'My goodness, that is one expensive laptop.'

'Yes it is, Sir. But it turns out we did get extra for our money,' Ashley said with a grin that lit up her face but died before I had a chance to reciprocate.

The picture on the wall changed to a close up of the PC's internal boards and chips.

Mark spoke again. 'The winning bid was from a company called *Action PC*, seemingly a conglomerate formed for the purpose. They used mostly off-the-shelf components that can be found in the majority of modern laptops and put them inside a specifically designed hardened shell casing. The product is a really good one. It was completely worthy of the job it needed to do, and it still is. However,' he paused and using a laser pointer, circled a small computer chip on the photo. 'The extra we got for our money is that they planted a backdoor access point into any network that this system would be plugged into. A specific piece of hardware and software designed to breach the main mobile network of the UK's deployed military. A task it's been happily doing for at least two years.'

It was so much worse than I had imagined. 'Our own, specially procured laptops are the gateway in?'

I got a series of affirmative nods back.

'Surely we can take this company to the cleaners? Get their executives arrested? Can we still hang people for treason? Or throw them in the Tower?'

Mark inclined his head to Ashley.

'I checked, Sir,' she said. 'The company was dissolved shortly after the buy went through. The contract hadn't called for any form of maintenance program to be instigated. In fact the ongoing support for the laptops was sourced to a completely separate organisation. One that, if it came to it, probably would be as surprised as we were to find this backdoor.'

I went to speak, but Ashley continued. 'As for the executives. None of them are UK citizens.'

I felt the knots fall from my stomach, to be replaced with a dull and heavy ache. 'Please do not tell me we placed a procurement for vital military communications equipment with…' I hesitated. It was too ludicrous for words. The projector screen gave a small flash as the next picture appeared on the wall. I looked up to see a very stylised and well-rendered image of the Chinese flag.

*

The hard bass and techno-mix of Sophie Ellis-Bextor's *Shoot From the Hip* album filled my head. The Bose headphones provided me with complete isolation and immersion into her voice and lyrics. I figured I'd chosen it subliminally as the randomised playlist brought me, *It's a Mixed up World*.

I was sitting in my favourite armchair gazing out of my apartment windows at the Thames. Across the water, against a sky reflecting the lights of the city, the jagged spires of the Palace of Westminster. On my side of the river, the green and cream terraces of the MI6 building. Star of many a Bond movie, my immediate neighbour was probably the world's most conspicuous secret headquarters. Below me, what had once been one of London's biggest wharfs. Back when the port and the nation it served had been pre-eminent in the world. Millions of tonnes of cargo from around the globe, coming in to the heart of Empire. An Empire that was intrinsically embedded into the lives of billions. Now the wharf's waters were undisturbed by vessels. The unbroken, glistening surface lit by the ornate street lamps of the Vauxhall Bridge and the glow from a hundred up-market apartments, was nothing more than a picturesque accompaniment to a new-money lifestyle. The true heart of the wharf, the commerce that drove its being, was long gone. As was the Empire. Replaced with a country that bought its military hardware from a rival nation and was no doubt being laughed at for its stupidity.

I raised my glass to my lips and accompanied by Sophie's more mellow tones, singing *Nowhere Without You*, drained the last of the Stellenbosch Chenin Blanc. I concentrated on the stereo remote control and pressed the pause button at the second attempt, slipped off my headphones and made my way to the kitchen. Two empty bottles of the South African wine stood like silent sentinels to my evening. I glanced across the apartment to my open bedroom door and then back to my wine rack. I eased a third bottle out of its restraint and with a little awkwardness, managed to uncork it. I went back to my chair and, with headphones back on, I let the wine and the unique tones of Sophie's voice sweep away my concerns. The album's random playing seemed to sense my needs. *Party in My Head* beat its way into my brain and I wondered if Sophie reminded me of Kate Bush, or the other way round. I turned the volume up and wished I could unplug the headphones, to let the whole building appreciate the rhythm. But that wouldn't be the responsible, good-citizen thing to do. I was a good citizen. Even if most of my life had been spent in denial. Even if my country was being fucking stupid.

Party in My Head ended with a slow fade, replaced in a moment with the steady beat and synthesisers of *Another Day*. My tomorrow would be exactly that. A day to start fighting back. A day to secure our first little victory in a war I hadn't been aware of. I drained the rest of the wine.

*

I was in work ten minutes early and took my third set of paracetamol for the morning, rinsed down with a cup of Steph's coffee. Rob, Josh and Ritchie had beaten me in by about two hours and gave me a hopeful look as I enquired how it was going.

Rob pointed to the hardened laptop on his desk. A keyboard and secondary monitors were hooked into it and the twin screens above the black case were filled with lines of code.

'We have a second laptop up on an isolated part of the network down in Tidworth Barracks. If we can get the code to compile we can upload it and then send it on its way. If we have it correct then the backdoor access will be denied, the systems will be isolated and then we can kill the code that was there. It should take a few seconds but once it's done and proved, we should be able to deploy the fix to the whole network. Anytime a laptop is hooked on to the network it will be sanitised. Simple enough really.'

'I'll take your word for it, Rob.'

'Not me this time, Luke,' Rob said. He was the only one of the team to call me by my first name. Not that any of us wore uniform or bothered about rank, but the military members of the team still referred to me as, Sir, whereas Rob, a Civil Servant, called me Luke. I'd have been happy with all of them calling me Luke, but even I understood that there were limits to how flexible the military could be.

'Really, not you?' I asked.

'No. Young Ritchie did the majority of the design on this code,' he said pointing across the desk.

'Congratulations. I'm impressed,' I said.

'Ach, he's tae modest. Me and Josh dinny dae anything wi'out Rob. Ye ken that anyway. But it's good tae see it al' work.'

I gave Ritchie a nod, took a swig from my coffee and slowly allowed my brain to process what he'd said.

'Okay,' Rob said. 'We're set. Luke, you just have to give the word.'

Glancing around I saw Rachel, Ashley and Mark coming into the office and beckoned them over.

'Right Rob. Go ahead. One small step and all that. Our first time defending one of our networks by ourselves.'

Rob pressed the enter key and both screens went blank. Had Rob not said, 'Oh!' I wouldn't have known anything was amiss.

'Oh? That's not the sound I had been expecting.'

'Eh…no. That's because my screens going blank wasn't the effect I was expecting,' Rob said.

The telephone on Josh's desk began to ring.

'JOCCSy, Corporal Hen— Yes...of course...No...Fuck it. I'll get back to you.' Josh hung up the phone and looked over to me with trepidation. I didn't think it was because he'd sworn down a phone line.

'Problems?' I asked.

'That was Tidworth. Their laptop and the whole of their network within the office has shut down.'

'Rob? What's going on?' It was Mark Donoghue asking the question.

'I...I'm not sure Mark. I think...' Rob pushed his chair away from the desk and crabbed his way across to his own computer. He called both Josh and Ritchie to join him. Mark inclined his head towards the area in the office that held a kettle and a coffee filter machine. Rachel, Ashley and I walked with him. I knew, even after a scant few months, that when Rob, Josh and Ritchie got heads down on a problem, you gave them space to get on with it. They'd let us know as and when they could. In the meantime I could have another coffee, tidy up a lot of outstanding reports and hope that things would be okay. Hope and coffee. Empires had been built on the same.

*

We were back in the briefing room and all of us, including John Leofric, were seated around the table. Rob didn't stand, nor was he apologetic or submissive.

'The original programmer that placed the backdoor code into the laptops was extremely gifted. He'd embedded a booby-trap into the system that activated if his code was tampered with. It dropped its pretence of hiding and sent a destruct message to the network. It would spread in the same way as the backdoor program had, so in effect, every time another node connected to the network it too would be destroyed.'

'And how much damage has our attempt done?' I asked.

'Limited. We had Tidworth up to be the test for remote deployment of the fix, but we had instructed them to be isolated from the wider network. We knew there were risks and so it made sense to try out our fix incrementally.'

John shifted in his chair. 'So no real harm done if, and I assume we can, fix Tidworth?'

Rob agreed, 'Yes. We can fix it, but to do that we have to restore the original code, so the backdoor access will also be restored. We'll be back to square one.'

'Can your colleagues at Cheltenham help out?' I asked.

'They haven't seen anything this sophisticated either and they are really, really good at these sorts of code tricks.'

'So what do we do?' John asked in a tone that made me immediately aware I had misjudged this long-lunch break, carpet-collecting, former defence attaché. He had a steel to his personality that had passed me by.

Rob looked across to Mark Donoghue. The stern Flight Sergeant, de-facto head of my technical team, stated the truth without fanfare. 'We need outside help. The US cyber teams are probably the only ones that have defeated stuff like this before. We need that liaison officer.'

Leofric sat forward. 'Okay. Well, we are no worse off than we were. It was a good attempt. We just need to get smarter. Luke, you and I will be having dinner with a mutual acquaintance. He promised us an officer. He needs to deliver. Anything else?'

I answered for the team and we stood as John Leofric swept out of the room.

'I didnay ken he 'cud move that fast,' said Ritchie.

13

London, May 2005

Captain Daniel Stückl walked into my apartment like an all-American hero striding off the pages of a comic strip. He was taller than me by a couple of inches and his broad shoulders, slim waist, blond hair, blue eyes, perfect teeth and slightly tanned skin gave him a look so at odds with the usual inhabitants of London that I wondered if he had a cape under his perfectly tailored suit.

He pulled behind him a single case and over his shoulder carried a small backpack. I wondered had he been fully briefed that we wanted him for six months, or perhaps he just travelled extremely light.

'Luke, I presume. I'm Daniel Stückl, but everyone calls me Dan.' His light American accent carried no heavy overtones that I could place and the effect was for it to sound calm and melodic to my ear. He grinned and the expression was reflected in his eyes as I reached out and shook his hand. I wondered if he was attempting to break my knuckles, but his face betrayed no such intention. The man was simply strong. I reclaimed my slightly mangled fingers and waved for him to follow me, guiding him through to the main living room.

'Nice view,' he said, walking across to look out of the windows. 'This must cost a fortune for the military to hire.'

'I wouldn't know. It's paid for in the background, but I think it belongs to some old General who's spending his retirement up in the country and never plans to return. From what I gather he wanted it to go to some decent use, rather than some corporate banker.'

Dan placed his hand on the leather sofa and indicated the antique sideboard. 'And he left his furniture?'

I knew I had reddened, but there wasn't much I could do. 'Eh…No. The furniture is mine.'

He raised an eyebrow and flashed that grin again. 'Oops. Sorry. Didn't mean to offend in my first five minutes. I figured the chrome and black stereo system was yours and the television and all that,' he said, waving an arm in the direction of the kitchen, equipped with modern and, I thought, sleek looking appliances.

'Yes, they're mine too. What can I say? I like modern gadgets but antique furniture. It's a quirk I suppose.'

'Heck no. It's a good quirk. Kinda makes the place feel modern and homely. I like it.'

Strangely, having only just met him, I knew he meant the compliment and wasn't saying it for effect. I showed him to his room, off a short hallway past the kitchen. Each of the two bedrooms in the apartment had their own attached bathrooms.

'Nice,' he said appreciatively and dumped his bags before following me back into the living room.

'Tea, coffee, drink?' I asked.

'Oh no alcohol for me. I might have a coffee. Then I thought I'd have a shower, clean up a bit before I take a couple of hours out for my nightly Bible reading. I'd like to invite you to join me for that of course. Evening prayers are so much better when shared. Don't you think?'

My heart sank and my mouth went dry. I had no issue with anyone's religious views, but I had a massive problem with anyone foisting theirs on to me. Especially some holier than thou evangelistic military missionary. Inside my head I imagined a picture of

Steve Jäeger, laughing at my expense. I realised Dan was still look-ing at me for an answer. I shifted uneasily on my feet. 'Umm…Eh…Probably n—'

Dan's face broke into a wide smile and he laughed. 'Oh boy, Steve Jäeger said you'd react like that. He told me to keep it up for the first day until you could take no more, but man, you wouldn't cope for five minutes.'

'You complete bas—' I said and laughed with him.

'He also tells me you make a mean G&T. I'll have one of those if it's going.'

I felt my heart and mouth return to normal. 'Remind me to slap Steve around the head the next time we see him.'

'Yeah, I'd probably advise against that,' Dan said.

'Really? Do you know his background then?' I asked and made my way to the drinks cabinet, retrieving a bottle of Tanqueray Number Ten and then to the fridge to get ice, tonic and lemons.

'No. Not really. He was in Vietnam, that we're sure of, but we call him the mysterious Mr Jäeger. I mean me and the guys at the US cyber centre know him, for sure, but no one really knows who he works for. I have my suspicions though,'

'Me too,' I agreed. 'I reckon CIA at Langley.'

'I wouldn't argue with that,' Dan said.

I put some ice into a glass, poured a good measure of gin and held it up. Dan indicated a little less. I poured the second glass to his liking and reached for a knife and cutting board.

'So Steve told you I had requested someone, umm, let's say, normal?'

'Yeah. He said specifically that I was to stir you up on the Bi-ble-bashing thing.'

'Ah! But he did also tell you that this was a six-month tour?'

'Yeah. Why?'

'Well, you seem to be travelling really light? Say when,' I said and poured tonic until he waved for me to stop. It almost filled his glass to the rim. I put the smallest dash into my own. 'Cheers,' I said and handed his drink across.

'Cheers. And yeah, kinda light, but my orders to move only came through three days ago. It's been a bit rushed.'

'Three days? But this move's been in the planning for months.' I motioned him across to the wingback leather armchair and I sat on the couch.

'Yeah,' he continued. 'It was planned and we had a guy earmarked for London, but then things got delayed and put back and the first officer broke his arm and you know how the military goes. Yours and mine are no different I guess. Difficult for them to organise the simple stuff when there is no pressure. The second guy was due to leave next week but then we got word you wanted a specialist white hat.'

'A what?'

Dan inclined his head and I was reminded of the two Hungarian Vizsla dogs my family had kept when I was growing up. Big, powerful, strong and occasionally at a complete loss for what we were trying to get them to do. They'd tilt their heads and almost frown as if to say, 'Are you for real?' When they did it I'd laugh and stroke their broad foreheads. I resisted doing the same with Dan and thought a quick explanation of my lack of technical prowess would suffice. He didn't seem put out.

'I get it. You see the big picture stuff. I worked with a guy like you before. Very useful actually. Works well with what I do.'

'And what you do is…be a white hat?'

'You know in the old Western movies, when John Wayne and the good guys wore white hats and the bad guys wore black ones?'

'Not really,' I admitted. 'But I'll take your word for it.'

'White hat hackers are programmers that hack systems to test them, find the weaknesses and then fix them up.'

'And black hatters are bad hackers? Yes?' I asked and took a long sip of my drink. The light touch of tonic did nothing to dilute the edge off the gin. It was how the drink should be. Ice cold and with a kick.

'Yes,' Dan said and took a sip from his own glass. I couldn't help but ponder that it must have tasted rather weak given how he had preferred the measures. However, better to drink in company than alone. I waited for him to set his glass down on the table.

'And you have this white hat as a job in the US military?'

'Not quite. We have computer security specialists and I was *recruited* to be one of those.' The emphasis on the word made me wonder.

'Recruited? Specifically, or you joined up and they put you in there?'

He hesitated and looked at me from under eyelashes that I now noticed were much longer than the norm for a man. They were an almost feminine feature on someone who was most certainly not. It softened his expression and made it look almost sheepish. There was a story behind Captain Stückl's recruitment and he seemed open enough to telling it. 'Go on,' I prompted.

'Well...enlisting was the other option they offered.'

'Other?'

'I may have been caught hacking into some sites that I shouldn't have. I was offered to use my skills for the good of the nation, or see the inside of the Federal Pen in southern Illinois.'

'Seriously?'

'Yeah. I weighed things up and figured the furlough and the uniform were better in the Army. Seemed a shame to lock me up.'

'How old were you?'

'I'd only turned twenty, so no youth schemes or easy life options. The Pen or the US Army.'

I realised I'd been holding my glass halfway to my mouth, entranced by his revelation. I set it down gently. 'You must have been good at hacking?'

'Not bad,' he said with another sheepish grin. 'Then I got a lot better with the power of Uncle Sam behind me. They turned me into a professional white hat. I've spent the last few years shutting down attempts to infiltrate our systems. We've been successful enough, once we eventually found the incursions.'

'You mean Spartan Storm took you by surprise?'

'Oh yeah. It's rocked a lot of folk to their core. Leaving aside the politics of it. But we've made up good ground and have shut it down now. Even if all I did was shut the stable door after quite a lot of horses had already bolted.'

'Well, if that's what a white hat does, then yes we are in need of a white hat. A massive, ten-gallon, full-on Texan white hat please. We found a piece of probably Chinese malware in one of our networks and when we tried to delete it—'

'Let me guess, the whole thing imploded?'

'Pretty much.'

'Yeah, we've seen the same before.'

'Mmm, we hadn't and that's why we asked for help. In fact we pleaded for it and Steve Jäeger decided to send you.'

'I don't know who asked who to be honest. But, whoever it was my orders to move came through in a rush. Like a real rush. The delays and procrastination were gone. Three days ago, I was told by my boss to say my goodbyes and get on a flight to London. Said they'd send any other stuff over as and when I needed it.'

'Say your goodbyes?' I drained the last of my drink and stood, offering a refill to Dan.

'Eh, no. I'm good for the minute.'

Back behind the kitchen counter, I poured myself a second. 'Your goodbyes?' I asked again.

'Yes. My wife and little boy.'

'Oh! I see. I didn't realise…I mean, no ring,' I said pointing to his hand.

'Eh, no. No ring. And don't be sorry. I…'

He paused, taking a sip of his gin and looking a little uncomfortable. I'd usually have let it slide, but like earlier, I seemed to know his mood. I had barely spent twenty minutes in his company, but I sensed a deep-seated conflict within Dan Stückl. The thought of someone so recently met, in fact anyone, no matter how long met, sharing personal issues with me was one I would normally have avoided at all costs, but this felt different. I surprised myself by saying, 'It's okay. You can tell me if you want to. I won't be shocked.'

'Let's just say that I'll miss Ryan, my little boy…'

'Ah. I see. How old?'

'He'll be two this September. Sweet kid.'

'And you're going to be okay staying for the full six months that we asked for?'

'Sure am. Heck, if they sent me to Afghanistan it would be for nine and you guys have decent views and a whole West End full of theatres, so, yeah, I'll cope.'

I returned back to my seat. 'Are you hungry?'

'You cook as well?'

'I've been known to, yes. What of it?' I asked, allowing myself to grin as I said it. I was no good at keeping a straight face like he had with his Bible story.

'Heck no. Sounds good to me. I might go and wash off the airline smell and change if that's okay?'

*

'You can certainly cook,' Dan said, easing himself back in his chair.

'Thanks. I like to. Normally I don't do it that much. Dinners for one can be a bit sad and lonely. More wine?' I asked, proffering the Chenin Blanc.

Dan offered his glass across to me. 'Just a half for me and yeah, I get that.'

'You do?'

He hesitated.

'It's okay, I wasn't meaning to pry.'

'No, I guess if we're going to be sharing this space for the next few months the topic's bound to come up. Might as well get it said.'

I refilled my own glass and sat back.

'My wife, Shirlene and I had been together for a brief while when we were in high school. Then I was home over the Christmas holidays a few years ago and we met up at a party. One thing led to another and all of a sudden I'm getting a phone call saying she was pregnant.'

'Ah. And you thought the old-fashioned, honourable thing was the right thing?'

'Kinda. I'm told by most that you can't tell from my accent, but I grew up in a town called Onawa, some ways north of Omaha, Nebraska. A small town with smaller imaginations. People know everyone else's business and I knew that even though I didn't live there anymore, my folks and the rest of my family would suffer the shame that I got Shirlene in the family way and then ran.'

A question occurred to me and I almost asked it bluntly. Dan saw me stop myself.

'Let me guess? You're wondering if the kid was mine at all? Was she just doing this to use me as her ticket out of there?'

'Well, I apologise, but yes. Was she?'

'I wondered myself, but there was no way to know. No way to prove it. By the time I came home to see her, it seemed the whole town knew we were going to have a kid. I figured I could do worse. We'd had some good times in high school and she is a looker.' He reached out and took a drink of his wine.

'But?'

Dan looked back at me. 'Yeah, she has a nice butt.'

I felt my face colour red. 'Eh no! No that's not what I meant, I meant is there—'

'And good legs too.' He delivered it deadpan but I caught the slightest twinkle in his eyes.

'Ha! Very funny!'

He laughed. 'I can see I'm going to have a lot of fun with you over the next six months and yes, you're right. There was a but. I had moved on a lot from the boy I'd been in high school. Shirlene was still the same old Shirlene. With an added bonus that her temper had got a whole helluva' lot worse than when she was sixteen and believe me, it had been potent enough back then.'

'You still went ahead with the wedding?'

'Didn't seem to me I had much choice. It wasn't quite a shotgun affair, but Shirlene's family could have made life uncomfortable for some of my relatives, so yeah. I went ahead with it.'

'And I'm assuming it hasn't worked out too well?'

'Not really. We got a house on base, near DC, and I took to spending a lot of nights working late and having dinner on my own when I finally got home. Don't get me wrong, Ryan my son is great. And yes, he is mine.'

I frowned by way of asking him how he knew.

'Shirlene's Mom fell and broke her leg about six months after Ryan was born, so Shirlene had to make a quick dash home. I was good friends with some of the combat medical team on base. Me and one of the doctors used to play in the same softball team. I asked him for a favour.'

'He ran a DNA test?'

'Yep. Came back sure as. He's my boy.'

'Well that's good.'

'Yes. It is. And…'

I watched him drop his gaze. His hands, resting on top of the dining table were folded one over the other, but I could see the tension in his knuckles. 'You half wanted him not to be yours. That would have given you a way out?'

A half-shrug, a small sigh and then Dan looked up at me and gave a brief nod. I fought a powerful urge to reach over to him. He obviously felt guilty for his actions and any plan he might have had. I thought it seemed perfectly reasonable.

I let the moment stretch out before I asked, quietly, 'So things haven't improved over time?'

He laughed. A proper laugh, spreading to his eyes and raising his mood. 'Gosh no. Worse if anything. She shouts and smashes her way through arguments when I'm home and shouts down phone lines at me when I'm not. If I'd been the religious sort, I'd have prayed for a deployment just to get the hell away. I couldn't believe it when I got offered London. I'd almost got to the point of volunteering to go to Iraq.'

'Well, I'm glad you're here. Maybe it'll give you some space to think and I know my team can certainly do with your help.' I lifted the bottle again and reached across the table.

Dan covered his glass with his hand. 'I'm good, th—' He interrupted himself with a yawn.

'Bit of jet lag?' I asked, pouring the rest of the bottle into my glass. 'Or am I boring you already?'

'Probably.'

'You are a bit of a sod aren't you?'

Standing and looking down at me he nodded, gave me a wink and said, 'Yeah, but you'll get used to it. I think I might crash so I can be ready for tomorrow. I assume you'll want me to work for my keep?'

'You assume correctly,' I said.

It felt like he held my gaze for a slight moment longer than I expected, then he turned towards his room. As he passed the kitchen bench he glanced back, 'Goodnight, Luke.'

I listened as his door clicked shut and stared at the glass of wine in front of me. I wasn't drunk. Not near to it, but I could feel a buzz around the edges of my thoughts. A frisson that made the world seem kinder. Or less threatening. Less hurtful. I heard the words again, 'Goodnight, Luke' and saw the backward glance. But the words weren't being spoken by Dan. In my mind's eye I saw another blond, blue-eyed figure. He was sixteen, like me. Both of us boarders at Sedbergh. He'd only arrived that term, but had settled in quickly enough.

I'd been upset over something I could no longer remember and Matthew had come to stand next to my bed. He had told me not to worry and that if I wanted to, I could come and lie next to him, in his bed. It might make me feel better. I'd said no, but had wanted to say yes. He made no more requests and left, drawing the curtains which separated each bed space from its neighbour. At the last moment he glanced back and wished me goodnight.

The old school house was called after an even older school master. Evans had been his name and the dormitory had probably changed little since he'd stalked the classrooms a hundred years before. I lay awake, intrigued by Matthew and his offer. I waited until the sounds of sleep came from my dozen or so dorm-mates and quietly climbed out of bed. Barefooted, I walked silently half the length of the room counting the curtains and stopped. My heart was beating almost out of my chest and I willed it to be quiet. I slipped inside the curtains and reached for the blankets and sheet that covered Matthew. His hand covered mine. He'd been awake. Waiting.

I felt the warmth from his body and his breath on my neck as we cuddled together. It felt comforting.

'Luke?' He whispered it so quietly.

'Yes?' My voice sounded strange to my own ears. Like I was breathless.

'I had a friend at my last school. We used to do...things. At night. When we were together. Would you like to try them?'

I felt my heart race on like it would break free from my chest. My mouth was dry and my tongue stuck to the roof of it, but still I managed a hoarse whisper. 'Yes.'

14

London, May-June 2005

The obligatory introductions to the rest of the office took almost an hour. Dan was charming to everyone and deferential in the right amount to John Leofric, Colonel Charles and even Dave and Jim. I'd briefed him during our half hour walk to the office.

Steph fussed over him like he was her long lost son, a feat she still managed to do to me even after all this time, although I'm not sure Steph ever looked at me in the same way she looked at Dan. Rachel and Ashley were the epitome of professionalism when introduced, but I did catch the glance they swapped as Dan left them. Apparently the eye-candy in the office had taken a turn for the better, but at least they refrained from wolf whistles.

John Leofric was the final introduction and I thought Dan might have been in his office for an hour or more, but instead it was mere minutes before John escorted him back to my desk. 'Dan, Luke. I'll leave you both to it. I don't care how we manage it but I'm relying on you to get this sorted. I want that malware taken care of.'

'Yes, Sir,' we said at the same time and Dan grinned at me. Leofric departed back to his office and we were left standing on opposite sides of my desk.

'We'll grab a coffee and then make a start?' I suggested.

'Sure.'

I waved for him to follow me across to our coffee machine. 'We used to have a full kitchen in our old office, but all we have is this now. Mind you, don't be surprised if Steph keeps you so topped up with caffeine that you ping off the walls...How'd you take it?'

'Straight black coffee, no cream, no sugar, thanks.'

I almost corrected him that the Brits used milk and his chances of getting cream in his coffee were slim to none, but I thought he'd pick up those nuances in time. I poured the coffee and handed it over.

He sipped, grimaced a little and said, 'Okay then, where's the code you want me to take a look at?'

*

I'd occasionally watched Ritchie, Rob and Josh when they were coding. Ritchie and Rob were touch-typists, their fingers moving rapidly on the keys. Josh was faster than my staccato two-finger typing, but nowhere near to being touch. They would open up command line entry boxes on screen and type in a series of, to me, meaningless commands and codes. It looked complex and, the first time I observed it, intimidating. Now I watched from behind Dan's shoulder and realised that my three guys were in a different league. A much lower one. Dan Stückl called up command line boxes at a rate I could barely follow and his fingers hammered out code, making the click-clack of the keyboard sound like a machine gun on full automatic.

When I'd observed Rob, probably the best of our programmers, I had considered fretting about my lack of technical skills, but in the end was comfortable that what I brought to the team was complementary. Now, as I watched Dan I realised that not if I took the next decade to study computers and programming could I get near to the skills this man had. Without reference to any book or notes he swapped from screen to screen and let out the occasional 'Umm' or 'Aww'. As for my three programmers, they made much more admiring sounds. I even heard Ritchie say something which sounded like, 'No way would I have ever thought of that. No way.' But with Ritchie I could never be sure.

*

Three-and-a-half hours later, with the office wall clock ticking towards midday, Dan pushed himself away from the screens and walked back over to my desk.

'It's done. Well, it's ready to be done. One more command and the system will do what you want it to do.'

'Kill off the malware and spread throughout the network sanitising as it goes?'

'Yep.'

'Okay. But you haven't done it yet?'

He glanced towards John Leofric's office. 'Nope.'

It made sense to me. We both went to the old man's office door and invited him to be the one to instigate the command. He appeared quite touched by the idea and with a semblance of understated formality, obliged. The whole team gathered round as the system dashboard, which Rob and Ritchie had designed, showed the status of infected hosts on the network. One by one and occasionally in fast bursts the number decreased down and down. In under half an hour it hit zero to a combined cheer and a lot of handshaking.

'Each laptop that isn't on the system will be cleaned once it hooks in, so that's it,' Dan said reaching out and shaking my hand. He held it a little longer than would be usual and spoke quietly so only I would hear. 'Well, I say that's it. That's the first. The good Lord alone knows how many more infected systems you guys have. I know we had no clue when we first went looking and the answer was a real shock.'

I feared he was right, and I thought we'd be in for a long and possibly fruitless search, but if there were latent threats out there, we had to be the ones to find them. The only good news was that we'd survived with the malware this far and apart from, as Dan had put it, bolting the stable doors after many horses had absconded, there was no real urgency in our task. Not for the first time, I was wrong about almost everything.

15

London, July 2005

The bright, early sun of a cloudless July morning wasn't what woke me, but the ringing of my phone. From the other side of the apartment I could hear Dan's ringing too. The screen showed "Office – Mark Donoghue" and the time nestled above it, 04:37. It wasn't going to be good news.

'Hello.'

'We need you in, Sir.'

My phone was a standard cell phone and not secure, so the level of questioning I could manage on it was by necessity curtailed. I settled for trying to know how bad things would be when I got into the office. 'Level?'

'Critical.'

I felt a strange mix of fear and excitement. In the last few months we had found more breaches, like Dan had predicted, but each and every one of them had only ever been ranked as moderate to severe by the amount of data stolen. Research and development plans, defence spending, projected budgets, projected foreign policy statements, it had all been hoovered up and sent, via a series of increasingly complex hops across the world, to final locations that we were almost certain were within China. Each breach had been closed down, documented and the subsequent reports sent, and sometimes taken personally by John Leofric, to the Government departments concerned. Each and every time the Labour Party ministers in charge noted the contents of the reports and did nothing more. There was to be no overt reaction, no hue and cry in the United Nations, no retaliation. I started to feel more and more annoyance at the political inaction and the seeming lack of courage to react, but for the team's sake I said and did nothing. As an alternative I tried to get traction through the Air Force Intelligence headquarters again, but only succeeded in getting even more frustrated by Group Captain Halson. His pig-like voice intoned more patronising suggestions that I was a disgrace to my uniform and I managed, just about, not to tell him I had swapped my uniform for a very well cut Jermyn Street tailored three-piece that he wouldn't have the grace or style to wear and all in all he could go f…

Instead I concentrated on what we could do. One by one we closed down the vulnerabilities and moved on to finding the next. With each success we got more skilled, but so did our unseen adversaries. They were constantly updating and adapting. I remarked to Dan that it was like a fencing match. We blocked and parried and they continually adapted, seeking out weaknesses. He said it had been the same in the US, but that now the adaptations were happening more quickly. Like they too were evolving. It was harder and harder to protect the systems.

For the preceding two months we had noticed that each attack that we traced would re-route through many more locations before attempting the final step of penetrating our networks. The malicious code would piggy-back onto computers that had been taken over without their actual users being aware. Each one left a unique Internet Protocol address that should have made our job in finding the source and pinning it to a physical spot on earth easier. Instead, these multiple IPs made the process of tracking backwards that much more difficult. Yet none of the breaches we had found had tried to deny the use of a system either temporarily or completely. Each incursion had been made with the single goal of stealing data. I did often wonder what the men on the other end of this two-way battle felt like, knowing that the Brits had finally woken up and were fighting back. And we were definitely fighting back. The team was functioning well and gaining more knowledge with each operation.

Domestically, Dan and I had slipped into an easy cohabitation arrangement. We'd walk to work in the mornings and share lunches in the various outlets dotted around Westminster. In the evening, we'd retrace our steps and retreat to the apartment where mostly I would cook, we'd talk on a vast array of subjects, but I was acutely aware that since his first night revelations about his wife, he never allowed the conversation to stray into anything too personal. I would serve the food, we'd eat, I'd drink more than him and then he would retire to his bed leaving me to sit and stare out at the Thames. On my own, I wondered how I found myself in this strange circumstance and if I could ever do anything about it. Of course I couldn't. He was, albeit unhappily, married. Then I would drink a little more, listen to some music and eventually go to my own room. That's what had happened last night too, so this early phone call on a Monday morning woke me after only two and a half hours of sleep, but the single word answer of Mark Donoghue had me fully alert and rolling out of bed. After a swift shower and rapid pulling on of clothes I arrived into the apartment's kitchen as Dan was stepping out of his own room.

'Happy Independence Day,' I said and figured that the surprise breakfast I had planned to cook, including pancakes topped off with small US flags was going to have to wait.

'Whoop! Go USA,' he said in less than enthusiastic tones. 'Not only am I not getting a day off, but it appears we're doing overtime now. Hell of a start to the week.'

'Agreed. Any thoughts?' I asked as we took the lift down to the ground floor.

'I honestly have no clue, but it must be a new attack. Surely we couldn't have missed something big enough to be classed as critical?'

He sounded confident, but I could see from the deep furrow on his forehead, he wasn't. Instead of walking to the office, we hailed the first black cab we saw. There were benefits of making a commute at not yet five in the morning and with little traffic on the usually congested roads, we were there in a few minutes.

*

I was surprised to see Colonel Charles walking into the MoD Main Building's foyer just ahead of us. By the time we got through the security pods, John Leofric was also arriving. The four of us were quiet as we rode the elevator up to the JOCCSy.

Dan took a seat in front of a computer while Ritchie and Rob hovered at his shoulder, rapidly briefing him on the situation he was facing. I listened and watched but couldn't follow much of what they were saying and I knew from their expressions the same went for Colonel Charles and John. I looked across to Mark Donoghue, making it obvious that we needed some more information. He signalled for us to follow him into the briefing room. Despite not having been on a flying squadron, I did understand how aircraft operations worked. You had to if you were an Air Intelligence Officer, so I recognised the words that Mark was using in his briefing. Glancing around though, I could see from the faces of the other two that they had been left behind. I interrupted the briefing.

'N-O-T-A-M.' I spelled it out. 'It stands for Notice to Airmen. It's how you warn any pilot, civil or military about anything out of the ordinary and includes restricted airspace. Anything from places you aren't allowed to fly around or over, or air corridors that are off limits due to VIPs using them,' I said and saw even more confusion on their faces. 'Like if the President of the United States, or the Queen was flying from a to b. The NOTAM would show it as closed airspace. They also show closed runways, or air shows, or even firework displays. Anything an aircraft wouldn't want to fly into the middle of.' This time I got nods. I told Mark to go on.

'We also use NOTAMs to notify about military exercises and areas within the exercise that are closed off for specific purposes. In this case,' he pointed to the projected image of a map showing the UK, the North Sea and the coast of Denmark. About halfway between the UK coast and the Skagerrak a relatively small, rectangular shape was marked in red. 'This is an air-to-air refuelling box, designated Harald and in use for Exercise Northern Wall. It's a NATO exercise designed to help us work alongside the Baltic countries that joined last year. The concept is that the UK, Norway and Poland will test the defences of Latvia, Lithuania and Estonia. The air-to-air refuelling is to allow the Royal Air Force ground attack aircraft to refuel shortly after take-off and again on the return leg so that they have maximum time over the main exercise area that is here.' He clicked the mouse and the map view expanded to include the whole of the Baltic Sea. A much larger irregular shape covered the coastal area from Klaipėda in Lithuania to Tallinn in Estonia.

The screen changed back to the first map. 'At 01:00 this morning a four ship of RAF Tornado ground attack aircraft departed RAF Marham in Norfolk on a simulated bombing mission. First stop was the Harald refuelling area.'

'And?' I asked fearing the absolute worst.

'And there's no one dead or injured, so it's not that bad, but watch what happens to the notified refuelling area coordinates over the course of forty minutes,' Mark answered and allowed the screen to play through a series of images.

The rectangular shape of Harald shifted up the map in small steps, eventually ending up north-west of its original position by quite a distance. I followed the movement but didn't quite follow the implications. The frowns I saw around the table told me I wasn't alone.

'The NOTAM system warns people where the closed airspace is. It stops civilian aircraft straying into areas you don't want them, like where a huge refuelling aircraft is flying around in long, lazy circles whilst refuelling four bombers. The Tornados and air-to-air refuelling aircraft have different systems in place to allow them to find each other, so they weren't the issue, but by shifting the NOTAM coordinates you open up the possibility of a civilian aircraft flying right through the actual area. The chances of a mid-air collision or at least a near-miss are considerable. It's hard to take evasive manoeuvres when you're plugged into a massive petrol station in the sky.'

'My God. Did that happen?' Colonel Charles asked.

Mark Donoghue shook his head. 'No. Nothing untoward happened, but it could have.'

'How was the refuelling area shifted?' I asked.

'Someone hacked into the NOTAM system this morning at 01:10 and in small steps changed the latitude and longitude of Harald. It didn't change where the refuelling actually took place and it didn't move the military aircraft or cause them a problem but had it not been for a very sharp eyed flight operations officer at RAF Marham it could well have caused a huge issue later in the day. That area is meant to be operational for the next twenty-four hours. The part of the sky it sits in is on the commercial flight routes from Scandinavia to the UK. The whole point of the NO-TAM is to re-route any civilian traffic away from it.'

'And you're saying this was deliberately hacked?' John asked.

'Yes. We got an alert direct from Marham as the Ops Officer up there watched the NOTAM change in front of her. She was looking at the screen when the coordinates shifted. With no idea how or why it was happening, she contacted the RAF Police Computer Security Unit. They had no clue about any of it and after an hour or so of dithering, they rang me.'

'And immediate actions?' I asked.

'The Ops Officer had assessed it as a flight risk and aborted the mission and the air-to-air refuelling. Everyone turned for home. They landed back safely after a few hours of flying circles in the air above the valleys of Wales to burn off fuel.'

'Okay,' I said, relieved that there had been no mid-air collisions, 'What's the current situation?'

'As soon as I was notified, I called Ritchie and Rob in to see if we could find out what had got into the NOTAM system and more urgently, see if we could stop it from happening again. What they found is why I called you and Captain Stückl, Sir.'

'Go on.'

'This wasn't someone planting malware and making an exit. Whoever it was accessed the live system and manipulated it in real time. Ritchie and Rob tried their best but they couldn't block them. Each time they tried the intruder shifted their attack and penetrated again. Seemingly at will.'

'Are they still actively in the system?' I asked, getting to my feet.

'Yes, Sir. That's why I pointed Captain Stückl straight to the desk.'

We returned to the main office and stood behind the central cluster of computer terminals, home to Dan, Ritchie and Rob. Rachel and Ashley, each on separate phone lines on the far side of the office raised their hands in greeting. Josh came to stand next to me and offered me a coffee. 'You're meant to be on leave,' I said taking the mug.

'Yeah, but Mark said if I was around I might want to come in. Not the usual thing to be woken at half four with, so it sounded intriguing enough to forgo one day of lazing about. Although I might still nip off at lunchtime as there's a Midday Mozart recital at St Martin's in the Field. So what's occurring, Sir?'

I back briefed him on the state of things and then returned my attention to Dan. 'Can you talk?'

Without taking his eyes from the screen, Dan said, 'Yep. You up to speed on what's been happening?'

'Yes.'

'Whoever is doing this is still manipulating the data. This is way more dynamic and complex than anything I've seen before, Luke. It's like they're playing with us. Every time I shut off one attack they spring up elsewhere.'

'What are Ritchie and Rob doing?'

'Each intrusion is coming from a separate IP address. I want them to try and trace them backwards. Maybe we can—'

I noticed movement off to my right and glanced around to see John Leofric heading to his office. His bearing, as usual, was one of erect defiance, but even without seeing his features, I could sense his annoyance and anger. I wondered which Government department was going to be getting his wrath later in the morning.

'—sorry,' Dan continued. 'Whoever's at the other end of this, they're very quick and they're adaptive. I was about to close another port down and they jumped ahead of me. I'm beginning to feel like a string ball being knocked about by some lazily aggressive cat. What time are the first civilian flights from Scandinavia to the UK?'

Before I got a chance to react, Ashley, who I hadn't noticed come to stand alongside me said, 'The first flight out of Oslo left at 06:00 their time. So about ten minutes ago given they're an hour ahead of us. There's another 06:00 out of Stockholm to Newcastle. Both of those will pass through the area.'

'But we're not concerned about that anymore, are we? There is no refuelling, we grounded our flights?' I asked.

'Yep, but if they manage to move the NOTAM coordinates again how embarrassing is it going to be to Her Majesty's Government if a couple of commercial airlines keep having to fly around a constantly moving restricted zone. It'll be an international incident and people will get severely pissed and you know who will be blamed.'

I knew Dan was right. The government would blame the military and look to hang it on someone. The senior military establishment would blame the Air Force and the shit would slide downhill until it landed on an individual that couldn't get out of its way fast enough. Possibly the Ops Officer at Marham who had spotted it in the first place, but much more likely, us. Especially if Group Captain Halson had any say in the matter. He'd look to pin it on me and I had no doubt he'd take pleasure in calling it a failure of the JOCCSy to actually do their job. My thoughts were interrupted by Dan issuing orders. Each attempt to shut out the hacker was met with a small groan as they obviously found a new way in. I'd never really seen Dan work under intense pressure before, but he seemed to be the personification of calm within a storm.

'This is getting really tight, Luke. I'm only just managing to shut him out before he can change and upload new coordinates.'

I let my mind wander a little and took a step back. I knew what NOTAMs were, but I realised I didn't know how they were actually created. 'Ritchie, is the system to establish a NOTAM the same as what's used to edit and amend it?'

I watched the red-headed Scot push his chair away from the desk and propel himself across to another terminal. He punched at the keyboard and chewed the corner of his lip. The seconds ticked by.

'No. It 'isny. The system to establish a new NOTAM is separate. What are 'ye 'thinkin?'

'We've been fighting to stop them amending the refuelling area. But it isn't in operation anymore. We don't need it. So if we cancel it then they won't be able to amend it.'

Dan's fingers continued to touch-type but gave a quick glance over his shoulder. 'But they can still get in and amend any other notification in the system. It only deletes a single entity. That doesn't stop the intrusion.'

'I know. But it removes the ball of string that they're currently fascinated with. Can we do it and maybe buy ourselves some time?'

'That's easy. I can 'dae that 'frae here.' Ritchie called.

'Then do it.'

It took three clicks of his mouse. 'Done.'

Dan's fingers hovered over his own keyboard. There was silence in the room. I looked up to the clock on the wall and watched the second hand sweep a complete circle. It felt like a thousand of them. Dan began typing again, but at a much slower pace than before. Another minute passed. Dan turned in his chair and looked up at me. 'They've gone,' he said.

Colonel Charles leant across to me and, in his amplified way, whispered, 'How do we stop them coming back?'

16

London, July 2005

It turned out the answer to Colonel Charles's question was a lot easier than we expected. The defence mechanisms we'd deployed against the laptop backdoor incursions worked on the NOTAM system equally as well. By Tuesday afternoon we had secured it completely and drawn up an intense schedule to deploy our defensive code on to every network the military currently used or had access to. We needed Rachel and Ashley to smooth our path into the defence contracting companies so we could do the same to theirs, but with only a few minor bumps in the road I estimated I would have the majority done in weeks rather than months. The code was complex and adaptive, but at its heart it worked on the fact that the attacks were originating from Chinese IP addresses, although it was often extremely hard to trace the source. Hard, but not impossible. I was confident that if we could deploy it widely enough then we would start to gain the upper hand and the number of attempted incursions would fall rapidly.

My frustration was the continued lack of interest the Government were showing. John had demanded a meeting with the Minister following the NOTAMs breach, but had been turned down.

The deputy assistant secretary to the assistant to the Secretary of State for Defence had dealt with his request.

'The Minister is not interested in the day-to-day minutiae of operations. There was no major incident, the solution was straightforward and as such it is nothing that concerns him.'

Leofric had been livid and kicked up a massive fuss. Eventually the Minister relented. John, Colonel Charles and myself had been invited to a meeting on level three of Main Building at 10:00 on Thursday morning. Dan couldn't join us, as his monthly liaison meeting with the US Embassy staff in Grosvenor Square was at the same time, so Mark Donoghue would provide the technical expertise. I hoped we would see some real progress and the government might start to take notice. It boded well that the Minister himself would attend. Even the date seemed lucky; Thursday the seventh of July. 7/7.

*

As I was preparing to leave the apartment after breakfast, Dan wished me luck with the Minister.

'Shame you can't make it.'

'Yeah, but Mark will be fine. He knows his stuff.'

I knew he was right. 'Good luck with your lot. Still no sign of that last packing box?'

'Nope. The Embassy figure it might be in Wright-Patterson Air Force Base, Ohio.'

'Really? How come?'

'Thirty miles due east of there is a town called London. They think the couriers got confused.'

'Has anyone actually seen it?'

'Nope. Not yet. By the time they find it they might as well send it back to my home.'

I felt a tremendous ache in my chest. The intensity of it surprised me and I half-turned from Dan and took a breath.

'You okay?'

I coughed. 'Yes, just a tickle in my throat,' I managed between a few more coughs. I wasn't okay. I was shocked at how I'd reacted. The man was married for God's sake. Yes, we'd been getting on well and yes the atmosphere within the apartment was relaxed, comfortable even and yes, we would talk easily into the evening each and every day, but that didn't change anything. I'd wondered occasionally when he held my eye contact a little longer than usual, or touched me lightly on the shoulder as he wished me goodnight, but there was no reason to suspect he was anything but straight. Yet his mentioning of having to go home had nearly floored me.

He rose and stood behind me, 'Need the Heimlich or just a good thump to the back?'

I coughed again. 'No, I think I'm good. Thanks.' I turned back around to face him. His smile, broad and confident lit the room and made me want to reach out and hug him. Instead I took a step backwards and peered around him to look out of the window. 'It looks like a gorgeous morning out there, you going to walk up to the Embassy?'

'No, I'll tube it.'

'Listen to you. Talking like a native. A month or so ago you could only call it the subway.'

'That's your bad influence on me.'

'Glad to hear it,' I said and threw him a mock salute. 'Happy box hunting.'

'Happy minister baiting. I'll see you about lunchtime.'

*

As John, Colonel Charles, Mark and myself sat in our conference room and rehearsed our strategy for the upcoming meeting, a public-address alert tone sounded within Main Building. It continued for fifteen seconds. I cursed whoever had decided to hold an evacuation drill and checked my watch. 09:20. It would be touch and go if we would make it back into the building in time for our meeting. When the tone finally stopped and there was silence, I hoped it had been a false alarm.

Colonel Charles stretched across to the telephone. 'I suppose we better chec—' He was interrupted by the PA system again, and a voice that sounded rushed and stressed.

'Bikini Alert, Bikini Alert, Bikini Alert. There is a major terrorist incident reported within central London. Main Building is on lockdown. Operation Synergy is in immediate effect. I repeat, Operation Synergy is in immediate effect. All personnel are to remain in their current locations and are to stay clear of windows and external walls. All personnel are to minimise phone calls. Evacuation of Main Building is not authorised. I repeat, evacuation of Main Building is not authorised. More details will be provided as soon as possible.'

Mark pulled the keyboard of the conference room PC over and typed in the BBC website address. I reached for the projector remote control and turned it on. The PC screen came into focus on the far wall, revealing a main picture that showed a mass of emergency vehicles outside the entrance to King's Cross Station. The headline read, "Tube warning after 'bang' heard" Mark clicked on the link. The story, at odds with the picture, said that Emergency Services were in attendance at Liverpool Street Station after reports of an explosion which was possibly due to a power surge.

'They haven't a clue what's going on,' John said as he read through the scant report.

'Anything on the classified nets?' I asked.

Mark swapped screens and accessed the MoD network, but before he could click into the latest news section of the site there was a knock on the conference room door.

'Come in,' John said.

Rob walked in and glanced at the projection screen. 'It's not on the MoD yet. Cheltenham have the first reports and are coordinating the comms for it. I've just logged in to my terminal,' he said referring to the specific to GCHQ system he had access to.

'And what is it?' Colonel Charles asked.

'First reports are confused, but they think six suicide bombers have hit various tube stations across the city.'

For the first time in as long as I could remember I silently called on a God that I didn't believe in to protect someone that I desperately wanted to be safe. Outwardly I hoped to the same God that my emotions were not so transparent.

John took the remote control for the projector and shut it down. 'I would suggest, gentlemen, that we go back into the main office and be with the rest of the team. This could be a long day and I would imagine our meeting with the Minister is not likely to proceed.'

*

By 11:00 the initial reports and confusion had been distilled into some semblance of facts and I was growing more and more worried. Three suicide bombers had hit various tube lines and one had detonated his device on top of a London bus in Tavistock Square. The city was on the highest security alert and due to user demand the mobile phone networks hadn't coped. I had tried Dan's number multiple times as soon as we came out of the conference room but each time it failed to connect. I rang the US Embassy on our secure lines and whilst it connected, it was immediately put on hold and left there.

By midday the Main Building's lockdown had been relaxed and personnel were being encouraged to go home by whatever methods they could, given that the whole of inner London's transport network was suspended. Alternate accommodation and temporary sleeping bunks were being set up in the lower basements for anyone that would be unable to travel. Our team weren't affected as we all lived within thirty minutes of MoD, but Colonel Charles still advised everyone to go home early.

'You too, Luke.'

'Yes Sir. I was going to try the US Embassy again.'

'I can't see them answering. Not until much later. They're probably in as much of a panic as everyone else. Dan will no doubt be on his way back, even if he's had to make a massive detour, he'll be here before anyone takes your call. I'm sure he's fine and if there is bad news the Embassy or others will let us know soon enough. It was always the same when I wasn't much older than you and serving in Belfast. Bombs go off and you simply have to wait and see. Go home.'

He was matter-of-fact, yet not complacent or cold and I knew he was right. I walked with him to the main exit. All of the usual security precautions were in place but they had been augmented by at least half a dozen heavily armed police officers immediately outside the front entrance and as many again at intervals along Horse Guards Avenue. Turning into Whitehall revealed more armed police spaced at intervals along its length and I realised the whole of the road, from Trafalgar Square to Westminster Bridge had been sealed off. I parted company with Colonel Charles as he turned left for the bridge and I continued along Abingdon Street. The cordon extended down its length too and continued through to Millbank. As soon as I parted with the Colonel I took my phone out and tried Dan again. Still no signal. I walked across the Vaux- hall Bridge and made my way to the apartment, wondering why my heart felt like breaking into a hundred pieces.

*

I drank coffee and watched the non-stop television news. I listened to the wailing of sirens and watched emergency vehicles speed across the bridge in an otherwise deserted London streetscape. Gone were the hundreds of cars and taxis and buses. In their place, throngs of people walked along the footpaths, streaming away from the city centre and towards the outer transport hubs that were still functioning. I picked up my phone again and was about to press redial when I heard the front door opening.

I ran into the hallway and met him halfway. He had his suit jacket hooked over his shoulder, his tie was loosened, there were dark sweat stains under his arms and he looked tired, but other than that he just looked like Dan. There was no blood, no cuts, no injuries.

'Hi,' he said and gave a thin, tight smile.

I walked straight up to him and gave him a hug. 'Are you okay?'

He pulled me in tight and, dropping his jacket on the floor, patted me hard on the back. 'Yeah, man. I'm good. I wasn't really near it at all.'

'I'm glad you're safe.'

'Me too. I'm glad to be home.'

I stood back and quickly turned away. Walking into the lounge and through to the kitchen, I carefully wiped away the tears I felt on my cheeks. Dan slumped into the armchair.

'I tried to call, but there was no signal,' he said.

'Me too.'

'I headed back to Whitehall but they told me everyone had been sent home.'

'Yes. About lunchtime. Are you sure you're okay?' I asked, switching the kettle on.

'Nothing a cup of tea couldn't fix?' he said in an awful impression of Dick Van Dyke's cockney accent. 'Isn't that the right response for a Londoner?'

I picked up a dishcloth and threw it at him. 'Tea has got this nation through all sorts of drama, so yes. Right reaction.' I choked down the lump I could feel in my throat. The worry and anxiety I had felt couldn't be brought into the light. I had to be *just* a concerned mate. He was *just* another colleague. I tried to keep my voice light. 'So what happened to you?'

'I'd arrived in to Bond Street Station when it all started. Sirens were going off and announcements were being made that the station was being evacuated. There was a bit of a surge of people and it got a little hairy for a while because no one knew what was going on. Then rumours started that there had been a suicide bomber. I was above ground by then and tried to call you, but I couldn't get a signal. Then I started looking round me and figured I didn't want to be in a mass of people. Weird thing was that I caught myself looking at every face that even slightly looked Arabic. That's such a crappy thing to realise you are doing.'

'Understandable though.'

'Maybe. Maybe not. On the flip side, I was impressed at how most people were really calm. Guess you Brits do react well under pressure.'

'We've had practice.'

'Yeah. Guess so. Anyway, I didn't know what was going on, but I figured the safest place to be would be behind the walls of the US Embassy protected by a unit of Marines.'

'Smart man.'

'I think so.'

His face broke into a relaxed, proper grin and I wondered what exactly he would say if I leapt the counter top and kissed him. Instead, I turned my attention to preparing two cups.

'Strange though. Spent a lot of my morning thinking that it could have been the train I was on.'

I didn't respond. I couldn't.

'Spent quite a bit of my walk home, via various police diversions, thinking and wondering about the same thing. How life could be over before you get a ch…'

'Before you get?' I asked and waited, but his reply wasn't forthcoming. I made the teas and carried them into the lounge. 'You were saying?'

'Nothing much.' He took a cup and raised it. 'Cheers, Luke. How was your day? What did the Minister say?'

'Ha. Speak of the devil.' I pointed to the muted television where Her Majesty's Secretary of State for Defence was being interviewed on the grass embankment outside the Houses of Parliament. Dan picked up the remote and unmuted it.

'…cowardly and unprovoked attack that seeks to undermine the fabric of our multicultural and inherently tolerant society. We, in this country have seen terrorists try to bend our will and break our resolve before. We did not fail then and we will not fail now. I can assure you that Her Majesty's Government will use every resource, both civilian and military, to track down those behind this dastardly act and see them brought to justice. I urge all members of the publ—'

Dan pressed the mute button. 'Were you in with him when this all broke?'

'No. We never got a chance and once it was underway there was no hope. I can't imagine we're going to feature highly on his list of priorities now.'

'No. Probably rightly so,' Dan said and laid his head back. He was asleep in minutes.

For the next few weeks I couldn't get him to expand on his feelings or what was going through his mind after the events of that Thursday. He was certainly quieter than usual, but had I glimpsed what was occupying his thoughts, I would have been stunned.

*

I met with John and Colonel Charles on Friday morning. We decided that it would be pointless trying to get another meeting with the Minister at the present time. I was frustrated, because I knew the threat we were dealing with was strategic and undermining our very abilities as a nation, but I wasn't stupid. The immediate danger of suicide bombs and death on the capital's streets was always going to take precedence. As Dan had said, so it should. The Colonel sensed my mood. His advice to me was as it had been previously. Keep the team doing what we could to protect our networks as best we could. So I called them all together and we drew up a new and longer list of potentially vulnerable systems. Then we got to work.

17

London, August 2005

On Monday the 8th of August, four weeks after the NO-TAMs incursion, we had our first day with no attempted intrusions into any monitored network. It was so unusual that we spent most of the day running diagnostics against our dashboard software, but it was true. No attacks. The next day the same. By the fourth straight day I felt less paranoid that we were missing something and increasingly convinced we had won. I also realised that Friday would mark exactly three months since Dan had arrived. He was halfway through his deployment. Halfway to going back to the States. I felt that our success should be celebrated, Dan's midterm point should be marked and anyway, I didn't need many excuses for a dinner party. I called the team together.

'Tomorrow. Seven thirty for eight. My apartment. You're all welcome. No need to make excuses, turn up or not.' I saw Colonel Charles, Dave and Jim standing on the periphery of the knot of people and walked over to them.

'You're most welcome as well. You're still a massive part of this team.'

I like dinner parties. I like the obliged formality of them, even though I rarely set a dress code. It wasn't black tie and dinner jackets that made it for me. More the layout of proper crockery, heavy cutlery, sherry glasses and water glasses, white wine glasses, red wine glasses, liqueur glasses, each in their proper place. Even the cups and saucers and dessert knives and forks and spoons. It was the preparation and presentation of the food. It was the polite and quiet, though sometimes raucous conversations. It was why, when I had been on military establishments and hated the rigidity of uniforms and hierarchy, I loved the dining-in nights at the Officers' Mess. It was also why I had hosted dinner parties since my late teens. When most of my friends would make do with a trip to the cinema and a McDonalds, I would host dinner parties at the weekends for my closest confidants. My parents obligingly retreating to their holiday cottage in the Lake District. My predilection for being a host resulted in my Godparents gifting me a full dinner party set of crockery and heavy silver cutlery for my twenty-first birthday. They even threw in a vintage silver toast rack, for use on the suitably late-served breakfast, the morning after the preceding late evening. My contemporaries thought I was insane. I couldn't have cared less.

Leaving work an hour early on the Friday, Dan and I sauntered back to the apartment. The afternoon sun was still high in a summer sky unbroken by clouds. We navigated our way through Parliament Square, skirted the Victoria Tower Gardens, along Millbank and past the Lambeth Bridge. As we passed the Tate Modern and stepped down onto Riverside Walk the shadow of Henry Moore's Locking Piece sculpture cast strong, abstract shadows on the ground. Dan did as he usually did and reached up to glide his hand over the cold bronze. We continued on, around a cordoned off building site where some entrepreneur investor was sinking Lord alone knew how much money into the building of two curvy and modernistic apartment blocks. Prime real estate on a prime location, the corner of Millbank and the Vauxhall Bridge. When finished, the apartments would look back across the river to St George's Wharf, but for now they stood, half complete with two cranes hanging above them that, as I looked up, shaped a perfect cruciform.

'I never noticed those before,' Dan said and I dropped my gaze to where he stood. He was looking across the river towards the Vauxhall Bridge.

'Noticed what?'

'The statues,' he said, pointing in turn to the four pedestals separating the five spans of the bridge. On each one a massive, twice-life sized, bronze statue. The one second in from the bank we stood on, had two figures. It looked like a mother and child.

'Wow! Neither have I and I've been looking at that bridge for over a year. Do you think they're recent additions?' I asked it and knew as the words came out of my mouth that they weren't. These statues were part and parcel of the fabric of the bridge, which meant they'd been there for a hundred years. Yet I had never once registered them. I pondered that Dan and I had walked this path every weekday and most weekends for three months and he'd never noticed them either.

'The one nearest to us is a bit strange. Pointing down into the river like that,' he said.

I considered the first statue, the one closest to the north bank. I could see it in the finest detail even though it had to be over fifty metres from where I stood. It was a female, dressed in a long flow-ing robe and in her left hand she held a book. I was reminded of the Statue of Liberty, but this Vauxhall liberty wore no crown and her right hand held no torch. Instead it was pointing down at the water of the fast and free flowing Thames. Her gaze, also unlike her New York sister, was not aloft but followed the pointing of her hand.

'What do you think she represents, the first one?' I asked.

'No idea. But perhaps she was a warning to children not to go swimming,' Dan said and chuckled in the way he did. Low and melodic, like his neutral American accent, which I still warmed to despite our weeks of cohabitation and our increasing familiarity. I watched him as he stood in profile to me, staring up at the bronzes on the bridge. The sun reflecting off the water seemed to frame him in its glow and I wished the world could be different. He broke my thoughts with an upbeat, 'C'mon or they'll be nothing to serve to the starving hordes.'

I gave one last glance to the rather foreboding pointing statue and the swirling water that broke around the bridge pier she stood atop. I also registered that there was a spotlight mounted under each one of the bronzes.

'They light up, at night,' I called after Dan.

'Great, if there's others on the far side we can take a look later.'

*

Everyone turned up. Even John Leofric, which somewhat surprised me. He was impressed with my apartment and commented at length on the table, chairs and other antique furniture I had within. I got the distinct impression that my ability to have tastes that we shared was going to count more towards him extending me an invitation to join his club at some point in the future than anything I might do in my career. Class was a strange, misunderstood and rock solid part of the British establishment. The boundaries might have blurred and the new money that came and went might try to suggest it was lessening, but it really wasn't. I knew I'd been born into an upper-middle class family and I knew that I liked the finer things in life, but my father had made sure I never forgot that only three generations earlier, my great-grandfather had been a hands-on builder. With his wealth came the push to ensure his kids did better than he had. He sent them to one of the best boarding schools in the country, and they did the same with their sons and my father had done the same with me and my brother. I was very grateful he had as I lifted the crystal decanter and poured another glass of wine.

My dining table was a reasonable size, but the thirteen of us couldn't possibly fit around it comfortably, so I had elected to make a less formal buffet dinner. The table played host to food, drinks and crockery and everyone helped themselves from the central serving dishes filled with fried chicken served on a bed of roasted pumpkin salad and one stacked with corn on the cob. It was my small nod to Dan's heritage and he'd seemed to really appreciate it when I finally revealed what I was cooking. He had offered to help and I had managed to deflect his attempts by allowing him to cut up the pumpkins. For a computer whizz he struggled with anything remotely creative in a kitchen. But that was okay.

In the background, playing at a level barely audible, I had loaded six CDs into my stereo system's carousel. I knew Josh would comment on it. It hadn't taken too long.

'Vivaldi, Bach, Purcell and Handel? I wouldn't have thought you a Baroque fan, Sir.'

'Ah, yes. It's my guilty secret. Although I thought I'd keep the volume down tonight, there is nothing like the power and majesty of a piece of Handel or even Corelli played with gusto on a full pipe organ. I used to love it.'

Josh considered me with what I presumed was a perplexed look. 'You say that like you've got personal experience. Did you play?'

'I did. Piano at first and then pipe organ at my school.'

'Really? I'm impressed, Sir. How far did you take it?'

'Oh. I was okay. I got all my exams. It's just a little difficult to keep one's hand in. Pipe organs aren't exactly easy to come by.'

'Woah. You're too modest. If you got all your exams, you must be seriously proficient.'

'Let's just say I was okay. Anyway, I figured some background Baroque would be easier on Colonel Charles and the old man than some other options.'

'Which were?' Josh asked.

'Nineties dance and techno beats,' Dan chipped in from behind me before I got a chance to answer.

'You ever hear of the Pet Shop Boys, or Sophie Ellis someone or other, Josh?' He asked with an overly exaggerated tone of depression.

'Oh God! Really? And he makes you listen to that, Sir?' Josh asked, feigning a look of horror.

'Okay, okay. You can both knock it off. I was thinking of putting some Amadeus on for you later, Josh, but you've blown that now and as for Mr Hee-haw country and western partner here, you can forget about any Patsy or Dolly being played tonight.'

*

The evening was winding down. The banter and the good-natured teasing had continued unabated but now the conversations were quieter. It seemed like an ideal time. I gently tapped the side of an empty glass and after pouring myself another refill offered the assembled dozen to join me.

'Eight months ago we were given the task of forming a new team. Three months ago we could barely keep our heads above water. Now, we seem to be gaining the upper hand at the very least. I'd like to thank you, Sirs,' I made direct eye contact with John and Colonel Charles, 'for supporting me in setting up the new team. I'd like to thank you,' I looked to Dave, Jim and Steph, 'for supporting our new arrivals, and,' I looked to each of my "magnificent seven", 'I'd like to thank you for everything you have done to make our journey so successful in such a short period of time. Finally, a huge thank you to Dan, for your expertise and assistance. I can't believe three months have gone so fast. Here's to us!'

'To us.'

*

Josh, Ritchie, Rachel and Ashley were the last to leave. I closed the apartment door and went back inside to find Dan standing at the main windows.

'Everything okay?'

He spoke without turning.

'Yeah. I thought I'd check out the statues we saw earlier. There are four more on this side. All different but, you're right. They're lit up at night.'

I joined him and gazed out towards the bridge. The four lit piers seemed so obvious when you knew what you were looking for, but without cupping your hand against the window to counter the apartment's lights, they could still be lost in the reflection. I reached across and turned off the living room lights. In the darkness the statues were revealed in stark relief against the side of the bridge and the river. Overspill and a reflection from the bronze cast a pool of light over the piers they stood on and it seemed like four golden halos hung over the otherwise pitch black water.

'I never knew you played piano,' Dan said.

'I guess it never came up. There's a lot you don't know about me.'

'I guess.' He let out a soft sigh.

I kept my eyes on the bridge. 'Are you okay.'

'Tired. That's all.'

'It is late.'

'No, I don't mean that type of tired. I could do with a few days off I think.'

I half-turned towards him. 'We could do that. We could take next week off if we wanted. You've had no time off since you got here and I haven't had any leave since Easter.'

He shifted his gaze from the river. The lights from the city allowed enough illumination for me to see his features clearly. He smiled. 'And what would we do?'

'That depends. Do you like fell walking?'

'Eh, I don't know. What's fell walking?'

'Sorry. Hills. It's hill walking. We call parts of our countryside, the Fells. It's beautiful country. My parents have a holiday home in the Lake District. It's about as far removed from London and cyber as you can get.'

'I like the sound of that. And you know your way around these Fells?'

'Yes. You sound surprised.'

'Well come on, Luke. You don't strike anyone as the out-doorsy, Grizzly Adams type.'

I turned to face him full on. His mouth was only inches from mine. I felt my heart kick but forced my voice to remain flat. 'I said fell walking in the Lake District. It's not exactly Alaska. There are shops and cafés in the villages. We don't actually have to hunt and kill our supper.'

'Ah, I see. So outdoors in a civilised, English manner?'

'Of course. Although we'll let an untamed Yank sample it if you think you can manage?'

He laughed. That low chuckle. 'How big are these Fells?'

'It's physically a bit of a challenge but we're meant to be up to that, aren't we? Us young military officer types.'

He reached out and squeezed my bicep. My heart lurched and I was aware of a bead of sweat sliding down the length of my spine.

'I suppose you'll be able to handle it,' he said as he held my arm.

'I suppose.'

Turning his head to gaze back out at the bridge he sighed and said, 'I've been thinking a lot since the bombings on the tube.'

'I know. You've been holding a lot inside yourself.'

'More than you know.'

'Tell me.'

He faced me again, still holding my upper arm. 'For a very short time that morning, maybe less than a minute, I wondered if I might get killed. If I would die in an explosion that I wouldn't see coming. Before I had decided to live.'

'What do you me—'

I never got to finish my sentence as Dan leaned in and kissed me. Still holding my wine glass I enveloped him in my arms as he pulled me closer. His body pressed into me and I gripped him harder. I tried to process thoughts but could only give in to the feelings rising within me. As I began to return his kiss with more and more unbridled passion he roughly broke off, away from my searching mouth and took a half step backwards. My heart, still pounding, almost shattered. Oh please, God don't let him regret this. Oh please, God do not let this be the end of us.

I let my arms unfold from around him and with bowed head, looked up, waiting for his words of disgust and derision. Instead, I felt his hand take mine.

'Come to bed, Luke.'

18

The Lake District, August 2005

Glenridding village nestles on the southern shores of Ullswater, with Place Fell facing it across the water and the mighty rise of Helvellyn to her back. I'd been coming to our holiday home on Easter and autumn breaks with my family for as long as I could remember. We would spend our summer vacations in the Bavarian Alps of Oberammergau, so I was equally familiar with the German mountains, but the English Lakes made the perfect getaway at short notice for Dan and me.

I lay in bed and listened to him making tea in the kitchen. It was a culinary expedition I knew he could manage and as long as he allowed the boiling water enough time to properly draw out the flavour of the leaves, even he couldn't go far wrong. I realised with a moderate shock that I was happy. Happier than I had felt in a long time. The previous four days had been a bit of a whirlwind. Friday night to Sunday morning had gone by in a blur of twisted limbs and sweating bodies. It seemed Dan had little in the way of reservations about his new-found life choice. The sex had been rough, gentle and everything in between. I hadn't felt an intensity towards a lover quite like it before, but I also knew it might well have been the heightened risks we were taking. He was married, yes, but much more than that was his job and worse still, his own family's reaction if they were to find out. He hadn't realised I wasn't playing with the same concerns until Sunday afternoon, when I managed to untangle myself from the bedsheets long enough to ring my parents to ask if I could use the cottage in Glenridding.

They were as good as usual, 'Of course. No, we shan't be using the cottage next weekend.' Even though I knew they used it almost every weekend, but I decided not to argue against my own cause. Neither of them asked anything about the fact I was going away to the Lakes with one of my colleagues. Dan had been surprised. He'd been even more surprised to learn that my parents and brother knew I was gay.

'When did you come out to them?'

I rejoined him in the bed. 'Before I joined the military.'

'And how did they take it?'

'My father and brother shrugged and said it wasn't a big deal. My mother took a little longer to adjust to the idea, but she's fine now.'

'But no one at work knows?'

'No. I don't think so. But then again why should they? It isn't like we flaunt heterosexuality or homosexuality at work. We don't mention it at all. I mean if people are married or in a relationship they'll talk about their partners, but if you don't have a partner then it's hardly a subject that comes up for discussion.' I let my hand trace over his chest. 'Come to think of it, no one has ever asked about my sexuality at work. So I've never had to lie about it.'

'You're lucky.'

'I guess. Although…' I paused, my hand still on his chest, remembering back through a lot of years to a small Royal Air Force Station and a cold Sunday in October 1997 when I was being interviewed to join the University Air Squadron. The interviewing officer read out a statement that said, to be homosexual within the RAF at that time was illegal, and I calmly lied that I wasn't gay. It dawned on me, looking at Dan, that my first step into my military career had been taken on the basis of the biggest lie I had ever told.

'What's up?' he asked.

I decided to deflect. 'Oh nothing. I was just thinking, Steph keeps asking me if I've found myself a nice girl, but that's because Steph is Steph. I can't imagine she'd react differently if I told her I was on the lookout for a nice boy. She'd probably offer to go looking with me.'

'But surely she'd have to tell someone if you did that?'

'Sorry?'

'What would they do to you if they found out?'

I'd been perplexed by his question and then I realised what he meant. 'Oh, no you have it wrong Dan. The military knows now. I mean the personnel side of things and those who approve my security clearances, and the commanders within Air Intelligence, they already know I'm gay. It's not illegal in the UK military anymore. Hasn't been for five years.'

He stared up at the ceiling. 'Oh. I see,'

I'd propped myself up on an elbow and considered his physique. Tall, muscular, strong. He was everything I had fantasised about since I'd first laid eyes on him. I'd spent many a night over the previous three months imagining the possibilities, but had not once made any form of play towards him. I knew we'd been getting on well, but his kiss on Friday night and what came after had taken me by complete surprise. A good, fantastic, amazing surprise. But now I wondered if he had only felt secure thinking I had as much to lose as him.

'I understand. You can't possibly have any of this revealed. You're still working under "don't ask, don't tell", aren't you?'

He nodded.

'So if this came out, your career would be over.'

He rolled over to face me. 'Not only that, Luke. I joke about religion with you, but in my family, it's no joke. Shirlene's family are even worse. We come from a part of Nebraska that makes the Bible Belt look like a loose cord tied around a heathen.'

'Okay, I get it. But don't worry. We'll be discreet.'

He'd shuffled closer and kissed me, gently this time. 'Thanks.'

We hadn't talked much more, but the rest of Sunday had passed quite quickly.

We'd left for the Lakes the following morning and now, early on Wednesday I'd suggested we actually leave the cottage and see some of the surrounding countryside. Dan had leapt up to make tea. I heard the toaster being pushed down. I figured simultaneous tea and toast might be a stretch and rolled out of bed to help.

*

The majesty of the surrounding peaks, looking down on the village like benevolent giants, had impressed Dan when we had gone for short walks to the local shops, but now, standing on top of Helvellyn, after a three-and-a-half-hour trek up footpaths, gravel tracks a final steep scree wall, he looked awestruck.

'My God, it's magnificent. I never imagined England could have this type of country.'

I turned full circle, slowly looking out on ridge after ridge, interspersed by deep valleys, stretching to the far horizon. I wondered how anyone from ancient history must have felt when faced with this view. The mountains looked to be never ending and although today the sun was shining and I was in boots, shorts and a shirt, I knew how rapidly the weather up here could change. It didn't need mid-winter to make the mountains treacherous. Those early tribes that ventured through this landscape on a journey to new lands must have wondered if they'd ever find a way through. I wondered if I would have given up faced with what looked like insurmountable odds. I decided, probably. Those small bands of families, or perhaps whole tribes, must have been extraordinarily brave. I doubted I could have matched them.

I felt Dan come to stand next to me. Brief shadows from fleeting white clouds flitted across the vibrant green of the hills, scarred and broken by rock escarpments and scramble paths of shale and loose rock. We weren't alone on the peak. It was August and whilst the mountain might have been the third highest in England, she wasn't a hard climb. Anyone with a reasonable level of fitness could make it up here and there had been a dozen or more people, most in groups of two or four, who had been ahead or behind us on the paths. Now they too were taking in the view they'd worked for. I felt Dan slip his hand in mine.

'Thank you.'

'What for?' I asked, gripping his hand tighter.

'For bringing me here. For showing me this.'

'You're welcome.'

'And for the last few days.'

My heart sank. 'You say that like the last few days are going to be put behind us?'

'No. Not at all. The last few days are the only ones in my life where I've been honest with myself.'

I kept hold of his hand but took half a step back and faced him. We'd had a whirlwind few days, but we hadn't talked in any depth about his motivations. In fact, other than him being surprised that I was not in the closet, we hadn't talked about much. 'Here, on top of a mountain?' I asked.

'What?'

'Pretty spectacular place for you to come out. You Americans can't do anything in a small understated way, can you?'

He mock punched me with his free hand before his face took on what I thought of as Dan's serious scowl. 'When did you know you were gay?'

I didn't answer straight away. Instead I turned back to the view and checked my watch. It was half one. I took a quick look up to the sky, orientated myself and by dragging his hand, orientated Dan too. 'About twenty-five miles as the crow flies in that direction,' I said pointing to the south-east, 'is Sedbergh School. It was, probably still is, arguably the pre-eminent public school in the north of England. Well, this side of the Pennines.'

'The what?'

'This side of the country. Durham would claim to be the best over on the east coast, but Sedbergh is the one for the west. The men in my family have gone there for generations. I did too. I was a boarder. Living in for whole terms. I met a boy called Matthew when I was sixteen. We fooled around, but nothing really serious.'

'Did the school know?'

'God no. It would have been instant expulsion. Everyone jokes about public schools in England being hotbeds of sodomy, and from when I was sixteen until I left, I might well have agreed, but it was sodomy far out of sight. Not even your US policy of "don't ask, don't tell". Just straightforward denial.'

'But you figured yourself out back then?'

'I suppose so. I denied it in public, but yes. I had boyfriends and I never felt any attraction to girls. Never tried to force myself to feel anything towards them either. By the time I was at university I'd had a few serious partners. A broken heart or two. Standard stuff. I don't think the heartbreak is any different if your first love is a girl or a boy.'

'And then you came out to your family?'

'Yes. I'd found out that I could apply to the military and they would pay me through the rest of my university degree. I'd thought about being a pilot but in the end was heading for intelligence. I'd been warned that part of the process would be an in-depth security clearance interview. I decided that if I was going to answer the questions honestly, to some random investigator, then I should be honest to my family first.'

Dan stepped in close to me. 'Your quite brave really, aren't you Luke?'

'I wouldn't have said brave. Lucky. The law had been changed. The British Military was embracing a new way of thinking. I was on the right side of history.'

'You still had to tell your family. The law doesn't affect what they think or feel.'

'Yes, I suppose. But that still doesn't make me brave. It only makes me luckier. I had a family who I knew would stand by me.'

'Really? You knew?'

'Wellll,' I allowed the word to draw out. 'I was fairly sure.'

Dan leant in and kissed me. When he pulled back I waited for him to glance around, to check to see if we'd been seen, but he didn't. We were more than three thousand feet up a mountain, but I was still impressed. 'Now that's brave, Dan. A public show of affection.'

'Seems that you have changed me, Mr Frankland.'

'Seems maybe I have, Mr Stückl. What do you think we're going to be able to do about it?'

That serious scowl overtook his handsome features again and I regretted the one question too many.

'That I don't know.'

*

It was early Friday morning when our idyllic retreat came to an end. I'd rung Steph on the Monday prior to us leaving London to let her know we were going on leave and to get her to sort out the paperwork. I told her we'd be back in two weeks, so when I saw my phone light up with the office number, I knew something serious had gone wrong. No one calls you on leave to discuss niff-naff and trivia.

'Sir, it's Mark.'

'Hi. What's up?'

'Steph said you and Captain Stückl were going fell walking. Is he with you?'

'He is. Hang on I'll put you on speaker.' I pressed the button and set the phone on the kitchen table.

'Hi Mark, what's up?' Dan called.

'Our friends are back, Sir. Looks like they hadn't really gone away. Rather they had moved house.'

I shared a look across the table. Dan shrugged. Without being able to get into details, we were limited on the questions we could ask.

'Are they doing what they did previously, Mark?'

'No. They still can't do that. Our old work is holding up. But they've shifted their interests. I wonder, do you think you could make it into the office sooner rather than later?'

I glanced again to Dan. He stepped forward. 'If it's that serious, we can be back today.'

'It's that serious, Sir.'

19

London, August 2005

Marseille was the new China. Or at least it was with regard to the IP addresses of our latest cyber-attacks. It took us until late afternoon to get into London and on arrival we'd been met with statistics that showed far from our Chinese adversaries giving up, they'd merely moved their base of operations. Our efforts had been targeted to stop attacks from the Chinese mainland. These new incursions were coming direct from various proxy locations, each one tracking back to the south of France. It was also apparent that the attack vectors themselves had changed.

I grabbed a coffee and followed Rachel, Ashley and Mark into the briefing room.

'They haven't tried to breach any systems, Sir.' Mark began.

'So what are they doing?'

'We had a tip off from GCHQ that a number of their staff had received spam emails.'

'We all get spam. I have no idea how many offers to purchase weird things come into my inbox on any given day.'

'Yes, but these are different. These aren't your standard "delete without thinking" phishing emails. These are specifically inviting you to a conference that would be a perfect match with your job and potential interests,' Rachel said, sliding a printed sheet across to me.

The email looked like it was from one of the many businesses that organised such events. I must have received similar at least once a month through the official MoD email system.

'Or,' she continued, sliding another sheet across, 'Offering a discount on books or DVDs or CDs that the individual likes.'

'Hang on,' I said whilst scanning the second sheet. 'Apart from the fact that these look perfectly legitimate, how the heck could they know what to entice someone with? That would mean they know them.'

'Yes. And no,' Rachel said.

I gave her my best look of bemusement, 'Go on.'

'Sir, you recall your short time on the Defence Debriefing Team,' she asked.

I had no problems recalling it. The months spent with them during the summer of 2001 had been an absolute revelation and full of experiences I could never forget. I'd been fresh out of initial Officers' training and had a six-month gap before the next intake for the Intelligence School. The military had to find something to do with people like me who were not fully trained. I couldn't see why they didn't send me home on full pay, but instead they had a thing called a "holding post". Somewhere they could send you where you would hopefully do little harm. My posting had been based out of Whitehall, London, which I had loved, but centred on debriefing Iraqi refugees coming into the country. Some we knew were genuinely fleeing from Saddam's henchmen. Some we were sure were Saddam's henchmen. Trying to ascertain who was who and trying to get useful information from the real refugees so that we could pin down Saddam's supposed weapons of mass destruction was not easy. I quickly learned that the British Defence Debriefing teams didn't use torture to get information but a much more subtle mix of questioning techniques. Not that the British hadn't used torture in the past, but since the 1970s they had realised the results gained from such techniques were marginal at best. People will tell you what you want to hear if you hurt them enough.

I was sure that my role for the few months was going to be administrative at best. Pushing pieces of paper around and making tea, but quite quickly they let me observe some of the interviews from an adjacent room fitted with a video monitoring setup. I'd been amazed at how much you could get from a person, the "subject" as the team referred to the interviewee, with very precise questioning. Rachel had been one of the more experienced interrogators on the team and before long I was sitting in alongside her on interviews.

The conditions in the refugee centres dotted around the country were not for the faint-hearted. I was disgusted that the British Government could tolerate people being held in the way they were, but I was even more appalled to know that so many supposed refugees were being allowed into the country with no form of official sanction or control. It had been Rachel that had told me to pick my fights. Getting stirred up over things we had no control over wasn't worth it. Much the same advice that John Leofric gave to me on a daily basis nowadays. I had taken hers and now John's lessons on board, but the ineptitude of my supposed political masters still angered me.

I brought my thoughts back to the present and answered Rachel. 'You have something specific in mind?'

'Yes, Sir. You know that if we could find a way into a person's lifestyle then we had a chance of getting them to talk. It's why we bugged the detention centres and sent some of our own people into them in disguise. Then we used any snippets we gained when we went back into the interviews. If we knew someone had a son or daughter, or elderly relative back in Iraq, we could use it as a little leverage to open them up.'

'I remember. But we had access to them. If you're saying these emails are using that same type of strategy, how are they getting the information in the first place?'

Rachel looked across the conference table to Mark, who slid the cover off the projector. A picture of a computer screen appeared with a long list of names running down the left hand side. I'd never seen anything like it before.

'I said we got a tip off from GCHQ. They found the first suspicious emails three days ago. Our first ones showed up this morning. That's why we called you back. But Cheltenham reckon the emails could be dating back months. They've been theorising how the Chinese could have got such specific information and they came up with this. Are you familiar with it, Sir?'

I shook my head and if Mark was distressed that I knew nothing about whatever he was showing me, he hid it as well as usual.

'It's a screen shot of UseNet. What's called a distributed discussion platform. Discussions are grouped into categories and it works like a massive bulletin board. People post an idea and then others interact with them and add their posts onto the bottom of the original.'

'Okay,' I said. 'And this is new is it?'

'Eh, no. It's actually been around since 1980.' Mark said and I was impressed he managed to keep the disbelief that I had never heard of it out of his voice.

'Right. Well I'm glad it hasn't taken me too long to catch up.' I saw the three of them grin. 'You're being serious though, 1980?'

'Yes, Sir. It was one of the earliest ways that academics, government officials and the military communicated together on the fledgling networks that eventually grew into the Internet. UseNet was pretty much the beginning of true network collaboration.'

'And it's still in use?'

'Yes. Only now it's open to the whole Internet.'

I looked at the list of names running down the screen. 'What is rec dot arts dot startrek?'

'Exactly what you would think. It's a board full of posts about *Star Trek*,' Ashley said and handed me another sheet of paper. 'These are the top boards on UseNet as of today. It quickly went from a scientific exchange of ideas to a freedom of speech model where anything and everything could be discussed.'

I scanned the list and saw alt.sex, alt.drugs and a myriad of other titles that testified to how quickly something could go from the academic to the sublime. 'Okay, but how does this get us to sending emails to people in GCHQ?'

'By default the types of people in GCHQ or the US military or even my RAF Police units that were interested in computers would have been on UseNet. I know I was,' Mark said.

Rachel leant forward and pointed to the list I still held. 'If you go into enough of these boards or the group discussions that they call chat rooms, then you'd be able to pick up a lot of background information on someone. Like we used to in the Debriefing Team, but even easier because you're anonymous. You could pretend to be anyone you wanted to be and given enough time, you could begin to pick out individuals of interest.'

'Alright, Rachel. I'll buy it. I spark up an online conversation with Mark here and I find out he likes *Star Trek*. So what?'

'Then over time, if Mark isn't switched on about his personal security you learn a bit more about him. You discover he works for the Electricity Board, or Local Government, or he's in the Army. It doesn't really matter, the who and what isn't important. You are really only after his email address. Preferably a work email but that isn't really important either. Then you send a targeted email that you know will have enough details in it to make it look completely legitimate and it will also contain an attachment or a link.'

It dawned on me in a rapid fire series of images that flashed inside my head. 'That's genius.'

There was no response. I looked at all three of them in turn and realised they had no clue I had worked it out. 'You click on the link or open the attachment and whatever computer you are on at the time is compromised by whatever code they have embedded. They copy the data off that computer and if you've been stupid enough to send an email home from work to yourself, they will have that email address or potentially hundreds of others. If they are on a work's computer, you will have infected the whole network.'

'Yes. Exactly,' Ashley said and didn't manage to hide her surprise that I had worked it out. 'Given the data you acquired you can start to target others. Ideally, with enough time and resources you can start to target senior players in your particular area of interest.'

I sat back and looked up at the briefing room wall where we had hung a map of mainland China. 'And we know exactly who has enough resources to do this, don't we?' I asked rhetorically but all three nodded anyway. 'How much damage do we think they've done?'

'Rob says that GCHQ are satisfied their systems are not compromised at all, but they are concerned that if these types of targeted emails continue, it's only a matter of time,' Mark said. 'They've even come up with a special term for it; Spear Phishing.'

I considered the name and had to admit it was well chosen. This was no wide net cast around to catch the unwary. This was a directed and well-thought out attack. It was also frightening to think that an awful lot of people on the many floors of the building where I now sat were not really computer literate, yet had access to computers. I wondered how easy it would be to send one of them an official looking email with what looked like an innocent attachment, only to have them compromise the whole system from within. We'd spent months securing the walls and gates of our castle and now someone was going to kill us by allowing a carrier pigeon to bring in the Black Death. 'I'm open to suggestions, but I can only see to start a campaign that will educate our people within the MoD and further afield. Is there much else we can do?'

Mark gave a half-shrug. 'Rob, Josh and the guys in the US thought they could write some code that would stop people opening attachments, but even if it can be done it would severely hamper normal operational use of emails. So, no, there's no quick fix, but yes a training and awareness campaign would be a good start.'

'Okay. But surely if the emails are being traced back to Marseille we can enlist the French to our cause?'

Rachel sighed. 'You'd think, but my experience of our opposite numbers in Calais when we were debriefing refugees, was that they aren't the most cooperative of allies,'

'I'm going to hope they've changed. I'll have a word with the old man.'

I stood and they followed me back into the main office. Dan was staring at his screen. Rob and Josh alongside him.

'Have you ever read Sun Tzu?' he asked as I walked in.

'Partially. Why?'

'I've said they've been adapting, but it's more than that. They've been flowing like water, seeking out the easiest pathway into a system. Now we've blocked up the gaps, they're going for the weakest link of all.'

'The people?' I asked.

'Exactly.' He swivelled his chair around to look across at me and I discovered something I hadn't known about myself. I could compartmentalise my feelings. This man who I had made love to not twelve hours ago was back to being Dan. US Captain, colleague, computer expert. Although it wasn't a completely airtight compartment as a small part of me could still envisage his body and another part of me started to consider what tonight would bring. I shut the thoughts down and turned towards John Leofric's office.

His door was ajar as usual, but I still knocked. He called me in and I brought him up to speed on our newly evolved threat.

'And you would like me to…?' He left his sentence unfinished.

'I'd like you to get the French Military Attaché in here and ask him for help.'

'That's not exactly how these things happen, Luke. But I can arrange for a friend of mine at Box 850 to sort out a liaison get together.'

John was old school and like a lot of the Civil Service he still referred to the Secret Intelligence Service, known by the public as MI6, by their old postal address box number. Even though they'd moved from Century House to Vauxhall Cross a decade earlier.

'If that's how it has to happen, then yes, please, Sir.'

'We may need a few others to join us, I think. Makes for a more convivial gathering. Can you ask Rachel to recommend a few names that she trusts from her previous lives?'

I wasn't surprised that Rachel would have worked with MI6 before, but I was mildly surprised that Leofric knew her background. The old man never ceased to amaze me. 'Certainly, Sir.'

*

Vauxhall Cross, the building that was home to the SIS, MI6, Box 850 or whatever other name you wanted to call them, sat right beside my home in St George's Wharf, so Dan and I had a walk of less than a minute from door to door. We still left with twenty minutes to spare as we'd been told by Rachel that the security procedures to get into the building could be a bit demanding. She wasn't wrong. It took almost fifteen minutes to get names confirmed and passes issued. Eventually a small and wiry member of the security personnel on duty, all of whom wore suits instead of uniforms and most of whom I thought looked seriously and aggressively scary, escorted us up to an empty conference room on level five. The large space was dominated by a floor to ceiling glass wall that afforded a magnificent view over the Thames towards the old Battersea Power Station. Its panoramic vista made my apartment window, with exactly the same view, seem quite small in comparison.

'You ever been to Langley?' Dan whispered to me as we made our way towards the central tables in the room, which were laid out with finger food, plates and pre-filled glasses. I had been expecting Leofric to arrange a sit down meeting with the French, but he'd told me apparently this would be for the best. I figured I was in no position to disagree.

'No, can't say I have.' I answered and picked out a glass of white. I took a sip. It was room temperature and atrocious. We walked over to stand next to what I knew were triple-glazed, bulletproof window panels that were specially coated to allow a one-way view only.

'It's isolated on the west bank of the Potomac. I mean, it's near to DC, but not stuck in the middle of the city shouting here I am. What were they thinking when they made this place?'

'God knows.'

'They were thinking that their old headquarters were as secure as a clown's trousers and a nice new audaciously designed building would be a statement that they had nothing to fear.'

I recognised the voice and turned to see its owner reaching for a canapé. 'Steve Jäeger, what brings you here?'

'Oh, you know. This and that. We got hit with the same emails as you guys. Well, not exactly the same, obviously, but the same concept. And of course I thought it was time for me to come say hi to Dan,' he said reaching out to shake our hands in turn.

The door to the room opened and Rachel entered accompanied by a man I thought I recognised from somewhere but couldn't place. She, as usual, looked like she had walked off the pages of a fashion magazine and he was much the same. Both were tall, slim and carried themselves with an air of grace and confidence that was undeniably alluring. They looked so well matched I wondered if he was her partner and I had maybe seen him at a function at some other time, but Vauxhall Cross wasn't exactly the place you brought your other half. I managed not to smile too much as that thought occurred to me and Dan crossed the room still talking to Steve.

'Good evening, Sir.' Rachel said.

'Call me Luke, Rachel. For tonight, while we're in here.'

'Okay. Will do. This is Andy Gibson,' she said and took a half step back. 'You might remember he used to come down to the debriefing centre when you were there.'

Her prompt allowed me to recall where I knew him from. 'Yes, of course. I remember you, Andy. You were an SIS liaison officer. I assume from you being here, you still are?'

'I am. SIS that is. No longer doing the liaison role but your boss and Rachel thought it might be good if I attended tonight. I had quite a while working alongside the French and they thought I might be able to help out. I also have a passing interest in China.'

Behind them the door opened again and John Leofric came in accompanied by three men I didn't recognise at all. Rachel leant across to me. 'The man on John's left, is Jeremy Vigroux, the French Defence Attaché to London. The taller and older of the two on his right is François Brecheteau and the other is Lionel Gueroult. They're both DGSE.'

'French Foreign Intelligence? Are they usually based in London?' I asked. Rachel looked to Andy.

'No. Those two have come in especially for this. Which in itself tells you something's a bit weird here. For the French equivalent of me to be sent to a meeting is one thing,' Andy said, turning slightly so he was directly facing me and away from our new arrivals. 'But this would be the equivalent of me and my boss's boss's boss being sent across to Paris. Seems like a touch of overkill.'

The door opened again and another three people who I didn't recognise came in. Andy waved them across and introduced them as Francis and Robbie from SIS and Will from GCHQ. Each apparently had an interest in what they called the socially adept way with which the Chinese were going about this email attack. I almost commented on their lack of surnames but thought it was probably best not to. Being paranoid about their security seemed like a favourite past time for both SIS and GCHQ, but they had bothered to show up and so I could cope with their clandestine approach.

I waited until John and, I thought interestingly, Steve Jäeger had made the introductions. I'd been briefed by John that afternoon to make small talk, chat with the various people in the room, by all means chat to the French, but not to raise any issues concerning the Chinese attacks with them. That would come in good time.

I sipped the white wine I had picked up at the start of the evening, which had now reached above room temperature, and nibbled on a variety of the hors d'œuvres. The small sausage rolls were as hard as bullets, the filo pastry ham and cheese pinwheels were limp and the cucumber slices, topped with Lord alone knows what, were as thick as my thumb. I was pleased to see that the SIS caterers were in every way as dire as the MoD's. No doubt it would not put our French guests at ease, but it would allow them a sense of cuisine superiority.

Mostly I spoke to Dan and Rachel, but occasionally I would hear John and Andy speaking in fluent French to our guests. Again Leofric had surprised me, but not quite as much as when Steve Jäeger joined them and also spoke the language in a way that to my ear sounded like immaculately pronounced French. It served me no purpose whatsoever as my linguistic skills were limited to Frère Jacques. I was a little envious of not only John and Steve but also Rachel who I already knew was fluent. I consoled myself with the knowledge that Dan, like me, was bereft of any Gallic flair.

After about half an hour, the younger DGSE agent, Lionel, casually made his way over to me. We shook hands and swapped banalities about life, London, Paris, the weather and the Six Nations Rugby that had happened earlier in the year and in which France had narrowly come second to Wales. As he recounted in his heavily accented but precise English, how the French should never have lost to the Welsh in the Stade de France, I noticed Dan disengaging himself from a conversation with Will, and making his way across the room. I made the introductions and Lionel finally got around to saying something I was interested in.

'You believe these incursions are coming from Marseilles?'

'Yes, we do. And it would be great if we could work together to put an end to them,' I said and sipped again at my white wine. I was impressed with how well I'd nursed it.

'I don't think there is a realistic hope of anyone of interest being in Marseille. I think that our Asian friends are, how you say, pulling the wool?'

'Perhaps,' Dan added. 'But we can trace fairly specifically the IP addresses and it wouldn't take too much effort to mount a joint operation.'

'Ah but you are only an American liaison. Yes?'

I was surprised at Lionel's dismissive tone, considering he'd been in conversation with Steve Jäeger earlier. I was about to interject, but Dan answered first.

'Yes. That's right. But I'm also a fully integrated member of Luke's team, so it would be a joint operation. His team, including me, and whatever assets you can bring.'

'I think it will probably not be possible. I am sure that you are being led down a false pathway. But this is why we do what we do. Nothing is straightforward or simple. It is what it is. No?'

I took a breath and wondered how I was going to convince this annoying little shit that he was wrong and we were right, but I never got the chance. He finished his drink, set the glass on the table and walked back to join his countrymen still in conversation with John and Steve. I almost followed him across the room, but Rachel's hand on my arm stopped me.

'Don't, Luke. There's something not quite right here.' she said quietly.

'What, obnoxious French men? Seems quite usual to me.' I said through what I realised were gritted teeth. Lionel really had annoyed me in a remarkably short amount of time.

'Yes, but more than that. I expected this to be fairly smooth, but John and Steve are failing to get any traction. It's like the French want us to be struggling against whoever is behind this and aren't prepared to assist at all.'

'But how can they? We have the evidence that it's almost certain the attacks are originating from computers located in their neck of the woods.'

'Yeah. I know, but Brecheteau, the senior DGSE guy, just said to Mr Leofric and Steve that he reckons the Chinese are playing with us. Like a cat with a ball of string.'

I put my glass down on the table and moved to block Rachel's view of the French party on the other side of the room. 'Sorry, Rachel. Are you certain of what you heard?'

Rachel inclined her head and gave me a puzzled look. 'Umm, yes. Why do you ask?'

'He said like a cat with a ball of string?'

'Yes. Well, no. He actually said like an aggressive cat with a ball of string.'

I thought back to early July and pictured the scene that had played out in our office. Dan at the computer, Rob beside him and

Richie halfway to another terminal. Josh and Ashley standing beside me. Colonel Charles off to one side, Leofric in his office and Rachel on a phone line on the far side of the room. Out of earshot.

I shifted my gaze to Dan and from the look on his face I knew, before I asked, what his answer would be.

'Did you by any chance mention that phrase to the French tonight?'

'No. Most definitely not.'

'What are the chances, do you think?'

'That type of phrase in this context. It's possible. But that almost exact phrase. I wouldn't have thought so.'

'No. Me neither.'

Rachel was looking puzzled. I leant in and asked her to discreetly fetch John for me.

The Entente Cordiale meeting broke up twenty minutes later. The French had said no to any cooperation and we were fairly sure we knew why.

20

London, August-September 2005

The counter-intelligence division of GCHQ took twenty-two minutes to discover seventeen bugs placed throughout our office and briefing room. They extended the sweep to the whole of the MoD Main Building and after four days had turned up an impressive array of listening and video devices. Only one section of the basement levels that had not been refurbished during the recent works was free of surveillance equipment. Given how many contractors had been used on the project I was told the chance of finding out who was responsible was practically nil. Not that we needed to find the person who planted them, we already knew it was done by our French cousins across the Channel. I was appalled and outraged, seething in fact, but John Leofric shrugged it off.

'It's part and parcel of the game, Luke. You think we only spy on our would-be enemies?' John asked, relaxing back in his office chair.

'I get that, I do. I'm sure we spy on all sorts of people I should hope we spy against the French, given we've fought against them more than most, but surely we should be making some sort of protest?'

'We will. At the highest levels.'

'I'm sorry, Sir, but what does that actually mean?'

'Our Prime Minster will speak to their President.'

'And then we'll throw some of their diplomats out, like we do with the Russians after things like this?'

'No. That would send the wrong message to those like the Russians and the Chinese. We might have spats with our friends, but we keep them quietly in-house.'

'So what will we get by way of satisfaction?'

'Ha! Would you like us to challenge them to a duel? Perhaps you could shoot that annoying little greasy one?'

'Lionel? Happily.'

'No Luke, sadly no duels. No satisfaction. Although I have no doubt our politicians will get some form of concession from Paris, but we will likely never hear about it.'

'But they'll cooperate with us on Marseille now, surely?'

John leant further back in his chair and gave me what I imagined he thought was his most benevolent smile. I liked and admired the old man, but with his pronounced overbite any smile, benevolent or not, looked a little threatening. 'We shan't be asking them to help with the Marseille problem.' He held his hand up to stop me speaking.

'We can't trust the French and our Government are still not interested. Neither for that matter are the US Government at the moment. I could postulate that they are concerned with the direct and immediate threats posed by extremists or that there are great strategic intrigues of which I know little and understand less, but for whatever reason, we are on our own. With one exception.'

'Steve?'

'Yes. He is feeling equally isolated and equally at a loss as to why. However, he is a handy chap to have at our disposal.'

'Business as usual then?' I asked. 'Try to keep the networks safe and secure and roll out some computer awareness training across the building?'

'Exactly.' John stood and came around his desk. 'Don't underestimate what you are doing either, Luke. I am most impressed.

You've come a long way in a short time and Dan has helped us enormously.'

I felt my heart skip a beat, but kept my voice neutral. 'I couldn't agree more. Shame he's going to be going soon.'

'Yes. Yes it is, however, according to Steve, he's more than willing to extend out the deployment.'

I felt a wave of happiness surge through me. Its intensity caught me by surprise and with it, I realised how far I had fallen already. Again, I kept any emotion out of my voice. 'That would be great. Is it possible?'

'Since Steve and I discussed it, I've had Steph looking into the admin side of it. Seems that the original liaison post that was established years ago is a RAF and US arrangement. The ultimate budget holder on this side of the water is still Group Captain Air Intelligence. Do you know who that is?'

My elation turned to dread. 'That would be Group Captain Halson,' I said and this time could not keep the emotion from my voice.

'Oh! You don't make it sound too good. Bit of a stickler is he?'

Bit of a complete arse, was the response that came to me, but I manged to say nothing and merely nodded.

'Well, I'll maybe give him a call nearer the time when we need to make a decision. I'm sure he'll be reasonable.'

I didn't relish John's chances but at least I didn't have to interact with Halson on it. In fact I was happy if I never had to see the tosser ever again. I certainly didn't expect him to march into my office three weeks later.

*

In the first few days of September the British Army's largest training exercise of the year kicked off throughout the country, but predominantly within the confines of Salisbury Plain. Four infantry brigades, two armoured brigades and an Air Assault Brigade set about each other for what was meant to be ten days of intensive warfare training. The troops, either recently back from Iraq or

Afghanistan, or about to go out to one of those two active theatres, were well versed in close-quarters urban warfare, but they still had to be trained and exercised for other types of war fighting and Exercise Anvil_05 was the way to ensure those skills hadn't been diminished. In addition to the fighting arms, the Army's logistic and wider support tails were also being put to the test. It was a complex and expensive series of events, planned for months, and closely monitored by the Army's highest command structures and the Permanent Joint Headquarters.

At 14:30 on the Friday, only five days into the exercise, an order came out of Erskine Barracks, about four kilometres northwest of Salisbury, from the email account of General Sir Dickie Wattman, Commander-in-Chief Land Command. It stated that the exercise had already fulfilled its objectives, that the troops had conducted themselves with tremendous aplomb and as such the exercise was being ended early. Commanders were to immediately pass the order to their subordinate units and congratulate their personnel on a thoroughly well done job. Each and every one was to cease and desist and stand down. Leave was granted for all personnel for the following weekend. It ended with the line: Anvil_05, Endex Endex Endex. For those involved the prospect of living in a muddy trench, or the inside of a tank, or in a wet tent for another five days compared to the prospect of a warm bed was an easy choice. By 16:30 most units had recovered themselves off the exercise area and the troops were either driving home for the weekend or breaking open their first few beers in the on-base bars.

That same afternoon, Sir Dickie had been attending a briefing in the Permanent Joint Headquarters bunker, near Northwood, London. At 14:30, emerging from seven storeys underground into the cold grey sky of a typical British autumnal day, he climbed into the back seat of his official car and his driver began the battle against Friday afternoon traffic. Despite clogged roads, they made it back to Salisbury in relatively good time. Sir Dickie strode into the subordinate command headquarters of the Air Assault Brigade with ten minutes to spare for what he expected to be a 17:00 summary brief on the day's activities and an overview of how the exercise was going so far. What he found was an impromptu bar-b-que serving up slightly overdone sausages and burgers with accompanying bread baps and bottles of Heineken. He was, to put it mildly, quite put out.

After a good few minutes of confusion, some raised voices and at least one tirade of profanities, the stressed and confused officer in charge of the Air Assault Brigade handed over a copy of Sir Dickie's own email. He swore no knowledge of it and the proverbial shit hit the fan.

I knew nothing about any of it until Monday morning. Dan and I had enjoyed our weekend as much as we had any other since we had started sharing a bedroom. On the Sunday we had even gone to the V&A Museum and spent hours standing up looking at other things as opposed to lying down looking at each other. On the Monday we'd strolled to work and settled in for what I assumed would be another week of trying to keep our networks safe. We'd arrived, as usual, earlier than our official 08:00 start time and I was already halfway through my daily scan of the open source reports and newspapers by the time the rest of the team were turning up. John came past and said good morning on his way to his office. Colonel Charles, Dave and Jim were heads down on the crossword, some things hadn't changed, and Steph was busy. Doing what I was never sure, but busy nonetheless, flitting about the office checking and straightening and being Steph. On her way past the office doors she was almost bowled over by an incoming Group Captain Halson. I glanced up at Steph's hurried, 'Sorry' to see Halson sidestep her with no apology and continue heading directly for me. I managed to get to my feet before he arrived. He stopped on the other side of my desk and slammed his two hands down on it. His brow glistened with sweat and made his face appear as shiny as his off-the-peg suit.

'I'm surprised you haven't packed up your desk already?'

His tone was surly, perfectly normal for him but slightly louder than I would have cared for. He was only three feet from me. I offered out my hand, 'Good morning, Sir.'

He ignored it. 'I have said it before and now you have proven it. You are an absolute disgrace. An embarrassment. I thought you were meant to be here protecting the MoD networks and computers…'

I was entranced. I'd been shouted at and worse during school and basic training but never by a Group Captain and never in front of my whole office. Out of the corner of my eye I could see Dave, Jim and Colonel Charles looking up from their cryptic clues. No mean feat to have disturbed them. The Colonel, who was the equivalent rank to the Group Captain was looking a little shocked and confused. I realised he would have no idea who this stranger in our midst was. The rest of the team were equally stunned. No one had reacted. Even Dan seemed completely at a loss. I realised Halson hadn't let up.

'…thousands if not tens of thousands of pounds wasted on a massive exercise and they couldn't just start again, half of them had gone home. All down to you not being able to do your job. No, you can't even do that. Swanning around in London in some swanky apartment at God alone knows what cost to the taxpayer. Parading in your fancy suits with your fancy attitude. You are and you always were acting way above your station and your place in life. Well you're done for now you supercilious litt—'

'ENOUGH!'

The volume of the shout made me jump and stopped Halson dead. Everyone turned to see John Leofric striding out of his office door. It was like years had fallen away from him as he covered the distance to my desk. He glanced down at the visitor's pass that Halson had clipped to his suit lapel.

'My office, now Group Captain.'

'And you are?' Halson said with barely a glance towards John.

'Someone who outranks you.'

It was said in a controlled manner but with an underlying tone that left no doubt Leofric was in charge. I watched the doubt creep into Halson's eyes. He turned his head towards Leofric. The old man, who had at least four inches height advantage over this squat pig, continued to stare down at him. Halson managed to mumble, 'Yes, Sir.'

The two of them went to John's office.

Colonel Charles, Dan, Mark and Rachel came over to me. 'Are you okay, Luke?' Charles asked.

'Umm, yes. I'm fine, Sir. Just not quite sure what that was about.'

'I think I might know,' Josh called from his desk a few feet away. 'I have a mate who works out of Odiham, on the Chinook helicopter fleet. We were meant to be going out in London this weekend but he couldn't make it. Some big Army exercise on and the Chinooks were providing airlifts for the troops. But he rocked up on Friday night. Apparently the exercise had been cancelled.'

'How's that our fault?' Dan asked.

'Don't know, Sir,' Josh said. 'I checked and there's nothing on the official MoD notice boards, but it ties in with what that man was shouting about. Who is he?'

I explained to Josh and the rest who the Group Captain was. Colonel Charles put his hand on my arm. 'Don't worry about him. The old man will deal with that. We need to find out what went wrong with the Army. Come on Jim, Dave, get on the phones to your old contacts. Find out what happened.'

I was stunned. Dave and Jim folded away their crosswords and each picked up a phone. Rachel too. With no official mention of any issue on the computer networks we would have to rely on the good old-fashioned grapevine.

It turned out the Army grapevine was swift. It took less than five minutes for the story of the cancelled exercise and the argument in the Air Assault Brigade's headquarters to be divulged to Dave, and Jim, and Rachel by three separate people. Rachel's contact also revealed that the Army's computer security team had been called in. They were the equivalent to the RAF one that Mark Donoghue had run before joining me. He got onto his erstwhile opposite number. He was still on the phone when John's door opened and Halson walked out. Without as much as a look towards me the Group Captain left the office.

John Leofric waited for Mark to hang up the phone before calling the whole team together. 'I have told the Group Captain that he is never to address any member of this team in such a manner again. I may have added a few other asides that you don't need to know. In turn, he informs me that a computer network breach is responsible for some disastrous end to an exercise. What do we know?'

'I've just come off the phone with the Army Comp Sec team, Sir.' Mark said. He recounted the story we knew so far and then added, 'The general assumption and indeed, the General's assumption had been that someone had broken into his computer whilst he'd been in London and sent the spurious email. The hunt started for the individual, but the Army Comp Sec team found that no one had logged on to the General's account. They had confirmed it by Saturday lunchtime and by Saturday night they had contacted Royal Navy and Royal Air Force computer security units that they suspected a network breach.'

'And why didn't the Army contact us?' John asked.

'They had no clue we existed, Sir,' Mark said and as soon as the words were out, we knew it was true. The MoD and the military, who were meant to work with one another, so often worked in isolation. 'They reported it to the people they knew. Basically sideways into the Navy and Air Force.'

'And it landed on the Group Captain's plate on Sunday evening apparently,' John added. 'He could barely wait to come here this morning and blame us. Well, you,' he pointed a finger at me, 'for it all.'

'Technically, he's right,' I said. 'The deployed military email network is under our remit.'

'Perhaps, but as we are still discovering, the whole of the UK reaction to networks is as fractured as our network design. It will take time,' John said and I was very grateful to him for it. 'Still, we should take over the investigation now we know of it. Carry on.' He turned away but as he did so he laid a hand on my forearm and inclined his head for me to follow. Aside from the rest he continued. 'Do not worry about that man for now. But do keep your wits about you. I've seen his type before. He's mean-spirited and petty. Be careful. In all things.' He spoke low and as he finished he made direct eye contact with me and then glanced across to Dan.

I had no response to give. The surprise that he had worked out Dan and I were more than colleagues was overwhelming. My face must have reflected my inner thoughts.

'No, it's not obvious. No, no one else knows. I had my suspicions, and you just confirmed them, but that's okay. He is the same rank as you and there is no law against what you are doing. Having an affair is not exactly the best situation to find yourself in, but that is his issue, not yours. However, you know what would happen if it was revealed to the US military, don't you?'

I nodded. I knew only too well. Dan would be out of here. Stripped of his rank, dishonourably discharged from the US Army.

'So be careful, yes?'

'Yes, Sir and…thank you.'

He walked away and I went to the coffee machine. If ever I needed caffeine it was now. I looked across the office and saw every one of my team either busy on their screens or on phones, apart from Rachel. She was walking towards me with a print out in her hand.

'Can you sign this, Sir? It's a request for the Commander-in-Chief Land Command to give us his network login details so we can go through his email accounts.'

'That was quick.'

'Turns out the Army Comp Sec team are delighted to hand it over to us. Couldn't get rid of it fast enough. They reckon that whoever touches this will end up being in the firing line, so as far as they're concerned we can have it.'

*

Three hours later Dan and Rob had proven that the email had been written within the General's account, using his logon details, but not from within his Salisbury Headquarters or anywhere else in the UK. He'd been hacked and his details compromised. From there, remote access to his PC accounts was easy and regular.

'How long?' I asked.

'Since he responded to an email about five weeks ago,' Rob said and pointed out the culprit on screen. 'Apparently the General was specifically invited to a conference in Virginia that was going to cover the new programs concerning Mine-Resistant Ambush Protected vehicles.' Rob handed over a print out. 'This came in at the tail end of July, so that ties in with GCHQ thinking this has been going on longer than we thought.' He handed me another print out. 'This is the actual conference invite from General Dynamics Armoured Division. The conference is real, but where the General signed up to was a trojan'ised website. He was well and truly socially engineered.'

'Can't blame him for thinking this is the same and legit.' I said, comparing the two piece of paper.

'No, I guess not. You can blame him for using an official email account to sign up to an external conference though,' Rob said.

'Yes, but he's a four-star General. You going to tell him?'

'Eh, no. That is well and truly above my pay grade.'

'Yes, mine too. But great work, Rob. I assume we have secured the good General's account?'

'Yep, all done,' Dan said. 'Now we need to trace where it came from and see if we can find any other examples. Then perhaps we can write some code to weed any like-minded attacks out, hey Rob?'

Rob didn't respond. I looked over to him and he was staring intently at his screen. 'Rob? Everything alright?'

'Eh, yes. I think so. I mean, I…Eh, can you…Eh, give us a minute, Sir?'

Rob never called me Sir. Dan pushed his chair around so that he could look at whatever was so distracting. I saw him frown as Rob pointed out a line of code on the screen.

'Mark, Ritchie, Josh,' Dan called and I took a step backwards. The four of them began opening program boxes on their screens and the office printers started whirring into life.

'Do I need to be concerned, Dan?'

'No. Not at the minute. We'll let you know.'

*

It was almost three in the afternoon when I heard Josh, quietly and with no dramatic outburst say from the other side of the room, 'Well, fuck me.'

Mark, Ritchie, Rob and Dan stood up as if their terminals were on fire. I watched them as they stared at the screens and then Dan waved me over. He pointed out a block of text that to me looked like a completely random character set. 'This is the header and footer of an email that you normally don't see. It's in the background and carries the send and receive information the message needs to get from sender to recipient.'

'Okay, looks like gobbeldy-gook'

'It mostly is, but in 2004 the British Government adopted the DKIM protocol to validate their emails. Everyone within Government, MoD and the Services use it. If your email address ends dot gov dot uk then DKIM is meant to protect it.'

'And DKIM is…?'

'Domain Keys Identified Mail. It's a system that is meant to verify that the domain name an email claims to be from is in fact correct. It's designed to verify and confirm message integrity.'

'And someone has broken it?'

'No. They didn't have to, they used the General's login so the email was authenticated because it was from him. His account at least.'

'So the spoof emails that we're getting, they've had their DKIM broken?'

'No, Luke. Slow down. Let me explain.'

'Sorry.' I hid the smile that threatened to sweep over my face when Dan gave a wink that only I saw.

'DKIM is a pretty robust, sophisticated encryption code. The spoof emails that have been targeting us are coming from domains that don't use it and are therefore vulnerable, but that's by the by. The General's did use it. This is what it looks like normally,' Dan said and handed me a printout of the text on the screen. It contained a solid block of characters, including lower case and upper-case letters, numbers and various punctuation marks.

'You said normally?'

'Yeah. Normally this block of characters is accompanied by a final checksum that the receiving computer can test and verify to prove that the email is legitimately from where it says it is. If it isn't the email is discarded.'

'Okay. The General's wasn't discarded so this was okay?'

'Yeah, but look at this,' he said and handed me a second piece of paper. 'This is a DKIM block and checksum from a usual email.'

I held the two pieces of paper side by side. Neither of the text blocks made any sense and the rest of it, that I presumed was the checksum Dan spoke off, seemed equally as mystifying. I was about to admit failure when I noticed that the General's email seemed to have a slightly longer header block. 'This one's got more random numbers and letters?' I asked more in hope than conviction.

'Exactly. That's what Rob noticed when he looked this morning. It has an extra line. A line that does nothing to interfere with the DKIM but is just there. Hanging about, doing nothing, but it's disguised to look like a random header checksum.'

I could hear a tremor of excitement in Dan's voice. I was baffled at how I had managed to fall head over heels for a computer nerd, but there it was. 'And?' I asked realising he was bursting to tell me.

'We went and checked every other spear phishing email we've been able to identify. The extra line is in each one. Even the non-DKIM ones. It's been disguised differently, but it's there.'

'And what does this extra line mean?'

'Well that was the problem. It's encoded, but it's always encoded the same way. We decided to test if it was using a simple substitution cypher, but that came up a blank. We chewed it over for a while and then we asked Rob's buddies down in Cheltenham to help. They identified is as using a new cypher key that was published last year. It's called Roo and was submitted to the EU Ecrypt network, it's a fas—'

'Dan,' I said stopping him cold. 'That's really interesting, I'm sure, but what does the extra line say.' I felt a tang of regret for interrupting him. He'd looked so excited and now looked a little crestfallen. 'Tell me the interesting stuff later, hey? For now, what does it say?'

He picked his bottom lip up quickly. 'It's a message. It says,' he turned to Josh who handed over a piece of paper with a line of pencilled text.

2616 401 302

I looked at the paper then back at Dan and the rest of them. I turned the page over. It was blank, as was I.

'It took a while, but eventually we wondered if the 2616 might refer to the Request for Comments that defined the Hypertext Transfer Protocol in 1999.'

I knew my blank stare hadn't altered.

'Don't worry about that, Luke, it's a paper that lays out how HTTP works on the net.'

'Okay…and the 401 and 302.'

Dan turned to Rob. 'We think they're status codes from within the protocol. The 401 would translate as an unauthorised request and 302 is to move permanently.'

Rob seemed incredibly pleased with their work. They all did. None of them said anything more, but they stared up at me. 'I'm sorry guys, you'll have to give me a clue, you've been looking at this for hours, I've just been handed it. What are you telling me?'

'We think it's a message. Directed to us. Ever since they shifted their base of operations from China, every attack or email generated into us has carried that same code. We simply hadn't seen it.'

I looked back down at the numbers on the page. 'You think this says it's an unauthorised request for them to move permanently? Oh! … Oh I see…' My brain conjured the words and it finally clicked into place. 'No way?' Seriously?'

'Yes,' Dan said, his face breaking into a grin when he knew I had reached the same conclusion. 'This is a request to us. This is from one of their programmers and he's asking for asylum.'

21

London, September 2005

We convened a meeting of the team in the briefing room and for nearly half an hour swayed between belief, doubt, cynicism and wariness. In the end it was Colonel Charles who asked the fundamental questions in clear terms.

'Can we answer this without compromising the safety of whoever is on the other side if they are legitimate, and without compromising ourselves if they aren't?'

'We think so,' said Dan with a note of caution.

'And do we have a plan if we establish they are for real?'

'That we do, definitely,' Rachel said. 'We can get them into the standard safe house setup for a full debrief. Like we would with any defector.'

The Colonel checked with the old man. John gave a single nod. 'Then let's reach out and make contact, Luke.'

The meeting broke up and I followed Dan back to his desk. Ritchie moved his screen round so that we could watch the commands he was typing.

'You sure this will work?' I asked.

'Not in the slightest,' Mark said, watching the screen.

'Good. Glad to hear it.' I said and noticed I didn't get the usual grins or half-laughs from any of them. Ritchie stopped typing and turned to me.

'It's ready, Sir. I canny tell if it'll dae what we want it tae, but we can send it.'

On the screen was what looked like a standard email receipt. The type of thing I got back from every email I sent on the MoD systems. This one looked the same, but had been composed by Dan, Rob, Ritchie, and Josh and made to look like an automatically generated one. It had within its header an extra line, encoded using the same cypher as the original message from our possible Chinese defector. The number string in plain text was written in pencil on a notepad next to Ritchie's keyboard:

2616 202 101 91.243.70.250 14:00

Dan had told me it used the same Internet Protocol as the incoming message, 2616, and the status code 202 meant "accepted". Code 101 meant "switch protocols" and the 91.243.70.250 was an IP address for a server in Berlin that hosted Internet Relay Chat rooms closely associated with UseNet. If our defector wanted to chat securely all he had to do was go onto the Berlin server at 14:00 and we would have a chatroom established that he could find.

I had wondered how he would know what time zone we meant, but Rob assured me that any time on a network, if not qualified, was always GMT. If our contact was in Marseilles he would be two hours ahead due to European Daylight Savings. My last concern was that Dan had shown me the Berlin server and it hosted hundreds of chatrooms. How would our guy know which one to visit?

'Because at that time every day, which is from now until we get a response, we'll go in and open a new chatroom called 2616 407.'

'Which means?'

'Proxy authentication required. If he's as clever as we think he is, then it should be child's play for him to suss this out.'

'Sir?' Ritchie's question brought my focus back to him. 'Dae I send it?'

'Nothing ventured, I suppose. Go ahead.'

Ritchie depressed the ⌐-shaped key on his keyboard and the email disappeared from his screen. I checked my watch. Ten minutes to wait until the first window.

I returned to my desk and tried to concentrate on some minor tasks. It was useless. The whole office seemed unable to settle and at 14:00 GMT, which for us was 15:00 British Summer Time, we gathered in a roughly formed semi-circle behind Ritchie and Josh. Both of their screens showed a blank white space with a small box where text could be entered at the bottom and on the top right a larger box that displayed two usernames. The first was Ritchie's chosen screen name, Niccolò, the second was Josh's, Maffeo. Ashley had contributed them to the puzzle. They were the father and uncle of the more famous Marco Polo but it was these two who had been the first named Westerners to reach modern-day China. We hoped our Chinese contact would be versed in his history.

'And we're sure this is completely secure?' Colonel Charles whispered in his usual loud voice.

'Yes, Sir.' Mark answered. 'If you're not in an IRC chatroom then you can't see what's going on inside it. If you are in, then your username pops up on the top right. There's no way to circumvent it. At that point we can interrogate the username and find out their location and even the type of system they're using.'

'That's why we have both of the lads inside,' Dan said. 'One to type the chat and the other to investigate who they're chatting to.'

The Colonel looked satisfied and we returned to our silent vigil. I checked the office clock on the wall and watched the second hand sweep round. It was the only movement in the office. I glanced back at the screens. The thin black cursors blinked in the text entry box. Ritchie and Josh sat poised, fingers gently resting on their keyboards. More silence. I checked the clock again. Not even a minute past three. Time, it seemed, was as tense as us and as fraught with its passing. A name appeared in the username box. *Dodgy_rodge*. There was an audible sharp intake of breath across the whole team. Josh sat forward, ready to type in what we hoped would be a suitable challenge to our visitor. Something they would know and be able to respond to. I realised I was biting my lower lip and felt the sweat on my palms. *Dodgy_rodge* disappeared from the username box before Josh's first keystroke was made.

'What happened?' I asked.

'Drop-ins. People pop their head into a chat room to see what's occurring. If they aren't interested they drop back out,' Josh said and relaxed back into his seat.

I stayed tense, balanced on the balls of my feet. Willing a name, any name to pop into the box. The second hand swept on. After three minutes I felt the tension beginning to dissipate. After eight we were deflated. After ten, defeated.

'Perhaps tomorrow,' Mark said.

Ritchie and Josh closed down the room and deleted it.

I decided to call it a day.

*

Dan came and stood behind me in the kitchen. His arms slid around my waist and I nestled my head back against him.

'What are we having?'

'Pork and corn fritters with sweet potatoes.'

'Sounds fantastic,' he said.

I stayed leaning into him.

'Teach me?'

I let the pork mix drop back into the bowl and turned around, staying within his arms. 'Seriously?'

'Yeah. I need a hobby and you always cook for me. I think it'd be nice to do it together, or for me to treat you occasionally.'

'See, there you go, surprising me again.' I said and turned back around to continue preparing the meat patties.

Dan nuzzled his head down onto the back of my neck. 'How do I surprise you? Well apart from my obvious prowess in bed.'

I twisted into him and he pushed back against me. 'I was seriously surprised at how naïve you were for a grown man,' I said and let him bite the back of my neck in retaliation. After a few minutes, I finally managed to stammer, 'Okay, okay, I give in. Stop it, or we'll get nothing for dinner.' He raised his head and held me closer. We stayed like that until I needed to move to the cupboard to get some olive oil. Dan took a seat at the kitchen bench.

'But you did surprise me,' I said. 'I'd expected that when the rest of your stuff turned up there'd be x-boxes and PlayStations and computer geekery galore.'

'Nah. Never my thing. Well, not since I was a lot younger and was hacking my way into prison. Now computers are just my job. I don't bring them home.'

'Yes, I know, but it surprised me.'

'Sometimes you make me feel…'

I turned away from the stove top and crossed the space to be close to him. 'What?'

'Aww, it's silly, but you play piano and organ, you go fell walking and mountain climbing and last week you told me you're a qualified scuba diver. And you cook. I can program computers. That's it.'

'And you can make me feel like I've never felt before.'

'Yeah, well, like I said, that's a given,' he said and leant across the bench to kiss me. 'But I think I'd like to cook. So, will you teach me?'

'Of course. In fact, not only will I teach you but we'll go shopping together, properly, for fresh ingredients and when Christm—'
I stopped myself and turned away. There would be no Christmas. Dan's six months would have finished by then. I felt a pain in my gut, but there was no point in torturing myself. I couldn't do anything about it except make the best of what we had. Dan came behind me again and I handed him a wooden spoon. 'Your first lesson, then. Pork fritters.'

*

Our Chinese friend didn't show up on the Tuesday. Nor on the Wednesday. By the Thursday I was beginning to doubt he ever would. The first notable thing was on the Friday afternoon when, for the first time in as long as I could remember, the whole team was still in the office at three o'clock. By five past the hour he still hadn't showed. I let my mind drift to plans for the weekend.

Throughout the week, the email phishing attacks had continued unabated and each one still contained the extra coded line. At ten minutes past four, as Dan signalled for the boys to shut the chat room down, the latest spear email arrived into Ritchie's inbox. Colonel Charles leant forward and said, 'Do you still have that false receipt you sent, Ritchie?'

'Aye, Sir.'

'Send it again. Now.'

Ritchie did as he was asked. Almost immediately an email came into his inbox. He clicked on it and interrogated the header block. Rob looked over his shoulder and called out the character sets to Dan who typed them into a program they had written which would decode the sequence.

2616 200 408 5

'They're the status codes for OK, request timeout. I don't know what the five is,' Josh said.

'Maybe he wants us to give him five minutes?' Rachel suggested.

'Makes sense, open the chatroom up again,' Dan said and I felt the buzz ripple around the room.

I'm not sure I'd ever felt the drag of time as slow or as tortured. I checked the wall clock and the second hand seemed to be moving like thick treacle had been poured onto its cogs. I looked from Josh's screen to Ritchie's. Both showed the chatroom, the username box empty but for Niccolò and Maffeo. In between their two desks, Dan and Ashley sat side by side at Dan's workstation. Each of his three monitor screens showed a different active program. One was the decoder for the header blocks, one was a track and trace program for IP addresses and one was our own firewall monitoring system to ensure whoever we made contact with didn't try to do to us, what we were going to do to them. I checked again. The second hand had moved a quarter of the clock face.

John put his hand on my shoulder. 'Relax.'

I realised I'd been standing on the balls of my feet, bouncing on my heels. Silent, but noticeable to anyone who had looked my way. I forced myself to take a deep breath and settled myself. I imagined the Sedbergh School pipe organ. My feet and hands in perfect symmetry as I played my way through John Hughes' great theme for *Cwm Rhonda*, while the school choir sung Williams' words for, *Guide me O Thou Great Redeemer*. I loved the tune for its calming effect on me as I played, juxtaposed with the rousing nature of the words when sung in the chapel. My atheism never worried itself with the dichotomy, neither did my Englishness. I saw the notes swirling and dipping their way through my mind's eye and I stopped looking up to the clock.

Anon97 popped into the username box.

'We're on,' Dan said.

The musical notes disappeared and I felt a surge of adrenaline course through me.

Ritchie typed our pre-agreed sequence to find out if this was our would-be defector. We'd gone over it so many times even I knew the status code meant "Proxy Authentication Required".

407

Ashley slid her chair across to be next to Ritchie. She, our only Mandarin and Cantonese speaker, was prepared for either of the languages, whether written in traditional characters or in the Romanised Pin Yin. Instead the text entry area of the chat room flashed up a plain English response.

What do you want to ask?

Ritchie didn't falter:

Which system was compromised by moving Harald?

NOTAM

What exercise did you stop?

Anvil_05

'Their IP is masked and being re-routed,' Josh called without looking up from the screen he was rapidly typing commands into.

'There's currently no backward intrusion into us,' Dan called, also head down and focused on his own screen.

'Ashley, you're up,' I said quietly.

She reached forward and typed,

Ni na bian shi shen me shi jian?

16:14

'Okay, so they know the details of the intrusions, they speak Chinese and according to their current time, they're one hour ahead of us,' I said. 'We're at the point of no return. Ask them the big ques—' I was interrupted by a new line of text on the screen and Ashley saying, 'Oh my good God!'

'What does that say?' I asked.

Ashley sat back and swivelled her chair around to face me. 'Lú kè zài ma? It means, is Luke there?'

22

London, September 2005

I sat down at Josh's desk and pulled the keyboard towards me. Whoever was on the other end of the chat had started by communicating in English, so I typed:

Yes, I am here, how do you know me?

I read your emails - for a while

Who are you?

A soldier. In specialist PLA unit

What is your role?

Cyber Unit – my task to cause maximum disruption to UK

Our networks?

More than that – embarrass you as country. Gain foothold inside industry base. Discover potential contracts and agreements you wish to secure worldwide. Allow us a position to take advantage by under bidding you

What do you want?

Exile

A couple of the team let out a 'Yes!' I looked over to John Leofric. He motioned for me to continue. Rachel said, 'Remember, you need to establish that we can trust them. They need to give us something.'

What do I call you?

The cursor flashed in the text entry box, but there was no response. I looked down at the keyboard and moved my hands onto the keys again, but Rachel touched me lightly on the shoulder. 'Wait. Give them time. Names are precious. They might not want to reveal themselves so quickly. Have patience.'

I brought my hands back and rested them on the desk. The cursor kept blinking. I tried to will my heartbeat to match its steady rhythm. I wasn't even close to succeeding.

Call me ZZ

Okay. If you want exile, how do I know you are who you say you are? How can I trust you, ZZ?

I lead a team that is set up to cause networks you defend maximum damage. Your team is more effective than before. You become a problem for us. My best path if not for real is to let you fail. Let you be destroyed

Alright. But we aren't failing. You just said so.

No. But you will

How?

Are you on own?

I looked around me at a gallery of expectant faces. 'Do I lie?'

'No!' Rachel said. 'Even if we're positive that he is incapable of seeing inside this office, we need to be able to establish trust and rapport as soon as we can. He knows you aren't alone. He knows there are at least two others from the original usernames in the chatroom. Be honest for as much as you can.'

No, I'm surrounded by my team.

*If Director Leofric there, you send team away and stay –
you and Director Leofric*

The fact they had used John's official Civil Service title was disconcerting enough, but my stomach churned as I thought of the only thing that John and I had in common, outside of the team. His knowledge of Dan and myself. Before I got a chance to comment or ask for advice, Rachel began to move everybody away.

'Stay focused, Luke,' she said, using my name as she had done when I was such a junior officer and she had guided me through her interview techniques on the Debriefing Team. 'If you don't want to answer a question, then don't accept it. Just move on. Don't give too much away that they can use. Keep control of the big items that you want to know. In this case, why we would grant them exile and what they can do for us. And don't forget to get a verification established.'

I nodded and watched the whole team move away to the far side of the office. Except John. He came to sit next to me.

Okay. Only myself and the Director now. How are we failing?

*I read a lot of your command emails - have access to many
accounts. The Director has meeting next Monday. With
Group Captain Halson*

I turned in my chair, 'Do you, Sir?'

John had gone quite pale. 'Yes. I want to discuss the extension of Captain Stückl's exchange post. That doesn't constitute a fail. That is strengthening our capabilities.'

I ignored the rush I felt with the thought that Dan might get to stay longer and turned back to the screen.

Go on.

Halson been in email contact with others. He want you removed. His budget pays for positions in your team - he want withdraw funds - see team collapse

'How on earth can they know that?' John asked.

I typed in exactly that question.

I read Halson email too. Have access to his official account – he writes other emails to other people about you – he not like you – he say very bad things about you

How can you read his emails?

Not important – but he not clever with passwords – I can also access his home computer – if I not genuine I let him make you fail and send you away

So how can you help?

You and Director still on own?

Yes

Halson home computer. He has bad passwords set. Easy to break. He has some photos on computer. Bad photos. He has some bad habit – wait

A box popped up in the middle of the screen. The accompanying message said, "User *Anon97* has shared a file with you, do you want to view it?" I yelled across to Dan. 'Is it safe if I view a file that I've been sent through this chat?'

'Yes, we've isolated the chat rooms from our network. At worst you'll compromise that PC, but we'll do a full format on it afterwards anyway.

'Thanks.' I clicked on the file.

'Fucking hell!' John said, before I had managed to process what I was looking at.

The image was of a mostly naked Group Captain Halson, on all-fours, with a muzzle across his mouth. A chain led from a studded collar around his neck to a pentangle-shaped metal frame work. In the foreground was a woman dressed in what looked like a rubber basque, stockings and high heeled shoes. In her right hand she held a whip. In her left, a large dildo that was inches from the Group Captain's posterior.

'Oh!' Was the extent of my reaction initially. 'And there's me thinking most of the reason he detested me was because I'm gay.'

'Well…' John said, tilting his head to the side to contemplate the image. 'I think he might just be an angry little man full stop, however…whilst this is a little disconcerting, I'm not sure it's illegal. I'm also not entirely sure I'd be comfortable mentioning it to the Group Captain,' John said.

'Me neither,' I said, as more text appeared on screen. It seemed ZZ was ahead of us.

Lady in photo. She charge. Halson pay her from separate bank account. Separate from his wife and his. He also pay her for other things. She send him other photos, to make sure he come back to her

A new file popped up on screen. I clicked on it and John was the first to react again. This time he simply said, 'Well. That's the one. I think we have the Group Captain's balls and his career in our hands.'

A glass table reflected the same woman, in different attire, standing over the Group Captain. His head was almost touching the table top and a rolled note was linking his nose to the first of four lines of white powder neatly aligned on the smoke-glass top.

You use this to stop him shut you down?

I was intrigued by ZZ's thinking.

Yes. We can use that. Why did you make just me and Director see this?

You need to control information. Not need team to know

John gave a small nod. 'Appears our Chinese friend is very aware of how to blackmail people.'

'So we believe him?'

'I think so,' John said. 'But what else does he bring to us if we get him out?'

Again, I typed John's question.

I lead my team. I know how they work and what they do. I can stop them from hurting your networks. Set them back a long time

Why would you do this?

Another delay in their answer. This time I waited a little more patiently.

I have own reasons

Do we believe him? I asked.

'I think so,' John said. 'We have no reason not to. Go ahead and confirm his location.'

Are you in Marseille?

Near, yes

Why are you in Marseille?

Many reasons

Why?

You begin shut out all our home locations – reroute not work as effective – so we look for somewhere you not suspect attack from – somewhere with large Chinese numbers – somewhere we fit into. Also we need to be in time zone closer to you to make things easier

What things?

I tell you all when safe. Not when still here

'I think we're at the point, Sir. What do you want to do?'
    'Make the offer,' John said.

You want asylum in the UK?

Yes

Can you get yourself out of your location and come to us?

No. I need my family to come too

John indicated that I should delete the text messages relating to Halson and minimise the photographs. Then he stood and waved for Rachel to join us. He pointed at the last message. 'Can we arrange for the family to come out of France?'

'As long as we're not talking about a tribe of extended second and third cousins, then probably.'

I started typing:

How many?

My mother and brother

Rachel said, 'That's easy...logistically. But that's based on my knowledge of previous defector debriefs. You'd still have to get this cleared by the Foreign Office, Sir.'

'I think that will be okay, given the likelihood of the intelligence value we shall gain,' John said. 'Go ahead, Luke. Make the offer.'

Okay. We will make arrangements to extract you and your Mother and Brother from Marseilles. You need to advise us of how many PLA assets are there and if you have internal security that we need to know about.

Security not issue here. I can make a place and time for me to be so you can come get. But you not understand. My family not here

I hesitated to type it, but I knew I had to.

Where are they?

Hong Kong

'Stall,' John said. 'We'll need time to set that up. It's a whole different ball game.'

We can't do that right away.

I understand. But I have to keep working if here. I have to keep my team on job that is meant to happen

I know

You don't. Attacks so far are nothing to what is coming

What attacks are coming?

No. You can't know. If you know people will suspect. You need to get me out of here but family too. You contact me this way if you have news. Every weekday, same time, I check. Yes?

'Do I confirm?' I asked, looking between John and Rachel.
   'Yes. We'll just have to figure it out,' John said.

Yes. Okay. Only on weekdays? Not weekends?

Weekday. We not work weekends. Suspicious if I use PC on weekend

'Holy moly, they're as lazy as us,' John said and laughed.

I go now. You not let me down, Luke. I can help you so much

Before you go. Next time we talk. I need to be sure it is you and that you are not compromised.

Compromised?

Being forced to type under duress. If you have been discovered.

Ah – then you ask me for password. Wait

I did as I was asked and watched the black cursor on the white screen. My mind was trying to process how on earth we would manage to spirit a Chinese defector out of France, let alone his family out of Hong Kong. My thoughts were interrupted by new text appearing.

You ask if me. I answer "Society and Civilisation" if I am being forced I answer "Monarchy and Kings"

The username *Anon97* disappeared from the chatroom participant box.

'How the hell do we extract two people from Hong Kong?' I asked, looking up at Rachel.

'With difficulty, but it's not impossible,' John answered. 'We go talk to a few folk that do this sort of thing all the time. Fancy a trip to Northwood?'

'Umm, the Permanent Joint Headquarters?' I asked, a little confused.

'The very same and more specifically, the Director of Special Forces.'

'DSF? Don't we have to run this past the government first?'

'How much interest have they shown in any of this to date, Luke?'

'None, Sir.'

'Exactly. I suggest we get the wheels in motion and by the time it is planned and ready to be carried out, there shall be bally little the politicians will be able to do.'

'But we'll still need to convince DSF to set things up?'

'Ah, yes we will, but Brigadier Addrian will be keen.'

'He will?'

'Of course. Ex-cavalry. Not quite the Household Division, but you can't have everything. Still, a Royal Hussar and,' John leaned over to whisper in a conspiratorial tone, 'a member of my club. I do not foresee any problems.'

*

I had my reservations about John's old boy network coming through, but two days later, on the Sunday afternoon, I sat in on a meeting that included the Director of Special Forces, Brigadier Addrian, the RAF Special Forces liaison officer, Wing Commander Rowanne Gale, a Major from 22 SAS, whose name was only given as Sean and who'd come up from Hereford, a GCHQ expert on Hong Kong who went by James, and Andy Gibson, the man from SIS who had attended the cocktail reception for the French. It seemed he had more than a passing interest in China.

I was used to the "heel-dragging, unable to organise a leaving party for a colleague within three weeks" type of military. I'd never been exposed to the can do, will do attitudes of the people who sat around this table. The meeting only lasted forty-five minutes. By its end I was, yet again, stunned by how much I had initially underestimated the capabilities of John Leofric. 'When is our earliest go date?' he asked.

'We need to sort out a refueller for the Hercules but we could be ready to launch in twenty-four hours, if we know where the assets are.' Rowanne said.

'I can't get you that information until at least 15:00 tomorrow,' I said.

'Then realistically we're looking at Tuesday,'

Sean added, 'My lads need some planning time and I'd prefer we weren't doing it in the back of a Herc en route to the target. So, yes, Tuesday would be practical.'

'Is this really time critical?' Rowanne asked.

John hesitated to answer. 'Luke?'

'Not absolutely,' I said. 'I mean if the French location was compromised and they shifted their base of operations, then it might be, but not at present. Why, what are you thinking?'

'There's a regular diplomatic bag flight in and out of Hong Kong every week. It goes via a couple of hops, through Europe, the Gulf States, Sri Lanka, Singapore and then to Hong Kong. Arrives in there on a Monday night, so this week's flight is already on its way, but we could use next week's as a cover. Arrive in as usual on the Monday night and put the aircraft unserviceable. Have the crew stay overnight.' She used her fingers to make air apostrophes around the word crew.

'Sean?' John asked.

'Yeah. That works for us, on the assumption the assets are in a civilian location and we can lift them without interference. We could pick them up on the Monday night or the Tuesday morning. If we use one of the embassy cars it makes it even easier. Put the two of them in the boot and no one gets the opportunity to stop us. Deliver them straight up the back ramp of the aircraft and then we can get out of there. I see no obvious concerns.'

John's attention turned to Andy and James.

'Only real issue is if you do get stopped. We can't have any form of engagement between British Forces and Chinese nationals in the streets of Hong Kong,' Andy said.

'That's understood,' Sean agreed.

'We can run a surveillance sweep on the usual channels for you and allow your people relatively good situational awareness,' James said.

'And I'll put our local safe house on alert, just in case you need to divert,' Andy added.

'Alright. And the French end?' John prompted.

Rowanne took the lead again. 'It should be relatively easy. You said they'd have a preferred spot for their pick up?'

'Yes,' I confirmed.

'Obviously, we'll need to know that, and they'll need to know when we clear Hong Kong airspace. At the agreed time, they move to their rendezvous and we can drop a 7 Squadron Chinook over the Channel and pick them up, if the geography allows, or we can have a car pick them up and take them to a spot where we can fly into.'

'And if those options fail, it's a little piece of fortuitous luck that HMS Lancaster is in Marseilles for a port visit and work up to a joint UK-Canadian-French exercise. She'll be there for the next month, so we could get them through to the port and lift them from there,' James said.

I looked around the room to see what was next, but no one spoke. Instead, they looked at John. 'Are we done?' he asked and got a series of nods from around the table. 'Do we have a green light, Brigadier?'

I considered the Director of Special Forces. He was the only person wearing military uniform and the bright red flashes on his collar proved he was indeed a 1-star in the British Army. It was just as well, for had he been in a suit I would have struggled to believe someone who looked so young could possibly be so senior.

John had back briefed me on the man. A former SAS troop commander, a survivor of multiple Northern Ireland tours, one of the first company commanders to enter Bosnia in a peace-keeping role, followed up with tours in Afghanistan and Iraq and now, director of the Special Forces of the UK. I'd been impressed. I was even more so on meeting him. He was both debonair and rugged. A man who I imagined could converse on a wide variety of subjects at a dinner party and then, if need be, take a dessert spoon and use it to kill you in one of fourteen ways.

'Yes. I'm happy to give the green light, but you still need to get us a final go ahead, John.'

'Agreed.'

John stood up and I realised, that was it. The rest stood too and John guided me from the room.

'That can't be it?' I said as we walked towards the exit of the Joint Headquarters.

'It is as far as we're concerned. Mostly. We will have to get them the locations of ZZ and the family, but after that it's down to them. We don't need to know the hows and wherefores. They'll sort that out between themselves, but the less we know about the tactical elements, the better.'

'And the final go ahead?'

'From the Foreign Secretary?'

'Yes.'

'I'll leave it as late as I can,' John said. 'But I don't imagine she will cause a problem. Once something like this is in motion it's usually too hard to stop and she's a bit of a weak spirit at the best of times.'

I was relieved. John would look after the political side and I would make contact with ZZ and tell him it was a go. In a little over a week we would have an asset in our grasp that could potentially destroy the Chinese incursions into our networks.

Before that though, there was the small matter of a Group Captain who was about to walk into an ambush.

23

London, September 2005

John started the meeting without me. Halson had stormed his way through our office, not even deigning to look in my direction. Leofric welcomed him like an old friend. Steph, who had been briefed that she was to be nice, indeed overly nice, to the man she had called, 'A pompous ass' was to bring them coffee after precisely five minutes. Office mum and all-round great administrator she may have been, but Steph was also extremely sharp. She knew something was afoot, even if she didn't know exactly what, so she played her part happily. Five minutes after the coffee was delivered, the office door opened and John asked if I could spare a moment to join him. I picked up a leather folder that I had kept a close hold of throughout the morning, walked in and took a seat. Halson was to my right, John behind his desk.

'Luke, the Group Captain has some concerns about your fitness to run my technical team.'

'Oh. And they are, Sir?' I said and shifted in my seat to look at Halson.

'You are out of your depth, you have little to no technical expertise and quite frankly, the RAF Intelligence branch is not getting adequate value for the amount of resour—'

'Sorry, Norman,' John interrupted. 'I may call you Norman?'

'I…well…I would rather, with Flight Lieutenant Frankland here, that you call—'

'Excellent, so Norman. The thing is, before you repeat to Luke what you have already bored me with, there are some matters I'd like to go over.'

I watched Halson bristle and begin to rise out of his seat.

'Bored? I think that is outrageou—'

'Luke, if you would be so kind.' John said.

I opened the folder and handed the now standing Group Captain the second photo ZZ had shared with us. He went white. Or rather an ashen type of grey. No words came. He was transfixed and I noticed the slightest of trembles run through him. The paper in his hand shuddered.

'Sit down Norman,' John said quietly. Halson sank slowly back into his chair. I glanced across to John and he held a finger up to his lips. We let the silence drag on as Halson continued to stare at the picture. After a few minutes he spoke without looking up.

'Where did you get this?'

'That's not the right question, Norman.'

Halson still didn't raise his head, but I could see his features harden. His narrowed eyes, reminding me even more of the pigs his voice always brought to mind, stared down at the photo. I imagined he was willing it all to disappear. Instead he asked, 'What do you want?'

'Yes, that's the question you should be asking. Young Luke will take us through that,' John said and held his hand out towards me. It was my cue.

'We would rather not let anyone see this image, Sir. As you have so often pointed out during your career, imagery can be a game-changer. It is the ultimate tool to convince people of a situation. This image would most certainly do that. As you are well aware, illegal narcotics, especially Class-A ones like cocaine, are a straight ticket out of the military. However, you being dishonourably discharged, with no pension or legacy to fall back on is not what we want. Were it to occur it would simply mean someone else would take over your role and we would have to convince them that my team and what we do is important and worthwhile. Instead, we would rather you stayed in your post and served out the rest of your time until your pension. No one need know of this.'

He still didn't look up from the photo in his hand, but through gritted teeth managed to whine, 'You're talking about blackmail?'

'Yes.'

The directness of John's single word answer finally brought Halson's head up. He appeared bemused and bewildered.

'I see no reason to sugar-coat it. It is blackmail. Exactly. Carry on Luke,' John said and pointed Halson to look towards me.

'My tour of duty will not be curtailed and instead will be extended out to May 2007. The exchange tour for Captain Stückl will be extended by six months and we would like the bill for such to be picked up by your budget. We would also like your full support if and when we need it at joint Service conferences, meetings or any other forums that may arise from time to time. Having the head of Air Intelligence back what we are doing would send a strong message.'

'And what else?' He said. His bewilderment now galvanising into an undisguised fury aimed at me.

'Nothing. That's it. Me left alone, Captain Stückl allowed to stay for longer and your support.'

'How do I know you won't come back for more?'

'Because I say we won't,' John said, before adding, 'and anyway, your retirement is in what, two years? No one is going to care if you snort half a tonne of cocaine up your nose at that juncture.'

I was aware that Halson hadn't taken his eyes off me. I tried to return his gaze but without making it into a staring competition. He frowned, like he was in deep thought. I couldn't see what his dilemma was. He was busted and had no real choice in the matter. All he had to do was agree. He thrust the image back towards me and I allowed it to drift slowly to the floor.

'Fine. You can stay in your post, Frankland and I'll support your team if asked.' He rose to his feet and straightened his jacket.

'And Captain Stückl?' John asked.

Halson walked past me to the door of the office and turned. 'I'll go one better. His exchange is due to end when?'

'November,' I said, suspicious of what Halson was up to.

'I'll push through paperwork to turn his exchange tour into a proper posting. You can have him for a full two years. In return, you ensure that image never comes to light.'

'Yes,' said John.

'Do I have your word, Director Leofric?'

'Yes, Group Captain. I give you my word,' John said, struggling to conceal his irritation at the pomposity of the man.

I barely managed to hide my delight at the thought of Dan being here for two years, but constrained myself to leaning back in my chair and smiling up at the Group Captain. He leered back at me with a hint of smugness and left. It scratched at my consciousness off and on for the rest of the day, but in the end I dismissed it as me misreading the defeated expression of a defeated man.

*

With Halson gone I tried to busy myself with work. It wasn't easy. I desperately wanted to skip across to Dan and tell him what we'd done, but John had been absolutely clear that no one was to know. No one. Especially, I was not to confide in Dan. John made me give my word. I did, but it didn't change the feelings of euphoria I had bubbling inside me. We could have Christmas together, and the New Year, and spring. Perhaps we could go away again, for a proper break. I was sure Dan would be delighted to have his tour extended, to spend even more time away from his harridan of a wife, but I also knew he'd have to go back to the States to see his little boy. But that wouldn't be for too long, a week at most and then he'd be back with me. Filled with excitement, I managed to make the morning pass, took lunch with Dan in a café five minutes from the office and then we gathered the team together for a pre-brief before we contacted ZZ.

It seemed a little surreal that we were about to arrange the defection of a PLA programmer, and his family, but I'd already been contacted by Rowanne with the flight plan and timings of the C-130J Hercules in and out of Hong Kong. It would be done, as she had suggested, under the guise of the scheduled diplomatic flight, and be a much simpler solution that trying to get four SAS troopers into Hong Kong on a British Airways flight and much, much simpler than trying to smuggle two Chinese nationals out on any of the civilian airlines that flew from Hong Kong to London.

All I had to do was establish the locations of ZZ and his family. The whole team gathered and Josh, Ritchie and Dan rearranged their desks so they could monitor and advise me in the chatroom. At the set hour I entered it using the name Niccolò. It took less than a minute for *Anon97* to appear in the username box.

Hello.

Hello.

Can you confirm your identity?

I am ZZ. Society and Civilisation

Okay. We are set. We can extract your family next Monday night early Tuesday morning. Prefer to take them at 3am Hong Kong time. Can they be ready?

Next week? Not tonight?

No, not tonight. Easier and safer to do next week? You can wait till then?

I realised I had no idea if he would be safe until then. I'd just assumed it would be okay. I felt a cold shiver run through me.

Yes. Next week okay. Gives me more time to get them organised, but time wi

The text stopped and I watched as the "but time wi" was deleted.

What were you about to type?

It okay. Not matter - next week okay

I checked my notes for what I needed to establish.

I need to know where your family are and where you are.

I send family address now

193

A box popped up on screen indicating I had been sent a text file. Dan leant across me and double clicked on it. It opened to reveal an address within the Sham Shui Po district of Hong Kong.

I will make sure they are ready. What do they have to do?

I don't know yet. I will tell you tomorrow. Now, you. Where are you?

In Gardanne, near Marseilles. In north of town. Near to Provence Power Station

Josh and Ritchie started opening up maps on their PC screens.

'There's quite a lot of open space around there, Sir.' Josh said. 'If he has transport I'll bet you could get a helicopter fairly near.'

Do you have transport?

No. But across street is supermarket. I meet car there?

We need to get you at same time as we get your family. 3am on Tuesday morning in HK will be 9pm Monday evening with you. Is shop open at 9pm?

No. But pharmacy shop next to it is. I can go there

Okay. I will confirm with the people who will come to get you. I will contact you same time tomorrow?

Yes. Thank you Luke

I shut the chatroom down and looked around me. I got a series of thumbs up and broad grins.

'Good work,' John said. 'Let's talk to our friends in Lyneham and Hereford so they can get their ducks in a row.'

*

By the Wednesday we had a working plan, simple in its execution but that made it all the more attractive. ZZ had confirmed his end and his family were ready. We had the address of the tower block in Hong Kong and of the pharmacy in Gardanne. One small surprise had been that ZZ's brother was only six years old, but the

Herc squadron said it wouldn't be a problem and the SAS lads said it meant they could fit him into an even smaller space if need be.

The aircraft would depart Lyneham early on the Sunday morning and our whole team would be in to monitor the operation and maintain as much contact with ZZ up until he got lifted out of France at 21:00 on the Monday night. Once they were back in the UK, they would be reunited in a SIS approved safe house and we would begin the task of debriefing ZZ at length. The smoothness of the plan added to the fact I knew Dan was about to be offered a full tour of duty made the week sail past. I could hardly remember a time when I'd been more buoyant, or full of optimism. Dan noticed, but I managed to deflect his questioning by saying the prospect of dealing the Chinese cyber battalions a severe blow was thrilling me. That and spending time teaching him how to cook seared beef.

On the Friday morning, John called Dan and me into his office. There was an email printout in military signal format on his desk and I knew it was going to be the posting notice. He asked us to sit down and for the first time I realised his face didn't quite reflect the expression I would have expected. I had imagined John was going to be delighted that Dan could stay and help us, yet his countenance was certainly not a happy one. It seemed to be a strange mix of emotions; far from smug, yet in the moment I was reminded of Halson's expression as he left this same office five days before. I felt nauseous.

'Dan, good news. I hope. We have been asked to grant you a full tour of duty, twenty-four months added to your initial deployment. The authorities in DC have been approached and confirmed that, as the Royal Air Force are picking up the costs, they are more than happy to foster this closer liaison and stronger ties between our two cyber-related units. It will also be seen as supporting the wider 5-Eyes cyber mission.'

I watched Dan's face light up. He glanced across to me and then back to John. 'That is fantastic, Sir. Outstanding. Aww, yes. Definitely yes. I'd love to stay.'

'Yes. Good. I thought you might be happy. The thing is…'

I saw John glance down at the piece of paper on his desk and hesitate. When he raised his head, he was looking directly at me. 'The thing is, it's been offered as a full tour.'

I knew it had, I'd been in the meeting when Halson offered it, so John's point was lost on me. I turned to Dan. He was still smiling as broad a grin as I'd seen on him. It made my heart jump as I realised that he really did want to stay with me. John began to talk again.

'It's a full exchange tour, and that means it is offered on the same basis as all US exchange tours within the UK.'

Dan stopped smiling. He frowned in confusion, as did I.

'What does that mean, Sir?' He asked.

'It's accompanied, Dan. It means that you will be given your own accommodation within London and your wife and child will join you for the duration.'

My world imploded.

24

London, September 2005

Halson had stitched me up and there was not one thing I could do about it. John reminded me later, when Dan was out of earshot, that he had given his word to not reveal the image if Halson made the posting happen. We'd both been played and we both knew it, but there was nothing to be done. I could hardly go and complain that Dan not be allowed to bring his wife over. I had no clue how Halson had figured it out. John counselled me that he might not have figured anything out at all. It might have been an unfortunate consequence of our request.

'Really? Do you honestly think he didn't do this on purpose?'

'No, Luke. I don't. Remember, I was the one who said to keep your wits about you. I said that Halson was a nasty piece of work, so no, I don't think this was anything other than him doing what he could to get back at you. However, I don't know how he knew, but you did say he was aware you were gay, so perhaps he took a reasoned guess. Regardless, I can't see you can do much about it and right now, I need you to be focused on work. Clear?'

He was right. Dan and I would have to figure things out, but our focus needed to be on ZZ. Monday was going to be a huge day. However, the weekend before then was going to be one of the few remaining that Dan and I could spend together. We decided to make the most of it and drove to the South Downs.

*

The journey was less than two hours to the upmarket hotel and spa we'd decided to treat ourselves to. It nestled on top of a modest hill halfway between West Lavington and East Harting; names that Dan had conjured with on the way.

'It sounds like something out of *Lord of the Rings*,' he said, staring out of the passenger window of the hire car we had taken for the weekend.

'Are you going to impress me by saying you've read the book, or disappoint me by admitting you've only seen the films?'

'Disappoint. Sorry.'

'I have the three books and the *Hobbit* back in the apartment, you know.'

'You have a lot of books that I'd be scared to touch.'

I glanced across at him. 'Seriously? You know that anything of mine is yours to use.'

'But your books are so grand. Do you have any that aren't leather bound with gold lettering?'

'Of cour—' I stopped myself and brought to mind my book collections. The *Complete Works of Shakespeare*, in twenty-one separate volumes, found in an antique shop, leather bound, gold lettering. Separate editions of all of Tolkien's works, the same. Churchill's twelve World War Two histories...the same. Hardy's complete works. The Greek Myths. Dickens, Thackeray, Trollope...I resigned myself to the fact he might have a point. 'I have a few paperback biographies of politicians,' I offered meekly in my defence.

Dan laughed and I moved my left hand from the wheel on to his thigh. He covered my hand with his and lightly gripped my fingers. We continued in pleasant silence for a while and I was struck by how comfortable it felt. The ability to just be with one another, not to have to talk, not to have to do anything other than to breathe the same air and be calm. It was something I'd grown to adore. He'd told me about how anxious and fractious living with

Shirlene could be. I had always tried to allow him calm and space, but now, knowing our time was limited, this ability to just "be" was more important than ever.

We drove on and green vegetation gradually began to dominate over the greys and browns of the cityscape I had become so used to. It was strange how much I loved London. I'd grown up in the north-east, but not within the urban centres of Sunderland or Newcastle. I'd visited them often, but my home had been in the leafy suburbs surrounding them. Then Sedbergh had been so remotely rural as to be on a different planet from London. I treasured reclaiming my outdoor life, my fell walking and skiing were precious to me, but I truly loved London. Or rather…I liked living there. I truly loved Dan.

'What are you grinning at?' He asked.

'Oh, nothing really,' I lied.

He paused and I thought we were heading back to mutually happy silence, but then I felt his hand grip mine a little tighter.

'You know, I never planned this, Luke.'

'I know…neither did I. Falling for a married man wasn't exactly on my list of things to do.' I looked across to him and flashed a half-smile.

'No. But you have been with men before.'

My smile disappeared. 'Yes. I told you. But never many and never as part of the gay scene.'

He was quiet again, but something was niggling at me. 'Dan, I'm exactly the same as you. You think we're different, because you've had a girlfriend or two, you have a wife. But you don't get to choose who you're attracted to. It's a random act of nature. If I believed in a God, then I'd blame him…or her. But I'm more inclined to believe it's the magnetic force of atoms and electrical sparks and micro-signals in our brains that do for us. I think we have as much control over them as we do over the formation of galaxies.'

'You're saying I had no choice but to be attracted to you?'

'Yes. To a point. You had no choice over the feelings that hit you. The feelings that cascaded through you and made you want me. If we could prevent the feelings we probably would. Life would be simpler.'

He gave a laugh, but it was discordant with the look on his face. 'So you're saying we have no choices? Life just happens?' His voice had raised a notch.

'No! Not for one minute. We have a choice, but it has nothing to do with the feelings and emotions we're hit by. Our only choice is do we act on the feelings or not.' I realised I had removed my hand from his and was gripping the wheel tighter than I needed to. I relaxed my shoulders. This wasn't worth an argument. 'Look, Dan…when I was a young man at school, I couldn't have predicted that the feelings of attraction I would have would be to men. You couldn't predict yours would be to women.'

'I could have.'

'Okay, predict isn't the right word. You might have guessed the majority of men were attracted to women, but you couldn't know you'd be one. The knowing is the thing. But you *were* attracted to women and you married one. You married one out of millions and billions. Yes, the odds were reduced because you had to physically meet her and that cuts down the numbers, but you had no control over the original feelings that caused you to fall in love.'

'So my only choice was to act on them?'

'Yes.'

'And with you? Are you saying I had no control over how you made me feel?'

'Of course not. You're only human,' I said it in hope and was rewarded by his deep and tender laugh. He clasped my hand again and moved it back to his thigh.

'My only choice was acting on those feelings?' He asked.

'Yes. And you did nothing for ages. Did you?'

'No. I guess not until the bombings. Then I had to.'

'Exactly. We do nothing most of the time. I've repressed my feelings about men for the majority of my life. I lied in my first interview for the Air Force. I denied my true feelings and my true nature for years. It's not healthy, by the way, keeping all that angst inside, but sadly, it's easier.'

'For you?'

'No. For society, or for the sake of careers, or for families.'

'But your family loves you.'

'Yes and do you know how lucky that makes me? My father is that strange mix of middle-class money and working-class ethics. He runs a successful construction company that's been in our family for generations and he's a season ticket holder for Sunderland Football Club. He can mix with highly educated, refined executives and poorly educated, rough-as-guts bricklayers and labourers, yet he'll speak to each with total respect and dignity. His various social circles share one common thread, they're predominantly male and with that comes predominant attitudes. Some of which are definitely homophobic. It wouldn't have been a massive surprise if he'd shut me out, regarded me as damaged goods or perverted, but he did none of that. He gets it.'

'Gets what?'

'That two men can fall in love as easily as a man and a woman can. Or a woman and a woman. The mystery of attraction is that, a mystery. That's why it's called falling. It's not, "I carefully climbed down into love". My dad got the simplicity of that fact. We have no clue who we will fall for.'

'And your mum?'

'Mums are mums. I'm her son. Naughty and irreverent or well-behaved and respectful, drunk or sober, gay or straight, it matters not. I'm her son.'

The traffic on the dual-carriageway suddenly slowed. One of those random unexplained jams that appeared from nowhere and would disappear just as quick, but it made me step on the brakes. I moved my hand back to the wheel and checked my rear-view to make sure I wasn't about to be slammed into by a truck, although I knew that I'd be able to do as much about that as about me falling in love with Dan. It was like he had read my mind.

'You said two men can fall in love…Are you in love?'

My mouth went dry and my tongue stuck rigidly to the roof of it. I could feel the spread of heat up my neck and into my face. I concentrated on the traffic and kept looking ahead.

'Well?' He asked.

I finally managed to speak. 'That's an unfair question.' The car inched forward. The silence now was distinctly uncomfortable. I willed him to say that he had the depth of feelings I had. Instead the traffic crawled and we said nothing for minutes that felt like hours.

'I don't think my parents are going to be as accepting if they discover what I've been doing.'

'You don't know that.'

'I really do.'

The traffic freed up and Dan turned the car's radio on. The DJ's musings and meanderings filled in for our conversation and I wondered if Dan would ever be able to admit what I knew, deep down, were his true feelings.

*

We spent Saturday going for a long walk up to the summit of Buster Hill in the glorious weather afforded by what was proving to be an Indian summer. On Saturday evening we took our time over an indulgent meal in the hotel's fabulous French restaurant and then took even more time over each other back in our room. As we lay together, satiated, in the dark, he rolled against me and nestled his head into my shoulder. His voice was barely above a whisper.

'I'm sorry that Shirlene's coming over and all this will have to be hidden away.'

'Hiding isn't anything different to what we've been doing. We don't exactly flaunt ourselves out and about, do we?'

'I suppose not. But you know what I mean. We'll have to be even more discrete.'

I felt my stomach flutter. 'Discrete? You mean you want this, us, to continue?'

The mattress sagged as he pushed himself upright and turned on the bedside light. 'Of course. How could we not continue?'

He looked genuinely perplexed that I had suggested otherwise. I hoped my relief and excitement, butterflies and knots were invisible to him. 'I thought that once she was here, you'd…'

'I'd what?'

'Well, just go back to…being you?'

'This is me, Luke. I've been thinking a lot about what you said in the car on the way down here. I can't choose who I'm attracted to, just what I do about it. I know this is going to sound weird, but I'm not gay.'

'I don't think I ever said you were.'

'Yeah. I know that too. But I'm not bisexual either, I don't think. Not in the truest sense of the word. I think I'm straight, but for you.'

'Straight with a bend of Luke?'

'Maybe…Luke-sexual? How's that sound?'

'If it means we can still share time together, it sounds great to me.'

He switched the light off and rolled into me again. He fell asleep in my arms and after a short while, I eased myself out from under him, laid his head on the pillow and quietly went into the en suite bathroom. I unzipped my wash bag and took out a 500ml bottle of gin. It wasn't that Dan didn't drink. He did and we had enjoyed two rare bottles of white Châteauneuf-du-Pape with our meal, or rather he had enjoyed half a bottle and me the rest. Nor did he comment adversely on me having a few G&Ts of an evening in the apartment, so he didn't mind me drinking at all, but…well this was just easier. He was asleep and I simply fancied a small nightcap. It wasn't that I needed a drink. Nor was I hiding the fact. The hotel minibar prices were always outrageous and I'd guessed that their gin would probably be of a lesser brand. I'd brought this little bottle of Tanqueray Number Ten just in case, but Dan was asleep and it wouldn't be fair to disturb him. I unscrewed the top and set it down on a towel next to the sink. I hadn't brought tonic and retrieving some from the minibar would also risk waking Dan…and he'd looked so peaceful. My first swig from the bottle coincided with my first tears. The full weight of what Halson had done finally found its mark and the prospect of losing Dan pressed down on me. Even if we could share elicit moments, he'd never be as completely mine as he had been. Worse even than him having to go back to the States, would be him still being in London, working with me every day, but not being with me properly. I reached for one of the hotel's thick flannels and between drinks, stifled my sobs. I didn't want to disturb him. With the tears came the realisation that I still couldn't tell him I loved him.

After a quarter of an hour, my silent tears finally stopped and I felt drained. Exhausted. I carefully screwed the top back onto the empty bottle and replaced it in my wash bag. I squeezed a fingertip of toothpaste out and painted it over my gums. Then I slipped back into bed.

*

On Monday afternoon we had the full team assembled in the office, an open line through to 47 Squadron's planning and operations room in Lyneham and another to Brigadier Addrian's office in Northwood.

The first milestone was to check in with ZZ. I opened the chatroom at our usual time.

Hello.

Hello. I am ZZ. Society and Civilisation

Are you set?

Yes

The aircraft will arrive into Hong Kong in one hour, 11pm Hong Kong time. Are your family ready?

Yes. They know to make their way to the street entrance of their tower block at 3am. My mother has been told to wear a red headscarf

We still need names, ZZ. We need to verify her identity.

The reply was not instant. I worried, but Rachel, as she had done before, cautioned me to be patient. 'This is the point of no return for him. As soon as he tells us names, we can trace them. We will know who they are. The act of defecting might be when he gets into the car we send, but in effect it is now.'

I took a breath and waited.

Her name is Veronica. Veronica Wai. My brother is Ethan. She has an old British Hong Kong Passport. She can show that?

I looked over to Ashley. 'Hardly Chinese sounding?'

'No, but most Chinese, especially in places like Hong Kong, Malaysia and Singapore have anglicised names as well as their Chinese. There's nothing unusual.'

I returned my focus to the screen.

Good. That is good. And you?

Yes, I will be at shop

We need your name ZZ. We need to know how to identify you.

Lily

No ZZ. We need your name.

That is name. My name is Lily. Lily Wai

'Oh! He's a woman.' Ashley said and broke the tension in the office. I heard a few laughs.

'Shame on us,' Steph said. 'Assuming he was a man all this time. Of course she's a woman.'

'This is going to be even better than I thought,' Dan said from over my shoulder.

I glanced up at him. 'How so?'

'Not exactly an equal opportunity society, the Chinese. If she's the team leader like she said, then she must be a phenomenally talented programmer.'

I started typing again.

Sorry my mistake. I didn't realise.

Most do not think a girl can programme computers

Yes. Sorry.

It okay. Never mind

So, we get your family and once we have them, we contact you and you move to pharmacy - - you be on here at 21:00 so I can let you know

No. We no use PCs at night time. Suspicious if I try

'Shit!' I hadn't expected her not to be able to be online. Plan B then.

Okay, give me a phone number.

No. We not allowed phones. Only phone is PLA secure line in main room we use

I stayed staring at the screen, 'Anybody? Any suggestions? We're too far along for this to be a problem.' The room stayed quiet. I spun in my seat to see a series of shrugs. I turned back to the screen, trying to figure out how we could let Lily know she should make the rendezvous.

Luke – you still there

Yes, just trying to think how we do this –

You get my family and I go to pharmacy – I trust you

'Simple is always best,' Colonel Charles offered.
     'What happens if there's a glitch?' Ashley asked.
     'Don't put that in her mind. Agree and move on,' said John.

Okay - you go to pharmacy at 9.00pm your time – we will have your family and we get you – but it means this will be our last communication until you get extracted

Okay – no other way – I sorry – there is one cell phone here but is the Major in charge. Do you want me to steal it?

'No, we don't,' said Rachel from behind me. 'It's too risky.'
     I referred to the notes that Sean had emailed to me from Hereford.

No – don't steal phone – We have identified already that the pharmacy has a car park. A car will pull up to the front of the pharmacy at 9pm – two men will be inside it. One driving, one in back. The one in the back will open the rear door. You walk to car and get in.

Okay. Thank you

Good luck Lily

I shut the chat room down.

'And now we wait,' said Colonel Charles.

*

At 16:55, Director John Leofric, using all his official clout and a security protocol that I hadn't been aware of, rang the Foreign Secretary's outer office and got an appointment with her for 19:00. 'Enough time to tell her and too late for her to bother doing anything about it,' he said, picking up his umbrella and slipping on his overcoat. The Indian summer had finally surrendered its grip on the capital.

*

At 18:00 I sent Josh, Ritchie and Ashley out on a pizza run. They were back half an hour later with five family sized boxes. The team dug in and then resumed what we'd been doing for the previous few hours; milling about the office, distractedly waiting. Once she'd eaten, Ashley took over from Rob monitoring the open line from Lynham. I shared a wry smile with Dan. I could see the tension in his features. I knew he would see it in me too. And in everyone else. There were a few muted conversations, but mostly we were quiet.

*

At 19:35 London time, 20:35 in France, 02:35 in Hong Kong and less than half an hour before the extraction teams rendezvoused with Lily, Veronica and Ethan Wai, my desk phone rang.

'Luke, it's John?'

'Yes, Sir?'

'It's off.'

'What?'

'I was wrong. I misjudged her completely. The Foreign Secretary is apoplectic. She has ordered an immediate termination of the operation. Her people are on to Hereford and Lyneham. I'm sorry, Luke. I've tried but…I…I don't understand what is going on…I'm sorry.'

I looked over to where Ashely sat, the phone receiver in her hand and I watched her features reflect at first confusion and then a strange mix of anger and sadness. She was speaking rapidly, but quietly, into the phone. Then she took it from her ear, stared at it in disbelief and slowly put the handset into its cradle.

'Sir,' I said to John. 'We can't get word to Lily. She's going to be completely isolated.'

'I know. I'm coming back to the office. Sit tight.'

I hung up the phone and saw Ashley coming towards me. She stopped halfway and shook her head. My expression had told her I already knew.

*

The phone rang twice before he picked it up. 'Stephenson.'

'It's Mary. I need to ask a favour.'

'Yes?'

'Your chaps and my chaps, don't always see eye to eye, do they?'

'It's been known for them to become disgruntled with one another, yes. Why's that Mary?'

'I need to keep an eye on some people, but I'm afraid Vauxhall Cross is involved and I can't ask them.'

'And so you want to borrow some of my Thames House people to do your snooping?'

'I wouldn't ask if it wasn't important, Duncan.'

'I'm sure. Meet me for lunch and tell me all. If you flirt with me and butter up my ego, I'm sure I can lend you a few people to keep an eye on things for you.'

'Why thank you Home Secretary.'

'See, you're halfway there already, Mary.'

*

I couldn't sleep. Neither could Dan. We sat up the whole night, desperately trying to understand why the Foreign Secretary would have stopped what was an amazing intelligence coup. If Lily was even a tenth as good and as knowledgeable as we hoped, she could render a major blow to Chinese cyber warfare capabilities, but the Right Honourable Mary South, Secretary of State for Foreign and Commonwealth Affairs had been extremely clear. She expressly ordered the immediate termination of the operation. John had re-counted that she had leapt to her feet, shouted at him and de-manded that on no account were SAS troops or RAF aircraft to be involved with the extraction of Chinese citizens from Chinese sovereign territory. With no prospect of pulling Lily's family out, John counselled that we would have to abort pulling Lily out. The Foreign Secretary said that she couldn't care less. John had tried his best. He argued until he could explain and convince no more. In the end the Foreign Secretary had given him a clear choice. Abort the Chinese operation and if that meant the French one too, then so be it, or tender his immediate resignation and when the Chinese nationals reached the UK, she would immediately have them deported back to mainland China. John figured that could well be a death sentence for all three. He also determined that to fight on from within was better than being completely shut out. When he got back to our office, he'd briefed the whole team on what had happened. They and I were glad he had decided to stay. Had he walked then goodness knows who would have been put in his stead.

None of it took away my feelings of desperation for Lily's safety. We had exposed her to a rendezvous where no one had shown up. She might have completely compromised herself to make the 21:00 appointment. We had hung her out to dry.

I had opened the chatroom, in case she was able to reach out, but there had been no messages. We set out a roster to keep the room open and active and I told the rest of the team to go home. To get some sleep. Dan and I arrived back into the apartment at about midnight. When we weren't discussing Lily, we had to dis-cuss his tour of duty, but Dan's responses were monosyllabic. I felt myself sinking lower and lower under an oppressive black cloud. As the sun rise broke over London, I got showered and dressed and prepared to head back into work. Dan had to go to the US Embassy to begin the paperwork of bringing his family over. I kissed him and wished him luck, even though a smooth administration process was the last thing I wanted for him, or me. Watching from the apartment window I saw him cross the Vauxhall Bridge. As he reached the far side and disappeared from my view I felt a wave of nausea and just made it to the bathroom before I threw up. My nerves were shot. Adding to my anguish about losing what Dan and I had built with each other was my dread that we might have got Lily killed.

I cleaned myself up and only to take the taste from my mouth, opened the drinks cupboard. There was no gin. I had meant to get some last night but the off-licence we usually frequented had been shut by the time we'd been heading home. Instead, I gulped down a couple of glasses of Polish vodka.

*

The chatroom remained quiet and the day had dragged. The team was listless and I had reread the same set of articles about ten times. None of it had gone in. Dan had come back from the embassy. His weak thumbs up telling me it had gone as expected. Mark and he then tried to get a complete sweep of the network underway but no one's heart was in it. Even John, normally resolute and confident, appeared to be at a loss. Only Steph showed any spark and thank God she did. By mid-afternoon I was observing how she was going to each of the team in turn. Spending a moment or two, or more with them. As she sat at each desk, I could see the spirits of the individual perk up. I intercepted her halfway to the coffee machine.

'You are a marvel, Steph.'

She reached out, took my hand and guided me away from the rest of the team. 'They feel let down by the system and they're frightened. No one knows who, if anyone will be on the other end of that chat window later. They feel saddened and hurt. So do you. The thing is, that's okay. But you can't expect them to pick themselves up if you, Colonel Charles and John are feeling sorry for yourselves as well. So until you get your head back in the game, I'm here.'

'Care to share what you've told them?'

'I haven't. I only asked them how they're feeling. Whatever they told me, I said it was okay. They're allowed to feel like that, but they also had to start planning what else we might do, depending on if Lily gets in touch later. They each have particular talents. They need to think what they can offer to the team.'

'None offer what you do,' I said. 'Thank you.'

'Don't be silly. You'd have done it too if you'd seen disappointment and disaster within teams as many times as me. It's an experience thing and you're still very, very young. Teams are like good marriages. Ups and downs, but as long as you realise the strength is in the bond, you get through. You'll find out one day.'

I couldn't help myself. The sigh escaped from me and I felt my shoulders slump.

Steph reached up and patted my cheek. 'Oh now don't you worry about that too. You'll meet a great girl one day and the two of you will make a beautiful couple. You're a handsome catch, Luke. I've often thought, if only I was thirty years younger.' She gave a long chuckle and propelled me towards the coffee.

*

At 15:00 UK time, I walked over to the screen with the open chatroom. Josh stood and offered me the chair and the whole team formed around behind me. We waited. The single word, hello, hung on the screen as it had done since the preceding night. About thirty drop-ins had been in and out of the room over the course of the day, but all had been deflected away and the chat window reset. The cursor blinked.

Hello

Rachel leant towards me. 'Be cautious. Take it slowly. Do not reveal too much.'

I nodded and typed,

407

211

I felt a massive wave of relief and heard a veritable chorus of 'Thank God' 'Yes!' and 'Fantastic' from behind me.

Are you okay?

Yes – sad – you not come

I am sorry – our operation was compromised

You not get my family – you not get me – ever?

I am so sorry – I cannot see anyw

John Leofric reached over, grasped my hand and stopped me typing. He took the seat next to me and slid the keyboard in front of himself, deleting the last few words.

I am so sorry – This is Luke's boss, Director Leofric. It was my fault, but if you can be patient, we are going to get you out of there. Can you be patient? Are you and your family safe for a while?

I stared at the screen and then at John.

'We are not abandoning her. She is too good an asset. So we are all going to keep on doing our jobs and I am going to figure out some way to make this happen. Are we all clear?'

I led the whole team in an almost perfectly synchronised, 'Yes Sir!'

We are safe. Yes I wait. But I say before. If here, I have to work

I know, you have to do what you have to do. We will be in touch through same mechanisms as soon as we have a plan.

Okay. Well then I wish you good luck next week

'That sounds ominous,' John said.

What do you mean?

I cannot say. You knowing will make me not safe. Make it dangerous for me. Maybe even mean we have to move again. I help when there with you. Not before

I understand. We will be in touch as soon as possible

Anon97 dropped out of the chat. John stood up. 'I would suggest we try to prepare ourselves for whatever is coming our way.'

'We're on it, Sir,' Dan said and immediately I felt the whole mood of the team swing upwards. Even my burdens seemed reduced by half. It was better than nothing.

Steph dropped by my desk shortly afterwards. 'See, the old man's head is back in the game. You follow his lead and we'll be fine.'

I agreed and over the next few days, she was right. We were fine; relatively. The networks we were responsible for suffered no live attacks and the training program we were rolling out across the building was stopping a few of the spear phishing attempts, but I still knew we were, on some levels, completely compromised. Lily had been able to read my emails, John's emails, Halson's and probably many more. We still had no clue how she was doing that or how to stop it. On the Thursday, John told me he would be disappearing off for a few days, expressly stating that he would not be telling me where he was going or why. I wondered if he was off to France himself, but he said that no, he was too old to be playing at that game. He just had a few people to catch up with.

The US Embassy advised that Dan's wife and child could probably come out on the 15th of October, only two weeks away. They would have a house sorted for the family by then. It would be in Nine Elms, literally a ten-minute walk further along the river from the apartment. We started considering that perhaps we could still share our commute to and from work and, if Dan arrived a little early each morning, we could share more besides. The thought brightened both of us up. He was having to make more phone calls back to the States above his usual once a week check in that he had set as a routine since his arrival back in May. Each time he came off those calls I could see his spirit had been sapped. Now, as he had to speak to her on a daily basis to advise on the move and the things that Shirlene should be doing, he would hang up angry, sad and tired. Even somehow, scared. I worried for him. I tried to talk to him, but he would change the subject, shut it out as a reality. He detested her but he loved his son and he could see no way to separate from her without losing him. I reckoned we deserved a weekend at home in the apartment, lazily whiling away Saturday and Sunday, me teaching him to cook and both of us looking after one another. It was exactly what we needed to counter the previous week. Sadly, by mid-morning on the Monday, our stress levels were back through the roof.

25

London, October 2005

Ashley got a phone call at 08:55 on Monday the 3rd of October that told her the Royal Navy's fleet wide communications system had failed ten minutes earlier. Every computer controlled node of every vessel within home waters had shut down. All deployed vessels, in the Gulf, the Mediterranean and further afield were unaffected, but within Portsmouth, Plymouth and all the other Navy harbours, bar one, the result was a comprehensive disabling of a warship's ability to function as anything other than a glorified passenger vessel.

The one unaffected base was Her Majesty's Naval Base Clyde, otherwise known as Faslane. It was home to the UK's ballistic missile submarines, the nation's Strategic Deterrent, and operated on a secondary network that was encrypted differently. It was also protected with much more rigorous firewalls, but as Dan, Mark and the rest scrambled to assist the Navy I couldn't help seeing a different picture.

I wondered if Faslane hadn't been subjected to an attack on its networks as the response from Her Majesty's Government would have been vastly different. A compromise of the UK nuclear fleet would be seen as a strategic threat to the country. It would demand a response. As it was, the Navy network falling over was a minor inconvenience. I saw, for what I thought was the first time, the rationale behind this whole approach of the Chinese. They had robbed millions of pieces of data and were leapfrogging their industrial capability based on stolen proprietary information and vast amounts of Western research and development. Now they were probing the military capabilities in order to establish weaknesses and exploitation corridors, but all of it was done at an acceptable level. They merely wanted to have the knowledge, if and when they might need it, but they didn't want to escalate it to a point where there had to be a response.

That was still the one thing I could not fathom. Why our government was not taking any action. I understood their lack of engagement in the immediate aftermath of 7/7, but now, months later, they still were not getting involved...in any way.

But then again, no one was. I had to believe that the Chinese were doing this to not only the UK, the US, the Aussies, the Kiwis and the Canadians. They had to be going after the French and the Germans and whoever else was worth the effort, but no one was clamouring about the state of affairs. I wondered if the citizens of Rome had felt like this as Nero played his fiddle.

At 09:05 we received word that the flight lines at RAF Coningsby, Leeming and Leuchars were grounded due to a software glitch in the Multifunctional Information Distribution System. In effect, the whole of the air picture that they relied on to be effective fighting aircraft had been whited out. They would be able to fly, but they certainly couldn't launch any aircraft to work with tankers or airborne command and control as they would have no way of communicating their positions to them. The significance of the bases involved wasn't lost on Mark or me. They represented the Royal Air Force's Quick Reaction Alert capability. All of the RAF's air defence assets were effectively grounded and had been since 08:45.

A minute after the RAF contacted us, we learnt that Ajax Squadron of the Royal Tank Regiment based in Tidworth but currently out on Salisbury Plain, supposedly trying to re-establish a part of their training which had been missed when Exercise Anvil_05 had been cancelled, were seeing the computer controlled aiming systems in their Challenger II main battle tanks cause randomised offset errors in the aiming algorithm. One of the most sophisticated heavy guns in the world was reduced to being as accurate as a blind man at a fairground rifle range.

The team logged all the calls and I watched them trying desperately to take some form of control back over the compromised systems, but each time they came up short.

At 09:30 we got a call to say that the LOCE system, a US provided NATO intelligence platform had had its entry webpage hacked. Instead of the LOCE insignia and mission statement it was now, and had been since 08:45, displaying a picture of a kitten.

We had no remit over LOCE, but it was another two fingers up at us as LOCE was hosted within the UK. Its main servers resided on an RAF station in Cambridgeshire.

I saw increasingly frantic efforts being made by Dan, Rob Josh and Ritchie, whilst Mark and the rest were on phones to Cheltenham, Vauxhall Cross, Tidworth, the RAF units and the Navy bases in Portsmouth. Steph set a cup of coffee in front of me. 'Lily warned us.'

'Yes, Steph, she did. And there is nothing we can do about it. The only good news is that if we can't recover control then we might have a shot at convincing the damned politicians to do something. But, I doubt it.'

'Why doubt? Surely this is significant enough?'

'I'm not so sure. This is a demonstration of capability but nothing that is significantly hurting us. I wouldn't be surprised if the ministers manage to sidest—' I stopped as I was suddenly aware there was silence in the office. 'What's going on?'

Colonel Charles said, 'The Army are reporting all their systems are back.'

'Air Force too,' Mark said.

Ashley, Rachel and the rest confirmed the Navy and NATO had also seen the attacks end. Everything was back to normal. I checked my watch. 09:44. Exactly 59 minutes from when the incursions had been simultaneously launched.

'Seems the cat has got bored and we've been let out of its clawed clutches.' Dan said.

I felt completely deflated. We had been shown an ultimate demonstration of our vulnerability and there was nothing we could do, other than once again, close the damned stable door after the fact. I hoped John was having more luck.

*

As Dan and I walked home that evening the first wintery squalls of rain and cold winds raked their way along the banks of the Thames. Umbrellas were useless, turning themselves inside out at whim, so we simply put our heads down and strode as fast as we could. By the time we got into the apartment we were soaked to the skin.

'Shower?' Dan said with a glint in his eye that for the first time since the morning raised my spirits.

'I couldn't think of anythi—'

I was interrupted by his phone ringing. He checked the number. 'It's the Embassy.'

I glanced at my watch, 18:00. 'Bit late for them to be calling? You better take it.'

He answered and wandered off to stand next to the main window. I watched him, silhouetted by the city lights and felt my emotions swirl in a confused mix of despair and delight. I needed him in my life and I couldn't bear the sadness and hurt he was subjected to, even on phone calls with his wife. How would he cope when she was here and he had to live with her? I wanted to protect him, but I had no clue how to do that. Instead, I went in to the bedroom, stripped off my soaked clothes and walked through to the en suite. As I turned on the shower Dan came into the room.

'The embassy has found a house. They said that given the urgent nature of the request for me to have my tour extended they were happy to step up the date of the move.'

The noise of the water wasn't loud enough. I wanted it to drown out whatever was coming next, but it couldn't. Just like I couldn't protect Dan. Like I couldn't make the world be the way I wanted it to be.

'Shirlene flies in on Friday morning.'

I stepped into the flowing water and hoped it would hide my tears.

*

For the next couple of days Dan was busy arranging his move into the townhouse that the US Embassy had secured and that Group Captain Halson's budget was paying for. I seriously pondered fire-bombing it. Perhaps that would delay the move? Perhaps cancel it? Instead, I helped him as much as I could. In the evenings we cooked together and made love. In the mornings, we made love, had breakfast and went to work. I knew that we might be able to do the same, even when Shirlene arrived into London, if we were careful. We planned our Thursday night, our last night together.

A meal. Dining out at our regular haunt of the Pico Bar and Grill, under the railway arches opposite the MI6 building. Quirky and intriguing, the whole Portuguese-styled restaurant used to rattle as the Eurostar train passed over on its way into Waterloo Station. Being only a hundred metres from the apartment it hardly felt like a night out, but the menu was functional, and Dan loved that he could get a US-sized T-Bone for substantially less than the usual London prices. The screens that would usually have shown any Portuguese football match were thankfully off tonight and the background dance music at a level that kept me, an appreciator and Dan, a loather, both happy. Despite, or perhaps because of its foibles, we both loved the place and the bar was well-stocked. More importantly to me it meant I didn't have to cook and neither of us had to clean up afterwards. That meant more time for each other.

At 04:00 Dan rolled out of bed and took a shower. Shirlene's flight was arriving into Heathrow at 06:35 and he was going to be picked up by an Embassy car an hour earlier. They'd even arranged a rental vehicle for him for a few weeks until he could get his new residency status, insurances and a long-term lease sorted. I'd compared it to the lack of help the Brits gave their people and decided torturing myself with more injustices wasn't helpful.

I got up and made tea. The stereotypically British answer to moments of crisis and disaster. English Breakfast for me. Earl Grey for Dan. I knew exactly how he liked it. I knew how he liked his toast, too well done for me. I knew that he liked a scrape of butter and a thinner scrape of orange marmalade. I knew he would come out of the bedroom, slide his arms around me and kiss me on the side of the neck.

I knew my heart was tearing itself in two.

*

The door closed and I was left alone. Dan would be on leave for the next ten days. Settling his wife and child into their new home. I would go to work like nothing had happened. In fact, I would go to work outwardly happy that Captain Stückl would be with us for much longer than we had first thought. I would go to work. For all of next week. But not today. Today, in just over an hour, I would text Mark and tell him to let Colonel Charles know that I was ill. Something I'd eaten. I was sure I'd be fine. Probably a twenty-four hour thing. A little gastro. Nothing to worry about. See you on Monday.

I shifted the occasional table to in front of the couch and on it, arranged my medications of choice. I couldn't see any other way to get through the day. Or the weekend.

I finished my second cup of tea before pouring my first gin. I added the smallest dash of tonic and the ice cold alcohol bit into my mouth and throat, dispersing the warmth of the tea and applying the first dose of numbness to my mind. The first glass of the day was always my favourite. The alcohol's surging kick seemed to enter my bloodstream almost instantly. I felt the lift in my heart rate, the adrenaline punch to my body, the ice cold and warmth spreading through my veins. The accompanying sigh was like a lover had caressed me tenderly. Like Dan was back beside me. I lifted the glass again.

*

It was daylight. I couldn't tell if it was morning or evening as an overcast sky was hiding any clue. Still, overcast or not, the brightness of the light made me squint and close my eyes again. The vibration of my Nokia phone continued. I searched for it, eyes still scrunched closed. I tried to remember where I would have put it. The vibrations stopped. I started to relax back into the couch, but then they started again. I swept my hand under the cushions. I'd been listening to a message Dan had left me weeks before. His voice, happy and laughing, asking me to get bread from the shop. I'd listened to it a few times. I must have hung up and drifted off. The vibrations continued. I played my hands over the couch and down the side of the seat, managing to recover the phone and answer the call before it rang off.

'Hello?'

'Luke, it's John Leofric. Where are you?'

I sat up and regretted it. A half empty glass of gin was in front of me, sitting strangely central to an Olympic-esque pattern of rings, each one glisteningly sticky and surrounded by empty tonic bottles, their twist caps scattered like confetti.

'At home, Sir. Sorry, I'd dropped my phone.' I reached for the glass and took a swig. It helped to clear my head.

'I need you to come to a meeting.'

'Now, Sir?' I looked about. The clock on the sideboard said half seven. I wasn't sure if I'd wound it recently. I stood up and looked over to the kitchen. The clock on the oven read 00:00. Neither one told me what day it was.

'Yes now, Luke. Can you drive? I've never thought to ask you before?'

'Yes, Sir. But I don't have a car down here. It's garaged up with my parents.' I walked unsteadily into the bedroom and retrieved my watch. It said 13:12 on Sun 9th. Two days. Almost two and a half.

'You'll need to catch a train then. Get the first one you can up to Welwyn Garden City. Ring me back on this number when you know what time you'll get in. I'll arrange a car to meet you. Okay?'

'Yes. Eh?'

'I'll explain when you get here.'

'Do I need to bring anything? Is this a formal meeting?'

'No, just you and no, it's casual. Right, shake a leg.'

The line went dead. I shrugged off my dressing gown for the first time since Friday morning and held myself under a cold shower. The sharp needles of the water stung and numbed my body, the memories of Dan stung and numbed my mind.

26

Welwyn Garden City, October 2005

A shower, a lot of toothpaste and a taxi later I'd caught the 14:21 out of London Kings Cross and made Welwyn within half an hour. John was waiting and led me out to a Ford Mondeo. 'We'll talk when we get to where we're going. Alright?'

'Yes, sure.'

The driver, a small, wiry guy with short hair, didn't speak. I got a courtesy nod from him as he made brief eye contact with me in the rear-view mirror. Five minutes later we had transited out of Welwyn, crossed west over the A1 and sped through a couple of small hamlets, whose names I didn't catch. Five more minutes and we were turning into a grand, tree-lined driveway. The long curve of which straightened to reveal a two-winged mansion of a house. Left and right of the property were manicured gardens and formal, geometric topiary groves. The whole place looked expansive and expensive. Very expensive. The car stopped in front of the massive main doors.

'Let's go,' John said and I followed him up the entrance steps. 'What is this place, Sir?'

'One of many back-up emergency planning hubs. In case centres of Government were ever targeted.'

None the wiser, I kept alongside him as the front doors swung open. I was briefly aware of a young woman dressed in jeans and a jumper, but John was already taking the main staircase two steps at a time. I hurried after him, along a corridor and into what I imagined was going to be a formal dining room or perhaps a library. John opened the heavy oak door himself and when I entered the room I was amazed.

Overall, I may have been right. It could once have been a formal dining room, or a library, but now the long and wide space had been turned into a modern operations room. It reminded me of the one in Qatar, but with a notable exception, this room had windows. Three large windows on the southerly facing wall that afforded an exceptional view of more formal gardens laid out to the rear of the house. The north wall was covered in maps, notice boards, briefing boards, white boards and pinboards. The westerly wall, directly in front of me, was home to six flat screen monitor displays that together formed a video wall. I'd seen one like it, but smaller, in Waddington, and I knew that each screen could display a separate feed, or on occasion, be ganged together to provide a single unbroken picture. Currently all the screens were blank.

Filling the floor space were eight desks; three each to the left and right sides and two in the middle of the room. Each desk was home to two seats and each seat position had a myriad of screens and telephones on it. No one was filling any of the seats. Instead, a small knot of three men and two women stood at the far end of the room around the only other furniture, a rectangular table, its top covered in maps and pieces of paper. I recognised three of the five.

'Hello, Luke,' Steve Jäeger said and held his hand out.

'Hello Steve. Is this where I say, fancy seeing you here?'

'Probably. You know Sean and Andy,' he said and I got a raised hand in greeting from Sean, the SAS Major and Andy Gibson, the SIS man who I was now realising was an expert on both Chinese affairs and the way the French Intelligence Services worked.

Steve turned to the woman on his left. 'This is Lorna, and this,' he indicated the man on the far side of the table, 'is Jack.'

Lorna shook my hand, Jack gave a half wave.

'Lorna works with me and Jack is a civilian consultant.'

Jack looked colossal. I'd once watched a US Army team take on a US SEAL team at American Football in the dust and desert within the base at Qatar. The Army team had been made up of big guys. The SEALs had made them look tiny. Jack looked like he could have held down his own place in the SEAL team.

'A consultant? Should I ask on what?'

Steve laughed. 'We'll leave that to John to tell you.'

The top row of screens on the video wall lit up. A map of southern France on the left, a map of the world in the middle and a detailed satellite image of Hong Kong on the right.

John stepped to the front of the room.

'Luke, you are going to have to brief Lily on what we're going to do.'

'Okay, Sir. And what are we going to do?'

'Well, our governments, Steve's included, are being extremely strange over the whole Chinese cyber capability. We believe the correct thing to do is to lift Lily out and use her to help us fight back. However, you and I both know that we were expressly ordered not to proceed.'

'Yes, I know.'

'Well, I have been thinking about that and given that I was the one the Foreign Secretary was yelling at, I recall exactly the words she used. She said that on no account were SAS troops or RAF aircraft to be involved with the extraction of Chinese citizens from Chinese sovereign territory.'

I looked about the table. 'So we're going to use American aircraft and troops?'

'No. We put it forward to our command chain and were also refused,' Steve said.

'Oh! I see, so what is the plan?' I asked.

'We're going to privatise the operation,' Sean said. 'Andy and I will provide our knowledge for the Hong Kong side of things.'

'And I'll go in and get them,' Jack said. 'I have a few guys who can help.'

'But how will you get Lily's family out if you have to fly in commercially?'

Steve turned over a photo that had been on the table. It was of a Bombardier Challenger 604 business jet.

'And you have a spare one of those on you, do you Steve?'

'No. But Lorna and I know a man who does.'

'It still doesn't get Lily's family through Hong Kong security,' I said, a little annoyed that I was having to drag information out of them. I could feel the pounding in my head starting again and I knew I needed about four paracetamol or one stiff drink. I wasn't going to get either stood here. I stifled my frustration.

'The owner of the jet has a number of enterprises and business links with Macau. Because of these he flies in and out of both there and Hong Kong on a regular basis. He's a bit eccentric, a latter day flamboyant showman. A few generations ago I imagine he would have sold snakeskins and natural remedies out of a horse-drawn wagon. Lots of promises, but mostly smoke and mirrors.'

'And what's he selling to Macau?'

'A different type of life-enhancing experience to high rolling Chinese gamblers from the back of a private jet. Our interest is because I'm fairly sure he doesn't get stopped by customs entering Hong Kong and I know for a fact he has a clear drive from Downtown to airborne when he's leaving. We can take advantage of that.'

'And he's agreed?'

'He doesn't know yet, but he will. We have, or rather, Lorna has a little official leverage we can use.'

'Which is?'

'Which is not necessary for you to know,' Lorna interjected.

Her face was neutral but I got the distinct impression asking more would be a mistake.

Steve rested his hand on her forearm in what I took to be a calming effort. 'Suffice to say he'll play along with us if he wants his US businesses to stay profitable. Isn't that right Lorna?'

She nodded.

'And the French end of things?' I asked wondering how the hell I had found myself in a stately home, decked out to look like a military operations centre and planning a freelance extraction mission on a dodgy plane owned by a potentially dodgy bloke.

'Pull up a seat and we'll take you through the whole thing,' John said.

*

It was after 2am when Steve dropped me back into London. I was grateful, tired, humbled by the talents of the people I'd met and as soon as I looked up to my apartment, heartbroken again at the thought that it would be empty. Steve pulled away and I gave a wave to the back of the car.

I checked around prior to swiping my access card against the security reader of the apartment building's foyer. The complex's concierge was only employed during the day, so at night the main door was locked. Checking behind me before swiping the card was a habit I'd got into after there had been a home invasion in a nearby block. They'd sneaked in behind an unwary occupant, forced them to ride up in the lift and open their apartment. At this time of the morning I didn't expect to see anyone on the street and sure enough it was empty, but for a couple in a car parked a little way along the road. I hadn't noticed them before and it was only as I glanced back that the glow of a streetlight picked out the passenger. It was of no consequence, they were in a nice car and too far away to run over and assail me before the door would close and keep me safe. I let myself up to the apartment, swigged down a handful of headache tablets, set my alarm and fell asleep.

*

She had just sat down at her opulent wood-panelled office in King Charles Street and sipped the first of the dozen or more cups of coffee she would use as fuel to get through the day, when the secure phone on her desk shrilled.

The direct line light flashed, not a call being handled by her assistant but a straight connection to one of her Cabinet colleagues.

The scrolling text display on the telephone's screen painfully revealed letter by letter, "T h e H o m e S e c" She picked up the receiver. 'Foreign Secretary.'

'Mary?'

'Duncan, how good to hear your voice.'

'I can detect your cynicism you know. I wonder why on earth I help you sometimes.'

'You keep hoping you'll get lucky, Duncan. Now, what heralds the call?'

'My chaps have some information for you. Photos too.'

'Ah, I see. Breakfast on the Terrace?'

'Sounds lovely. See you then.'

*

In some respects, the military is great. I could have ordered Mark to ensure all the team were out of the office by 15:00. Or, I could have advised Colonel Charles and he would have ordered Mark. Either would be as effective, but the military didn't work on blind orders and unquestioned following. Not usually. Usually it required explanation and reason. In this case I asked Colonel Charles for advice. He suggested that honesty was always the best policy. I called the team together.

'I'm going to be talking to Lily over the next few days. You all need to be out of the office when I do. I can't tell you why and I don't want to have to lie to you. All I can ask is that you trust me and believe that I have our team's best interests at heart.'

I'm not entirely sure what I thought their reaction would be, but I got a complete set of 'Sure, no problem boss.' back at me. It was rather an anti-climax.

At 15:00 I logged in to the chatroom. By 15:15 I had briefed Lily on our plans to extract her and her family. By 15:20 my life had taken a very complicated turn.

27

London, October 2005

The inside of the Bombardier Challenger 604 business jet was almost as I had imagined. Leather reclining seats, high-gloss cabinetry, a glamorous, uniformed flight attendant called Mary-Lou and, through the open cockpit door, a high-tech and satisfyingly reassuring modern glass-instrumented flight deck. I'd only really got one detail wrong. Mary-Lou was actually called Betsy. A fact I discovered when she introduced herself, took my jacket, my leather duffle bag and offered me a drink.

'Gin, if you have it.'

'Oh I'm sorry, Sir, we only have orange juice or Coors Light,' she said, in an accent that would have rivalled Scarlett O'Hara's for its southern drawl. She opened the full height bar to reveal that she spoke the truth. I could see three cartons of OJ and the rest of the space was stacked with beer bottles. I don't like beer that much and this wasn't even proper, full-strength alcohol. Still, needs must.

'A beer please, and I'm Luke.'

'Certainly, coming right up and I appreciate y'all telling me your name but Mr MacLellan wouldn't approve. He likes a little formality, so I can call you, Sir, or Mr?'

'Ah, I see. Well it's Mr Fra—' I stooped myself and felt my face flush red. Betsy gave me an odd look, tilting her head and widening her eyes. 'Sorry, Sir?'

'Pearson. Mr Pearson,' I said. 'Or Sir, I guess.'

She righted her head and seemed to accept my correction without hesitation, turning away to pour me a beer in the luxury galley. As she did, I looked through to the cockpit where I could see a sliver of both the pilot and co-pilot as they set dials and checked lists. I had piloted single engine, light aircraft during my flying training with the University Air Squadron. Three great years, when I was meant to be gaining a Law Degree with honours, but what with the Squadron life of flying nearly every weekend, social functions and training nights at least twice a week and my first introduction to a proper, hard-core drinking culture, I had ended up scraping a pass in my law studies. Although, in compensation, the Air Force had funded most of my university years and paid me a wage as soon as I'd agreed to join up. Not as a pilot though. I could fly, but I knew I didn't have the extra aptitude needed to be a fast-jet military pilot. So I'd opted for Intelligence, but my flying training meant I knew that up front in the 604's cockpit, the man with his cropped black hair was sitting in the pilot's seat while to his right, the woman with a cascade of golden blonde hair, was the co-pilot or more correctly, the first officer.

Betsy handed me my beer, the colour of which didn't come close to matching the deep tones of the first officer's hair. I took a sip. Weak, but cold. Better than nothing. I placed the glass into the ready-made holder next to my seat, sat back and waited.

After ten minutes a Mercedes E-Class came to a halt opposite the aircraft's front steps. The driver got out and opened the car's rear door. The first thing I saw was a brown leather cowboy boot touching down onto the tarmac. The man that followed was heavy featured with a heavy build, dressed in jeans, an open-necked, white-collared shirt and a brown leather jacket that came to his waist. I was somewhat disappointed he didn't have a Stetson. He walked directly to the steps of the aircraft and a moment later hustled into the aircraft cabin.

'You ready?' He called into the cockpit.

'Yes, Sir,' the first officer replied.

'Well then let's go. A beer, Betsy,' he said and handed his jacket across to her. I could see his jeans sported a brown leather belt with an oval black and silver buckle which had an intertwined monogram as a motif.

'Yes, Sir, Mr MacLellan, right away.'

I stood up as he passed Betsy and walked down the length of the cabin.

'You're Luke?' He said holding his hand out.

'Yes and you're—'

'Stuart Campbell MacLellan the Third. Call me Mac. Pleased to meet you. How's the beer?' he said, and tried to crush my hand in his grip. I was reminded of Dan's initial handshake with me. He had been strong and hadn't been trying to prove anything. Mac however, was pressing deliberately. I could see it in the flex of his cheek muscles and the smallest of twitches to the side of his mouth. I held firm, relaxed my shoulders and broadened my smile. 'The beer's great,' I lied.

He let go of my hand and took a seat on the other side of the cabin from me. Betsy placed two beer bottles in front of him. He drained the first in a single hit and handed her the empty. The jet's engines started up and the cabin door closed.

'Let's get this plane in the air,' he called out towards the cockpit.

I tried to place his accent. Unlike Betsy's, it wasn't a full-on southern drawl. There was an edge to it, a strangeness to his vowels.

'Lorna and Steve tell me you weren't expecting to be on board,' he said.

'No. I wasn't. I'd expected to be monitoring things from behind my desk.'

'Which is where?'

I pointed out the window of the jet as it taxied to the end of London City Airport's runway. 'About a mile in that direction.'

'You in the military?'

I was surprised by his question. I thought Steve would have briefed him, but obviously not. I decided, as I had with Betsy, the fewer of my details I shared, the better. I answered, 'Yes.'

'Yes? Is that all you're gonna tell me?'

'Yes.'

Mac gave a short snort of a laugh. 'Another one, just like that son-of-a-…ah hell, no skin off my nose. So, why are you here then?'

'The people we're going to lift out of Hong Kong. Our contact didn't trust that we wouldn't let them down again. She insisted that I go and collect them in person. No deal if I didn't.'

The aircraft joined a queue of small business jets and came to a halt. Its engines throttled back, their noise decreasing to a lower pitched whine. Betsy came to help me with the executive seat's harness. Mac closed his eyes and asked, 'Do they know what you look like?'

'Sorry?'

'The people in Hong Kong. Do they know what you look like?'

'Eh, no. Why?'

'Why didn't you say you'd go, but send someone else?'

'Because I need the contact to trust me and if I started off in a lie, then I don't think it would work.'

'Would be safer.'

'I'm hoping it won't be dangerous at all,' I said and wondered if I was managing to hide the nervousness bordering on fear that I felt every time I thought of the things that could go wrong. The whole plan relied on Steve and Lorna's certainty that Mac MacLellan the Third could waltz me through Chinese Macau and Hong Kong.

'You never can tell if it's going to be dangerous,' he said. The Chinese can blow hot and cold and you're talking about smuggling two of them out on this plane. Could be hairy…and you're flying in with no cover.'

I knew not to tell him that I was expecting to meet up with Jack and his team once I arrived in Hong Kong. They would have

arranged hire cars and hotel accommodation as well as having rec-
onnoitred the area around Lily's mother's tower block. 'I think the
fewer people on the ground the better,' I lied.

'You want me to arrange a driver at least for you in Hong
Kong?'

'No, it's okay. I already have one arranged to meet me.'

'Your call I 'spose. But hairy if you ask me.'

I felt a real surge of panic. What the hell had I let myself in
for? I tried to swallow but my throat was suddenly dry. I reached
out for my beer.

Mac gave another snort of laughter. 'Ha, lighten up kid. Your
face looks like a baby moose facing a grizzly. I'm only joshing with
ya. There's no danger. Geez-Us you look like you could use a dia-
per. Ha!' He reached across the aisle and offered his beer in a toast.
I thought about perhaps chucking my beer over him, but settled
for chinking my glass against his bottle and mustering a smile.

The aircraft engines increased in pitch again and we trundled
forward, lining up for take-off.

'More seriously, though son, you a good flyer?'

'Yes, why's that?'

'Tail end of the typhoon season. We're probably gonna be flying into one. Smooth to Dubai and smooth most of the way to
Macau, but I've seen the forecasts. It's meant to be getting mighty
bumpy when we get nearer.'

'Is this another little joke?' I asked.

'No. Straight up,' he said and I had no idea if he was suckering
me again.

I slapped the armrest of the chair. 'This looks a robust enough
aircraft, Mac. I'm sure we'll be fi—' I was interrupted by the sound
system playing at a high enough volume to drown out the engine
noise. I instantly recognised the song as *Take Me Home, Country
Roads* by John Denver. I was bemused and my face must have registered the same.

'Never take off or land without it,' Mac shouted, tapping his
hands and feet to the tune. 'It's my good luck charm. So don't you
be worrying none about any storms. We'll be a-ok!'

I gave him my best smile and seriously hoped the pilot and first officer were not relying on a musical accompaniment to do the hard work for them. The engines spun to full throttle and in my mind's eye I could see the pilot holding on the power and then slipping the brakes once clearance was given by the air traffic controller in the tower. I hadn't expected to be pushed quite as far back in my seat. The acceleration of the business jet was way beyond anything I'd felt in a commercial airliner. I involuntarily gripped the arms of my seat a little tighter than usual and as the music cut off I heard another snort from Mac. When I looked across he was staring down at my slightly white knuckles.

'Good flyer, eh?'

I relaxed, 'I'll cope Mac. The acceleration surprised me, that's all.'

We angled up and levelled out at a cruising altitude of 37,000ft, according to the in cabin display, again achieved in a much faster time than I was used to. Mac was once more looking quite intently at me.

'Imagine putting an 18-wheeler engine into a go-kart. Or an Indy-500 engine into your Mom's compact saloon. That's what you've got here. Jet engines on a small airframe. Flies high and fast. Relax, we'll be in Dubai in just over six hours.'

Betsy delivered another beer to Mac.

'Do you play cards, kid?' he asked, slipping a box of playing cards out of a side cabinet next to his seat.

'Not really. Solitaire occasionally.'

'Well God damn this is gonna be a slow day.'

'Perhaps you could teach me?'

'I don't think so. I can't teach you how to play poker and then take all your money. There's no sport in that,' he said and once again drained one of his beers in a single hit. Betsy arrived to remove the bottle and replace it with another almost immediately. Weak beer or not, the man liked a drink. I wondered why he didn't opt for a full-strength lager and get more effect, but decided against asking. He pressed a button and a television display rose up from the desk in front of his seat.

'Do you like football?' He asked.

I didn't really, but I figured that from London to Dubai, then onwards to Macau and Hong Kong was a long time to be in this man's company and have nothing to talk about. So I lied, again. 'I don't mind it.'

'Which team?'

'Sunderland. It's where I was born.'

'Sun who?'

'Sunderland. The Black Cats?'

'Where the hell do they play out of?'

'The Stadium of Light, in Sunderland, England?'

'No kid. Geez-Us. American Football. Not soccer. That ain't no sport.'

I wasn't sure which I wanted to correct first, his grammar or his pompous ass attitude. In the end, as I rather needed his jet, I decided to do neither.

'Umm. No. Sorry, I don't follow American Football.'

'Well, I guess I'll get Betsy to show you how to work that television in front of you and you can watch whatever you want. There's about a thousand films in the system. I'll be over here watching proper sport. You could join me, learn a thing or two about one of the great teams in the world.'

'Go on then, who are they?'

'The Dallas Cowboys, son. The Cowboys. *Theee-eee* most successful football team in the world. Eight Super Bowl appearances and five victories. No one even close to that number of final appearances.'

I wasn't completely bereft of knowledge on American Football. Dan had mentioned it on occasions as he looked for the results in the Monday papers, but it was no longer shown on British TV, like it had been when I was younger, so I had no idea which teams were good and which were bad.

'And you're a hard-core supporter?'

'Yes, Sir. I always back the best.'

'So they're your home team, like Sunderland for me?'

'Hell no, boy! I ain't no Texan!' He seemed quite annoyed.

'Oh, sorry. I mean the country music taking off and now Dallas?'

'I have a house there. Spend quite a bit of my time there, that's for sure, and the place did make me a chunk of coin, but I'm not American.'

'You aren't?'

'No kid. I'm Canadian. Calgary, Alberta to be precise. Proud to be…strong and free. You ever been?'

I shook my head.

'Great place. Stampedes, parries, open spaces. And a good deal of oil.'

'Maple Syrup and the Mounties?' I said, hoping to recover favour by mentioning two of the few things I knew about Canada. Mac's face did not brighten.

'The Mounties, yeah, but Maple syrup? In Alberta? Oh no kid. That's all those damned Québécois Frenchies that make the most of that stuff. I mean…nothing better on bacon, but it ain't produced in Alberta. You have some holes in your knowledge. Well I aim to fill one in. Let's show you some real sport.' He swivelled the screen around.

I watched as two teams that seemed to have a hundred players on each, ran into the middle of an immense stadium. 'So who's playing who?' I asked.

'This is the Cowboys versus the Philly Eagles. Sunday's game. Round five of the season.'

'Do you know the result?'

'Well sure son, I was there. I have a box in the Texas Stadium. Great view, I'll point it out if the cameras pan across it.'

'Okay, so you're watching it again, because…'

'Because you see more on the TV recording.'

He said it like it was the most obvious thing in the world. I was a little more impressed that he had been at a game in Texas on Sunday and now, on Wednesday morning, he was taking off from London to fly me to Hong Kong. If this was how the other half lived, I liked it. A loud brash, untypical Canadian he might be, but his lifestyle was looking attractive. I leant on the arm of my seat and said, 'Okay. Dallas in blue I guess, with the Lone Star on their helmets?'

'Yes, Sir. Now this here, this is the kick off to start the game.'

I settled in for the flight and an induction into Gridiron.

*

Mac had mentioned the thousands of movies on the aircraft's video system. He hadn't mentioned the years' worth of archive football matches it also stored. By the time the strains of *Country Roads* played again, signalling our arrival into Dubai for a quick refuelling stop, I had watched last Sunday's game, which finished in a comprehensive, 33 to 10, victory over the poor Eagles, and followed it up with the back to back Super Bowl wins of 1992 and 1993. Seemed to me that the Cowboys were not bad at all, but the start stop nature of the game was strange and I wondered what the average Rugby player would think to all the padding, protection and helmets that the US footballers wore.

*

After departing Dubai less than an hour after arriving, Mac insisted I watch Super Bowl XXX when the Cowboys ran out victorious over the Pittsburgh Steelers by 27-17. By now I not only understood the game but knew a number of the Cowboys, especially their quarterback, Troy Aikman, by name. Mac was impressed.

'Hell, kid, you come out to Texas anytime you want and I'll treat you to a box seat. Even introduce you to Troy if he's around. He commentates on the television nowadays, but he most times makes our home games. Nice kid. Californian, but we'll forgive him that.'

I smiled along with the joke that I didn't really get and then said that I might catch some sleep. Mac called Betsy to turn two of the front seats into an almost full sized double bed. I slept fitfully, often waking in a sweat as my mind raced through the multitude of things that could go wrong. Eventually I must have managed to sleep a little deeper, because I was wakened by the strains of *Country Roads* as we made our final approach into Macau. Betsy took care of turning the bed back into seats and I took my original position across the aisle from Mac. He didn't look as if he'd slept at all. Another beer sat in front of him, the liquid gently sloshing from side to side, but not as much as Mac's weather forecast had predicted. Through the cabin windows was a night sky full of thick cloud and the occasional, far off, lightning flash. I hoped the tail end of the storm had passed us by. I also hoped that my agreeing to do this wasn't going to be the stupidest thing I'd ever decided.

After landing, we taxied for a long time across a well-lit causeway that, from my limited view through the cabin windows, appeared to dissect a lake. The further we taxied the more my heart pounded in my chest. Mac was on his feet long before we came to a stop. Betsy helped him into his jacket and handed me mine and my bag. I felt sick.

Mac led me a step or two away from Betsy. 'Calm yourself, son. Calm yourself. These guys out here know me. They're gonna do a rudimentary check. That's all. They ain't gonna care who you are or where you're from if they think you're with me and you're here to spend big money. Besides…' he reached into his jacket pocket and pulled a thick roll of US Dollars. 'This is what they're really here for. They make my passage through customs and immigration swift and easy and I make their lives a little kinder.'

The aircraft taxied straight into a well-lit hangar and came to a halt, the jet engines wound down and Betsy opened the cabin door. It folded forward and became the aircraft steps. As soon as they touched onto the ground, Mac bustled down them and I followed. It was cold, the wind was fresh and swirling around and my ears still hadn't cleared so the noise of it and the surrounding airport seemed muted. In the corner of the hangar was a black Range Rover, a grey sedan and a bright blue police car. The red flash down its side, the standard emergency light bar on its roof and the word, "Policia" painted on the rear wing gave it a very European feel. I wasn't sure what I had expected, but not that.

At a table to the far right of the police car sat two men wearing white shirts with yellow insignia on their epaulettes. I thought they must have been freezing. Standing behind them were two police officers wearing heavy jackets, and emerging from the grey saloon car was a suited, much older looking man.

Mac changed direction and headed straight for him. 'Muhai. Good to see you.'

'Mr MacLellan. Good to see you too.'

The two men shook hands and as Muhai's back was to the officers at the table, Mac handed the roll of notes over to him. He slipped them into his inside jacket pocket and continued to shake Mac's hand before leading him across to the table.

The two I suspected were Customs Officers stood and gave a small bow of their heads. Not as low or as formal as I'd seen Japanese people do, but polite. The two cops stayed standing behind and disengaged. Muhai took a seat, opened the desk drawer, took out a stamp and an inkpad and held his hand out. Mac handed over his passport. Muhai flicked through it, not checking anything other than to find an empty page. He raised the stamp and with one bang on the inkpad and one on the passport he was done. Mac thanked him, thanked the still standing Customs Officers and walked off towards the Range Rover.

I swallowed hard and stepped forward with my passport in my hand. Only it wasn't.

Steve Jäeger had briefed me that no one would bother checking any friends of Mac too rigorously, but they would still need to see a passport. He and Lorna had provided a set of dummy details and more worrying to me, a genuine looking British Passport, in less time than it would have taken me to come up with an alias. Mind you, the alias they had picked was my great-grandfather's surname and I wore his signet ring that had been passed down to me. I had wondered at the use of Luke as a first name coupled with a surname that was within my family, but Andy, the SIS officer had reassured me that the closer to the truth the better. Especially using my real first name as I would react properly if people called me by it.

'Welcome to Macau, Mr Pearson,' Muhai said.

'Thank you,' I answered and surprised myself with how firm and calm my voice sounded.

'You have been before?'

'No. First time.'

'I am sure Mr MacLellan will show you a very good time. I hope you are lucky.'

'Thank you.'

The passport had been made to look like I was a seasoned traveller. Muhai flicked through to an empty page and with another double bang of his stamp, it was done.

The nearest Customs Officer reached his hand out and I handed my bag over. He weighed it in his hand a couple of times, asked me in heavily accented English if I had any firearms, to which I said, no, and then he handed it back, gave me a small bow and held his arm out towards where Mac stood next to the open doors of the Range Rover.

'Thank you,' I said and walked away.

'Get in the far side, kid,' Mac said as the driver stepped out to close Mac's door for him. I was surprised to see the vehicle was right-hand drive. Once I was in, the car accelerated out of the hangar and onto the airport's inner perimeter road.

'Aren't we waiting for the crew?' I asked, catching a last glimpse of Betsy making her way off the aircraft.

Mac looked sideways at me as if I was mad. 'No. They stay close to the airport. So they're ready if I need them.'

We were clipping along at quite a speed and didn't appear to be slowing for the upcoming security barrier. The driver, a big man with a shiny bald head, a thick neck and shoulders that were wider than the expansive Range Rover's seat, flashed the headlights twice and the red and white barrier swung up without delay. We swept onto a main road, braked harshly, u-turned and then accelerated towards a roundabout.

'They drive on the left here?'

'Yep. Just like you Brits.'

'I thought they drove on the right in China.'

'They do son, they do. But not here or in Hong Kong. One of my life's regrets is that my Scottish forefathers didn't make the whole of Canada do the same. Would have loved to see the Yanks try to figure it out when they crossed the border.'

To my left I could see a forest of cranes, each one illuminated to not only show their height but to light up the construction company name. There were dozens of them. 'What are they building?'

Mac ducked down and looked across me. 'Casinos, son. You ever been to Vegas?'

'No.'

'Every casino in Vegas wants a part of what they have out here. Some already have. We're going to the Sands. They were one of the first to make the investment, opened last year. Now the Venetian, MGM, Wynn and a whole heap more are making their moves. Couple of years from now this place is gonna be bigger than Vegas. Way bigger.'

'Seriously?' I was genuinely surprised. Chinese communism and Western decadence didn't seem a match made in heaven.

'Damn straight. You mark my words, if you have money to invest, this is the place to do it. High-end hotels, high-end chauffer services, high-end services of every kind, if you get my drift.' He tapped the side of his nose like he was letting me into a major secret.

I didn't really get his drift. 'Surely the Chinese Government will have something to say about this?'

'They do. They love it. It's the government who are driving the whole rodeo. Money talks and there's a lot of money down here. Biggest gamblers on the planet are the Asians. Always have been. Bet on two flies running up a window. Hell I've seen a man in this town put four million on a single spin of a roulette wheel.'

'Did he win?'

'Nope. Walked away like he'd lost ten bucks.'

We took a sweeping right-hand bend and the lights of the cranes and the buildings fell behind us. The road kept straight as an arrow, and the yellow-neon light stanchions lining each side seemed to soar up into the distance, but beyond them was pitch black. I realised it was a bridge and craned my neck down to look between the seats and out of the windscreen. 'Wow, that's some construction.'

'Three miles near as dammit. Longest bridge they have connecting Taipa to Macau. Can't recall its name. Filipe, you remember?'

'The Amizade Bridge, Mr MacLellan. It's Portuguese for Friendship,' Filipe the driver said in heavily accented English that I guessed made him also Portuguese.

'Keep watching out, there's a hell of a view coming up,' Mac said.

As we topped what I imagined was the apex of the bridge I realised we were only a quarter of the way across. The roadway sloped back down and then rose again. It was constructed like a stretched out W. The lights of Macau provided a magnificent back-drop.

'Clever little bastards the Chinese,' Mac said. 'Soon as they negotiated the handover of Macau from Portugal, just like they did with Hong Kong from you guys, they started on contracts for massive construction projects. This here bridge was one of the first ones.'

'Have you been coming here long?' For the first time since I'd met him, Mac hesitated in answering me. He looked out his side window.

'A while. Now, you know what you have to do when we get here?' He asked, switching the topic.

I glanced forward to Filipe.

'Don't you worry none about Filipe. He and I go way back. Trust him like a son, ain't that right Filipe?'

'Yes, Sir, Mr MacLellan.'

I wondered if he made his real sons call him Mr MacLellan, but decided not to ask. 'I check in and wait for you to call my room.'

'That's it. Keep yourself a low profile. Order room service. Watch the in-house movies. Book a massage. Hell, order a special Macau massage.'

I had no clue what he meant but decided not to ask. Mac kept on talking.

'I'll meet the guys I need to and we fly out this evening. You get to be a high rolling gambler.'

'What happens if your real high rollers want to ask me about the games I play or to be honest, anything about gambling?' I asked, worried that the plan Steve and John had come up with to cover my appearance in and out of Hong Kong might be weak at best and massively flawed at worst.

'They won't. Gambling's a solitary affair, kid. It's not a team sport. You don't swap tactics with your fellow players. You don't give a damn about them. You don't want to know how they did 'cos winning more than you is a balls ache to learn about and losing more than you never gets admitted to. Anyways up, they'll probably be half drunk. In fact, you make yourself smell like you've had a few and you'll fit right in. Splash some of the hotel mini bar on as cologne before we leave.'

I agreed, but doubted I'd waste good booze like that.

We came off the second apex of the Friendship Bridge and after a long sweeping left hand curve I could see the tall tower of the Macau Sands Hotel, glistening like a golden beacon. Its name illuminated in a faux Arabian script looked both trashy and classy in equal parts. We drove in under the tower to the covered parking bays in front of the main reception. Two uniformed concierges opened our doors and greeted Mac as Mr MacLellan. The taller of the two reached for my bag, but I declined.

'It's okay, I'll carry it.'

We were escorted into the marble floored foyer, but instead of being led to the reception desks under their cedar-lined ceiling, we were taken into a private lounge off to the left. Inside, a uniformed waitress stood in front of a bar that ran the full length of the tennis-court sized room. Two white leather couches, trimmed in the same deep maroon of the waitress's waistcoat, sat either side of a glass and marble low-level table. Two guest cards, one pre-filled with Mac's details, one with the name "Luke Pearson" lay on the top, next to two Montblanc fountain pens. Before we had even sat down, the waitress set a beer in front of Mac.

'Coors Light, Mr MacLellan,' she said. Despite her looks, she spoke without a trace of a Chinese accent. 'And for you Mr Pearson?'

I looked behind her and saw a distinctive round, black bottle. 'I'll have a Hendricks gin with a splash of tonic please...?' She turned a little and allowed me to see her name badge. 'Alix. Thank you.'

As she stepped away, Mac said quietly, 'Don't screw up your signature.'

I signed a clumsy scrawl across the designated space and set the pen down. Mac put his in his pocket and caught my expression.

'You really haven't travelled in the right circles, kid. These are complimentary.'

'These,' I whispered, 'are Montblanc fountain pens. They must be worth five hundred pounds.'

'Probably. What's that, about a thousand US bucks?'

'Yes.'

'So that's a single ante into a single game for the people I bring to this hotel. Less for the Chinese guys who I make sure keep coming back time and time again. Pick it up and put it in your pocket.'

The waitress arrived with my drink. She held a small crystal jug and as she began to pour the tonic into the equally fine crystal low-ball tumbler said, 'If you would tell me how much, Sir.' I stopped her almost as soon as she had begun.

We waited not more than five minutes. Long enough to have a drink and I imagined, if you were a normal traveller used to this type of reception, long enough to relax you a little. Perhaps it was designed to start the process of relieving whatever stress you had accumulated flying in on your private jet from your equally luxurious yacht in Monaco or home in the Hamptons. For me, I managed to have my drink, but the nervousness of hopefully making it through the second check of my identity was doing nothing to relieve any stress. I was sure my passport would stand scrutiny if called on, but the next twenty-four hours were going to take me way outside of my comfort zone.

The door opened and another concierge came in. His heavy French accent adding to the cosmopolitan mix of Macau.

'Hello, Monsieur MacLellan, it is good to see you again.'

'You too Julien. You too. We good?'

'Oui, Monsieur, if you would be so kind, I shall escort you to your suites.' The waitress picked up our registration cards and handed them to him. He gave each no more than a cursory glance and we followed him to the door. I picked up my bag and was right behind Mac, thinking that the second check of my identity had been passed easily, when the waitress called, 'Oh, Mr Pearson, Sir.'

I froze. I felt her hand on my arm and could do nothing but turn slowly. 'Yes?'

'You forgot your pen, Sir,' she said and handed me the Montblanc.

*

The laptop and Nokia mobile phone I carried inside my duffel bag looked perfectly normal. The specialist software they both hosted wasn't and Lorna had insisted I never let them out of my sight.

'They'll stand up to a quick visual inspection, but if anyone gets time to open them up they might figure it out. That's not the real concern.'

'What is?' I asked, whilst also wondering exactly who she was. Steve had never introduced her more than saying she worked with him, but Lorna had played a major part in putting this clandestine operation together. Especially after Lily had insisted that I get involved directly.

'The Chinese have been known to do what the Russians do,' Lorna said, handing me the laptop. 'Anyone checking in to a hotel and leaving their bags will get them back in good time, but any electronics left inside will have picked up a hitchhiker. We don't want that. So keep it with you, yeah?'

I'd agreed and she'd shown me how to use the equipment. I sincerely hoped I could remember. I was about to find out.

The laptop linked to the encrypted Nokia phone. I turned them on and synched them the way she had shown me. Then I poured another drink from the suite's mini bar and waited patiently for the system to run its checks and establish a secure link. I had no clue where the software had come from, but I suspected that it had been borrowed, loaned, begged or stolen from NSA, the US equivalent of GCHQ. Wherever it had come from I was assured it was robust enough to provide secure communications, even from within China. I knew for certain it hadn't been officially requested for my use, as officially, I was on leave for four days visiting my parents. Likewise, I couldn't hope to use any of my team's equipment, as they'd been specifically kept out of the planning. If all of this went badly wrong, they had to have deniability. Only John Leofric and I would take the fall on our side of the Atlantic.

Once the tell-tale chirp sounded, I opened a browser window, typed in the sequence of numbers I'd memorised and navigated to the correct Internet Relay Chat room. I checked in using the pre-arranged name and number, "Traveller5179". It was 05:00 local time but my body thought it was still 22:00, as it was in London. I wasn't sure who was on the other end as the username in the chat only displayed "Home".

Hello – who's there?

Hi – Steve here - can you confirm

Sheffield Hallam

My chosen password was the university I'd attended. If I'd been compromised my password was to be Durham School.

Good evening – or good morning, good trip?

Morning, dawn in about an hour – not bad – very flash – I could grow to like it

I'm sure - Okay on to business

Steve took me through the plans again and I confirmed my end. We were still on track.

You're due to check in with Lily in 16 hours. Get some sleep. Good luck

You too.

I logged out of the chat room, disconnected the phone and shut down the laptop. Dawn was cracking through the heavy grey clouds and my fitful sleep on board the plane was beginning to catch up with me. I pulled off my clothes, climbed into bed and turned the TV onto CNN. The news anchor was announcing yet more repair and rehabilitation delays in the US as almost two months on they were still trying to cope with the aftermath of Hurricane Katrina. President George W and his wife had arrived into New Orleans on Air Force One to discuss what more could be done. The pictures showed them waving at the top of the aircraft steps. I was asleep before they reached the tarmac.

*

Thirteen hours later, as rain and wind rocked the hotel and the last vestiges of light were seeping away from a sky so heavily laden with storm clouds that it didn't need the night to bring darkness, my room phone rang.

'You ready to go?' Mac asked.

'Yep.'

'Lobby, five minutes.'

I was there in half that. Mac and four Chinese men, two conservatively dressed and two dripping in gold chains, large jewel-set rings and dark sunglasses, were shaking hands with the French concierge from earlier. I stood outside the knot and observed. Only the Chinese with the jewels were talking and shaking hands. I allowed my gaze to linger and it was soon obvious by their stance and how they themselves were aware of their surroundings, that the conservatively dressed pair were security for the other two. I decided not to give them any reason to look too closely at me and walked towards Filipe standing next to the first of two Range Rovers pulled up at the front doors.

The distance from Macau to Hong Kong is forty miles by air, yet commercial airlines take over four hours at their fastest to make the journey as they go via one of a number of Chinese mainland airports. There is a ferry service that takes over an hour but is not for the luxuriously minded and only runs infrequently during the day. Apparently, according to Mac, plans for a jetfoil catamaran ferry were being discussed, but it would be a few years and, much more ambitiously, the designs for a bridge and tunnel linking Macau to Zhuhai and on to Hong Kong were being drawn up, but I thought the chances of that were slim. It would cost billions and take decades. If the Chinese Government was anything like our own there was no way they'd invest in something that they'd never see the end of.

That left a private jet to make the trip in a little over seven minutes flying time. The taxiing out from the Macau hangar and into the Hong Kong one took longer than the flight. I had initially thought it meant a high-profile business man could avoid the hassles of commercial travel, enjoy his gambling in Macau at be back in Hong Kong by the evening. Now, having seen the two men in the back of my Range Rover and the two Mac was accompanying in the other car, I was doubtful of the businesses being represented. The bejewelled pair were what I imagined senior men within the Triads would look like. I knew little about the organisation, other than the myths and legends that had built up in popular culture, but I knew enough not to ask stupid questions. They didn't talk to me at all. It suited me fine.

A quarter of an hour later I was walking up the steps of the Challenger 604. This time, there were no Customs Officers, no immigration officials, no police. There was no need. This was a short hop from one part of China to another.

Betsy greeted us, the pilot and first officer were back in their seats and we were on our way in minutes. As we made the long taxi back to the main runway, isolated as it was on a strip of reclaimed land on the eastern side of Taipa Island, the rain and wind seemed to increase considerably. The two principal Chinese, who had been chatting to each other since they boarded, went quiet when the first big gust rocked us.

'Don't you boys worry none. Y'all know that my lucky charm will get us up and down, safe and sound.'

They laughed and went back to talking, but I wasn't so sure. The problem with a single runway was that you had no option about the direction you took off in. If that meant a crosswind, which in this case it did, things could get decidedly scary.

We turned, ready to take off and the aircraft felt like it was a scale model, being poked by the pudgy fingers of a disinterested child. The engines spun up to full throttle and to the accompaniment of *Country Roads*, being sung along to by all four Chinese, in a manner which I had to try hard not to laugh at, we battled our way down the main runway. The buffeting seriously worried me, but Mac seemed unconcerned and I doubted even he could have influenced the Air Traffic Controllers to allow us to depart if the crosswinds had been beyond safe limits. Although I couldn't be too sure. The man seemed to have everyone in his pocket. We struggled into the air, I watched the lights on the Friendship Bridge pass from sight and we turned into the wind, towards Hong Kong. Everything became a little calmer. We had hardly gained any height and the song had barely finished when it started up again for our approach into Hong Kong International. At least we were landing into a headwind. We touched down without incident and taxied to the Hong Kong Business Aviation Centre. By the time we got there, parked up in a brightly lit hangar the twin of the one in Macau and allowed the engines to shut down, I'd been in the plane for twenty-three minutes. Seven of which had been airborne.

Mac slapped me hard on the shoulder and led the four Chinese down the aircraft steps. From my small cabin window I could see two waiting Range Rovers and a BMW X-5. The Chinese again went two and two; security and a principal into each of the Rovers. Mac climbed into the first car and pointed for the driver to go. Only when they had all departed did I make my way down the steps to the BMW. Its black tinted windows masked the occupants from any onlookers.

I climbed in to the front passenger seat and nestled my duffel bag between my knees. The driver put the car into gear and we set off.

'Good trip?' Jack asked from behind me.

'Not bad. How are we looking?'

'Good. I see no issues. Other than the storm might make things a bit uncomfortable.'

As if to underline his words, as the car left the cover of the hangar a torrential downpour hammered against it.

28

Hong Kong, October 2005

B en and I had been dropped at the Metro Hotel in the Sham Shui Po area. The single room had been booked and paid for by Jack earlier and we bypassed reception on our way up to it. His other two colleagues, Todd, a specialist driver, and Mikey, another "consultant" who was even bigger than Jack, were in the Holiday Inn about three blocks further south. The BMW was tucked away in valet parking. The Metro was a far cry from the Sands of Macau, but it was three minutes' walk from Lily's mother's tower block and I wasn't going to be here that long. The only reason I needed a room at all was to make a connection with Lily back in France. At 21:00 local time, I opened a chat room and typed "hello". Almost instantly the cursor gave a startled jump.

Hello it is ZZ - Society and Civilisation

Hi, it is Luke

Are you in HK?

Yes – is everything ready with your family?

Yes

And with you?

Yes – I go to pharmacy again – you not let me down this time – you promise Luke

Yes I promise – we will not let you down this time –

Good – for you now in China –

Her threat wasn't lost on me. It hadn't been lost on John, Steve, Lorna or Jack when we had reconvened after Lily had insisted that I go and fetch her mother and brother myself. We knew that it was a massive risk and that potentially she could hand me into the Chinese authorities, but we could see no way that she would have been able to engineer the opportunity and saw no reason why she would have gone to such lengths to get me. I was hardly her UK equivalent. Perhaps Dan with his white hat hacking skills, but not me.

In the end we dismissed it as a viable risk, but we also knew we had to come through this time, or there was a small chance that Lily might wreak revenge by announcing to the world I was in Hong Kong.

Yes – trust me Lily – I will get your family – in 6 hours

Okay – I go now

The username *Anon97* disappeared and I lay back against the bed's headrest.

'So we're still on?' Jack asked.

'Yes. Although…I am beginning to get a bit worried about the storm.'

'Why?'

'We came over a bridge on the way in from the airport?'

'Yeah, the Tsing Ma.'

'I went over a long one in Macau, they seem to like long bridges out here.'

'That they do. Is that a problem?'

'The one here is a suspension bridge,' I said.

'I guess so.'

'Do they shut it in high winds?'

251

'Fuck!' Jack said. 'I don't know.'

'It's the only route to the airport, isn't it?'

'Yeah. There are no alternatives.' Jack switched the main light off and eased the curtains open. The room looked north, up to the mountains surrounding the city. Lightning, both sheet and fork was clearly visible and the downpour hadn't let up. 'The bridges must be built to withstand typhoons out here?'

'You'd hope so,' I said without feeling much hope at all.

'Well that's good. Thing is, according to the news program I watched earlier, this is the tail of a tropical storm. Not even strong enough to get a name. Just number twenty of the year,' he said.

'Really? This doesn't warrant a name?'

'Nope, so a real typhoon must be something else. I've never been in one. Not too sure I'd like to try, but I have to hope that if this isn't one, then the bridge will be open.' He let the curtain fall back into place and turned the lights back on.

'Do you want to sleep?' He asked.

'Eh…no. Even without the sound of the rain and wind, my nerves are jangling. Why, do you?'

'I might catch a few hours. My alarm's set,' he said pointing to the digital watch he wore.

I got up from the bed and took a seat at the small desk. Jack lay down on top of the covers, his feet dangling over the end. I had to admire his calmness and his ability to not worry about something he had no control over. He was sound asleep in five minutes. I stayed wide awake and fretted about rain and wind. I switched the lights out and pulled the curtains apart enough to watch the lightning.

*

We left the hotel at 02:45 local time and walked into the teeth of a gale. By the time we had gone half a block I was soaked through and my duffel bag was almost blown out of my hands half a dozen times. I clutched it to my chest and pressed on. The overhang of shops and apartment blocks proved to be no use at fending off the rain, which was more or less horizontal. The wind whipped it into stinging darts, while instant and monstrous claps of thunder followed each intense lightning flash. The street, wide enough to accommodate three traffic lanes on either side, was bordered by decrepit looking high-rise blocks, and the noise echoed off them like it was trapped in a canyon. The high-mounted street lamps running up the road's central reservation shook and bent and the neon lamps flashed and sparked.

On the right-hand side, halfway up what must have been a 12-storey building, an old air conditioning unit had come loose. It hung by what seemed a single bolt and added a banshee-like wailing and grinding of metal to the rest of the orchestra. I didn't blame the occupant for not trying to lean out and fix it. If it fell it fell. I hoped it would hang on long enough for me and Jack to get past it.

At the corner of Kweilin Street the single canyon turned into a crossroads and the wind whipped around viciously. A telephone box, its glass shattered and metal frame twisted by a small tree that had been uprooted from a mid-pavement planting space, was desperately hanging on to its foundations. Street signs flexed and bent and hundreds of cardboard and plastic boxes whirled high in the air or raced along the road. We hurried on and were offered a little respite until the next junction with Yee Kuk Street and the cross-wind coming down the side street almost knocked me over.

Jack put his hand out to steady me. 'Are you alright,' he yelled.

'Yes. Keep going.'

We were almost bent double but we eventually reached the T-junction with Tung Chau Street. Above us, adjacent to the original road, a modern flyover of a freeway allowed the trapped canyons of air to finally barrel out, giving them an escape route, letting the wind's intensity lessen. It did nothing to diminish the amount of rain.

On the left of the junction, a modern, clean tower block that wouldn't have looked out of place next to my apartment in St George's Wharf. On the right, twenty or thirty floors of 1960s or 70s vertical misery. It was this one that Lily's family were in. A corner shop, literally set into the foundation corner of the building was boarded and shuttered. Next to it, a metal-framed door with a reinforced glass top half. It led to the tiniest of spaces, off which was a single elevator and another door to stairs. Jack and I crowded in, happy to get out of the wind and rain if only for a brief spell. The neon lamps of the freeway provided enough residual light for me to see my watch. It had taken us seven minutes to walk what should have taken three. We waited and I worried that we'd not even get to the airport.

At 03:00 the lift door opened and a small woman stepped out. She wore a red head scarf and a long, close woven coat. In her right hand she held a single plastic bag. A young boy held her left hand. He was dressed in boots and jeans and an anorak with the hood zipped up firmly so that his face was barely visible.

I shuffled back and allowed her into the space. 'Veronica?'

'Yes. You are Luke?' She asked and proffered the plastic bag. Inside was a plastic lunch box and a few cardboard containers of juice. At the bottom was an old blue coloured passport. I took it out and held the photo up to the glass of the door. Veronica took her head scarf off. The passport photo showed a strikingly beautiful young woman, with strong features and a confidence in her eyes. The woman in front of me was older, her face lined, her hair greying, but as she looked back at me, her eyes held the same look as the photo. Confidence, perhaps even rebelliousness. I saw the mother and I knew her daughter.

'And this is Ethan?'

'Yes.'

I kept the passport but gave her the plastic bag back. 'Is this all you want to take?'

'There is nothing more.'

'We're good to go, Jack,' I said.

He pulled his mobile out and sent a pre-drafted text to two different numbers.

Veronica replaced her head scarf and as she did, Ethan hunkered in next to her legs.

A minute later the headlights of the BMW illuminated the torrential rain and small rivers of water flowing down Tung Chau Street.

'Ready?' I asked Veronica.

'Ready,' she replied and lifted Ethan into her arms.

I held the entrance door and Jack ran to the car. Even he struggled to hold the rear door open against the gusts while Veronica climbed in with Ethan. I ran out and slid in next, then Jack. He slammed the door and with Ethan perched on Veronica's knee we set off. No one spoke. I glanced to Jack. He shook his head. I checked my watch. It was 03:02. Minutes ticked by. The car drove fast but legal, wind-buffeted and rain lashed. My eyes flicked between my watch and Jack, 3:03, 3:04, 3:05. Each time he responded with a small shake of his head and my concerns mounted about what the hell was happening in France.

*

Lily had excused herself from the large kitchen table before dinner had finished.

'Are you okay,' Major Shao had asked.

'Yes. I'm fine,' she answered with a tight grimace and walked through to her bedroom. Unlike the other four, this was exclusively hers. Being the only female on the team had advantages. The Major had his own room of course, and the other seven soldiers shared the remaining three. Not that it meant they were crowded. The large house on the corner of Rue des Azalées and Rue des Hortensias was airy and spacious, with a swimming pool in the rear garden. Lily had been reminded of her old home in Hong Kong. The one she and her family had been ripped from because her father had been declared an enemy of the State. She'd thought she'd lost everything. Then she'd lost Paul and knew true devastation. Yet here she was, half a world away. Rising each morning, taking a long, hot shower, dressing in feminine, civilian clothes, walking through to a beautiful slate-floored kitchen so tastefully decorated and superbly equipped. Hearing birdsong and, when the winds blew from the north-east, smelling the fragrance of a forest less than half a kilometre away. France was beautiful and her life was easy.

Their cover was simple. The massive Provence Power Station, with its incredibly tall chimney, was over twenty years old. Its coal-fired generators were in need of an overhaul and preliminary work to convert them to burn other fuels. A Chinese company had won the contract. Lily knew they had won it thanks to the endeavours of her team a year before, when they had hacked into the contract bids database and undercut all other companies.

Now, the small commune of Gardanne had over two hundred Chinese living and working in its midst. The company had rented large houses north, south, east and west. There were minibuses shuttling the workers in and out on three rolling shifts. The town was benefitting immeasurably from the influx of commerce and the local press and population were won over by the politeness of the workers and how they conducted themselves. Lily knew why they were so well-behaved. Strict penalties faced you at home if you were unruly. To bring shame on the People when abroad on a State-sponsored contract would be met with severe punishments. The workers were warned before they left China and regularly since arriving in France. Work, earn, spend, be friendly, fit in. The company sponsored local events and school competitions and guided tours of the work being done. They hosted a public festival to celebrate the Chinese and French people and their close relationships. All the workers were given the day off and had to be in attendance.

All bar eight.

Major Shao, Lily and the rest of the spearhead section of the PLA Cyber Unit Battalion 60288 had slipped into the town easily. They even had passes and high-visibility uniforms with the Power Station logo on. But they kept an eight-to-five roster and their work was worth more than a thousand power station contracts. Sergeant Wai, team leader had been the first name down on the deployment order. Outwardly calm and dedicated. Inwardly, still seething with the State and the People. As soon as she'd arrived in the pretty town, she knew it was her chance to take revenge.

Lily lay on her bed and tried to calm her thoughts. It was still light and there was another two and a half hours to wait. She regretted not stealing the Major's phone, but now, even if she did steal it, she didn't have a number for Luke and her mother didn't possess a cell phone. One of the restrictions the family were still forced to live under. There was a home phone, but Lily knew it was monitored. So she would have to trust again, as she had done the first time. The time she was left standing outside the nearby pharmacy, hopping from foot to foot, desperation creeping up and overtaking her. Then, when she could wait no longer, she had trudged the short walk back to the house. She'd been gone twenty-five minutes when it should have taken her ten. Major Shao had been severe in his consternation. He had taken her aside from the rest of the team and demanded she tell him where she had been. What she had been doing. She held out a paper bag and said, tearfully, 'I'm so—sor—sorry. I thought it would be next week, but it started too soon. I had run out. I ha—had to buy,' she forced him to take the closed bag, 'these. I had to ask the pharmacist if I could use their toilet.'

The Major had looked into the bag and the open box of tampons, with one missing from the four rows of nine, had a physical effect on him. He recoiled and almost threw the bag back at her. Lost in a world that he knew nothing of, he stammered an apology of sorts and a warning that went badly for him. 'Don't do it again. I mean. Not. Well. Not *that*. I—I don't mean, don't do that ag—I mean. You obviously have no way to stop tha—I mean…don't go out like that again. Take someone wit— I mean…'

Lily could see the horror that she might ask him to go for a walk with her stop that train of thought. In the end he asked if she was alright.

'Yes, Sir.'

'Fine. We shall say no more.'

When she'd got to her bedroom and with no knowledge of why the British hadn't taken her, she cried and panicked all night. Had they picked up her family? Was a telephone call going to make Major Shao arrest her? Would she and her family be reunited in a prison cell? The morning had dawned with no such calls. No arrest. No news at all. She had to assume the British hadn't picked up her family. Or if they had, it hadn't been discovered yet. She had to know. After they had finished breakfast, she'd taken Major Shao to one side.

'Major. I am sorry about last night.'

'I said, it is done with. No more need for anything to be said,' he stammered in renewed embarrassment.

'Yes, Major, but I am afraid my, umm, my, cycle is not as usual this month. I know I have already used my weekly call home on Sunday, but I would like to talk to my mother about this. Could I perhaps—'

'Yes. Certainly. Ring home,' he said and pointed her to the front lounge space of the house that had been turned into their operations room. The one landline they had connected sat next to encryption devices which allowed it to be used for secure communications back to China, but the soldiers were also allowed to use it for a weekly call home. It was obviously monitored and all calls recorded, still, it was the only way. Her mother would answer, or not. Of course she had answered and played along with the cues from Lily. A meaningless conversation that simply told Lily she and her family were still safe. When she hung up, she still had no clue why the extraction had been cancelled, but Luke would tell her when she went back into the chatroom.

Now, seventeen days later, she was going to risk it all again. On blind faith that her family would be picked up from Hong Kong, although she had tried to put her own guarantee in place by insisting Luke went to get them himself. Not that she could prove he was actually there, but she hoped he was. She had a gut instinct that he was trustworthy. And if he wasn't, this time she would destroy him. This time she would release the emails and phone conversations she had logged on him and the American, Stückl.

The thought caused her to catch her breath and sit up. Her father would be delighted she was striking a blow against the communists, but he wouldn't approve of her destroying an individual's life because of his lifestyle. She felt her father's disappointment that she would even consider such a thing and knew she wouldn't use the material she had against Luke or the American. All she could do was make a silent wish that things went well and the spirit of her father would help guide her.

She lay back down and tried to quieten her mind. It was useless. Thoughts and fears cascaded through her and sapped her energy. She rolled from side to side and willed the time to pass.

An hour to go. The date number on the watch face showed the 13th. A lucky number for her culture. She hoped it would be the same for the British.

*

At 20:45 she joined the rest of the unit in the front lounge. Slightly smaller than the one they used for an operations room, it still accommodated the eight of them comfortably. The only issue was most of them didn't speak French, so their TV viewing was restricted to DVDs sent from back home.

The Major moved up on the couch. 'Ah, Sergeant Wai. You have missed the beginning, but come, join us. We received it today directly from the Army's Film Unit. It's "*On the Mountain of Tai Hang*", you know?'

Lily did, but frowned.

'The best picture winner at last month's Golden Roosters? It swept lots of awards?' He continued, keen for her to be enthused.

Lily was familiar with the Sino-Japanese war movie, but she continued to frown. 'I'm sorry, Sir. But I don't think I'm up for that at the moment. Umm, Sir, could I have a word?' she said and took a step out of the room.

'Corporal Han, pause that will you?' The Major called as he got up.

Lily had hoped he would have been distracted by the movie, but now he was going to devote his attention to her. That was a pain. She knew it came from her being the most experienced on the unit. The Major never ignored her.

He joined her in the hallway to the kitchen. 'Yes, Sergeant?'

'Sir, I need to go to the pharmacy again.'

He hesitated and his expression seemed to falter between confusion and concern. 'Are you ill?'

'Not ill, Sir. Just cramping.'

'And you need to go to the pharmacy…?'

'I need magnesium tablets, Sir.'

'Really?' What for?'

Since agreeing with Luke to go for a second attempt at extraction, Lily had spent a lot of time coming up with her reasons to get out of the house. She had figured the Major might have been embarrassed by her previous cover, but he wasn't stupid. He would know the actual cycles of a woman's body. He was married back home. Her excuse relied on him not being completely ignorant of a woman's body.

'Well, Sir. You know a couple of weeks ago I had my p—'

'Yes, yes, Sergeant.'

'Well, it's been a couple of weeks, Sir. I get cramps sometimes, when I am ovulating.'

The Major tried to give his best look of concern and only managed to give a look of despair.

'Especially after a particularly heavy peri—'

'Yes. Yes. Certainly. I understand. So you need magnesium. Do we not have any in the first aid kit?' He asked.

Lily watched the red flush spreading up from his neck. 'No, Sir. I'm afraid not. I also, well I need a few other personal items,' she added, desperate that he wouldn't send one of the other soldiers in her stead.

'Right. Okay. No need to detail a list.' He held his hand up and Lily went to turn away but the Major turned first.

'Corporal Han?'

The heavy-set Corporal, originally from Hulun Buir in Inner Mongolia, leapt up from his seat. 'Yes, Sir?'

'Go with Sergeant Wai, please. It is late and she has an errand to run. I don't want her to be alone.'

'Yes, Sir.'

Lily's heart sunk as Han, a small mountain of a man, moved past her and grabbed his coat.

'Thank you, Sir,' she said to the Major and gave him a weak smile. She knew if this worked he would probably die. Her heart ached for him and his family. He was a nice man. But then again, her father had been nice too. So had Paul. She stiffened her resolve, as she had every day since she had been dragged from her home. Pulling on her jacket, she led Corporal Han out the door.

The walk down Rue des Hortensias took three minutes. On the way they joined Rue des Capucines and passed a small monument dedicated to the memory of the Sixth Group of Foreign

Workers and to the Spanish Republicans who had fought within the French Resistance in World War II. One of the Privates had translated the inscription in the first weeks they'd been here. Lily had been inspired by the notion of small groups of people doing so much damage to authoritarian regimes. She had researched about the resistance, the foreign workers and the disgrace of the Vichy government as and when she could and always mindful to cover her tracks. As she had with every chatroom session she had shared with Luke. Free access to all of the Internet was something she was looking forward to in England.

Han was a cheerful big guy. He chatted amiably with her about the start of the war movie he and the others had been watching and how pleasant an evening it was. By the time they'd exhausted that conversation they were already at the pharmacy. It sat mid-row in a small shopping complex, home to a supermarket, newsagent, hairdressers, beauty salon, a women's boutique, a café and a real estate office. All of them, bar the pharmacy were shut. The large well-lit car park was empty save for three cars and a motorbike, all parked in front of pharmacy.

Lily checked the shop's wall clock as she walked in. Six minutes before nine. There were only two other customers in the place. A man in full leathers, with a motorbike helmet tucked under his arm, and an older woman who was in conversation with the pharmacist. A younger woman sat at the till, halfway along the main counter.

Lilly picked up a metal basket and started moving up and down the aisles. Han followed her until she stopped at the rows of sanitary products. He hesitated, looked at the shelves and then quickly walked off towards the men's product aisle. She checked the clock again. Five minutes. She checked her watch. Either both were frozen, or time was moving this slowly.

After traversing the aisles a couple of times, carefully studying the product descriptions for numerous items and adding a few to her basket, the clock hands finally and excruciatingly slowly, slewed their way to nine o'clock. She walked down to the free-standing product carousel that stood just inside the doorway. Her fingers revolved the display's inflatable neck pillows, money belts and power converters, but her eyes were fixed firmly on the car park. A medium-sized sedan pulled up, parallel to the store fronts. Lily prepared herself. She watched the vehicle closely, she held her basket loosely, ready to drop it and run. The front passenger door of the car opened and a harassed looking woman stepped out. Lily could see a man in the driver's seat. The interior light showed a child's car seat in the back and a crying toddler, almost bright red in its face, fists balled and swinging in the air like it was boxing an unseen adversary. The woman shut the door behind her and walked towards the shop. The car pulled away to park. Lily let out the breath she'd been holding and then jumped in fright as Han put his hand on her arm.

'Sergeant? Are you okay?'

'Yes, why?' It came out forced. She could hear the stress in her voice. She tried again. 'Sorry, you startled me. Yes, I'm fine, why?'

'I was asking if you had everything, but you seemed to be away in a world of your own,' the Corporal said. His round face and soft features held no malice. She liked him as much as she liked the other members of her team. He was a good programmer. A couple of years older than her, he'd been talent-spotted at Beijing University. The PLA had allowed him to finish his degree and then recruited him into the cyber units. She wondered if he would be held accountable as the Major would. She hoped not. Though if he was, she would feel regret.

She was about to answer that she only needed a few more things, but she and Han had to step out of the way of the harassed mother entering the shop. As the door was swinging closed, Lily saw the reflection of another car pulling up out front. It parked parallel as the other had done, but was facing in the opposite direction, towards the exit of the car park. The nearside back door opened from the inside and was left ajar, hardly noticeable, barely a crack.

Lily fought to control her voice. 'Ju-long?' she asked, using Han's first name and stepping forward so that he, with his hand still on her arm, had to turn into the shop, away from the door. 'Can you ask the pharmacist for a packet of paracetamol? The strongest they have without needing a prescription?'

'You aren't feeling well, are you?'

'Oh, I'll be fine. It's a bad headache, that's all, but if you get them then I can finish up and we can leave.'

'Umm. How do I ask for paracetamol in French?'

Despite the tension she could feel coursing through her, she laughed. 'Between our team we speak almost twenty languages, yet here we are, and neither of us can speak the local tongue. Your English is okay though, isn't it?'

'Not too bad.'

'Then try that and point at your head a lot.'

Han chuckled and his round face beamed down at her. She was suddenly hit with a wave of remorse. If she ran and he did nothing, he most certainly would be punished. He might be killed. Her father's disappointment washed over her again. She reached out and patted Han's arm. 'Good luck.'

He took it as encouragement for his interaction with the pharmacist and walked away.

She moved to the rear most aisle of the shop and glanced up at the clock. Now time had gone into fast forward. It was three minutes past. The car wouldn't wait for ever. She picked up a bottle of shampoo and looked through to the shop's main window. The interior was reflected and she could see the pharmacist, still talking to the old lady, while the harassed mother waited impatiently to one side. Han stood slightly behind the two and Lily could see he was still chuckling to himself. The man in the leathers had set his helmet on the front counter and was talking to the pretty young woman on the till as she scanned his purchases. CCTV cameras covered the whole of the counter area, from where prescriptions were put in, to where they were dispensed. At least two of the cameras covered the spot where Han stood.

Her decision was made as she surveyed the people in the tableau. Lily put her basket on the ground and rehearsed in her head the movements she needed to make. Then rehearsed them again. A deep breath. Another look at the reflected scene. It would give Han a reasonable defence. She had to try to give him that. Another breath and then she walked down the far side of the shop, cut across the middle aisle and came out opposite the till. She turned right and with her stronger left hand grabbed the biker's helmet off the counter. As Han turned to face her with his still beaming face, she swung as hard as she could and brought the heavy helmet up in a perfect arc. It hit the tall Mongolian between his right cheek and temple. His nose broke and blood sprayed up into the air before splashing the pharmacy's white shelves and the harassed mother's pale face with a vibrant slash of colour. Han's eyes rolled back in his head and he collapsed to his left like a felled oak. Lily froze for a moment as his bulk careered into the nearest shop display and sent a hundred tubes of Vitamin-C tablets cascading across the tiled floor. The crash broke the spell that had held her and she ran for the door. The biker flailed his arm at her but she ducked under it, threw his helmet at him and almost ripped the door off its hinges in her fury and panic. She headed straight for the car, its rear door now fully open. Leaping in almost sideways, she managed to slam the door shut as the car accelerated out of the car park.

Lily struggled to sit upright as the car took a sharp right. A fierce left hander threw her halfway across the back seat and into a grey-haired man. He helped her sit up and she finally was able to reach for the seat belt.

'Hello Lily, I'm Steve. Would you like to speak to your mother?'

*

Jack finally gave me a thumbs up. A moment later his phone began to ring, he spoke a few brief words and then passed it to me. I passed it to Veronica. 'It's Lily.'

The tears started almost immediately and even though I didn't understand the language, it was apparent Veronica Wai was extremely pleased. She let Ethan listen and the little boy spoke for the first time since coming out of the lift.

I let them talk for a few minutes and then advised Veronica we needed to keep things short. She would have plenty of time to talk to Lily very soon. I took the phone from here.

'Steve? You on track?'

'Kind of. We have a small change of plan.'

I tried to stifle the rising panic I felt. 'What's changed?'

'We're not heading for Calais. We had an alternate offered and I thought it might have been a struggle to get all the way through France if there were any complications. Good job as it turns out.'

'Why? What complications have there been?'

'Nothing important, Luke. A bit of a scuffle that I'll tell you about later. The change is that Rowanne, the SF liaison Wing Commander you met, rang me yesterday to advise she had a helicopter from RAF Odiham, supporting part of the Canadian French exercise happening in Marseille. It went unserviceable and being a Special Forces helicopter, they diverted to Aubagne.'

'Where's that?'

'French Foreign Legion Barracks. Half hour drive from where we picked Lily up.'

I was confused. 'Really? Will the helicopter be fixed in time?'

Steve's laugh surprised me. 'No Luke. The helicopter's not really broken. It's just sitting there waiting for us.'

'Oh, I see,' I said, even though I didn't. 'Why is it sitting there?'

'Because Rowanne was pissed that the original op was pulled and we left the asset hanging in the wind. She checked with John and he confirmed that the Foreign Secretary never said you couldn't use a RAF helo in France.'

'Good for her. So you're heading there now?'

'Yep. Legion base is secure and the helicopter crews work with them regularly. I'm even dressed in flying kit for the first time in a long, long time.'

I wondered again at who on earth Steve Jäeger was and what his background included. I'd find out one day. For now I checked out the window; ten more kilometres to the bridge. 'How will you get onto the base?' I asked.

'Our current IDs are good for Sean and me.'

I doubted Steve was referring to the nondescript ID he'd shown me all those months ago. I guessed he'd be showing whatever real ID would get him through a French Foreign Legion base. 'And Lily?'

'She'll be in the trunk by then. We get through the front gate, drive to the helo pad, up the ramp and away. No one other than Rowanne and the aircrew will know.'

As a plan, it was very good. If there were any squadrons in the Air Force who knew how to keep a secret, it was the Special Forces support squadrons. I began to relax. 'I think you mean in the boot, Steve?'

'Yeah, yeah, *toma-toe* – tom-aaa-to. How's it going with you?'

I had decided I would be straight with him about the storm and the possible bridge closures, but I didn't get the opportunity. Jack tapped me on the arm and pointed out the window. We were on the initial approaches to the Tsing Ma Bridge. Massive overhead signs showed large red Xs and arrows pointing away from the three main carriageways. I felt real fear as I saw police cars lining the sides of the road that the diversions pointed to.

'Steve, I'll call you back.' I ended the call and handed the phone back to Jack. I was aware he was suddenly tense. He pocketed the phone and I saw him balling his fists. The driver, Todd, was gripping the steering wheel so tightly I could see his knuckles whitening. There were uniformed police waving night-glow sticks back and forth, directing us down and away from the bridge roadway.

'How the fuck have they intercepted us?' Jack whispered to me. 'How can they have traced us?'

'Maybe it's just an educated guess. We were odds on to head for the airport,' I said, but I had no clue how they knew we had taken Veronica and Ethan. Surely they would have stopped Lily if they'd known? Maybe they'd tried. Maybe that was the scuffle Steve had mentioned. I felt a wave of tiredness sweep over me. On its heels, a wave of intense sadness for Veronica and Ethan.

'Boss, what do we do?' Mikey asked from the front seat and I could see him starting to reach for the front glove compartment. I had no doubt that these American "consultants" would be carrying some form of weaponry, though God alone knew how they had brought it into Hong Kong with them. I was about to protest, but Jack beat me to it.

'Slow and steady, Mikey. We have no choice. Just keep going. Follow their directions. We can't start a shooting war,' Jack said.

The tension inside the car was as electric as the lightning outside...except for Veronica. I realised she was looking down at Ethan and seemed unaware of the diversions and imminent roadblocks.

'Veronica, I am so sorry,' I said.

She glanced up and out of the windows. 'Why are you sorry? It is not your fault we have to use the lower deck.'

'Pardon?'

'Lower deck,' she repeated.

'I don't understand,' I said.

'Oh. I thought my English was good. Maybe I am out of practise?'

'No, your English is perfect. I don't know what you mean by lower deck.'

'Two lanes run inside the lower train deck of the bridge. All cars use them in heavy winds. It is noisy going through and the petrol fumes are heavy sometimes, but that is not your fault.'

As she spoke I saw the last of the large overhead electronic signs before we left the main carriageway. It confirmed what she had said. Todd relaxed his grip on the wheel and Jack, Mikey and I breathed again.

'There's an enclosed deck. Of course there is,' I said.

Veronica looked genuinely confused. 'Yes. Of course there is. Otherwise the airport would be inaccessible in high winds and we get a lot of those in the typhoon season. I have only been through the lower deck once. Many years ago with my husband.'

I was tempted to ask her so much about her family, but I knew that could wait until we were safely back in the UK, so I bit my tongue and breathed in the petrol fumes of the lower deck and thanked the Tsing Ma Bridge designers for their cleverness.

Twelve minutes after we exited from the lower deck we pulled into the hangar at the Hong Kong Business Aviation Centre. It was empty save for the Challenger 604. As we came to a stop next to the steps, Mac appeared in the aircraft's doorway and gave a wave.

I escorted Veronica and Ethan up the steps and then went back to thank Jack and his team.

'Didn't really have a lot to do. Did we?' He said.

'No, I guess not, but I appreciated the security. See you around.'

*

Ten minutes later the aircraft was taxiing out to the main runway. Mac and I retook our original seats. Veronica and Betsy were both fussing over Ethan.

'That big guy in the vehicle,' Mac said. 'Didn't look like no Chinese Hong Kong cab driver.'

'A bit of personal security,' I said.

'Big son-of-a-bitch, weren't he?'

'Yep. He has friends who are bigger.'

'I'm always on the lookout for boys like that. You might put him in touch with me someday?' Mac held his hand out across the aisle. 'Deal?'

I shook it. 'Deal…And you're sure this next bit will work?'

'Of course.'

I reflected on Jack's attitude to the rain and wind. I had no control over what was about to occur, but I knew that everything we'd done so far was all going to come down to the next half hour. I allowed *Country Roads* to wash over me as the Challenger 604 soared into a very unsettled sky.

*

Veronica and Ethan were temporarily hidden in the storage containers under the double bed that Betsy had made up. I was stretched out on top of it.

The hangar lights in Macau were as bright as ever, but as I craned my neck to see and not be seen, only a single car, a dark saloon was parked within it. We came to a stop and the engines were idled, not shut down. This was designed to be a very quick visit. Hong Kong to Macau, eight minutes flying time and an almost sideways landing, followed by a six-minute taxi to the hangar.

A Chinese to Chinese flight, so no officials on the Hong Kong side. Macau to Dubai was an international departure and had to be attended by an immigration official to stamp the passports. It was the same man who had met us on arrival, Muhai.

Mac sauntered off the aircraft with Betsy. He told Muhai that I was sleeping. I'd lost a lot on the tables and had drunk too much in response.

Betsy handed her own passport and the flight crews' over. Easier than them having to get out and into the cockpit. Standard procedure for Mac and his aircraft apparently.

After a series of vigorous stamps, Mac wished Muhai well and in turn the Chinese man waved him goodbye. Sixteen minutes later we were airborne. Another ninety and we left Chinese airspace. Within seventeen hours of leaving Macau, we were landing to the accompaniment of *Country Roads*, at Aberdeen's Dyce airport and taxiing to a freight hangar at the northern end of the main runway. Andy Gibson from the SIS was there to meet us and escorted Veronica and Ethan down to a waiting car. There were no officials from customs, immigration or any other departments. I grabbed my duffel bag, shook hands with Mac and Betsy, shouted a thank you through to the cockpit and walked down the steps.

As the car carrying Veronica and Ethan pulled out, a Mercedes carrying John Leofric pulled in and the window rolled down. 'Nice job, Luke. Get in. You must be exhausted.'

29

London, October 2005

The plan was simple. SIS would run the debrief initially and because it was an "off-the-books" operation they would keep Lily, Veronica and Ethan in an "off-the-books" safe house located on an isolated farm in a place called Old Clachnastrone, nestled in a meander of the River Spey, a mile south of Grantown-on-Spey in the highlands of Scotland. For places in the middle of nowhere much, it ticked all the boxes. I was to stay in a hotel in Grantown and be available when needed. What John hadn't told me was that Dan would be waiting in the hotel bar for me. I almost cried, but managed not to. Instead I gave him a hug and we managed to make it masculine enough so that the barman, a raw cut highlander, saw nothing untoward. As I stepped back I noticed that Dan's left eye was discoloured.

'What happened you?'

He raised his hand to the side of his head, 'Oh, not a lot. Unloading the van at the house and the door swung into me.'

'Are you okay?'

'Yeah, thick head, I'm fine. I got you a gin,' he said and slid a glass across the bar.

As I drank the perfectly mixed shot, Dan told me John had briefed the team on what had happened with Lily and asked any of them who had reservations to put in paperwork and he would see them transferred out. None had taken up his offer.

'And you?' I asked.

'He requested I come off leave early. They're gonna need me to sit in on the technical side of the debriefs, I wouldn't miss it.'

'And Shirlene and Ryan?'

He reached out for his own drink and took a long sip. 'Shirlene is Shirlene. Not a lot's changed. Ryan's Ryan. Happy as a two year old should be.'

'And you?'

'You asked already. I'm good.'

I lifted my glass and walked across to the table set into the hotel's bay window. Dan followed along.

'I know I asked before, but I'm going to ask again. And you?'

He sat down and in the motion his resolve of keeping up a front dissolved. 'I'm broken Luke. It's been a week and I have no clue how I'm going to cope with her?'

'You didn't get hit by a door, did you?'

He shook his head. 'This was as a result of me saying I had to go away, come up here, not that I could tell her where or why.'

'Did you hit her back?' I asked, strangely hoping he would say yes and dreading it at the same time.

'No! Of course not.'

I saw the barman look over. 'Okay, sorry. It was a dumb question.'

'And there's one other thing.'

This time I hesitated. He looked intense, his eyes and mouth hard set. I felt the pain tearing at my heart again. To look at him and not be able to hold him each and every day would destroy me. 'Go on,' I finally managed.

'She was here for one day and I was apart from you for that same day and I knew. As certain as I've known anything. I don't love her anymore, if I ever did. And I do love you.'

He said it so quietly and yet the force of his words almost knocked me from my seat.

'Really?' It came out too high-pitched and I sounded incredulous, even to my own ears. As soon as I'd said it I regretted it. He looked hurt. 'I'm sorry, I didn't mean that to sound the way it did…I mean…it's…well…'

He held me in a stare and I realised, as he'd told me, so I could finally tell him. 'Dan, I've loved you since I met you.' The smile that I adored spread across his face.

He lifted his glass in a toast and leant closer. 'We're the only two of the team here, by the way. John Leofric and Steve Jäeger are staying somewhere else, probably somewhere bigger and better.'

'I think this place is perfect.'

'Good, me too. Our rooms are apparently next door to one another.'

'How handy.'

'Luke, one last thing before we go to bed.' He gave me a look that was carnivorous. Any jet lag I had was brushed away.

'Go on.'

'I'm going to file for divorce.'

I felt a surge of happiness and a sharp stab of sadness. 'What about Ryan?'

'I'm going to sue for custody and once it's granted, I'm leaving the Service.'

'Custody?'

'Yeah. I'll get it too. She drinks, she cusses and she's violent. I can prove it and I have more money than her.'

I wasn't sure swearing and profanity would sway a judge, but then again, I didn't understand half of what Americans thought was acceptable or not. I was sure that Dan hadn't finished. 'And?'

'If I do it in the right order, I'll leave with all my benefits and then…'

'Yes, and then?'

'And then I'd like to live life as I always wanted to. As I should be living. I'd like to stay in England with you. For the rest of my life. Would you have me?'

'Of course.'

*

The following day was Saturday and John picked us up from the hotel early. We pulled into the driveway of the secluded farmyard with its magnificent main house hewn from granite, in time to see Veronica and Lily walking with Ethan between them swinging him up with every step.

I safely assumed it was Lily, not that I had actually met her. She was slim, petite, doll-like even. Most of what I had imagined. Straight black hair, longer than I had envisaged. I also expected her to be formal, regimented, reserved. When I stepped from the car, Andy Gibson, standing in the frame of the front door, pointed me out. Lily let go of Ethan's hand and ran across the open yard. Without words she jumped up and threw her arms around me. Slight as she was I took a step backwards, such was her enthusiasm.

'Thank you Luke, thank you. Thank you for getting me and my family out.'

'You are most welcome.'

'I will not disappoint. I will give you enough ammunition to destroy the Chinese. I promise.'

'I have no doubt,' I said, managing to gently ease her back down on to the ground. 'This is Captain Stückl,' I said as Dan got out of the car.

'I know,' said Lily and a strange look seemed to briefly cloud her features. I couldn't figure what had gone through her mind.

'Are you alright?'

'Yes. Of course, yes,' she said and the moment was gone. 'Captain Stückl. My former nemesis,' she giggled. 'Now my comrade-in-arms? Yes?'

'I hope so,' said Dan and he led off towards the main house.

*

By the Sunday night we knew about Lily's father, her journey to the PLA and the teams she had led. We understood their mission and the organisation of the cyber battalions. We knew that they were being directed by the very top of the Communist regime in Beijing. This was the proof of what Steve Jäeger had inferred to me all that time ago; State-sponsored espionage on an industrial scale. We knew what the next target sets were for her unit in particular and a snippet of what others were tasked with. We didn't know the overall strategy that was driving everything, but I was beginning to see flashes of light in a storm of grey circulating in my head. I knew, with more information and more time, I'd extract the overall concepts. For now, we had enough.

Andy Gibson convened a meeting with John, Steve, Dan and me. 'We need to get Lily and her family rehoused and into a protection program. Then we need to let you and GCHQ get her working on defensive and potentially offensive code. Steve, NSA will want to sit in on that?'

Steve agreed.

'First though, I think we have enough to brief Cobra,' Andy said. 'I warned off Sir Colin, last night,' he continued, referring to the Chief of MI6, 'and he concurred. We've issued a preliminary briefing note to all the usual suspects.'

I was delighted. Finally we were going to be able to raise the Chinese cyber threat to, as John had once said, the highest levels of Government. Andy's reference to Cobra meant the Cabinet Office Briefing Rooms and specifically room A, where high-level security meetings would be chaired by the Prime Minster. The membership of each meeting depended on the subject, but almost always included the Home, Foreign and Defence Secretaries, the Chiefs of MI5, MI6, GCHQ, Defence Intelligence and the Chairman of the Joint Intelligence Committee. Surely when they learnt of what Lily had told us they would finally react.

Andy continued, 'Sir Colin feels that, given the unorthodox manner in which this was all done, Cobra are going to want all the main players in the room.' He finished speaking and was looking directly at me.

'Is that my cue to say something?' I asked. 'Because I'm not quite sure what you're telling me.'

'Sir Colin wants you to be present. As well as Director Leofric, obviously.'

'Obviously,' John said. 'The Foreign Secretary will definitely want me there to answer for my crimes.' He laughed, but I knew the Minister would not be happy we circumvented her orders.

'Eh, you know that I'm only a Flight Lieutenant, right?' I said. 'I'm not sure I get to brief the Prime Minister.'

'I know, Luke, but to paraphrase what Sir Colin told me, you are the acknowledged leader of your team. You pulled them together from nothing in a little less than a year, you organised and led the defence of UK networks when no one else gave a damn and you orchestrated the extraction of a potentially valuable asset. He thinks you being in the room is the only way that the politicians do not go apeshit over the unauthorised nature of the operation.'

'You know I didn't plan that extraction, right?' I ended it with a smirk and the humour wasn't lost on Steve, John and Andy.

'Yeah, we do, and we know that you won't be the only one for the high jump if they don't see the value in Lily, but I can't see how they wouldn't,' Andy replied.

'Okay then. I guess I've come this far.'

'Great. There is one more thing,' Andy said.

'Go on.'

'Sir Colin thinks there's a possibility the PM will want to meet Lily.'

'What for?' I asked and then realised I already knew the answer. When I'd been involved with the Iraqi defector debriefs, the Prime Minister had occasionally asked to speak directly with the more senior figures that had come over from Saddam's Republican Guard or any of the government ministries. He seemed to think he could read the measure of the person by talking to them. I always thought he was a typical New Labour idiot, full of his own self-importance and believing his own hype. I saved Andy the bother of answering. 'No, it's okay. I know why he might want to talk to her. What about Veronica and Ethan?'

'They'll stay here. Lorna's going to come up and look after them for a day or two. It's a quick jaunt down to London and back up for Lily, she might not even be called for, but...' Andy allowed his sentence to hang.

I knew it was left there for me. 'But?' I asked.

'But,' he continued. 'This is still an unauthorised operation. I elected to be a part of it like the rest of you, but I can't drag in any other officers. Also, we're using this particular safe house because it is completely off the books. We can't use any officially sanctioned ones in London and we need to get Lily down there and prepared for a Cobra meeting on Wednesday morning.'

I realised all, bar Dan, were looking at me and I realised that Steve, Andy and John had already decided what was going to happen. Now all I had to do was agree. 'You want me to take Lily down to London, keep her with me and then pitch up for a Cobra meeting on Wednesday?'

'See,' Steve said, 'I knew he'd figure it out quickly.'

'Once the meeting approves the operation retrospectively, we can swing our whole protection program mechanism in to place. We can relocate the family and begin to really exploit Lily's capabilities. So you're okay with this?' Andy asked.

'Like I said, I've come this far, I can't see why not. Drive to London and go to a meeting. It's not flying into China and recovering a family,' I said with nonchalance.

Andy's face didn't reflect the humour I'd been hoping for this time. 'Remember Luke, she's technically in the country illegally and if she's as valuable an asset as you say, the Chinese will be looking for her. So low key. All the way. Look after her, you'll be her only set of eyes. Yes?'

I hadn't really considered that the other side might want to get her back. 'Yes. Low key. We go back to London, she stays indoors. I look after her. On Wednesday morning I go to the briefing and what? Does she come with me?'

'No. You got to Cobra and I'll come and babysit her in your apartment until she's called for, or not,' Andy said. 'If she is needed, I'll escort her myself.'

'Okay, then yes, I can do that.' I said.

'Great. I'll arrange a suitable car and you Dan and Lily can leave tomorrow,' John said.

I was delighted. That meant another night with Dan.

*

We left early on the Monday. John Leofric's idea of a suitable car for Dan, Lily and me to travel down in was a BMW 5-series, so the journey was pleasant enough. Lily spent most of the time gazing out of the windows at the scenery and occasionally asking questions about where we were. For a young woman who might have to meet the Prime Minister she seemed remarkably calm.

'He is British and polite. I have seen him on television and he seems a good man,' she answered when I queried her. 'He is not likely to hurt me or hit me or be aggressive to me, is he?'

'No, of course not,' Dan said.

'Well then there is nothing to fear.'

I snorted.

Dan apologised to Lily on my behalf. 'Ignore him, Lily. Luke is a bit of a Conservative and traditionalist.'

'I know,' Lily said.

I glanced into the rear-view mirror and made eye contact with her. 'How do you know?'

'I told you, I read your emails. I understand your sarcasms and inflections. Each cyber unit has advisors, linguistic advisors that help others who might not be as fluent. I am one of the advisors for English. My father and mother were both privately educated within the British schools in Hong Kong, so my brother and I were constantly being corrected, especially by my mother, to use proper English.'

'But when you typed to me in the chat room, you used…' I paused and tried to find the right words.

'Clipped phrases,' she offered. 'Like, I go now, write later.'

'Yes, why?'

'You not think I Chinese maybe if I write like I too fluent,' she said and overly emphasised her Asian accent.

Dan shared a look with me. 'You leveraged our stereotypes?' He said.

'Yes. Stereotypes can be useful sometimes. Harmful others.'

I knew then that I'd been played, but I didn't mind. Her abilities and her knowledge were more than worth the price of granting her and her family their freedom.

*

An hour after sunset, I pulled into the parking bays under St George's Wharf. Dan and I escorted Lily up to the apartment and into Dan's room. Dan's old room, I thought. Again, I got a stab of emotion, but this time it was much less. He was going to file for divorce. He was going to get custody of Ryan. Once he left the US military with their decrepit laws on sexuality, then we could live together openly as a family. We'd agreed that as soon as possible after his exit from the military, we would enter into a Civil Partnership. My life was almost perfect.

I walked him down to the foyer.

'I'll be here all tomorrow,' I said, 'but so will Lily, so I can't imagine we'll be able to get up to much.'

'No,' he laughed. 'Certainly not what we did last night.'

I felt the blush spreading across my face and was glad the foyer was relatively dark. I held him close and kissed him goodnight. 'Ring me,' I said. 'Or text, or send emails. Or all three.'

'I'm going into the office tomorrow, so I will ring you and I might even stop by on my way hom—' He stopped himself. 'On my way to the house.'

'Thank you.'

He brought me back closer and kissed me again.

He eased open the foyer door and made his way into the London night. Had I known what was coming, I'd never have let him go.

30

London, October 2005

Lily went to bed before ten. She still seemed calm about the potential meeting, but as we spoke during the evening, I could see the strain of the previous few days in her eyes, or perhaps it was the cumulative strain of years. At least she would have all day tomorrow to relax and sleep if need be.

When her bedroom door clicked shut, I went to the drinks cabinet and discovered a dribble of liquid in the bottom of a Tanqueray Number Ten bottle. There was a half empty bottle of vodka, but I wanted a decent drink. The local off-licence was open until eleven and it was only a fifteen minute walk down the road. Lily was safe in bed and I rationalised that stretching my legs would do me good. After all, I had sat in a car for half the day. I grabbed my coat and keys and let myself out.

As I reached for my wallet to pay for the three bottles of Tanqueray, I heard a siren pass on the street outside the off-licence. By the time I'd paid, two more had followed.

'Busy night for a Monday,' the shop assistant said and flicked his head in the direction of the passing police cars.

'I guess.'

It was London and sirens were a regular occurrence. I took my change, lifted the carrier bag to a reassuring clink of the bottles inside and left. Turning onto the Wandsworth Road I could hear the sirens up towards the river. Five minutes more and I could see the blinking and strobing of blue lights reflecting off the St George's Wharf apartment blocks and the low clouds that had not delivered with their threat of rain.

It wasn't until I rounded the final curve of the road that I realised the three police cars were parked nose-on to the kerb outside my block. Another siren sounded behind me, a different warble. An ambulance streaking up the road, passing me and braking to a halt next to the police. Paramedics jumping from the vehicle and entering the wide open security doors. The lights of the foyer blazing, and a man lying on the ground inside. I couldn't see him clearly, not from this distance, so I'm not sure how I knew, but I did, instinctively. My mind screamed it. I knew it was Dan. I heard the smashing of glass as I dropped the carrier bag and ran.

Two constables blocked the doorway with outstretched hands. 'Whoa, whoa stop. STOP!' They yelled and restrained my desperate lunge to get through. The senior Sergeant turned away from where the two paramedics were kneeling next to Dan. They'd already cut his shirt off and were applying large wound dressings to his upper left arm and shoulder.

I tried again to break through. 'Dan! Dan!'

'Luke, it's okay. I'm okay,' he called but his voice sounded far from okay. I pushed forward again.

The Sergeant stepped across to be directly in front of me. 'Calm down, who are you?'

'What's happened?'

'Sir! Who are you?'

'I'm Luke Frankland! He's my partner. What the hell's happened?'

'Do you have ID, Sir?'

I stared past him and saw Dan looking directly at me.

'Dan! What happened?'

The Sergeant spoke again, more forcefully. 'ID, Sir?'

I reached for my wallet and showed him my military ID. I kept calling for Dan, but the paramedics blocked my view and the police were moving me further away. The Sergeant took a hold of my arm and forcibly walked me back outside with the help of one of his constables. 'Let the paramedics do their work. You said you were Mr Stückl's partner. Yes?'

'Yes. I am. Now, please, tell me what's going on.'

'We're not quite sure. We got a call of a domestic violence incident.'

'From who?'

'From Mr Stückl,' the Sergeant said.

I put my hand into my jacket pocket for my own phone, why hadn't Dan rung me? It wasn't there. I'd not taken it with me. I remembered it plugged into a charger on the kitchen benchtop.

The Sergeant was still speaking, '...he said he was coming to your apartment as it was safe. He said he'd tried to call you but there was no answer, but it was still the safest place for him and the boy.'

'The boy? His little boy, where is he? Is he okay?'

'Yes, he's fine,' the Sergeant said and pointed to one of the squad cars I'd run past. A driver was in the car and a female police officer was in the rear nursing a toddler. I recognised Ryan from the photos Dan had shown me.

'What's happened to him. To Dan?'

'He's been stabbed.'

I'd never understood the phrase about legs turning to jelly before, but I did then. The Sergeant reached out and steadied me. He backed me up to the front of one of the other cars. 'Here, take it easy. Are you alright?'

I rested my weight on the bonnet and forced myself to breathe. 'How bad is it?'

'The paramedics will do everything they can for him and then we'll get him to hospital.'

I realised the Sergeant had used Rachel's trick. If you don't like a question, refuse to acknowledge it. It made me feel worse.

'Thing is, Sir.'

'Yes?' I distractedly nodded.

'The thing is, on the call that our emergency dispatch received, he said he'd already been attacked and was taking his son and going to apartment 71, here.'

'Yes. That makes sense. He used to live here too. He still has keys,' I said distractedly, still craning my neck to see what was happening in the foyer.

'Well we got here before him and used our override code to enter the building. I'm afraid there was no answer to our repeated knocks on your apartment door and given that he said he'd already suffered injuries and that there was a minor involved, we forced our way in.'

All my focus snapped onto the Sergeant. My mind instantly cleared of any distractions. 'You did what?'

He misinterpreted my tone. 'I'm sorry, Sir, but we had to. We had reports of a minor and we had no choice. We had only just entered when one of my constables radioed to say Mr Stückl had staggered into the foyer. So it really is only your door that was broken.'

'And where the f—' I stopped myself.

'Where's what?'

I saw the paramedics lifting Dan onto a wheeled stretcher. My mind was in freefall. I fought to remain in control. 'Where are they taking him?'

'Saint Thomas's Hospital. He'll be there in minutes.'

The paramedics began to wheel Dan out to the waiting ambulance.

'I need to talk to him,' I said and the Sergeant stepped aside.

'Dan. What the hell happened?'

'Shirlene.'

'The bitch stabbed you?'

'Yeah, she knows about us.'

I felt like a giant weight was squeezing my head. The pressure was crushing me. 'She knows?'

He manged a weak nod. 'I tried to calm her. Lifted Ryan up, tried to get her to back off. She stabbed me while I was holding him. I ran. Came here. Had to call the cops in case she followed. Sorry. Thought you'd be in. Sorry.'

He looked so vulnerable. I reached out and laid my hand on his left arm. 'I'll come to the hospital, I'll come, but…I have to…'

'I know. I'm sorry. I nearly…'

The paramedic eased me out of the way and she and her partner lifted Dan into the back of the ambulance.

'I'll come as soon as I can,' I called.

'You'll stay the fuck away from him you fucking faggot.' The scream echoed off the low clouds and cannoned off the buildings, the police cars and me. Dan struggled against the stretcher restraints, his face pale and clammy, now taking on a countenance of terror. I turned to see a woman, blonde hair plastered in sweat against her forehead, blood across her denim shirt and jeans, hands by her sides, the right one red and holding a kitchen knife. She had rounded the corner of the apartment block and was running straight for me. Dan's laboured breathing came in shallow pants and I registered his tortured cry of, 'Shirlene, don't.'

My feet were rooted to the spot as she closed the distance between us and brought the knife up. The blade, half coated in Dan's blood, reflected the police car strobes and showed up as purple in the strange mix of light. I watched Shirlene's eyes narrow and the spittle flying from her mouth as she growled and snarled like a feral animal. The knife began to angle down towards me and I didn't move, didn't close my eyes, didn't raise my hands to defend myself. It was too late.

Less than five inches from my heart the blade dropped directly to the ground. Shirlene yelped in pain as the Police Sergeant's expandable baton cracked against her wrist. In the same instant he had tackled her to the ground and two constables dived into the melee.

'Get that bloody ambulance out of here,' the Sergeant yelled at the paramedic still standing next to me. She needed no second prompt. The doors swung shut and I stepped back, desperate to follow Dan, yet mesmerised by Shirlene being subdued by the police. They had already cuffed her and between the two constables and the Sergeant she was being dragged up to her feet. She looked like a ferocious wildcat. Our eyes met.

'You fucking faggot. Get your own man. My husband knows what side his bread is buttered, you fucking queer piece of sh—'

'That's enough,' the Sergeant bellowed into her face and Shirlene was stunned into silence. Her shoulders slumped and the anger, so evident on her face moments before, fell away. All the fight went out of her in a single breath.

The Sergeant yelled again, 'Name?'

'Shirlene.'

'Shirlene what?'

'Stückl.'

'Get her into a car and caution her,' the Sergeant said in a gentler tone to the constables. 'Then get her away to the station. I want her charged with GBH for starters. Go on. I'll be right behind you.'

With her hands cuffed and the two tall constables practically lifting her towards a police car, Shirlene meekly submitted. I watched them place her into the back seat and a short moment later the car drove off.

I was alone and felt like my world had gone into some sort of crazy fast forward. Thoughts raced through my mind, none forming long enough for me to grasp. My heart was hammering in my chest, Dan was gone, Shirlene had stabbed him, tried to stab me, been disarmed, tackled to the ground and arrested, yet mere minutes had passed.

'Are you okay, Sir?' The Sergeant asked.

He was standing less than two feet from me. I hadn't noticed that he and a constable had come to stand next to me.

'Sir?'

My eyes focused on the scuffs in the Sergeant's uniform trousers, caused no doubt by his tackling of Shirlene. He'd surely saved my life. That single thought allowed normal speed to be restored, and, desperate as I was to follow Dan to hospital, I knew it was much more important to get upstairs and check on Lily. To do that I needed the police to be gone.

'Yes. Yes, I'm fine. Thank you. I mean, thank you for saving me. For saving my life.'

'Don't mention it.' He shrugged and I saw he was looking far from composed.

'Are you alright, Sergeant?'

'Me? Yeah. I'm fine.' He said distractedly whilst reaching into his pocket and producing a notebook. 'I assume you and Mrs Stückl have met before?'

'Eh, no. Our first encounter,' I said, trying and failing to add a light tone to my answer.

'She seemed to know you?'

I knew from my university days studying law that I would have to give statements. I knew that if they ended up charging her with an attempt on my life, I most definitely would be required to give evidence, but for now I also knew that Lily needed to be my priority. 'Sergeant, do you need me for anything else right now. Can we possibly do this tomorrow morning? I really want to go to the hospital to be with Dan.'

The Sergeant looked almost relieved by my suggestion. I think the full implications of his intervention against an armed assailant were only beginning to sink in. 'I'll need you to come to the station to give a full statement tomorrow, first thing, Sir.'

'No problem.'

'And I have some claim forms for you to fill in for your doo—'

I almost laughed. 'I don't care about the door, Sergeant. You saved me from being almost certainly stabbed. I think the door is the least of my concerns. Can I go?'

He closed his notebook and half-turned, but stopped and faced me again. 'Umm, there is one thing Mr Frankland. When we got here, Mr Stückl identified himself as a serving US Army Officer. He also gave us his address and the details of his wife.'

'Whom you've now met. A definite crazy bitch.'

'Well, certainly a very angry lady. Thing is, we'd already dispatched a unit to her address, but we obviously had just missed her.'

My mind was starting to race again. I needed to get upstairs and check on Lily. My frustration showed through. 'Yes, and?'

'I have to contact the US Embassy. He's a foreign national and serving military and now we've arrested his wife. She will also be classed as foreign military if she's here with her husband on a tour of duty.'

'Yes,' I said tersely, desperate to get upstairs. 'So what?'

'So, Sir. Before I joined the Met, I was in the Army. I've served on deployments with the Americans. When you said you and Mr Stückl were partners. You meant at work…didn't you?'

I felt my frustrations and impatience leave me as surely as the fight had gone out of Shirlene. The Sergeant had not only saved me from a knife, he was now saving me from myself. I closed my eyes and took a breath.

'I can ignore a lot of what Mrs Stückl was shouting, Sir. I can put that down to incoherent rage, but if I have to contact the Embassy, and I need to fill in a report, wording can be key. I know the Americans aren't as open on certain subjects as the Brits. So, can I ask you again, how do you know Mr Stückl?'

My eyes remained closed. I took a deeper breath and considered my answer. I hated all established religions. Their paedophiles, their hypocrites and charlatans, the corruption and the dishonesty, but I'd been schooled in religious studies since my earliest days in a classroom. I knew my Bible and the manmade bullshit it was made up from, yet now in the forefront of my mind I saw the passage from Luke's Gospel. Of course Luke's. Chapter twenty-two, verse fifty-four. I had no choice. I opened my eyes, looked at the Sergeant and said plainly, 'He's my work colleague.'

'Great. I thought so. I'll leave you to get to the hospital, Sir. But if you can come in and make a statement first thing tomorrow, please?'

I looked in to the foyer and the pool of blood in the middle of the floor. 'And that?' I asked.

'I'm afraid that will be down to the block owners, Sir. This isn't a crime scene. My colleagues are at Mr and Mrs Stückl's house. That's the crime scene.'

I tried to control my rising desperation to see Lily as I waited for the Sergeant and the rest of the police to get back into their cars and pull away. The sight of the small boy in the last car to leave made me realise I had no idea where they were taking Ryan. Some prospective stepfather I was shaping up to be, but I was going to have to worry about that later. I willed the lift to rise quicker. Coming out on the seventh floor I could see the remnants of my door hanging on its hinges. I eased my way past it and called out to silence. I kept calling her name and saying it was me. I entered Dan's old room. The bed had been slept in and the top sheet and quilt looked as if they'd been hastily thrown aside. I knew it was pointless, but I searched the room and the rest of the apartment anyway. Lily was gone.

*

Andy Gibson and John Leofric joined me inside half an hour. I called in the rest of my team too, but left the Colonel, Dave, Jim and Steph out of this one. We met in the apartment. John took me aside.

'I know about Dan. We can worry about the fallout of that later. For now, we have to find Lily.'

'I know, Sir. I can't imagine what she thought when British Police kicked in the door.'

'I daresay she was transported back to the night the Chinese took her father or when they killed her brother. If I was her I'd want to put as much distance between me and this place as possible.'

Andy had a map of London spread out on the dining room table. He was already sectoring the city and dividing it amongst my team. John and I rejoined the rest. As I leant over the map, my body facing the apartment windows I noticed more blue light strobes on the far bank of the river. It was another police car, parked up next to the construction site of the two curvy apartment blocks. I went back to the map. Lily didn't have money that we knew of, but we had to surmise she'd get some, so we decided to go for the major rail and bus hubs first. Try to stop her before she left the city. I was tracing my finger over the nearest when another siren and accompanying lights made me look to the window again. A second car had joined the first, but this one was parked on top of the bridge. I could see four officers, two on the bridge and two on the bank. I walked to the window and looked down. The four were shining torches onto the water of the Thames. I couldn't see it from where I stood, but I knew the bridge pier that they were gathered around was the one with the statue pointing into the water.

*

We gathered behind the tape and watched her body being lifted from the river into a police boat. Only Andy had an ID that could possibly sway a police officer to give out information, but that was all we needed. The description fitted. The team stood down. I went to Saint Thomas' Hospital. To Dan.

*

Steve Jäeger met me at the entrance to the ward. I was glad to see a friendly face, even if he looked as stressed as I'd ever seen him.

'You can't be here, Luke.'

'Get out of my way, Steve.'

He stepped up close to me and with no menace or threat to his voice, said, 'Do not try, Luke. Do not be stupid.'

I couldn't understand what he was doing. I went to sidestep, but Steve took hold of my arms. 'He's my friend, Steve, I want to see him.'

'You can't and you won't ever be allowed to see him again.'

'What the fuck do you mean?'

'His wife was emailed a file. Pictures of you and Dan, email transcripts and text messages you had sent to each other. She sent it to the Embassy.'

'I don't care. We were going to come out anyway. I don't care.'

'You may not, but the US military sure as hell does. His wife's been arrested for God's sake. The child is in a temporary foster facility until we can get him escorted back to the States to be with his Grandparents. This is a fucking disaster, Luke. Don't you see that?'

I hadn't. Right up until Steve laid it out as plain as the daylight that was beginning to come through the windows. I was exhausted. I thought Lily had been the disaster. I'd been wrong.

'You need to leave,' Steve said and taking me by the arm walked me to the doors of the hospital.

'Who emailed her the file?'

'I don't know. Not yet. But you have to leave. You can't have any contact with Dan. Not now, not ever. It's finished.' He pushed me back into the early dawn.

*

The green coloured awning covering the Terrace Café of the Palace of Westminster sits on the northern bank of the Thames between Westminster Bridge and Lambeth Bridge, and to the southern side of the part of the Palace that is the House of Commons. It is frequented by parliamentarians and, on occasion, their specially invited guests. It caters for breakfasts, lunches and dinners. It is especially favoured by the governing party and within that, the Ministers of the Cabinet get the best seats. When two of the four Great Offices of State in the United Kingdom dine together, they are guaranteed exceptional seats and faultless service.

They chose from the breakfast menu. They chatted about the weather, as the British are inclined to do. They asked after their families and their colleagues and their pets and their ailments. As they finished their meal, the woman, who smoked, walked into the open air section and lit a cigarette. From where she stood she could see, far to her right, the green and cream terraces of Vauxhall Cross. One of two intelligence services of the United Kingdom that answered directly to her. The bend of the river meant most of the Vauxhall Bridge was lost to sight. Her male companion joined her.

'It's done? Already?' She asked.

'They had an unexpected incident'

'I thought we were going to convince the PM it was a futile waste of his time? Take care of it that way.'

'She ran out of a fire exit door. Right across the front of the surveillance car. They had their orders. If an opportunity presented itself, they were to take it. Plain and simple, like we had agreed. Minimal fuss, no loose ends to follow. What did you want them to do?'

'Now, now. No questions like that. I didn't expect anyone to do anything. And I didn't agree anything. Neither did you Duncan. Did you?'

'No, Mary. I didn't.'

'Good.' She flicked the half-finished cigarette into the fast flowing waters of the river and blew out the smoke. 'Although, I imagine our friends will be very grateful.'

31

London, October 2005

Director John Leofric had been denied a meeting for a week. Eventually after many phone calls and much lobbying, he was granted thirty minutes with the Foreign Secretary in her office at the Palace of Westminster. The caveat, which was a surprise to him and me, was that I should attend as well. How she even knew my name was a mystery. Why she should want me there, a bigger one.

It was scheduled for 09:00. We arrived at 08:50 and were kept waiting until 09:10. When her private secretary showed us into her office he said, 'She needs to be leaving at 09:30, sorry.'

He wasn't. Then again, neither was I. I could say most of what I wanted in a sentence and a half, although John had warned me repeatedly to hold my tongue.

She was polite in her greeting as was I. John began and laid out the case of what Lily had managed to tell us and what we knew to be fact with regard to the Chinese threat to our computer networks and critical national infrastructure. We had long suspected, but Lily had provided the confirmation.

The Minister held her hand up. 'Now, remind me, this...Lily? She is this Chinese girl who drowned?'

'Hong Kong Chinese,' I said.

'I think, Flight Lieutenant Frankland, you will find that Hong Kong *is* China nowadays. I would have thought a professional Intelligence Officer would be up on his current affairs.'

I said nothing.

'So is she the one who is dead?'

'Yes,' John answered.

'Then how on earth can we corroborate what she has told us. Did she provide us with cyber warfare capabilities? Did she defend us against these alleged Chinese attacks?'

John and I remained quiet.

'Well!' The shrillness of her voice grated like a knife on a plate.

'No, Ma'am.' John said.

'No, Ma'am. Exactly. So all in all there is nothing to discuss.'

I could take no more. My tongue holding ended abruptly. 'But Ma'am, we have a clearly proven and well-evidenced history of Chinese atta—'

'Flight Lieutenant Frankland. Be quiet!' She stood and because of all the years I had spent in hierarchical institutions from boarding schools to the military, I reluctantly fell silent.

'Young man. You have brought a potential mountain of disrepute onto our shoulders thanks to your indiscrete and disgusting behaviour with a married member of the United States Armed Forces. I am informed that your unwilling and seduced victim will be returning to his home this week, along with his poor wife and we will not be getting a replacement in his stead. I for one am not surprised. I have checked with my Right Honourable colleague the Secretary of State for Defence and he assures me you have not breached any UK military laws, which in my eyes is a shame as I would have seen you run out of the Service for your actions. As for the Chinese *threat* as you and your team director insist on calling it, I am going to say this once and once only. From the very highest level, you are to know that it is not in the best interests of Her Majesty's Government to proceed with any actions in this matter. You will cease and desist all operations. Is that clear? And one final thing. The mother and brother of that dead girl will be deported to China tomorrow.'

She was sending them to their likely deaths and I'd had enough. The clarity of what I was about to do didn't come as a shock to me. I knew it was of and in the moment, and most importantly, I knew it was the right thing to do. The absolute right thing. For one surreal second I wished I was in full dress uniform, replete with a sword. I imagined the action I was about to take would have been more aesthetically pleasing. As it was I simply stood up.

'Ma'am, I believe you and this Government are traitors to this nation. I hereby offer you my formal resignation as a commissioned officer in Her Majesty's Armed Forces and I suspect, given your attitude, you will see that my resignation is actioned as soon as possible.' Unlike most spontaneous statements, it came out perfectly.

She wanted the last word. 'I will see it actioned today, you arrogant little shit!'

I couldn't give her it. 'You, Madam, are as common, undignified and as ineloquent as I always thought you would be.'

I walked out of her office and back to my apartment. I packed a bag of clothes and headed for the door. The MoD would arrange a moving company. They'd look after all the rest. For now, I just wanted out. As I got to the door I hesitated. This was the space where Dan and I had fallen in love. This was where we shared so many of our secret memories, known only to us. I felt the walls would retain them too and somehow it comforted me. But this was also where Lily had run from and I was supposed to believe that in her fear, she had fallen into the river. I would never be able to prove what I thought had happened. And anyway, did it matter? However she died it was such a pointless and stupid waste. I felt the tears start to roll down my cheeks, but I wiped them away. I had to remain strong. I had to hope when he got back to America, Dan would find a way to contact me. I had to hope that Veronica and Ethan would be safe. I had to hope for miracles and in my non-spiritual soul, I knew they didn't exist.

Walking back to the kitchen, I opened the drinks cabinet and stuck the gin bottles into my bag.

The nearest station was Vauxhall, south of the river, but I

wanted to pay my respects one last time. The morning traffic was heavy, as usual but the footpaths were not crowded. I stopped above the pointing lady statue and looked down into the fast flowing waters of the Thames. The official report had said Lily must have slipped on the river bank as she tried to hide under the bridge. Scared by the police who had crashed into the apartment, she'd fled down the fire escape stairs and out the rear door of the block. Across the road and down into the shadows of the bridge arches. The slippery bank, muddy, dangerous in the daylight, treacherous at night. She had supposedly stumbled, slid and fallen. The current had swept her downstream only to be caught in an eddy which caused her to hit her head on, and be caught up by, the spotlight stanchions that illuminated the downstream statues. Death had been instant. A small grace.

I found it all too convenient, but the alternatives that bombarded my thoughts made me feel sick to my core.

My phone began to ring. I retrieved it from my pocket and checked the display. Steve Jäeger. He'd tried to call me a dozen or more times since the night in the hospital. I'd rejected each one. This time I pressed accept.

'Luke?'

I dropped the phone and watched it spiral away into the Thames. It disappeared from my sight as surely as Dan had disappeared from my life.

Epilogue

For Immediate Release – Newsroute
London, November 2005

In 2004, the UK was the biggest EU investor for China and the third biggest EU trade partner of China, as their total trade volume reached 19.73 billion US Dollars, up 37.1 percent from one year earlier.

At the invitation of Her Majesty, Queen Elizabeth II, the President of The People's Republic of China arrived in London on Tuesday November 8th, 2005 to pay a state visit to Britain.

In her address at the State Banquet in the President's honour, Her Majesty The Queen, said:

"It is almost twenty years since we visited China and since then China's development has caught the world's attention and admiration.

I am pleased that so many young Chinese people choose to study and gain work experience in the United Kingdom and more and more British people now work, travel and study in China. We have a dynamic trade and investment relationship with British companies creating jobs in your country and Chinese companies doing the same here. Your visit allows us to draw attention to the flourishing relationship between the United Kingdom and China and to demonstrate the importance we attach to its development.

It is a relationship of great consequence to us, full of potential and rich in opportunity for the people of both our countries."

The President added the UK leg of his overseas trip at short notice and is expected to meet British Prime Minister Tony Blair and deliver a speech on bilateral and international issues on Wednesday.

End of Press Release

Coming Soon

Pick a Packet or Two

When a British bank, investing in emerging markets and hoping to help some of the world's poorest, starts haemorrhaging money, Luke Frankland is called in to find out who is to blame.

He soon finds himself in the middle of a multinational game of treachery, extortion and murder. His home life should be his refuge, but that is about to get equally complicated.

The second book in the Luke Frankland Trilogy.

Acknowledgements

Quite simply this book couldn't have been written without the assistance of the following people:

Thank you to Chris for the artillery advice. To both Pearl and Veronica for the Mandarin and Cantonese translations. To Martin and Jim for the Tornado fleet discussions. To Paul for the French translation and to the good folk behind the Ville de Gardanne's Facebook page for the confirmation of their local memorials.

With thanks to all my beta readers, including, Murray, Taryn, Banu, Howard, Lewis and Craig.

I'd also like to thank Emma for all your moral support and so many valuable introductions, let alone for your head-hunting exploits that changed my life.

And speaking of jobs, a huge thank you to both Christopher and Chris for allowing me the time and space to complete this novel whilst starting out on a new adventure with Recorded Future.

I'd also like to thank the NHS staff at the South Tyneside District Hospital. Without the care they gave me in April and May 2018, I would not be here today and the books would not be possible.

And finally, to my parents, and my brother Jamie, for your unconditional love and unstinting support.

Tim
London
June 2019

About the Author

Tim Hind was born in Sunderland and joined the Royal Air Force as a Commissioned Officer in the Intelligence Branch after reading Law at university. He is also a graduate of the UK's Defence Intelligence and Security School.

During his time in the Service he initially focused on the Middle East and then specialised in cyber warfare. He later joined Barclays Bank in a Global Information Security role with stints in the Middle East and emerging markets and subsequently headed up the bank's global cyber intelligence capability.

He then moved to America to lead another cyber intelligence team in his position of Vice President within a start-up cyber intelligence company that was sold in 2016.

Tim now lives in London and is a director of cyber intelligence teams located in Europe, the Middle East, Africa and the Asia/Pacific regions, who service clients globally in the public and private sectors. When not travelling the world for business or pleasure, he enjoys reading biographies, cooking, fell walking and skiing. He is also a qualified scuba instructor and, by his own admission, a commercial aviation geek. Despite all of these activities, he is most happy when at home surrounded by friends and family.

The Book Reality Experience

CPSIA information can be obtained
at www.ICGtesting.com
Printed in the USA
LVHW041632290519
619455LV00004B/679/P

9 780648 519850